C000059418

The Sun Thief
Crosswalk

Fifth Edition

ACKNOWLEDGMENTS

Technical Adviser
Mark McCandlish

DEDICATIONS

for Connie,
to SSLF for patience and support,
to my children for saving me,
to my brother and grandmother for watching over me, and
to RS, JC, and CR for returning, right on schedule.
And to JR for keeping an appointment
made so long ago among the stars.

Forward

I had a teacher once who used to say, "Life is terrible…, thank God!" There are times in our lives when we are left a legacy that, at first glance, seems small or perhaps unfair, or even, unfortunately, brutal. Such are the gifts of life to humankind. We agree to play our parts. At times we stand at the edge of an impenetrable forest, our angel hands us a machete and wishes us God speed. No matter how many times we'd like to veer off the path or hand the task off, if we are steadfast, miraculous things do occur. I am always humbled when I have the great good fortune to work with people who are islands of courage. They stand up knowing full well that doing so just makes them an easier target for opposition in whatever form that comes, and they speak their truth to the world. The incidents which propelled the writing of this book and the people I came into contact with because of it have changed me, utterly and forever.

First and foremost, I want to acknowledge the woman who died in a crosswalk on her way to church on a sunny Sunday morning on July 11th 2010, in the middle of nowhere Maine. That sacrifice started an avalanche of events and understanding that still reverberates and I hope continues to do so. It was quite an offering. Her name was Connie. She should be remembered.

Second, within the context of this book, I have to say that without my technical adviser, Mark McCandlish, this book would not have been possible. Without the enormous and selfless giving of his time and expertise, this book simply would not exist. It was one of the greatest acts of unconditional caring I have ever witnessed. Mr. McCandlish is also the role model for one of the major characters in the book, Charlie Shepard. For me, Mark and Charlie are virtually indistinguishable.

Third, there is a deep esoteric component to this book. I realized in short order that this component was the ultimate reason to write the book. Yes, we have a material situation on our hands that is unconscionable. The ultimate question is why? It is the very clearly definable battle between Light and darkness that we express here. We are, after all, the younger brothers of the angels. Relentless attempts are made to sever us from what sustains us spiritually on this planet; the sun, the seed, the soil... injuries to our etheric selves. Do not entertain for one moment any idea other than that we, the tenth hierarchy, are on the verge of making a profound leap as Spiritual Beings and that it is this that is under siege. I do not believe that anything but the Light will prevail, and any other conclusion is smoke, mist and mirrors...a handful of fear. So, to those of you out there who have walked and continue to walk with me down the esoteric portion of this path, *namaste*. I will always love you.

Cara St.Louis-Farrelly
November, 2012

Nevertheless, this is a true story

Bird of Paradise, or First the Dying.

She set the wide-brimmed red straw hat atop her short, iron-gray curls, some escaped here and there from under the straw. This was the kind of thing the old woman did just to attract attention. At this point, she did not mind cultivating an aura of quirkiness. She was fond of wearing bright colors for the love of the color itself now, which was a comfortable reason. For a long time, she had decked herself out vividly, displayed in colors so brilliant one could almost eat them. Then people would often remark on it and she could steer the conversation back to the years she lived in Hawaii. She did love to talk about that, even now. She just didn't feel she needed to make sure it came up anymore.

It was Sunday. It was July. The sun felt high even now at nine-thirty in the morning. The wide-eyed cat, whose eyes were always dilated with nameless anxiety, slipped into the apartment between her legs as she opened the door and stepped out into the morning. Her landlord, that hateful, smelly man, stood several yards away with a cracked, green garden hose watering dozens of tomato plants in white plastic buckets. She grimaced briefly at his terrible back, put one arthritic hand on the crown of her hat lest it fly away on a sudden gust of her disdain and grabbed the railing mercilessly with the other. Three wooden steps stood between her and the driveway; between "way up here" and "way down there". She hovered under an umbrella of fear; fear of breaking a hip and so maintained a pro-actively adversarial relationship with stairs and with damp surfaces. This day she wore her open-toed white sandals with the back straps. She would not drive. It was a mere block and a half to church, after all.

She waved without speaking to her next-door neighbors. They sat comfortably on woven nylon lawn chairs in their back yard, the old fellow with the Sunday newspaper scattered recklessly across his lap and onto the grass. Down the long drive she minced, skirting the big pothole, another mortal enemy, and onto the sidewalk. To her, it felt like breeching a coral reef from a lagoon to make the safety of open ocean; dicey, unsure, a little treacherous. Yet here she was once more, safe in the quiet lane on the orderly and well-measured sidewalk on her way to church.

The traffic on Main Street loomed ahead, relentlessly following its plumb line to the right and then a little further away, to the left. It was a small, small village but it was a tourist village and the summer holidays were in full swing. Still, when she arrived at the main street, it seemed traffic was fairly light. She saw friends across the road, other members of the plain, white Episcopal Church leaving their cars, mingling on the expanse of emerald lawn. Laughter drifted across the road toward her followed by bits of conversation. At the crosswalk, she stopped, prepared to wait, endlessly as always, until everyone came to terms with the inconvenience of having to stop for an old woman who just wanted to cross the little road and go to church. It seemed as if this act – this entire tableau – was so firmly rooted in the twentieth century that it almost wasn't visible to the naked eye anymore. This little play was an anachronism, despite the real live flesh and bone of the actors. And they did hate to slow their vehicles down like this. Oh, how they hated to slow down.

In the end they did, though. Three cars reluctantly slid to a stop, drivers resigned to this spectacle of old age that was to walk slowly across their field of vision. She had not liked to be that. Then she decided, to hell with them.

Just wait, she thought. In about five minutes, you'll be this old, too. Just wait.

She looked carefully and thoroughly left and right, then across the way as someone waved and called out her name. She smiled and shouted hello. Down to the asphalt and gingerly, slowly, across the lanes of traffic. Her hips were of no real use to her anymore. She walked in spite of them really. She was thinking of the giant yard sale scheduled for next Saturday, and that she intended to go. The white canopy tent was already stretched tautly on the church lawn. Her daughter, Christina, needed to borrow her car after church. She was within a few moments of reaching the other side, this little list knitting itself together comfortably inside her mind.

Then her feet were swept out from under her and her head slammed into something very hard. It was that simple, like being surprised by a rip tide in a gentle surf. She heard the deep crack of thick glass caving in. That was the extent of it for her, really. She was lying on the road ten or fifteen yards away from where she had been hit. A young woman, long blonde hair flying behind her, ran to her side, knelt down.

"Be still, don't move."

Someone else ran for the priest. Blood trickled, warm and itchy, from her ears and her hearing aids, the very expensive ones, the ones she fussed over so much, were nowhere to be seen. One poor leg was at an incredibly unnatural angle under the other and her right hip bone had torn right through her fragile skin. Far, far away she heard a man screaming. Many people had gathered around her now. The wail of an ambulance could be heard getting closer and clearer.

"She just came outta nowhere! I didn't see her!"

Over and over, she heard this from somewhere off to the side. The man who had run the old woman down careened around the street on desperately shaking legs, alternately screaming and falling on all fours to the pavement. One of the parishioners, an older man like most of them were, took charge of the blubbering, reeling driver.

"Now, you just be quiet," he said "Sit down. Sit down over here." The driver sank to the sidewalk and put his head on his knees. He trembled uncontrollably and cried loudly, unable to catch his breath. The village police arrived, sirens wailing at high pitch. An ambulance rode in their wake.

EMTs worked quickly and carefully on her shattered body. Surprisingly she was conscious and calm. Shock is protection for the body but also for the consciousness. The crew gingerly lifted her onto a gurney after her head was secured. She screamed a little when they lifted and straightened her leg. The open mouth of the rear of the ambulance swallowed them all and the door shut. It leapt away screaming out of the way, get out of the way, toward the hospital. Someone plucked a white sandal and a little beige hearing aid off the van's windshield.

She drifted in and out of consciousness on the ride to the hospital. In her fog, she thought she was sailing. She thought she was on a swift catamaran off the coast of Lanikai with a firefighter, a man who looked familiar, some rescuer. Sometimes the pain broke through and she cried out, aware again but only briefly. The ER doctor gave them permission to administer morphine over the crackling radio. It was a sweet sleep. She knew they would be calling her daughter, her son-in-law, her grandsons. Her granddaughter, Anya, had just arrived in Japan. She would not see Anya again, she knew that. That was a deep regret, for sure. In the year she had lived a few blocks away she had formed a good relationship with Anya. She loved her granddaughter dearly. She also knew how desperately she was injured; mortally. Her daughter – the only child left – was more than brave enough to let her go; make them honor her wishes, come what may. Of that, she had absolutely no doubt. She was not afraid to die.

Suddenly they were at the emergency room and all tranquility fled. The catamaran became a dust devil, sand through her numb fingers - fast and forever gone. The back door swung open and an ER nurse thrust himself into the back, grabbed her gurney and pulled. She slid. Her eyes opened very wide, her mouth gaped. She gasped noisily, taking in as much air as her lungs would hold, filled them, filled them, filled them... intending to shout to God himself. Then she lost consciousness until she was roused by the steady tone of her daughter's voice.

"Mother, we're here. I'm here. I'm paying attention; they're taking good care of you."

She pried open one now grossly swollen and bruised eye. There was the vague outline of a doctor, other people were there, murmuring. She felt someone grasp her hand, tried to speak. No teeth. Swollen tongue and lips.

"I... don't... want..." was all she could manage.

She was sure Christina would know what she was trying to say. No extraordinary measures, no heroics. Didn't matter if she managed to say it, Christina knew quite well what her wishes were. Then came exploding searing pain and she screamed.

*****

Christina and her husband, Otto, and their two sons drove calmly but with clear certainty of what would happen. She knew her mother would die that day.

"I actually think maybe she's already gone. I don't think she'll be alive when we get there." Otto drove. Hank and David were in the back seat. Their daughter was half a world away. It was sort of a guilty wish, she supposed. This would be so hard to live through.

"Mom," Hank said, "it would be very much like Gram to pull through all this and then be an invalid. I know that sounds harsh but...".

Of course, he was right and they all knew it.

They pulled up in front of the hospital, looked for parking. Quickly, they made their way into the emergency room. An older man sat behind an information desk.

"My mother was just brought in. She was hit by a car."

The man behind the desk turned his little plaque around and 'Information' became 'Will return shortly.' He led Christina, Otto, Hank and David through a few windowless hallways. An emergency room nurse intercepted them, guided them to a fairly large bay behind a curtain.

Christina wasn't ashamed of what she was thinking any more than she was surprised by what Hank had said in the car. Her mother had more than earned that reaction.

Goddamit, she thought, *this is exactly how it would end*.

She studied the monitor above her mother's head: blood pressure, heart rate, oxygen level. The woman had spent a lifetime being melodramatic and high-maintenance. There was going to be no drifting off in her sleep. No one had ever considered that possibility. It followed that this would be the final scene. Six months prior to this moment, she had assured Hank that when her mother passed it would have something to do with a car. These kinds of 'knowings' were common for her, others would have seen them as eerie and a little morbid. So common, in fact, that her children were not even a little bit surprised when they turned out to be true. They absolutely expected the things their mother said to come true.

The figure rested on the bed before her, face so very swollen and eyes bruised, a suction tube lay in the crook of her poor battered mouth and an IV snaked fluids into a vein in her arm. Her right side had clearly borne such a tremendous impact. She was by the grace of God mostly unconscious. Hank, David and Otto stood beside her.

"Mother, we're here...".

Then she lifted off the bed slightly, back arched toward the ceiling, and began to scream.

"Out, out, out...".

Christina ushered her boys – thirteen and seventeen – into the hallway and away from the horrible and violent reality of their grandmother's brokenness. Someone showed them into a small, private family waiting area. There were chairs, a telephone, magazines; a place to hide. They sat, held themselves onto the chairs with their hands, and tried so hard to collect themselves. Christina could still hear her mother screaming from down the hallway, plugged her ears with her fingers, clamped her eyes tight shut like a little girl. When she looked up again, Father Daniel had arrived and was with them. He sat beside her, face screwed up into practical hopefulness; firm but gentle.

"Listen," he was saying, "it looks bad, I know, but your mother is strong and scrappy and a fighter. It's going to take a while and it'll take a lot of care from you and from others but she'll come back from this." He refused to believe anything else.

Christina was so confused. What? How could people who knew the same woman and each other and sat in the same room really have such very different ideas of what came next? She dreaded what was coming. She certainly didn't want to immediately contradict him, he was doing his job.

I already know what I have to do, she thought. I've always known and it doesn't have anything to do with a long painful brain-injured recovery after being run down by a van at the age of seventy-four. Her poor body is crushed. She told me a long time ago, when my grandmother died as a result of a car accident, what I had to do at this moment. And I'm sorry because I don't know how you're going to take this, Father Daniel. And I'm sorry she never talked to you about it.

Then a surgeon - a woman with blond hair pulled back in a ponytail - rapped lightly on the door. Christina motioned her to come in. They waited expectantly. The surgeon leaned against the wall and sort of slid down on her haunches with a chart in front of her.

"So, now would be the time we'd be starting all kinds of extraordinary efforts to keep your mother alive. Pretty aggressive stuff... if you want us to do that."

Christina took over, as she had been trained all her life to do.

"Well, what are her injuries?"

"Broken neck and clavicle, broken hip. Many broken ribs, broken leg.   Intra-cranial pressure is rising because her head hit something. Probably the windshield. That's making her blood pressure fall rapidly because her brain stem is swelling at the base of her neck, shutting down the blood flow. The first thing actually would be to get in there and operate on the leg before she loses it."

Christina thought that was so strange.   The broken leg had top priority?

"Do people her age come back from stuff like this? Her right side seems to be crushed... seems like she has a very serious brain injury. I mean, I understand her head hit the windshield and you're saying the blood flow to her brain is cut off. Has been cut off for a while."

"No telling. Sometimes, yes. Sometimes, no. There's no pulse in the leg. She'll lose it if we don't get in there immediately." The surgeon's face was perfectly neutral.

Here it is.

Christina leaned forward, her elbows on her knees, her hands clasped in front of her. "Here's the thing, doctor. My mother told me what to do under these circumstances decades ago. She has an advance directive. There really isn't a decision to be made here, which doesn't make it easier, actually. But she made this decision for herself a long time ago... and now I have to do what she asked me to do." Her children were right here. Part of what had to happen now was that they had to see what you do in this situation.

The surgeon nodded. "Just keep her as comfortable as possible, then?"

"Yes," Christina answered, "please. She shouldn't have any pain, okay?"

A gangly, young surgical resident was sent to collect them. Her mother was calm again. Christina reminded them to keep her comfortable and pain-free so there was a regular, frequent injection of morphine. Her mother's arms flailed a bit at times. She had seen this before in the dying, reaching out toward the heavens, towards nothing the living could see. Her eyes opened periodically although Christina realized her mother couldn't see anything. She was tremendously near- sighted and had developed diplopia in the last few years; she had double vision. Christina thought it was sad, sad in the way that only someone else who was nearly blind could understand; that her mother couldn't see a thing in her last few hours of life. She couldn't see her or the children. God should grant people perfect sight in the last moments, He really should. Christina leaned in close. Once again when her mother opened her eyes, it was such a struggle against the injuries and the shock and the drugs. She tried to mouth a few more words. Her hearing aids were gone, so she couldn't hear much either, if anything.

The curtains parted and her friend Amy walked in. She stood beside her and hugged her. She looked stunned, a pale combination of pensive and shocked, as if she wasn't sure what to do but would be standing by for anything. Just to have shown up was courageous.

"I'm so glad you're here," Christina whispered.

"I was at church when Father Daniel made the announcement. I drove in right behind him."

Christina held her mother's hand, gently squeezed and felt the slightest of squeezes in return. Father Daniel had the other one. Hank pulled up a chair and sat at his grandmother's feet. David sat beside Christina. Father Daniel anointed her mother's forehead and intoned the prayer for the sick. She sighed.

If you think my mother is going to willingly wake up from this and face what would be coming... if she did wake up it would only be for long enough to kick my ass for not doing what she told me to do.

"Daniel," she asked firmly, "can we say The Lord's Prayer? It's important." She wanted it to be the last prayer her mother heard.

And so this small group who were attached to this old woman by blood or by life, this old woman who lay broken and dying, firmly and with great surety repeated this ancient token of passage, this translation from one thing to the next. Christina wondered what other people in other bays in the emergency room were thinking and feeling as they heard this prayer rise up and float over them. Was there a little boy with a broken arm next door or some other fairly run-of-the-mill emergency room malady? A stomach ache, maybe? What would they feel hearing God invoked so boldly next door like this? Such an achingly private thing to overhear.

She glanced over and realized that Hank, eyes red-rimmed suddenly, was crying silently. Tough guy, devil-may-care Hank, so certain his grandmother – whom he knew very well to be a difficult, difficult woman – would be fine eventually and complaining again loudly about everything under the sun. Hank knew for sure that if his mother had asked for this prayer to be said then his grandmother was going to die. There was no question.

Christina looked at her other son. David seemed to be collapsing in on himself, slumped over in the chair beside his grandmother. Needing to get him away, she bent over and laid her arms across his shoulders and around him.

Amy spoke. "What if I take the boys home with me for now?"

"Mom," Hank said suddenly, "I'm going to walk to Gram's after Amy drops me off and see what medications are in her bathroom... in case the doctors need to know." He stuck out his chin.

"Sure, son," she answered, knowing that Hank knew as well as she did what was happening but he had to do something. She was like that, too. She always looked for some way to act in the face of a situation that seemed out of control.

Then she was somehow, and inevitably, alone with her mother. There was no noise. Otto went to get coffee and make phone calls. The nurse stepped away. It was, as it had always been really today and how many thousand days before, just the two of them. Christina and her mother, lives so inextricably wound one around the other. The eternal, inescapable dyad. It had just been the two of them when Christina was born - no father in the picture - just them. They had never allowed themselves the consciousness of knowing for sure that that was how it would almost always be. There would be another child, a brother, but he had been dead for twenty years. In the end, it was always going to be just these two when one of them passed from this life.

Christina sat down in a chair beside her Mom's not-quite-so-beaten-up left side. She took her hand and laid her head on her mother's arm. Both extremities were cold and blue was making its way up from her fingertips. She thought she should look at that arm, that hand, memorize them, as if a child could ever forget the way a mother's hand looks. We first realize that our mothers are succumbing to time by the look of the hand; what once was young and supple…the strongest lifeline we could ever know…seems suddenly fragile and wrinkled and breakable. We say to ourselves, when did that happen?

"Okay, Mom," she whispered. "Okay."

And then her mother just stopped being alive.

Sie lebt nicht mehr, Christina thought. That's how the Germans say it, she lives no more. It's far more beautiful than, 'she died.' The nurse returned, handed Christina a scuffed black pocketbook belonging to her mother. No doubt it had been tucked in the crook of her arm as she made her way through the crosswalk. As she and Otto turned to leave, Christina kicked something, sent it sliding. It was a white strappy sandal lying underneath the gurney. She picked it up and walked away.

*****

It was July. It was Sunday. Just another day for George Walters, out on one errand, hopefully the only trip out for the day. He was coming back from the discount store where he bought cheaper insulin needles. He was in astoundingly bad health, even though he was only sixty-six. One trip would do him in for the day. He had taken his oxygen off to drive and could feel the difference. He would need to get home and get inside away from the heat, sit down and put it back on. Sit and breathe for a while. He did not smoke, had never smoked, but still had a chronic lung ailment. He was also deeply diabetic, so between his diabetes and the lack of oxygen, he needed to get home. The diabetes had cost him the sight in his left eye a few years previously.

The damned doctors and the state made him get checked out every once in a while so he could keep his driver's license. They would give him the once over and ask him some stupid questions that were none of their business, and then send a paper along to the state. Then he could get his driver's license stamped. It was just the eye, mostly. George had hit a few things because of his eye, that's all. He refused to stop driving; he would not willingly surrender his license. He had no wife, no children. He was an old Army man and had served in Vietnam from 1962 through to 1973. He could remember a time when he was sharp, when he could read and write, breathe and think. No more. He'd been sicker and sicker since he left the service. Since then George had been working at various things. He was a mechanic by trade, thanks to the army. A fellow didn't have to read much to fix engines. He didn't seem to be able to stick with anything and people had actually insinuated every once in a while that he wasn't too bright to begin with. But that wasn't right. George Walters used to be just a regular guy, he knew that. Something had happened but he damned sure couldn't figure out what had gone wrong.

Hell, screw 'em. I was smart enough to work on engines for the big shots. Smart enough for the army. Got a nice assignment in Virginia, too, in that office for a while. People don't know nothin'.

He definitely needed to get home. He was getting short of breath and felt the cold sweat of anxiety creep over him like it did. He looked over to his right. People were mingling in front of the church. Eyes back to the road ahead and something suddenly slammed his windshield, sharply, quickly but with a dull, heavy thud. Dead center and then off again, just that quickly.

What...?

George wasn't even completely sure he had seen something but the sound was real and the giant spider crack in his windshield was real. A dull thud followed by the cracked windshield. The moment of impact was lost to him; he might as well have been asleep.

He slammed on his brakes. He was overcome with the certainty that he had hit someone whether he remembered seeing a person or not. His stomach lurched. The same people who had moments ago been mingling happily beside him on the lawn were now panicked, running toward the street, running into the church. Several yards ahead, there lay a smudge of color in the street. If he stared and tried hard to focus, he realized it was the outline of a person. Yes, he saw someone lift an arm, grasp a hand.

Dear Lord, no!

And that was how easy it had been. One moment George Walters was a sick, belligerent old man driving home, getting by and then the next moment, two lives were hanging by a thread. Another interminable moment arrived. By now he was shaking so badly he was unable to locate the door handle on the van or make his numb fingers identify the outline, grip it, pull it. He had to get out and find out who he had hit, see if he still had time to change anything or if it was all a huge misunderstanding.

No-no-no-no-no!!!

The door swung open. He had turned the handle and collapsed against it. Falling, he caught himself.

The other cars that had stopped for the old woman to cross the street were still there. People had climbed out, some were talking on cell phones, others were converging on this ridiculous point in time and space where it felt like everything and everyone had hit some kind of concrete wall. Nothing was moving. Nothing was going by. The world had ground to a halt. Right here.

George was crying now yet continued to shake and scream 'No' in a high pitched, breathless sound.

She came outta nowhere! I didn't see her, I didn't see her! Oh, my God!

Police were there and an ambulance. Someone grabbed his arm roughly, pulled him toward the curb.

"Now, you just be quiet. Sit down over here."

His feet banged up against the curb as he was pulled to the side, his right arm reached down for the concrete and he sat.

"She came outta nowhere. I didn't see her."

"Hush now."

A female cop approached him; put her hand on his shoulder. "You alright, sir?"

What? What? NO!

"Were you driving the car, sir? Anybody else in the car?"

"It's my car. I'm alone."

Having established that George wasn't hurt, she asked him for his driver's license. Another cop started going through the blue mini-van and rifled through the glove compartment for a registration. He spotted the portable oxygen canister and brought it over to where George sat. The female officer asked George if it was his, did he need it, and when he nodded, she threaded the cannula over his head and put the nose piece in his nostrils. She turned the canister on, sat down beside him and started to make notes.

More village police arrived, parked their squad cars at strategic angles in the road. Some re-routed traffic; others moved onlookers away and set up a perimeter around the accident site. The crowd belonging to the church moved inside, they gathered where they had been going anyway huddled together in shock. Father Daniel made the announcement, there were gasps, and then he delivered a very unsteady sermon.

Outside George Walters found himself to be under arrest. He passed a breathalyzer test – no alcohol on board – but was so obviously incoherent and utterly incapacitated, slurring all the words that tried to escape his lips, wobbling when he stood in front of the officers, that he simply had to be charged with driving under the influence. He was informed of his Miranda rights and then driven, in handcuffs, to the closest hospital where many vials of blood would be taken from him and sent to a lab in the city for analysis.

"I'm sick, you know," he told them, "I needed my oxygen. I didn't have my oxygen...my medicines. They make it hard for me."

I had to drive. Otherwise who else will take care of me?

He grabbed the sleeve of the nurse as she left. "Hey… I can't read. I can't write. I used to be able to but somehow I can't do it anymore." The nurse pulled away from his grip.

He covered his eyes with his hands, began to sob in his own emergency bay in a different hospital in a world that had fallen to dust before his eyes. Poor George, who could no longer read or write. No one was there to pray with him.

George Walters was released on four hundred eighty-two dollars' bail. A squad car delivered him back to his apartment. The van was hauled off to the police lot and photographed as evidence.

*****

Christina turned the key in the lock that opened the door to the little space that had been her mother's. She had done this before with her grandmother and then with her brother. She knew what it felt like. It was a cool early evening and it was the first time she had been inside since the passing. She was on her own because, again, this was a thing so intimate as to be penetrated solely by her. She was aware of how her mother might feel about just who entered her home in the time right after she died. It remains a sacred space for a while.

Past the devilry that was the pothole in the driveway, up those three steps her mother was so afraid of; how unbearable to see dishes in the sink waiting for a rinse, toothpaste and a toothbrush on the sink, towels over the shower rod. An unused train ticket to Boston, dated for Monday, lay on the kitchen table. Unbearable. There was a bit of food in the refrigerator, not a lot because she could never seem to think far ahead anymore although for some reason she tended to buy four gallons of milk at a time, just in case. Her little radio sat next to the train ticket, always tuned to the public radio station. There were bath towels in the dryer. Christ, no one ever says, don't bother, you won't be back. No one tells you how it feels to walk into the living space in the wake of death. Life hadn't even vacated yet. Her old cat, poor thing, was hiding. Christina filled his water bowl and food dish. That was not enough to get him out from under the bed. He could no doubt sense the life lingering here like the scent of bread baking in the oven. He would refuse to come out until all his mistress's life had drifted away on the breeze.

Otto and the boys arrived, noisily, with Chinese take-out. They would have dinner with her mother while some of her mother lingered. It was their last chance at a private moment with her. She wished Anya were there. Christina envisioned her mother sitting on the couch wishing the boys wouldn't be so noisy, trying to get a word in.

Have dinner with us, Mom, because we know that you're still here. Before you get busy doing whatever it is you need to do now.

Before she passed out the little white cardboard food containers and the chopsticks, she set aside a fortune cookie.

"One for Grammy, right, gang? We'll put this in her pocket. For luck or for bon voyage or for remembrance… something like that."

"Mom, I want to open it," David said. "I want to know what it says."

"No, no," Christina replied. "Grammy can open it herself."

And then it was time to go and collect her daughter and bring her home. Christina took her mother's laptop from the office in the apartment on the flight to Seattle. A few days ago, she had been on this very same flight with her daughter, Anya. Mt. Rainier from the air, snow-covered and exquisite in July, its beauty reflected in the sheer delight on her daughter's face. They passed some time in Seattle together then she put Anya on the flight to Osaka. Her daughter, dark curls bouncing as she walked excitedly toward the gangway, she who was so excited, had turned and waved several times as she disappeared into her dream. She wasn't sure the boys would have done something like that. It was pure, unaffected Anya.

Now Christina was flying back across the country to meet Anya and take her home to her grandmother's funeral. She would write something about her mother on the flight. There wasn't a soul left alive who could do it properly as she had been inextricably connected to her - even during the periods of years when her mother ran away - for fifty years. There had been a lot of disappearing, a lot of running away. She would write it, though she dreaded the actual placing of one word after another – while she waited for Anya and then while they waited together for the red-eye flight back home.

Anya got the news over the telephone. She spent two days being stunned and then burst into tears and asked to come home. Of course, that's what she wanted to do. They were going to allow her to choose; the trip was the realization of a dream that she had apparently been born with. She, like her grandmother before her, was drawn to all things Japanese, but in particular to the country itself. Christina's heart bled for Anya, halfway around the world and faced with an impossible set of circumstances. Tender Anya, just fifteen, would insist on being with her family, just as all the children would have, wanting to help send their grandmother on her way. It was such a generous act on all their parts as she knew her mother had done very little to earn this affection from the young ones. They saw the very 'human' human who didn't understand what she was doing, had no idea, and almost never meant it to come out the way it did. They were able to be patient in a way that Christina was not.

Delta Airlines changed Anya's ticket at no charge and allowed her friend Patricia to stay with her at the gate until she left, despite security regulations. The trip from Osaka to Seattle was a very, very long one.

At the same time, Christina sat on her own flight and, using her mother's laptop, began to write about her – a vignette she hoped would be both true and capture some of the better essence of a very difficult, very complicated woman. What was crucial? How did Christina want to remember this woman because this broad stroke would put the punctuation on a life. She had been a musician and then a technical writer and editor. Her security clearance had been quite high. She had worked very closely with top Navy scientists in Europe and Virginia and Hawaii and despite all that, Christina was certain that right now what she and her mother both wanted to remember was the music.

So she painted a picture that still lived in her own mind and memory. There had been a lonely child growing up in a tiny, fairly impoverished farming town near the Ute Indian Reservation, one that sat on the Four Corners, in World War II America. It was the same house in which Christina had been born. By the mid-1950s her mother was a young woman. Christina could hear the plinking of the old Baldwin, the same spinet on which she herself had learned to play. She wanted people who barely knew her mother to see the dream, the art, the potential that propelled her, not the old woman who couldn't hear or see or tolerate other people, who had such a hard time anteing up a kindness; a thin, bespectacled girl sitting alone, feet barely touching the floor, at the very used instrument Christina's grandmother had purchased second hand. Sit down in the old chair on the other side of the tiny living room. See the little girl hunched over the piano, dirty blonde braids down her back, practicing until her fingers bled; see the little girl left in the care of her grandmother because her own mother could only find work in a town 45 miles away, who managed to earn the highest marks and, in the end, got into college on a piano scholarship; see the girl, a good-looking brunette now, working her way through college as the 'girl singer' in some friends' version of a Big Band. A crooner? No, that was a man, she was a torch singer, Christina supposed. See the young woman who went on to teach music.

Christina wanted people to hear the faint remnants of marching bands the way she did; echoes of small villages in the south and south-west; choral groups in dangerous inner cities; and children on the pueblos of New Mexico learning to sing. Her music was, before she gave up teaching, before she entered this other life and career. That's a snapshot her mother would have wanted. It was the snapshot Christina wanted. Her children wouldn't even have recognized this beautiful, impulsive, windblown character, long since left the stage. As Christina wrote it and read it over, a voice in her memory whispered, a gentle love-filled voice, bending over to say to Christina-the-little-girl, *remember me*.

After the old woman went to work for the Navy, she couldn't talk about most of what she did anyway. Christina would write about the woman far away and buried by time: the music teacher. The local people didn't know much about her and, even though she longed to be social and have friends, she couldn't seem to be anything but insular and unapproachable. She had been lonely this last year, Christina supposed. She had seen her mother in many places and under many circumstances, including just the two of them when no one else could see, and she was well aware that her mother had a public face and a private face. She would orchestrate this 16last piece and it would be true and false at the same time. The circumstances, the players, everyone – it would be above all else true for Christina – but it would be a truth that very few people in that room would have witnessed. It would help her family, it would help a community that had been completely manhandled by this accident, and it would help her mother. She was sure of that. She would write it and Otto would read it for her because it would be too close, too personal, because it was so achingly true. It was like opening the child Christina's battered little doll trunk from so long ago, the one where the clasp was not quite right anymore, and taking out wrinkled, folded, yellowing sheet music from another era. This music, this final piece, was the melody so thoughtlessly and easily discarded by her mother, saved somehow by a little girl with a battered old doll trunk, kept on a high shelf in the very back recesses of her memory.

And then they were home.

*****

The day she returned with Anya she received a phone call from the hospital.

We cannot accept any of your mother's organs for donation, they had said.

"What?" she replied, "Why?"

"Because your mother lived in Europe, well, England in this case, in the 1990s," the hospital worker sounded disappointed but as if she had heard this before, "your mother's organs are being rejected therefore."

"What are you talking about?" Christina said.

Her mother's organ donation was being rejected because of where she had lived and when. Absurd. The body was collected and prepared for cremation. It had, for some reason, been sitting in the hospital mortuary for three days while the organ donation issue was sorted out. Christina carried a suit of clothing over to the mortuary and instructed the gentleman handling things to make damned sure there was a fortune cookie in her mother's pocket when the cremation was carried out. She wished now she had sewn it into the pocket of her mother's pants.

Then it was done. No fanfare, it just happened. Her mother had been cremated. Christina arranged for half the ashes to be shipped to the Big Island where her friend who was a native Hawaiian and priest would carry the pretty little wooden box up the side of Kilauea to a secluded forest he knew and scatter them there among the trees and vines. The old woman would have loved that. She would take the other half to a second location on the Big Island herself but that wasn't possible just this moment. The next task was to go through her mother's home and clear it out. The hated landlord had called and asked when they'd have all the old woman's belongings out. So, she found herself sitting in her mother's office the very next day, looking through things. Nothing she found really surprised her. There were boxes and boxes with envelopes inside marked 'paid bills.'

Copies of her income taxes that went way back. Her mother's attention to her own finances was obsessive compulsive; she was so afraid of being poor again that she would have sewed every farthing she had into her own clothing and mattress had she thought it would help make her secure, she was so worried about being poor, although her definition of poverty was completely absurd. There was a phone and a printer/fax machine, her paper shredder. That damned paper shredder! Her mother shredded everything. For a long time she had wondered why her mother was so terrified that someone would see her social security number on something or a bank account number or credit card number. Someone might get hold of her phone bill. *Mother. For God's sake!* No one was that interested in stealing the old woman's identity and, frankly, although she had a nice secure retirement income, no one was going to live in Tahiti on what they could steal from her. It occurred to Christina now, though, that it was probably just a habit from her government days when, she was sure, employees with serious security clearances shredded everything. Still, her mother was always certain she needed to take extra precautions, certain she was a target somehow.

When the office was cleared out and she had settled which boxes and bits of furniture she was taking home with her, Christina moved on to the walk-in closet. On the shelves above the clothing were rows and rows of technical writing manuals. She took down three ring binders and found copies of the Naval Fact Sheet, the scientific publication from the Office of Naval Research in London where she had been editor from 1989 through 1991. This was just not Christina's thing. A writer herself, fond of writing novels and articles and poetry and even a screenplay, this obsession with grammar and punctuation and technical jargon and page presentation...it just made her yawn. She tossed just about all of it and it filled a very large trash can. She smirked when she realized how angry the landlord would be when he had to get that five hundred pound trash can out to the curb on trash day.

Serves him right. I hope he hurts himself.

She was down to college memorabilia and family photos. Her mother's clothes were hung in colorful rows of tropical prints with a liberal smattering of white. Anya would need to go through these as she loved to wear what she and her friends would describe as 'retro' clothes. Anya was an artist and so treated everything like an art project, even her clothing.

The van was loaded and she carried several boxes back to her house, unloaded them into a corner of the garage. Then she went back for the crystal stemware and the grey and white wedding china – these she would seal up and save for Anya. Her mother had said that's what she wanted long ago. Christina took the silver and her grandmother's pewter and the delicate china hot chocolate set with the pale pink flowers painted on the side of the cups and pot. She thought that was probably her grandmother's, as well. She found a scrapbook she had not known about until the funeral, with recital programs, play notices and home-coming souvenirs from her mother's school days. All of these things which Christina decided to keep, selected from everything, were a collection that belonged to a life so long ago and far away; a life her mother had dropped on the floor like an old unwanted toy and walked away from altogether. It had been Christina's life, too, once upon a time.

Back at the family house, she turned to her mother's personal effects and the stuff she had on her when she was hit. The minute they had returned from the hospital the day the old woman died, Christina tenderly tucked away her mother's pocketbook, which contained her wallet and her driver's license, a scarf and some coins, and the strappy white sandal in the top drawer of a chest in the closet under the stairs. It was too much to think about looking inside the pocketbook, it being such a deeply personal item. That day, inside her wallet, Christina found a slip of paper on which her mother had written the words, "My social security number", followed by ten digits. Her memory had grown so dim.

*****

August did arrive; it blew exceptionally hot and dry. Time was going by and time was powerful; it had to help with something. August was good for Christina's vegetables, as they could always be given a drink of water but not rescued from a deluge. The summer before had been so wet that seeds literally rotted in the earth where they were planted. Hank would be leaving for college soon, way too soon after his grandmother's death for

Christina. He had arrived just a few weeks after her younger brother died and now he was leaving just a few weeks after her mother died. This was obviously significant but she didn't have the brain-power or will to work it out right now. He and a friend had been out walking on the jetty a few nights prior, under an exceptionally pregnant full moon – the jetty all the parents insisted the kids stay off – and he had slipped, breaking and dislocating a finger and smashing a knuckle. It would require surgery and rehab and Hank wasn't old enough to know just yet what a liability that finger could be for the rest of his life. She did not like to look at his poor maimed hand, which 19had been whole and useful, and see it broken forever. Hank was too young to have anything be 'broken forever.'

David was at music camp on the lake. The plan had been: Anya in Japan, David at music camp and Hank had his first paying gig as an actor in a Shakespeare festival. Christina would be flying to Seattle to bring Anya home after a glorious three-week sojourn into the land of her dreams, Hank would be making his debut, and David would be attending his first serious music retreat. David, like his grandmother, wanted to be a music teacher. Her mother had been beside herself with pride and happiness and had intended to go with Otto and get David settled into camp while Christina and Anya were away. It was certainly fitting that she be the one to start David on this path. And then all of it had died, it seemed, murdered in the road that Sunday morning. Hank withdrew from the play out of shock, Anya had flown home devastated by the violence done to her family, and David went on to camp but there would certainly be an empty chair in the audience when he performed. So, yes, August had arrived but the tale, the tragedy, seemed stuck at the beginning. It had arrived hot, but not hot enough to warm their cold, cold grief or dry enough to dry the tears that still flowed, surprising Christina completely, like a river. It was, Christina thought, a story which had perhaps begun with its own ending. It was an impossible tale.

She took her mother's car to the shop and left it as it needed a few repairs.

"My God," the woman behind the counter said. "I'm so sorry about your poor mother." She shook her head. "I was driving by the accident that morning. Of course, we had no idea. Then I got home and, you know, the funniest thing... I saw this little jar of cranberry chutney in my refrigerator that she gave me and my husband for Christmas. It made me cry."

This scene was commonplace. It happened to Christina all the time now. No matter where she went in their little village, someone might stop her and tell her they had witnessed the accident. They were themselves so traumatized by what they had seen and it seemed they would always start to tell her something, open their mouths to form the words even, but then change their minds, as if the memory was just too terrible a burden for Christina. She was glad and grateful. She didn't want to know. As it was she was finding it hard to shake the image of her mother being rammed into by a mini-van and flying through the air. She hoped that stopped soon. It was like a film that ran in her head, over and over.

"You look just like your mother," the woman behind the counter was saying. "I can't believe it."

Christina laughed. "Well, more so now, I suppose. Shorter, older, grayer, it was bound to happen. Listen, you would know the answer to this question. I haven't transferred ownership of the car to myself, yet. The plates are good for another month or so. How does one even do that?"

"Call city hall and ask," the woman advised.

A few days later, she and Otto and Hank were making their way back from a visit to the hand surgeon, driving her mother's little white Subaru. They turned right out of the office complex and made their way east, always toward the sun rising over the ocean, which merged seamlessly with the early morning traffic in the small city north of their own small village. Christina was thinking about Hank's hand, worrying he wouldn't make the time or expend the energy to do physical therapy once he got to college.

"Mom, stop!' he said from the back seat. "It's just my pinky. It'll be fine."

A mid-sized silver sedan glided up beside them. It was an odd place to pull up, just as the road narrowed to one lane on each side and so it pulled them away from their conversation into silence. It was a stupid move on the sedan driver's part because there just wasn't time at this point to win a race of who gets to go first.

"Otto!" she said, nerves rising. "Watch out for this guy."

Otto continued on his course because experience and common sense and plain old self-preservation would force the sedan to slow down, once the driver realized they were already both in one lane. There was no merging left to be done. The guy kept coming. He wasn't trying to beat them; he was trying to push them into the on-coming traffic, it was the only place for Otto to go. He leaned on his steering wheel, sounded his horn loud and long.

Horrified, Christina looked at the driver, who hadn't reacted to the horn in the slightest. There were two men in the front seat of this generic four-door silver sedan. The driver was a big man, really heavy, thick skinned with longish black slightly curly hair, a black mustache and very darkly circled eyes. His nose was large, meaty and beaked. His belly grazed the steering wheel. He did not seem angry or intentionally violent in a recognizable way. It was as if for him their car did not exist, they simply were not there. That was the scariest part. This was not road rage. The driver did not see them. The driver did not hear them. If anything, she felt that she might be looking at some kind of black out.

"Otto! Let him go!" Christina was near panic. Angry drivers in oncoming traffic were leaning on their own horns and swerving out of the way. Otto slowed to a near standstill, waited until he could blend into traffic. Two weeks after her mother had been run over in the street, someone had tried to push her into on-coming traffic.

"Well, that was a hell of a thing to have happen at this point in time," she said, looking at Otto.

"Mom, relax," Hank said, although he was clearly shaken.

Right, Christina. That had to be one of the most unfair, unnecessary coincidences ever but it was just a coincidence. Relax.

It really had felt like murder. The incident...the driver's face...would not leave her memory. It had occupied a mere ten seconds perhaps but she would never forget it. What had the other fellow in the car looked like? Had there been anyone in the back seat? She really couldn't remember. There had been more than one person, she was certain. That face. The driver's face was all she could remember. It wasn't enough that her mother had been run over and killed, seemingly at random. Now she was faced with absurdities like the organ donation refusal, some stranger had tried to push them into oncoming traffic and they had absolutely no idea what had happened to George Walters. He had vanished.

Despite everything, they were nearly ready to take Hank to New York City and get him settled in his dorm room over Labor Day weekend. Life had to go forward, especially for the children. She thought Otto would have a harder time than she with this because she had been preparing herself mentally for a couple of years. It was going to hit her husband hard, he just didn't know it yet.

She would have liked to know more about the collision that had killed her mother and the man driving the car but so far no call to the local police station had yielded any results. Newspapers called her for interviews from all the surrounding towns. They mentioned Walters had been charged with driving under the influence and they wanted her to comment but inevitably they knew more about it than she did. She was simply unable to get information or an accident report from the local police. They read in the newspaper that George Walters, age sixty-six, had been charged with using a car as a dangerous weapon and with driving under the influence. They knew he was out on bail. That was it, nothing more. No call from the police, no call from the district attorney. Hank, especially, wanted to know more. He wanted to know what the guy was 'on' at the time if he was under the influence. Under the influence of what? Prescriptions? Illegal drugs? What? It seemed that Hank would not get his answers before he had to leave for school. Whatever might be going on relative to her mother's death, if anything, appeared to be going on without them.

Otto repeatedly called the local police. All they would say was that the blood tests were still in Boston or the DA had the reports and they couldn't give anyone any information about anything. Christina decided to hire an attorney. There were insurance matters to settle anyway since it was an accident resulting in a death. So they hired a fellow from a reputable firm – one they had already done business – and let him look into it. Meanwhile, they had to get Hank on his way. Christina hoped that the violence of the summer would not mar Hank's long-anticipated leap into independence. They had all suffered so deeply and so thoroughly and lost so much. They hoped that Hank would be utterly occupied, utterly distracted. That would be a good thing.

Then the suffering of August surrendered to the strength of September. They did seem to be moving forward, through time, if marking off the days could be trusted as evidence. IIt was a fine day to see Hank on his way. Hank had graduated a year early and had won a place in a prestigious program. It was such a bittersweet event. Christina spent a week laying out items in the dining room, covering the floor with logistical items, thinking and re-thinking, organizing, trying to imagine every contingency. It seemed as if she was preparing to send him into the desert for three months rather than Manhattan. Shorts, blue jeans, T-shirts, movement clothes, first aid kit, battery-operated radio, sheets, blankets, pillows, lots of socks, lots of underwear, all lined up neatly so that hopefully nothing would be left behind. Vacuum, laundry bags, text-books. In the end, Hank stuffed all his clothes into an army surplus duffel bag anyway and, with his bedding crammed in at the bottom, would spend weeks swearing he couldn't find it...or his underwear either. He couldn't have known that despite her aching feeling at watching him fly out of the nest, she was eternally grateful to him for having provided such an all-encompassing task, something to distract her from her place in time and space.

With the other two safely bunked down with friends, Christina and Otto loaded the car. Hank made sure he had his lucky necklace. They set off unafraid, excited and more than a bit melancholy into the autumn.

Christina took snapshots all day, thoroughly irritating her son. Hank sleeping at the hotel, Hank brushing his teeth, Hank in line with the other freshmen waiting for a shot at the dorm elevator. She and Otto had lived in New York for years and knew, for a young man like Hank, this was exactly the right place to be. His intellect, his opinions, his talent – all would be formed for better or worse in the messy, loud thick of things, just as it should be for him. New York would rough him up, like New York does. He would come out the other side of that as someone extraordinary.

The last conversation she had with her attorney before they left yielded a decision.

"Christina?" she had picked up the phone.

"Hi," she answered.

"Listen, I've talked to the village police, my assistant has called them several times. They simply will not release any part of the accident report or give over any real information, even to you."

Christina was stunned.

"Why? I don't understand. How could I not have any right to information about the accident that killed my mother?"

Her attorney chuckled on the other end.

"You do. I think the chief of police, who is sitting on all this, is a little confused. He says he's not releasing the information to anyone until the DAs office decides what to charge this guy with."

Her head was spinning. She sat down.

"Wait a minute. He's been charged. He's been in court already. At least that's what the newspapers said. How would I know? I mean, I'm just her family. And, frankly, how would the sole survivor getting a copy of the accident report affect anything? The facts of the case are plain. The facts aren't going to change just because I look at them. "

"No, of course not. It's a very public case; I think that might have something to do with it. Newspapers and all that. Maybe something's going on we don't know about yet."

There was silence.

"I'll tell you what I'll do for now. I'll write a letter reminding them of the Freedom of Information Act. They can still drag their feet if they want to but maybe it will help."

They hung up. It was as if George Walters had disappeared behind some impenetrable wall. She was actually going to have to invoke the Freedom of Information Act to get any details about her mother's death and the man who killed her.

"Well, I applied for two overseas positions this week," her mother was on the phone from Virginia.

"Great," Christina yawned. She was still in bed. It was Saturday. "Where?"

"Well, one is in London...".

Now she was awake. "Yeah! Pick that one. That's definitely the one you want."

"I still have to make the most-qualified list, you know. Which I haven't yet. And then there are a couple of interviews to get through, remember?"

"Ugh. Well, where's the other job?" "Cuba."

"Cuba," Christina repeated. "Why the hell would you want to go to Cuba?"

"Because it's warm. I'm worried that I won't be able to cope with the climate in London."

Christina buried her face in her pillow. She let her arm, phone included, drop over the side of the bed.

Moth-er!

She put the phone back to her ear.

"So, let me get this straight. You would rather work in Cuba, which is basically a leper colony to most of the rest of the world – quarantined, I thought, as far as the U.S. is concerned – than live and work in one of the most cosmopolitan cities in the world with all of Europe at your feet. Wait a minute. We have a military base in Cuba? How is that possible? I thought they hated us."

This was so typical of her mother. She'd spent a couple of years in Guam, another military armpit, and loved it mostly because it was intolerably hot and humid. She seemed to have loved it because it was utterly miserable. Christina and her brother spent the summer of 1977 there with her and it had been like living under water. It rained when it wasn't raining. She remembered driving her mother's little car to the summer job she had secured at a grocery store accounting office and driving through such a deep puddle that water leaked in through the driver's side door.

"Yes. Guantanamo Bay. And, yes. The climate is my number one priority."

"That's just dumb."

"Okay."

"What's the job in London?" Christina sat up, threw back the blankets. She padded to the microscopic kitchen in her tiny studio apartment and scooped coffee into the coffee maker.

"Editor for the Naval Fact Sheet. That's the tech and science bulletin the Navy sends around among all its scientists. It's a pretty big deal within the Navy anyway. I'd be helping the scientists write summaries of what they've been up to for the sheet. Whatever they're working on."

"What do scientists in the Navy work on? Weapons?" She filled the coffee pot with water at the kitchen sink and poured it into the coffee maker.

"Mostly, I suppose. Other stuff, too. I imagine I might be helping them edit other work, as well. I'd be located in the Office of Naval Research. But, like I said, I have to make the most-qualified list and the job doesn't close for a few more weeks."

Christina was trying to finish college... again. It was hard for two reasons. First, she was putting herself through and she had no money. Both her parents, who had been divorced for decades, seemed to have a fair amount of discretionary income but were unprepared to pitch in for her college expenses. They just didn't subscribe to that sort of mollycoddling, like many other things that her friend's parents did believe in. She was so used to it; she didn't even notice anymore. It was indistinguishable from anything else in a very thin but broad layer of resentment that always bubbled just below her conscious thoughts.

Second, she was a talented writer but didn't know if that's what she wanted to study. She had a ravenous curiosity, an unfettered imagination, and a rare gift for making ridiculously obscure connections between one thing and another but no real discipline yet when it came to the writing; her attention span just wasn't long enough. Her stories were never finished, her thoughts dangled carelessly – Christina's life threads weren't yet drawn together – they were very unruly and couldn't be braided or woven. So majoring in English would give her a lash under which to have to produce actual finished work and hopefully learn some form. However, she strongly suspected that at some point it was better to write than to study writing, which is otherwise known as 'reading.' The one thing that no one ever got around when it came to writing was that one needed to be able to establish a level of tension and concentration – like throwing a net out into the sea and keeping it open and filled with water, throwing a lasso out into the air and keeping it twirling endlessly or hitting a tuning note and sustaining the sound way past the point of reason. That tension had to hold all the way to the end of a piece, no matter how long. It was exhausting. It was like an itch just out of reach that never went away. It was an actual organ of deliberation, an organ of concentration and will, which has to be located and voluntarily developed. Part of it, too, is hearing the 'music.' There is music in words, one has to hear it, and then one knows the story is true. Without that, words issue themselves into the air and then clang to the ground, collapsing under their own weight.

She had no money and the financial aid picture was a little unfathomable at the moment. She was working as a scheduler for a carpet cleaning company, she had waitressed, tended bar, the usual student stuff. Her car wasn't working and she had no way to have it fixed so it was in a semi-permanent parked position in front of her apartment, like a metal and rubber sculpture erected there to commemorate her poverty every morning when she left. There was ramen in the cupboard and diet soda in the refrigerator. Her parents undoubtedly assumed that when Christina got tired of living on ramen and diet soda she'd surrender and jump into the mainstream with everyone else.

Her mother was working for the Navy in Dahlgren, Virginia, at Naval Weapons. That was all Christina knew because her security level prohibited her from talking about her work much at all. While it was fabulous that her mother was on the verge of being able to travel to exotic locales due to her work as a technical writer for the Navy, that sort of thing sounded like indentured servitude to Christina. Grammar for a living and dining out on punctuation successes? Break out the champagne, honey, we've got ourselves a semi-colon! No, thanks. Her mother, on the other hand, was just anal enough to thoroughly enjoy technical editing and just nervous enough to appreciate the relentless routine and security. She was also abnormally enamored of the military and considered herself to be a World War II buff. Was that because her own father had been in the army during WWII and wore a lovely, smart, crisp uniform just after he took a powder and left her and her mother to fend for themselves? Yes, it was. Her mother knew all this and couldn't stop herself. She didn't want to. Newsreels from the Second World War and headlines from the Cold War had shaped her reality completely. A very tall man in uniform who treated her like garbage was too close to being her Dad to resist. As a civilian woman working for the Navy, these men were available absolutely everywhere. Military bases were wallpapered with them.

On the other hand, Christina's father inhabited an easy chair in his living room not too far from her apartment and did come out once a year to play blackjack in Vegas but that was the extent of his world and had been for years. It was just plain difficult to find a way to take him into account.

"Also," her mother was saying, "this post requires a much higher security clearance so I'd have to go through that." Nothing to worry about there. Her mother always played by the rules. She was single. Her children were grown. She had outstanding credit, no debts, no encumbrances, no substance addictions, not one dirty little secret… nothing that would have smudged her character nor anything that could be used as leverage. She loved the military, loved a regimented environment, and accepted everything her country did as the absolute right thing to do. In essence, she was tailor-made to work for the military.

Six months later, as she sat down to a dinner of spicy ramen and diet soda, Christina got another call from her mother. The fellow who had originally been hired to take the London job had backed out at the last minute; she had no idea why. The job was hers if she wanted it. So she took it and in 1989, her mother moved to London, to work at Edison House near Marylebone Station for a three-year hitch. In the summer of 1990 Christina flew into Heathrow Airport to visit for a few weeks. She was also going to make a short pilgrimage to Ireland.

In general, the first thing Christina fell in love with was the sheer abundance of daylight in England in the summer. It was the latitude: a blessing in the summer, a curse in the dark winter. The coffee smell drifted through her mother's house at five in the morning and there was plenty of daylight already. The sun finally dipped below the horizon at about ten o'clock in the evening. Her mother rented a terraced house near the train station at Little Chalfont in Buckinghamshire, or Bucks as everyone called it. The United States Navy subsidized her rent and she was allowed to buy food at the PX and gas for her car on the nearest base at an extremely reduced rate compared to what the Brits paid. In addition to all that, she received her normal pay grade salary. Her two-storey living space was narrow and long and she had a big overgrown back garden that opened out onto a large grazing common although there was nothing but pavement in the front side of the house. The commuter train into the city was within walking distance although her mother always drove and parked in the car park because there were no pavements once she left her house and there was no mercy on the roads for either cyclists or pedestrians. It was a thirty-minute ride into the city on the 'fast Amersham', the express between Amersham and London. The train pulled into the well-appointed, clean and modern station at Marylebone, just a few streets away from the office. This particular morning, Christina was meeting her mother just before lunch. She was supposed to wait at the station because she had no idea how to get to Edison House. Her mother would collect her and take her to the office to be introduced around. Christina got off the train and found a take-away tea shop, ordered a cup of hot tea with milk and a chocolate muffin and sat on a bench just inside the street-side door, happily munching and sipping while she waited. There was a flower stall on the corner opposite her bench, overflowing with beautiful blooms. How lovely, she thought, to want to pick up a bouquet on your way home. She also loved that a person could sit on a city bus or train or in a station and hear an absolute symphony of disparate languages, for the study of languages unknown to her was one of the loves of Christina's life.

Eventually, she spotted her mother entering the station and rose to meet her. She was wearing the obligatory Burberry coat. It was a bit cool, that was true, especially for June, but maybe not extraordinary in England.

"So," her mother said, "it's this way." She turned right and crossed the street. Then they took an almost immediate left turn. "I thought I would introduce you to some of my co-workers, they're expecting us and then, if you don't mind, one of the scientists' wives wants to take you to lunch and show you around tomorrow. She and her husband are German."

Christina was puzzled. "Someone I don't even know?"

"Well, I ended up having a string of meetings I didn't know about and Lorna offered to show you around. You'll like her, I promise. Here we are." The sign read Old Marylebone Road.

They stopped in front of a red and white building "Edison House" was engraved on a gold plaque by the front door. They entered and climbed a narrow flight of stairs. It seemed as if all stairways in England were narrow and musty. A feudal remnant, perhaps, defensible from the top? Christina was introduced to several people immediately and shook many hands. She saw a man stand up from a desk in another room. He had aggressively disciplined short black hair and was clean-shaven and forty-ish and wearing a dress-white naval uniform. He turned away from them but she caught the right side of his face. He rolled his eyes. Obviously he was annoyed to have to stop what he was doing and greet her.

He turned, put on a smile and stuck out his hand. Christina took it. "Commander Scott," her mother said, "this is my daughter, Christina."

"Great to meet you, Christina," he said.

Yeah, I'll bet.

"Your mother's really been looking forward to this visit. Unfortunately, I have a meeting so you'll have to excuse me." He turned, put his uniform hat on, and descended the stairs, his white back disappearing anonymously through the door.

Her mother was taking the afternoon off. They would have dinner in the city and then had tickets to see Peter O'Toole do some play at the Shaftsbury Theatre in the West End. They took the tube from Marylebone to Leicester Square, all the while her mother chatting about the particulars of Underground travel in the city and which trains were a pain and which were better than most.

"Most of us can't wait to get home," she was saying, "if for no other reason than it's just too hard to get from point A to point B. We're none of us accustomed to relying on the Tube to get where we want to go. We miss our cars. We miss the big supermarkets. We really have to think too much."

Christina's mind drifted. Complaining was just a habitual method of communication for her mother. She seemed to have made friends here, that was good. She was more in charge of herself than Christina had ever seen her. That was a surprise. Her mother was, in a way, inhabiting her own body and life in a way that Christina couldn't remember ever having seen. Usually Christina had a far better ability to leap and damn the consequences; her mother tended to be hesitant and dubious and a little fearful, asking Christina's advice even when she was a child. Fending for herself in a completely foreign environment had done much to bring out the confidence in her mother and every little girl wants a mother who just clearly believes she knows what she's doing, even if it isn't really true. It is a child's primary source of security in the world. She liked what London was bringing to the surface in her mother. She had not even imagined the makings of it were in there.

They ate at a small Italian cafe not far from the theatre; a table for two looking out onto the street. The pasta came in a cavernous white ceramic bowl. There were shrimp nestled in noodles drowning in butter and Parmesan cheese. The street was narrow and cobble-stoned, with street lamps that would lightly illumine the evening later on. The narrow pavements were full of city workers who were now snaking around and pushing by as they hurried to catch their trains. She gazed at a small bookstore just opposite as she ate and half-listened to her mother, who was not eating, just sipping a cup of black coffee as was her habit. In London, she loved to order coffee before dinner or on its own because the British only drank coffee after dinner with a sweet and it tickled her mother to confuse them with her very American habits. In fact, the more bemused they were with her American habits, the more she loved shoving it into their faces. She was contrary all the way up to being unnecessarily rude and wasting everyone's time. Every once in a while, Christina would hang back and apologize to whoever her mother had just insulted for the sake of insulting them. She was quite used to it.

"Tell me about this woman I'm touring the city with tomorrow," Christina said.

"Lorna von Marshall," her mother replied, "she and her husband,

Wolfgang, as I told you, are German. They're a fair bit older than I am, she's probably sixty and he may be getting close to seventy. They usually live in Virginia, but he's been assigned over here for a special project. He thinks it'll be his last assignment before he retires. She's a sculptor. You should ask to see her studio sometime."

Promising.

"How did a German end up working for the U.S. Navy?"

"Wolfgang was in the German army. He was older, in his late twenties when the war broke out. He worked as a baker, on the front lines, serving food to the troops. In fact, he lost most of the hearing in one ear because he was standing too close to one of the big guns one day when it went off. Went to a polytechnic in Berlin before the war. Has several advanced degrees, one is in physics, for sure. He's brilliant. They're all brilliant but some are nice and some are bastards about it. Wolfgang happens to be nice. A lot of the scientists connected with ONR are Germans from the World War II era or from the Eastern Bloc. Most of what I have to do for them is help them with their written English and it's a little boring. Some of the stuff I see...," her mother closed her eyes and shuddered slightly, "well, it's scary. Damned scary." That was all she said about it and Christina knew well not to ask. "What does he do now, this man?" The pasta was warm and good.

The people outside were definitely worth watching.

"He works on the weather, atmospheric experiments. I don't know any details because I don't work with him much right now but I do know that sometime in the forties, maybe earlier, he went back to university to take an advanced degree in meteorology or atmospheric physics, I think. He didn't have any choice. They said you will be going back and you will be studying this... whoever they are. Probably the Nazis."

"I don't like your boss much."

Her mother stirred her coffee slowly.

"Well, I often wonder how many of the people I work with are spooks. Probably quite a few."

The Shaftsbury Theatre was like many other theatres in the West End, tiny, kind of dingy and corny, and old. Both the seats and curtains were worn velvet. Nevertheless, the benefit to this kind of cramped set-up was that no matter where you were seated, you were close to the stage. The house lights dimmed and the play began.

Peter O'Toole was wonderful, as she had assumed he would be. She had no affection for aging drunks so the story itself was unsatisfying. Still, it was a note-worthy event and she was glad to have seen it. He was good enough to make her wonder if he was telling his own story really. They caught the fast Amersham afterward to Little Chalfont; she slept well that night, waking as usual to the ever-present aroma of coffee early the next morning.

At twelve-thirty sharp she presented herself at Edison House, once again, and was ushered into a small windowless office, fluorescent overhead lights bearing down, where her mother sat with several printed pages spread out before her and two men, scientists she assumed, since they were not clad in uniforms, who leaned over the desk, deep in concentrated discussion. The lights beat down unnoticed by the little group underneath, but she detested fluorescent lights and so searched the room for somewhere else to rest her attention. Above the desk sat a row of books: the Chicago Style Manual, Navy technical writing manuals, Strunk and White and the like. One of the scientists was an older fellow, white hair tucked behind his ears a little in need of a trim, hearing aid conspicuous in his right ear. He had thick skin and a ruddy complexion; his eyes were blue and one could have said contained the possibility of affection but he was obviously extremely busy. Christina knew at once that this must be Wolfgang van Marshall. The Commander's office was again empty.

Then a small, thin woman appeared, clad in a beige trench coat, the belt obediently done up around her tiny middle. Her white hair was cut in a chin-length bob and she wore eyeglasses. She smiled and stuck out her hand, tucking her umbrella under one arm. Germans had such a wonderful habit of shaking hands no matter what.

"Hello," she said in fairly well-accented English, "I am Lorna Von Marshall. And you must be Christina, yes?"

"Yes," Christina took her hand and replied, smiling. One could not help smiling back at this little woman.

"I see you have met my husband?" she said. Wolfgang looked up and nodded. "We're going sightseeing, Wolfgang."

He stood up and shrugged, grinning, as if to say, sure, go and play, only leave me alone just now. It was an affectionate gesture, communication decades in the making. By four o'clock, they had seen much of the city and Christina was ravenous. Lorna was a wonderful guide and a lively and charismatic conversationalist. The city smelled of diesel fumes and everyone, literally everyone, smoked cigarettes as they walked. The Strand, the Royal Courts of Justice, and the College of London; they had seen many things that most tourists would have on their secondary list, the 'if we have time' list. Lorna seemed to know quite a lot about the various buildings they visited. Christina supposed that an American would have a very American list and a European, a very European list. Certainly, a German would have had their fill of churches and castles so they had seen law schools and newspapers and universities. Christina positively yearned to see Lorna's artwork.

"You must be hungry?" Lorna asked.

They headed for Covent Garden to eat something and to sit for a while. The restaurant, called The Grotto, was primarily decorated in pink and, dimly lit by rustic wall sconces, had a subterranean atmosphere. It was a charming, warm, friendly place, floor to ceiling, a pale skin-toned stucco. They sat together as old friends already, Lorna sipping Fra 'Angelico while Christina had a coffee, so comfortable they were together. Lorna was remarkably skilled at making a person feel quite at ease. They made arrangements for Christina to visit the von Marshalls when she returned from Ireland in a few days' time. Suddenly it was six o'clock and they needed to pay the bill and hurry back to Edison House where Christina was to be deposited so she could ride home with her mother. They hurried, laughing.

"Time has flown away without us," Lorna smiled.

Christina flew to Cork Airport a few days later, on the wings of midsummer's eve. Even more so than England, Ireland in June demanded long sleeves and pants plus a sweater or two. Lee picked her up at the airport in an old Volvo wagon. Lee, a childhood friend of her mother's, had grown up in the same little town in America. She was tall and slender, wore no makeup and had long black hair that was uncut and unfettered. Her Irish accent was very light. Lee threw her bag into the rear of the Volvo and not long after they were on their way Cork City gave way to the countryside. The diversion to Ireland for a few days was a gift, affordable because Lee and Thomas, her very married Irish lover, ran a bed and breakfast there and all that was required of Christina was a plane ticket and a few dollars in her pocket. Rural Ireland still existed in its own time, inhabited by farms and villages and fisherman and priests. And writers. Lots and lots of writers.

"There are more writers per square foot in Ireland," Lee was shouting to her over the noise of the old engine, "than anywhere else on earth!"

She slowed the car considerably for an obstacle on the road before them. As they got closer, Christina realized it was a cart pulled by a small horse, little more than a pony really.

"Gypsies!" Lee shouted.

They were right up behind the little cart.

"Seriously," Christina replied, "there are still gypsies?"

Lee downshifted noisily.

"Yes. Usually you see trailer caravans. This family has one of the old-style wagons."

They crawled along the road behind the wagon and pony. Lee decided to pull over and go into a shop to get some provisions, hoping the wagon would get far enough ahead of them that they might get home before dinner.

They stepped inside the shop, abruptly quiet after the noisy ride. Christina followed her along the aisles.

"People hate them," she said stopping to inspect a plastic-wrapped package of tongue.

"Why?"

"People say they steal, for one thing. I don't know, it's one of those ancient enmities. Ah-ha! Here we are." She located a package of pork then went on to buy a small bottle of Ribena fruit syrup. Then they waited for their turn with the cashier. "I think it may be because in many ways they live in the last century and that makes people angry somehow. That represents lots of things to people. Freedom, for one. They haven't readily embraced technology, for another, or the rules for modern life. They're self-sufficient, right? The modern world isn't everything it's cracked up to be... who wants to be reminded of that?"

They moved forward in line.

"You know, we don't often see money. Thomas and I do a lot of bartering, one thing for another. We have fields being grazed by someone else's cattle. Things like that." Lee laughed.

"Well," Christina said, "I've brought money to pay for my room and board. It's all yours."

She pulled fifty Irish pounds from her pocket and handed it to Lee. Lee clasped the notes between her palms and rubbed them together, as if she could start a little blaze with the cash by doing that. Paper money apparently was not totally necessary to make their lives work, but a bit of it was a treat.

When they pulled up to the cottage, Thomas swung through the screen door. He was smaller and thinner than Lee, with greyish brown hair and a beard that he wore in the style reminiscent of a medieval monk. Lee parked alongside an old uneven stone wall covered in moss. It was a low-slung house with old plaster and short ceilings. Christina put her bag down in the library; a duvet and pillows stacked there waiting for her among the books. There was a dining room, kitchen and bath on the ground floor. A set of French doors revealed an acreage and a view of an unkempt little glass greenhouse with a hectic array of clay pots stacked on shelves inside. In the far corner of the kitchen, Thomas had installed a hatch in the ceiling and a drop-down ladder. This was for unobserved escapes when they had guests or when Lee was simply done dealing with everyone.

The next morning, Thomas, an archaeologist, took Lee and Christina on a hike around the immediate area. He suggested she tuck a book into her pocket as they might have occasion to sit by the river for a while. They set off down a dirt road, in the direction of a gathering of red and white cattle, which all stopped what they were doing to watch the trio pass by. A hundred yards further on, the dirt road narrowed and the sides of the road become a grass-covered bank on either side.

As they walked, Thomas put a hand out and stopped them, motioning for them to listen. They did hear something, a scuffling followed by bleating. It sounded like sheep or goats. Sure enough, a moment later a herd of sheep rounded the corner coming straight at them. There were goats as well, some tiny kids, horns just disbudded. Some that morning, by the look of them, as there was a little blood crusted on the little stumps on their heads. There was nowhere to go, the sides of the road were high and the lane was narrow. Thomas picked her up and helped her jump for the side followed by Lee. There they perched as the flock passed noisily down the road under and away. They laughed at their predicament but the view was wonderful.

"What's over there?" Christina covered her eyes and pointed toward the horizon.

"Ah!" Thomas said, following her gaze, "That's Skibbereen. We'll drive in there in a bit. We'll get lobsters off the boat if someone is already in." As Thomas drove through Skibbereen, they slowed to a crawl allowing a priest on a bicycle to pass.

Thomas pointed him out and said, "The astronomical society here has a telescope over in that building behind the rectory. They meet once a month, next week in fact, after you're gone. Ah well, never mind. The priest is the President of it. Like the priest before him was."

Odd that a Catholic priest would be the head of the Astronomy Society here.

"The priest before this one lived in the rectory there with his mother. When she died they had to pry him out of the house. Three days he wouldn't let go of the body, screaming and crying he was. They had to carry him away, as well." Thomas tipped an imaginary hat to the priest as he cycled by them. The car moved along again. There were no lobstermen in just yet so they settled for a piece of beef and drove back to the cottage. They sat at the wooden table in the kitchen, wood stove burning behind Thomas. He liked to sit near the stove. Lee was at the sink preparing food.

"You know, Christina," Lee said, back turned, "I always feel that your mother was one of the bravest women I'd ever met."

Christina was taken aback. That was not a word she'd have used.

How brave is it to… never mind. I guess you just had to have been there.

Lee thought her mother was brave but Lee had grown up with their reality. Christina had grown up with the adult version, a reluctant reflection in a severely broken mirror. The two versions and their inner workings were probably never going to line up.

No matter what, the wilds of Ireland were places, it seemed clear, where the bottom still held. There remained a slice of arboreal forest intact in County Cork. One needed peat or wood to stay warm, a bit of land to cultivate, a boat that didn't leak, a good book to chase the cloudy days away. Cattle concerned themselves with your comings and goings and sheep could chase you up a tree. It was no wonder Ireland was filled with more writers per square mile than anywhere else on earth.

*****

"Come in, come in!" Lorna beckoned. Christina was ushered into the foyer. The front door was leaded glass. It was a typical feature in London houses that Christina liked and here it allowed an enormous amount of sunlight into the room without sacrificing privacy.

"Would you care for a coffee?" Lorna asked.

"Not at the moment, thanks," Christina replied, taking off her coat. Lorna took the coat and hung it on a rack near the door.

"I'm really anxious to see your work, if you want to know the truth."

Lorna laughed.

"Alright, then! We'll not disappoint you." She led Christina through the narrow hallway and opened a door. A long narrow flight of stairs led to what was a lower, garden-level room, as one had to ascend a flight of stairs to enter the front door from the street.

The studio lay at the bottom of the stairs. It was a bright room painted white to catch what light came in through windows in the front and back. All along the walls, on benches and on a work table were faces, masks mostly, but the occasional three-dimensional head either alone or in groups of two. A Madonna and child with what looked like an eagle or some other bird of prey attached to the woman's left shoulder, peering out into the distance, caught her eye.

"As you can see," Lorna said over her shoulder, "I am obsessed with the human face. I confess."

From Lorna's garden level apartment, an endless parade of feet and legs passed the front windows. It made for a fascinating pastime. They pulled up chairs and sat with a drink, conjuring up stories about the legs and feet that passed by. Clothes, shoes, gait, pace, all were fair game. Especially intriguing were the legs that stopped, turned and changed direction indecisively. Stocking Tales, Lorna called it.

"If one is very observant, one can learn so much from a person without even talking to them. It's really an art, this game of assessing someone based on their clothing, gestures and demeanor. There are so many of them sometimes right outside my window there, they remind me of the big dances we all went to in Berlin right after the war. Legs, legs and more legs! There was very little to do and no one had any money so everyone went to the dances. I was twenty-four and Wolfgang would have been thirty-three already. We met at a dance just like that."

"Is that a good story?" Christina asked.

"But, of course! I have only intriguing stories," Lorna laughed. "I was supposed to meet another young man at that dance. Actually, I wasn't even going to go because I didn't have a dress to wear. No money, as usual. But my friend, Ruth, who was rich, lent me a dress. Wolfgang stole me away from the boy at the dance and that was that."

The sculptures, faces and masks were made of granite or some other stone, clay or wood. Some had been formed with hands and fingertips, others were chiseled. Most of the faces had closed eyes. Some were ever so slightly open, and a few were open but the eye sockets were empty. They were meant to be slightly hidden in gardens or leap out at the unwary observer. Perhaps they wouldn't be noticed at all but simply blend into a tableau. Although Christina thought it would be good to see the soul behind the masks, she thought they were beautiful. She also thought Lorna was beautiful; a working sculptor in the heart of London was simply too romantic a notion to resist. Anyone with an imagination would make up details Lorna did not provide.

On the worktable lay a block of wood and a carving knife.

"I am working on a young woman right now, the face is there in the wood already, it reveals itself as I carve. My job is to get to know her and see who she is," Lorna said when Christina mentioned the rough, unfinished piece. "Perhaps she'll be a tree spirit in the garden; I'll finish her and hang her on a tree."

Christina's last day in London was bound to arrive, there was no stopping it. She was scheduled to lunch with her mother and the wife of one of the Eastern Bloc scientists at a restaurant in a hotel near the Swiss Embassy. The space was tidy and clean, decked out in ferns as was quite popular then. They ordered. Christina felt very melancholy about leaving.

Back to spicy ramen and diet soda, I suppose.

She and Lorna had promised to write. The von Marshalls were due to return to Virginia within the year.

"Have you had a pleasant visit?" her mother's friend asked.

"I have. Not really anxious to return home yet, I have to admit."

"Magda, are you going home for a visit soon?" her mother asked.

"I'd like to," the woman replied as a waiter set a bowl of consommé on the table in front of her. "I haven't seen my family in two years. The commander refuses to authorize time off for my husband."

Christina spread a white linen napkin across her lap.

"I think he's a horse's ass," she said.

Magda started, eyes wide. "Shhhh…!"

"Why?"

"You don't know who's listening."

George and the Dragon

"Most people don't realize it, and that includes most New Yorkers, but just outside the United Nations building is a statue. Right outside the visitor's entrance. It's a metal statue of St. George on horseback. In his right hand is a lance or a sword or something and he's got his arm cocked way back, ready to hurl the thing down. Under the horse is a metal representation of a dragon. You know what that dragon's made of, Unger?"

Two men stood in a doorway shielding themselves from snow. One man, mostly bald with a little closely shaved white hair remaining, thick-set, stuck his hands in his overcoat pockets. The younger man huddled over a cigarette, protecting his lighter flame from the wind.

"What's that, old man?"

"Missiles. Old dismantled missiles. Russian and American both. How do you like that? Old SCUDS." He chuckled lightly.

Unger smiled, pulled deeply on the freshly lit cigarette and inhaled smoke laced with cold air and snow, "Yeah. How 'bout that. See you tomorrow. *Vice Admiral*." He darted out of the doorway and headed down the street.

Alex Getz, retired Vice Admiral Alex Getz, sixty-eight years old, current advisor to Sceptre Corporation on all their defense department contracts, lingered in a doorway in lower Manhattan hiding from the snow. He was still in front of the Sceptre offices although the meetings were over. Not everyone had left the building, which made him wonder. He waited for as long as it seemed realistic to wait just to see who else might come out but no one else did. He needed a cab back to his hotel. He still had Christmas shopping to do. Every year it was this way. There was always a lot of business to be done before the end of the calendar year and he never remembered that he was going to hate shopping on December twenty-eighth. So he ended up doing it every year. He was deeply disturbed at the moment but decided to shop anyway to keep anyone he didn't want to suspect he was deeply disturbed from noticing. Go about your business, that was the first rule. It was his first rule anyway. Getz was at the end of his association with Sceptre. That was finished as of tonight. They were involved in chemical warfare which they had, apparently, been testing on larger and larger samples of the world population for decades and now Sceptre had a plan, ready to roll out, to test some of the most serious biological and chemical weapons on earth on living populations. They maintained that test populations would be relatively small, completely contained animal populations but it seemed to Getz that a group capable of crossing this line wouldn't think much about using 'chems' or 'bios' on anyone for any reason.

In Vietnam, he had seen the results of chemical warfare. He had made himself one of the foremost experts on chemical and biological weapons strictly for that reason. There wasn't even the excuse of an 'enemy' in this plan. There was no Bad Guy here, just unadulterated power mongering. Sceptre was the bad guy. It was enough that they had been dumping chemicals from the sky already in barely excusable amounts, really shaky stuff, barely tolerable, supported by the thinnest scientific data. Most of the data they claimed to collect from these long term experiments was cooked, biased and downright fraudulent. Alex had liaised with the Department of Defense, going on record that he thought this was unethical at the very least. This new plan was way over the line. It was due to roll out in the first few days of January, so he had very little time. He had years' worth of documentation in a box in his office at the Fitzpatrick Hotel on Lexington beneath the floorboards under the carpet.

The Pentagon didn't know that yet. Very few people could have accumulated such documentation, just the half dozen or so primary players. He was that well-connected, that trusted, and, frankly, he was running the show in key ways. He had been an advisor to three Presidents and was well connected at the Pentagon. They must have known this might be the straw that broke the camel's back. One word from Alex could snarl this project up forever with the military. They would almost certainly have difficulties with air space and the FAA without him. He would have to be very careful now. They would be waiting for the merest suggestion that he might sound the alarm. He was a White Hat at heart and now they knew it. Everybody knew it.

He returned to his hotel on foot after stopping at Bloomingdales for a few things for his wife. There was a fireplace, albeit a gas-powered one. He turned it on, slipped out of snow-filled shoes, and retrieved a shopping bag from the hallway inside the front door. He poured himself a scotch and sat down at the table. From the bag he took out gifts for his wife, wrapping paper, tape and ribbons. Carefully, because he was a man who took care, he cut two square pieces of silver flocked wrapping paper, measured to fit these gifts. He carefully placed each box precisely in the center of the wrapping paper and folded the paper up along the edges, creasing and pressing. Cellophane tape secured each seam. Just as methodically, he measured and cut ribbon, tied each package up with it and made a nice knot with the ends. He pushed the boxes to the side of the table and he was done. His wife was due back on the thirty-first.

Another scotch, this time by the window. He was on the eleventh floor. He pushed the curtain aside gently with his free hand, not too far, and gazed out into the whiteness. It was a habit to step back and away from the window at the slightest unexpected movement. The avenue was beautiful in snow, absolutely irresistible. Still some traffic on Lexington, despite the hour and the weather. Far below a taxi pulled to the curb. He let the curtain swing just about shut, a slit left open through which he watched the sidewalk below. A man carrying a yellow umbrella opened the door and as he got in he closed his umbrella, opened it then closed it again. He shut the door and the taxi pulled away.

The next day at twelve-thirty precisely, Rear Admiral Alex Getz entered La Caprice Restaurant on Fifth Avenue just opposite the Central Park Zoo. He sat alone at a table where he had a clear view of the sidewalk. He ordered fish and chips. As he ate, he saw the same man, the man from the cab the evening before, stop in front of the restaurant. He wore a Michigan State University sweatshirt, a Yankees cap, and a down coat and had a very big, very expensive camera slung around his neck. The city was full of tourists just like this. He stopped in front of the window of La Caprice for a moment, then crossed the street and disappeared into the zoo. The day was clear and cold and there was about a foot of snow on the ground in the park.

The two men met in front of the snow monkey enclosure. There were many people, parents and children, gathered here because the snow monkeys were receiving their Christmas gifts. Animal handlers positioned themselves inside the enclosure in order to narrate events. A pine tree had been placed in the enclosure and it was covered with fruit. The snow monkeys climbed the tree to get the fruit, sped off with it, kept it away from each other, devoured it whole, then swung back onto the tree for another treat.

Alex strolled up beside his contact.

"No matter what they're doing, they look unhappy don't they?" He laughed.

"They do. Downright gloomy." He raised his camera and began snapping photographs.

The message to Alex's superiors was that Sceptre Corporation was absolutely determined to roll out the operation, code-named Gray Quilt, no matter what happened or who objected. The fellow continued to snap pictures for a full minute, scanning the entire circumference of the snow monkey enclosure. He appeared to be following the monkeys as they grabbed bits of fruit from the tree and scampered around each other. Finally, he lowered his camera. He and Alex leaned on the chest-high cement wall that encircled the monkey habitat.

"A couple of monkeys here seem hungrier than the rest. They've been eating for two full days!"

"Greedy bastards!" Getz laughed. "Which ones?"

"Ten o'clock, they have a lot of black fur on their heads."

Getz casually looked to his left. Two men were indeed leaning on the opposite wall, just as they were, and they wore black knit caps. They were all watched, naturally, all the time but this was extra surveillance by unknown assets.

"Jeez," Getz said, "maybe a monkey ought to go out for a hot dog every once in a while if he's that hungry." *Bring me in for protection.*

Getz and his contact walked away from each other, they'd likely never see each other again. He stayed by the snow monkey enclosure for five full minutes, not wanting to appear spooked. The Sceptre people were already alarmed. He was vulnerable right now, at least for a few minutes. He had asked to come in, for protection. That was all he had to do. Being out in the cold was temporary but it was a very dangerous temporary. He knew everything. They would want him dead if they realized he was about to bring the program to a screaming halt. Dead men can't get in the way of anything.

The two watchers wandered off in the direction of the polar bear habitat. Alex would rather they stay where he could see them until his people showed up. He waited. This was wrong. His experience, his intuition, his military training… everything was starting to scream at him, *wrong!* His people would have been here almost instantly. They weren't showing up.

He decided to move out toward Fifth Avenue. He had to stay close to his original position but visible and surrounded by people. He began to move quickly. Still no sign of the watchers but everyone, anyone, could be a watcher at this point. A double line of very young school children holding hands and chattering loudly ambled past him, slowing him down. He passed the snow leopard cages, the penguin habitat, a utility shed loomed on his right. As he passed the shed, rough arms grabbed him from behind. Someone put him in a chokehold, he was cracked violently in the head and his legs went out from under him. Both men pressed their full weight down on him while one pulled off his shoe and sock in one swift motion and he felt a sharp jab in his right heel. That was the point. They were off him and running.

He sat up as quickly as he could and dug around in his pocket for his knife. He opened it, plunged the edge into his heel and, screaming, dug a hole out the size of a nickel. Whatever they put in there would be in a tiny ball bearing sealed in wax. The wax melted at body temperature releasing the poison. That way he might be miles away before he keeled over and died. He had a few seconds but he had to work quickly and be ruthless.

Where were his people? They weren't coming, the bastards. They were giving Sceptre the green light. He was out in the cold. Genocide was a 'go.' He'd been cracked in the head and now his foot was maimed and bleeding. He'd probably get a little shocky soon, as well. If he'd got the thing out in time, he might get a little sick, that's all. He was starting to spike a fever, he could tell. So even though he may have survived this attempt on his life, he was bound to be so sick for the next few hours that he'd be little more than an obvious target reeling around the city. Maybe they would hang back, think it was just the poison doing its work. Half a dozen substances came to mind but he pushed that thought aside. Either he'd been quick enough or he hadn't. He struggled to rise and staggered toward the avenue. People moved away from him, this old lunatic staggering into the avenue, barefoot, carrying a shoe, trailing blood. He propped himself up against the wall that lined Fifth Avenue on the park side. Many vendors sat in folding chairs behind displays set up along the wall despite the cold. It was Christmas and they sold a lot of trinkets and prints. Getz tried to stand and walk again after a moment, the cold was driving him now. One, two steps and he toppled over again, the world slid out from under him. He fell into a display of black and white photographs of the city.

"Hey, goddammit!" The vendor leaped out of his chair to try to catch the falling merchandise. "Watch out!"

"Oh," Getz slurred. What was actually coming out of his mouth? Not the words in his head. "Sorry."

"Are you alright?" the vendor realized there was something very wrong. Getz didn't look like a bum. He looked like an old man having a stroke.

"No," Getz stammered, "my car didn't come for me."

"Sit down, man," the vendor righted his chair and took Getz by the arm, lowered him into the chair.

"Cold," Getz whispered.

The vendor pulled Getz's sweatshirt hood up over his head. He poured tea from a thermos and helped Getz cup it in his hands, lift it to his lips and drink.

"Is there someone I can call for you?"

Getz shook his head. *No, don't call anyone. I'll just die faster.*

Two days later, on December thirty-first, the same vendor pushed a cart laden with his photos across Fifth Avenue to his spot. There was a crowd behind the wall, a hundred yards into the park, near a lake. He wanted to see; usually things like this in the park were a big deal. He pushed his cart along the path until the crowd was so thick he couldn't move it anymore. He wanted to see. Reluctantly, he left his cart on the path and pushed closer to the center of the crowd. A police boat bobbed about in the center of the little lake. They were pulling a stiff, bloated corpse from the water. Wet rope dangled from the corpse's neck. News crews were arriving. With some effort the heavy body was hauled into the boat and the police made for land. As they got closer, the vendor pushed his way toward the apparent landing point. He wanted to see. Central Park was his office and all the vendors would be speculating about this for days. He got one short look at the body. Even contorted by the filthy water filling his body and the remnants of poison, he could make out the features of the old man with one shoe.

*****

June 9, 1966. Midshipman Alex Getz left Annapolis for the last time as a cadet. The previous day he had graduated with his class, which was the first to use the new stadium for the ceremony. He was to report to the aircraft carrier USS Hancock, eventually, as an ensign. First, he had been assigned rather mysteriously to temporary duty at the Pentagon in the Navy's Center for Naval Operations. This would have to do with two things: his university major in Operations Analysis, an applied mathematics degree, and his father, a naval attaché in Saigon.

For today though, and just for today, he was a regular guy, just a twenty-one year old college graduate. His parents had already caught a Braniff flight back to Texas. When he was finished in Washington D.C., he would drive down as well, taking a leisurely six days, six days to think about what lay behind and what lay ahead, and six days more than he had had to himself in a great long while. Four years ago he had turned down a number of other college offers when he selected the Naval Academy. He was brilliant, gregarious and an all-American tight end. His senior photograph in the yearbook – *The Bag* – seemed to reveal, if one could go by the photo alone, a young man who wasn't merely serious. The corners of his bow-shaped mouth did curl up slightly, although it didn't seem to be a smile. His eyes promised something altogether mean or even possibly brutal. His general countenance, if one looked long enough, seemed to demonstrate a shade of betrayal mixed with fury. The six days he spent cutting a diagonal across the country was a time he meant to finalize his feelings about Vietnam. Everybody talked about Vietnam all the time. It was their war. He thought he would also marry Donna either before he left or when he returned, he would leave that up to her.

Donna was his high school sweetheart waiting in Abilene. She was gorgeous, blonde, she wore white gloves and a hat to church every Sunday and was profoundly practical. She would not marry him just because he was leaving for Vietnam, she would marry him when she decided the time was right. She would not graduate from Abilene Christian College until the following spring anyway. Most of the cadets swaggered around bellowing their impatience to end up in-country. Not Getz. The whole subject left him completely cold. He was assigned to an aircraft carrier, his specialty computer-guided ship-to-shore missiles. For him it was an exciting, state-of-the-art field. Lots of technology to work with, computer systems that were brand new, and his ability to use his considerable mathematical prowess, sitting on a ship far, far off-shore. COBOL was everyone's darling at the moment and he was truly gifted in the new science of computers. His degree and talents made him exceptionally desirable to the Navy in areas of strategy, operations, and intelligence and there really wasn't anywhere else to practice his skills.

His final grades were poor but in no way reflected his intelligence and capabilities. It was a shame, he thought, because he had tried like hell as the years went by and the war drums beat ever louder, to make himself seem unfit for command. It had not worked. He was often in trouble, a member of the century club early on – having completed more than one hundred stints running in circles in the yard as a disciplinary measure for demerits. He liked to drink. He liked to play football. Nevertheless, his superiors considered him to have been cut from true leadership cloth. There was so much to leading men in combat that had absolutely nothing to do with grades, with college. Today the day after graduation, he couldn't have cared less about leading men into battle.

The reality was he did not 'believe' in the war. It was not logical. It wasn't patriotic. As far as Alex could make out, it had nothing to do with the United States. The cold fury in his eyes, hardened like steel over the last year, had come when a classmate revealed to him that their fathers served in the same office in Saigon and had done for several years as naval attaches. Between large tumblers full of scotch in a little dive in rural Virginia, the other cadet let slip what he should not have known to begin with; their fathers were part of a Naval group in Vietnam established specifically to assist the French with their war until the French gave up and went home, agitate between the north and the south and generally keep the war going for as long as possible. No peace was wanted, thank you very much. Sometimes another person, with a slightly different slant on the facts – facts you may have had all of your life – can utterly remake one's understanding of something.

There was no honor in what his father did for a living. Yes, his father had spent the majority of his time in Saigon since 1959. His mother stayed in Texas for the most part since neither of them considered Saigon a place for the family. Periodically they did mount an expedition to Japan, where the elder Getz would meet them for R&R. He came home periodically as well, bearing Asian trinkets and long, wonderful yarns about his work.

Getz made his way to Washington D.C. and reported to Naval Operations as ordered. He was situated in a room with half a dozen other young military men. The room was filled with what was considered to be the very best electronic equipment, used almost exclusively for surveillance. Suddenly he wondered whether he'd been stationed on the Hancock to conduct surveillance or fire missiles. He would be rather relieved to be shunted off to surveillance. Like all the others, he believed that when it was necessary he'd be able to push a button he knew damned well would almost instantly kill hundreds of people. They were aware that many of the casualties would be civilians. If he had a choice, though, he'd rather never have to find that out about himself. Four weeks later, he was en route to Abilene to propose to his girlfriend and say goodbye to his mother.

It was while sitting at the Formica table in his mother's kitchen eating chicken fried steak with Donna that his life changed dramatically and forever, although he had no way of knowing at that moment just how profound the changes would be. Although he was adept at the 'good ole boy' stuff that made him popular at Navy or in a locker room, he was not a man for overt sentiment. He was a careful, methodical man. Donna appreciated that. He refilled her glass with lemonade before she asked him to, then setting the pitcher back down on the table, he took a black, velvet ring box from his shirt pocket and pushed it toward her without a word. The only detectable change was the slight cupid curl on his lips which had, during his time at Annapolis, passed for a smile. She was expecting a ring, they both knew it. They both knew what her answer would be. She picked up the box with her left hand, placed a forkful of mashed potato in her mouth with her right hand. When she was done, she lay her fork down, opened the box and slid the diamond solitaire inside onto her finger. It was quiet, it was careful, it was done.

In return, Donna slid an envelope across the table in his direction. She had discreetly tucked it under her placemat waiting for the right time. It was from the Department of the Navy and those sorts of letters always frightened her a bit. Alex took the brass letter opener from the drawer behind him and carefully slit the letter open.

Dear Ensign Getz;

This is to inform you that a change has occurred in your immediate assignment. Please report to NAVBase San Diego on 1 August, 1966, for deployment to the Vietnamese National MilitaryInstitute in Da Lat, Vietnam. There you will take up your assigned post as post-secondary instructor to the cadets in Operations Analysis and Advanced Mathematics. Congratulations.

It was 'signed' by the Secretary of the Navy.

Getz set the letter down on the table. Donna picked it up and read through it.

"Teaching?" Donna asked.

"Apparently."

"Well, how do you feel about this? It's better, probably. Right?"

"I don't know," Getz was truly stunned. "I keep being re-routed. The question is why? To what end?"

They finished their dinner quietly, each busy with thoughts that had never entered their minds before this. The dishes were done and put away.

They walked toward the center of town, as they did every evening when Alex was at home.

"When you've graduated, you could actually live with me... if the circumstances were right. I assume they'll house me on campus or near enough with other teachers." He looked at her expectantly. It was an almost unheard of luxury for an ensign to have his wife with him on assignment.

"I think I'd like to do that," she replied," if the circumstances were right."

August in Vietnam is so hot, even the locals want to rip their own skin off. Getz was used to hot but Texas hot, the hot of the southwest, with the occasional muggy night thrown in. *Da Lat* was unique in that it sat fifteen hundred feet higher than the rest of the country and temperatures there rarely exceeded spring heights. It was an old French town built on the Swiss model. He had indeed been quartered with the other men on the academy grounds. The Vietnam Military Academy had been a two-year institution since the 1950s. Just this year, the program was advanced to a four year college.

The instructors were all American and represented the Army, the Air Force and the Navy with Marines falling, as always, under the auspices of the Naval instructors. The entire life of the academy was modelled on West Point. Every cadet, upon graduation, spent one year attached to one of the military branches within the United States. The goal seemed to be the making of a large well-trained cadre of American-trained Vietnamese military officers, expertly trained in intelligence and, one hoped, as loyal to the U.S. causes as to their own. Back from their year in the US, graduates would be seeded within the Vietnamese military.

Ten months after he arrived, and two weeks after Donna graduated in Abilene, she joined him in *Da Lat*. She was absolutely fearless and he was proud of that. She arrived on her own clutching a single, neatly-packed suitcase. They were married by the chaplain, an Air Force man. Ensign and Mrs. Getz were at that time the only married couple on campus. The exception was the commandant but he was Vietnamese and lived elsewhere. The military academy was an elite school; *Da Lat* had been built as a resort. The average temperature in August was a mild seventy-five. *Da Lat* was famous for roses and cabbages and mild temperatures while the rest of the country baked. Getz felt guilty every day knowing his classmates were engaged in the battle and he was teaching Vietnam's spoiled elite how to be intelligence officers. Even after a few months he had no idea how this assignment had come to him.

Donna loved the cacophony of open air marketplace where she bought fresh vegetables, fruit, flowers and books. She bought silks and sewed them into curtains and dresses and shirts. People swam and played golf. There were gardens everywhere, mostly carefully trimmed and sculpted and loved. Alex had no idea whose Vietnam this was. Getz' classes went well at the academy. His pupils had an affinity for advanced mathematics as they were generally screened to be such. He taught them Cobol programming language, as well.

Seven months later, on January 31, 1968, the Vietcong launched the *Tet* Offensive. It was the only battle to have serious effects on *Da Lat*. They stayed at the school during the offensive protecting their charges and guarding the school. Within a week of the end of the hostilities, the US retaliated by drenching hundreds of thousands of acres of forest and jungle in Agent Orange, ostensibly to clear out guerrillas. From that point on the produce and meat and milk were contaminated with the neurotoxin pesticide. Spraying kept up periodically for months. The reason was unclear to Getz as it made no sense after a while. They just seemed to be spraying for the sake of spraying, just to see what would happen. They ate it, they drank it, they breathed it right along with the Vietnamese. In September of 1968, Donna gave birth to their first child, Molly. Molly was born blind with severe hydrocephaly. She lived for nine months then, by God's grace, she passed away. Donna once again packed her single suitcase, very neatly, and very much on her own, all the courage drained from her, boarded an airplane for Abilene. They never saw or spoke to each other again.

Alex remarried. He rose through the ranks until he became a Vice-Admiral. He fathered a healthy son and made his home in Virginia, where he became a high-ranking intelligence officer and finally advisor to three US Presidents. He was a major player in almost all the big civilian defense contracts. He became very much involved in the business of the Sceptre Corporation just after Vietnam, during the theater that came to be known as the 'Cold War,' and throughout the oil-driven altercations in the Middle

East. Sceptre was one of if not the largest supplier of chemicals to the US military. Although he was their most highly placed liaison to the Pentagon, Getz never again entertained the slightest romantic notion about neither what his country's mission was abroad nor the goals of the companies that provided the government with what they demanded. He watched and he waited, ice in his eyes and the corners of his mouth turned slightly up, resembling faintly a Cupid's bow.

The Pilots: Firebombers

"Two good nozzles. Looking for max."

"Three-fifty."

"Everything's going to be wonderful."

"And it's raining down through two-sixty...". The gauge read +2.600.

"Cal, shut down that sprinkler." "Roger that, boss."

'Boss' was Tim Verzet, Jr., age thirty-nine, captain aboard this simulation of a Boeing 747 being tested as a Very Large Aerial Tanker firefighting vehicle. His friends called him 'Flyer,' the nickname bestowed upon him by his father.

This particular set of tests was both boring and exhausting. For one thing, they were holding the airplane very close to the ground – firebombers called it the 'edge.' VLAT aircraft spend their critical time at the edge because that's where things burn. The goal is to hit a blazing target, which is something of an art when moving at one hundred and fifty to two hundred knots. These pilots hit the target with a belly-full of flame retardant, a moment firebombers refer to as 'pulling the trigger.' Terrain was a big deal in these tests for two reasons. Any pilot who forgot to climb before banking, taking into account the relative size of his ship, would likely sheer a wing completely off his plane. Already at suicidally low altitude in rugged terrain, bad judgment in this arena made a crash inevitable although the 747s turned out to be a lot more maneuverable than anyone anticipated. To prove they could fight fires alongside the smaller, faster planes, these VLATs were required to maneuver far more aggressively than other passenger aircraft and that made Tim's arms and shoulders ache, even in a simulator.

The second factor dictated by terrain but also by season was the wind. Air by itself is not dangerous, but air careening off a mountainside is, and updrafts and whirlwinds caused by the heat of a fire or wind roaring through a gorge can trap aircraft and make the crew feel like they're inside a washing machine. Turbulence can throw anything that isn't fastened down around the inside of the aircraft like a weapon and readily knock the most seasoned pilot unconscious by bashing him senseless against the insides of his own plane.

Tim rubbed his face wearily, got out of his seat and stretched his arms high over his head.

"I'm getting coffee," he said.

The only thing left to do today was a visual inspection of the 747 parked at *Pinon* Airfield. The retardant delivery system itself had to be gone over physically. The electricians were tracing every line to the ports and back to the power boxes. He'd read the spec manual last night before bed. He was required now to check the gear as installed and make sure it lined up with specifications. He was mandated to then do an in-depth review and checklist of maintenance. Tomorrow, he would fly several more simulations. The simulations were created after long interviews with pilots in the field and analyses of records of both large and small disasters. The Forest Service had thick files of accident reports in which aircraft simply broke apart in the sky, succumbing to stress. Later in the week he would green-light aircrew training and maintenance training practices. His part in this NASA-run project was just about put to bed. There had been four phases to complete.

Phase One: a thorough interviewing of pilots in the field on these aircraft and, critically, interviews of aerial firefighting pilots themselves. Pilots were grilled, wish lists compiled, complaints logged about how particular aircraft handled during fires that had been. Half a dozen teams were performing the same tests on this bird, the Boeing 747. Several other teams were analyzing the McDonnell-Douglas DC-10 for the same job. Those were the lucky crews. They were in the air. These birds were not competing for one spot; they were both being brought into the United States Forest Service's firefighting stable. Sooner or later actual flight tests would be performed on the 747s and he would be one of those pilots. It couldn't happen soon enough for him. The elements of this test short of getting the aircraft up in the air were his definition of death-by-plodding.

Phase Two: analysis of existing performance data, more plodding.

Really they were just going over the initial flight worthiness tests already performed by the makers.

Phase Three: get in the simulators and evaluate handling and performance under different conditions and in different terrains. Better certainly but not the real thing. Approaches and drops were simulated, flight under restricted visibility like a pilot would encounter in dense smoke, landing gear responsiveness, altimeter and airspeed references were varied, with gusts and turbulence, the firebomber's primary enemy, applied brutally. Flyer, his first officer and his flight engineer flew simulated fire attacks going up-slope with any number of variations and downslope as well, with numerous randomly selected variables. Phase Four consisted of the results of actual flights of the DC-10s. Those were underway now. In the end, based on the given that expert flying was the baseline, the only real concerns specific to these enormous planes were that they would need a special staging ramp during prep to get into the air and that they would inevitably create a lot of wake turbulence for other, smaller aircraft also on the scene. There was therefore never any discussion of one of the big ships being the Bird-Dog – the lead aircraft – but rather it was assumed they would fly at the rear and bat clean-up, so to speak. Other than these considerations, both planes performed at the top end of the desired range. The dispatcher would simply have to decide in the moment whether the descent angles were too great for planes this large in a given terrain.

Tim couldn't wait to get into the big ones. He'd trained his entire life for this, born and bred to be a pilot and a firefighter, like his father. He was tall, almost too tall to fly. He had light brown, wavy hair which he wore a little longer now that he was out of the military. His ears were a little like open car doors and his nose was a little big but somehow the package worked. He was slim for his height and tended to amble, a trait which hid well the internal combustion engine that drove him always to go higher and fly faster. It was the part of him he was always trying to tame. He was thirty-nine years old but looked ten years younger than that. Flyer left the military to do a lot more firefighting than was possible on an Air Force base, where pretty tight safety is maintained. He started out at Cal Fire, the California-based aerial fire fighter division based in Redding. California was an exceptional training and testing ground as the kinds of trees native to

California – mesquite, eucalyptus, Ponderosa pine, vegetation that was little more than brush – were oily and highly combustible. Mountainous terrains, deserts, sprawling but densely populated cities, some flatlands... all were available in California. He flew T94s, T95s, Grumman S2Ts, he was rated on the P3 Orion thanks to the military and he was eventually rated on the DC-6, DC-10 and 747. He wore a bomber jacket given to him by his Dad in 1988 upon the occasion of earning his pilot's license, which his Dad had helped him earn by teaching him to fly.

His Dad, Tim, Sr., had been a firefighter and a paramedic in British Columbia who would tell you he was a firefighter who used the plane as his tool. Tim, Sr. looked a lot like Errol Flynn and had been around long before there were rules or best practices for firebombing. He was a pioneer in creating those rules through sheer experience and a lot of luck and he had seen his share of fellow pilots die in fire attacks. Flyer, on the other hand, was an impulsive pilot in love with the endless horizon. He loved to fly and he preferred to go fast. Unlike his Dad, he was a flyer who happened to fight fires. Both of these men, though, subscribed to well-known basic rules of flight for firebombers: try to stay in the middle of the air; do not go near the edges of the air, the edges consisting of ground, buildings, ocean, trees and interstellar space. Flying around the edges is truly dangerous.

It was odd for someone of Tim's nature to be able to perform the calculated, thoughtful flying involved in aerial firefighting. There was an inordinate amount of time spent sizing up the situation, the fire and circling the fire looking for an exit. Impulsive pilots ended up dead. He saw this necessary control as a personal challenge, a way of defeating the emergency itself by slowing down and staying calm and detached. They used to talk about making the fire 'lay down.' This was Tim's way of making his internal fire lay down. His Dad would say, this is a job not an emergency. Not that he downplayed the expertise required from these pilots. The fires were dangerous and hot and the terrains often ridiculously difficult. Crews flew eight hour stretches of continuous dumps. The job was, in fact, demanding and treacherous. People who wanted to keep flying either stayed in the service or went into commercial flying for about the same wages that fast food cashiers make. Many of his friends slept in cargo planes or lived with their parents or worked two jobs just so they could jockey for a spot with major airlines who weren't hiring anyway. Not that firebombing paid well, but it was at least gratifying as a profession.

Thankfully, the day finally arrived when the pilots got to shake out the 747s. No matter how one looked at it, this was an exciting ship. It had a range of five thousand miles and a drop length of twenty-five thousand feet in segmented drops. It had a loiter time of three hours, meaning it could hang out airborne for a while until a fire was properly evaluated and either an air attack plan was devised or it was sent home. The reality was that this supertanker, using six strategic refuelling locations across the country, could drop ninety thousand gallons on multiple targets within the space of about sixteen hours. It was going to be the major player in any air attack on any fire in all but the most rugged terrains. When he imagined what this ship would look like as part of a firefighting team, he saw it as something like a massive great white shark swimming up behind. Dedicated, muscle-bound, unstoppable merely began to describe it.

On a beautiful, hot Saturday morning in August in the northern New Mexico mountains, Alpha Crew climbed into a cold, dark 747 cockpit. Tim Verzet was commander of this ship, Cal Penderton was first officer and Lee Phillips was flight engineer. They ran through the pre-flight checklist, turned the power on and fired up the systems. Within half an hour, they were airborne. Tim repeatedly flew an elongated, lazy horseshoe approach to a football field nearby. Dotted at regular intervals on the turf were hollow white plastic collection tubes, about three feet high. At the upward end a collection cup would collect fire retardant as it plummeted down and measure the liquid. There needed to be a fairly even distribution of red-dyed liquid in each collection tube allowing for wind variations. They sank to one hundred and eighty feet each time on a short path to keep lower speeds, a maneuver that seemed like inviting catastrophe each time it was observed from the ground. No matter how many times they witnessed this maneuver, because of the sheer magnitude of the aircraft, those on the ground were sure they were watching a leviathan plunge to the ground, an impact which would be accompanied by the scream of twisting metal and ripping seams. Then, miraculously, at the last conceivable moment, the beast would heave back up into the sky.

On their approach to target, Tim called for full flaps and adjusted the engine power to keep a controlled flight path. He did love flying this bird. Cal called the altitude as they descended. Several hundred feet off the ground, Tim gently pushed the nose up, leveling out at about one hundred eighty feet. He held it at a three-four degree nose up attitude and one hundred fifty knots airspeed.

"Stand by…", Tim called.

Tim punched a 'pickle' button on his control yoke – pulled the trigger - and pushed all four throttles forward maintaining a slight positive angle of attack as twenty thousand gallons of retardant blast through four twelve inch ports on the ship's underside. The liquid was driven by eight tanks of pressurized air and the entire belly-full was away within ten seconds, which is good because at one hundred eighty knots the plane is over and past the target fast. The 747 checked out.

Tim spent that evening packing his duffel bag at the base pilot's quarters. He would return to Redding the following day to finish the last month of his contract and then, on the first of October, he was officially a firebomber for Bluesky Airways at *Pinon* Airfield in the middle-of-nowhere, New Mexico.

*****

Tim kept a Piper Supercub at *Pinon*. It was his own personal lift home, the Volkswagen Bug of the sky, but the Supercub had two distinct features that made it Tim's commuter of choice. First, it could take off and land on anything fairly flat in a short space. Second, it was equipped with an obscenely oversized engine and so it was fast and fun to fly. That simple. He took off in the morning with reports of storms in California. That was absolutely typical of summer in California, and August in particular. Besides, New Mexico was known for its low-level treacherous turbulence. It was either fly home in the wind or take a bus. His car, a very old Volvo four door sedan, was in California.

Over Redding, he encountered a fair bit more bumping around. There was definitely a big storm out there somewhere. For now, the sky was mostly blue with a thick layer of constant white haze at the horizon level. Visibilities had been diminishing for the last decade, one assumed from a level of pollution building in the atmosphere generally. Standard visibility expectation used to be forty miles. Now the standard was ten. For a pilot who felt that all the way to the horizon was all the way to the end of the world a seventy-five percent reduction in standard visibility was something to mourn. He sailed over islands of houses, high schools, swimming pools, playgrounds, all pocketed in green areas. Cal Fire base appeared and he set the little plane down, rolling uneventfully to a slow taxi. He parked the plane out of the way. There were a few other personal aircraft parked here. Any pilot who had the choice would choose the air rather than the ground. Engorged, black clouds gathered in the distance to the southwest coming up behind Bully Choop Mountain.

Tim pushed through the door into the office and dispatch.

"Hey, Flyer!" a middle aged woman sat behind the desk wearing a headset. "You're home!"

"Yeah, you can't slack off all summer, can you?" Tim grinned.

He ducked into the locker room to call his Dad. Tim Verzet, Sr., age seventy, now lived in peaceful retirement on several hundred acres near Lake Helen in the Cascades. Helen had been his wife's name; that's why he bought the place. Everybody called the elder Verzet, "Huck", even Tim. Snow-covered Mt. Shasta was his view with Lassen Peak a hundred miles in the distance. Lassen Peak was still an active volcanic site complete with intermittent steam and bubbling mud.

Huck grew vegetables, flew a little, worked with his friends in the area who were foresters on evaluating the viability of the plant life and water… essentially puttering in his own very specific and disciplined ways. He also kept bees. Anything that flew was of interest to Tim's Dad. Tim's mother had passed away when he was ten and so it had been the three of them – Tim, Tim's Dad, and every so often, Jeff, the son of a man with whom Huck had flown for years – and airplanes for as long as anybody could remember. Unofficial son, Jeff Brandenburg, was an aircraft mechanic working for a major airline at Dallas-Fort Worth. His Dad had passed away when Jeff was two. Jeff spent many years in and out of trouble, had run away and not been seen for several years, then resurfaced one night in the winter at Huck's door. Jeff would have been humiliated to be thought of as an orphan or a charity-case, so he came and went, touched base with

Huck, loved that Huck just let it lay there. Tim straddled a bench between two rows of lockers and punched numbers on his cell phone.

"Verzet!". The response when his Dad picked up the phone was always the same. It was hard-wired, like his telephone. His Dad needed and appreciated a hard-wired telephone. This was an old house with an old and trusted infrastructure. Up in that area, one needed all the communication options one could get in the winter. His Dad operated a short-wave as well.

"Dad!"

"Flyer? Where are you?" His dad was happy to hear from him.

"Back at Cal Fire, Dad."

"How'd everything shake out in New Mexico?"

"Really well. Those dogs are definitely going to hunt," Tim used one of his Dad's favourite expressions. "I was thinking when I'm done here in about twenty-six days, not that I'm counting, I'd come up for a few days before I head down to *Pinon*. That okay with you?"

"Sure thing, son," his Dad was clearly excited but, as they both did every time, 'made the fire lay down.'

"Great, I'll call you before I come."

Tim unloaded his flight bag into his locker and then headed back to dispatch. That's where all the news would be current. For one thing, there would be good weather information on the mass of black that appeared to be moving toward them. Indeed, several dry lightning storms had been reported over the last twelve hours with no end expected. These storms could produce hundreds of lightning strikes with no moisture behind them. Any rain associated would evaporate long before it hit the ground because the air was just too hot. Cal Fire had an intricate and beefy system of ground firefighting resources but the air attack would be called first. They would get there faster than anybody, start a defense and relay vital information about a fire that could only be seen from the air. The firebombers never put a fire out but they often made it possible to put a fire out.

Dispatch reported that the day's fire hazard was extreme. Lines of storms were passing over dense forest to the south. Lightning strikes and small fires had been reported over the last few hours. It was possible, even likely, that a hundred fires would pop up and, in a worst-case scenario, converge into one super inferno, turning quickly unmanageable. The aircraft would be in the air long before then spraying retardant to ring smaller fires, laying down retardant near populated areas in the anticipated path of the fire, making critical observations for command to be relayed to ground crews and, if necessary, intervening in situations in which a fire threatened a crew on the ground. The Santa Ana winds blowing through California every year were devil winds and could turn on a ground crew in the blink of an eye, surrounding the hapless team and creating for them an island in the fire they hoped would not be the last place they'd ever see. All the firefighters underwent extensive training and had experience under those conditions. Luckily, the *Santa Anas* swept through far to the south. Northern California saw white-hot grass fires and lightning free-for-alls.

At three-thirty that afternoon, dispatch sent Tim and three other pilots into the air. They were all in S2Ts. Tim knew this would likely be the last fire he fought in this small plane. It was a good plane, a reliable, tough little fire horse.

"Roger, Bird Dog."

Tim was not the lead plane on this mission. The Bird Dog instructed them to ring a wild patch creeping up on the primary fire line. Logistics was already out there setting up a very large base as they anticipated a very large fire. Hundreds of ground crew, bulldozers, a kitchen and tents and hydration supplies... they were all there. Cal Fire had a can-do attitude and nothing else would suffice. He lifted off with a full belly, just over nine thousand gallons in this case, aimed himself at the fire and flew over it, gauging landmarks – two was the rule – so that he would know exactly when to pull the trigger. He marked his escape route, off to the southeast. He came around in a wide circle then aimed himself right back at his points of reference. Firebombers do not chase smoke or look for the flames. They identify and look for landmarks that they have already identified. He came level with his landmarks and pulled the trigger.

"Bulls-eye," the radio crackled. It was the lead plane.

They continued to offer air support for four hours. There was something about this fire. They all knew it almost right away although no one was talking about it yet. Despite being driven by the merciless *Santa Ana*, despite the constant incidences of lightning and almost no rain, there was a ferocity about this fire, an ungodly aggression, which Tim had never witnessed before. It was as if someone were pouring invisible gasoline on the flames. They would not lie down; they roared and screamed and writhed. He was very glad not to be on the ground and very concerned about the people who were. This fire was being driven by something beyond their experience and no one wanted to entertain the idea that somehow there was a new breed of inferno.

As he was picking up his sixth load, the Bird-Dog 's voice crackled across his radio.

"72. We've got a crew getting ready to deploy. You're the closest air support."

"Ready to deploy?"

The firefighters would be throwing out the orange tents, reminiscent of mummy-style sleeping bags. They'd enclose themselves in these on the ground and wait for help. If they did not run out of oxygen, the bags would hold against the fire up to five hundred degrees. Then the glue in the bags itself would start to melt.

"Roger that, 72. It's a burnover. The space is getting pretty small up there."

He was aloft as quickly as he could be and heading single-mindedly for the coordinates given. It was in times like these – all too many of them – when his Dad's voice echoed in his head.

"This is not an emergency. It's a job." That kind of attitude and level-headed thinking had saved him more than once. Hurtling pell-mell into a fire to rescue a crew was likely to get the pilot killed, as well.

He found the crew trapped on an island. The fire was a demon taunting them. He could see the crew had just about made it all the way into their bags. There was very little time but he made one circle around the island, giving them all a minute more to secure themselves. He laid down a strip of retardant along the flank of the island. He knew others were behind him. They would each make a drop ringing the firefighters, even directly on top of them if it seemed like the reasonable thing to do.

"Bulls-eye, 72."

Belly empty, he turned and headed back to base. He was there, just after dusk, when a truck brought the terrified, exhausted and grateful crew back home. They looked as if they'd been beaten nearly to death but they were alive, charred and singed and black, but breathing. They were bloody but that wasn't from the burn over. All crews got scraped up and cut pretty badly in a wildfire. When he put his head on his pillow that night, knowing that the fire was still completely out of control and growing, he relived what he had seen from the air that day and bent his mind toward marking indelibly this type of fire, this level of inferno, he'd never witnessed before. He wanted to know what was going on. There was always a way to make a fire lay down. Sometimes it took a month but he had never seen anything like this.

This fire became catastrophic, intense and uncontrollable. By the next morning, five thousand acres were ablaze. An unnatural wind continued to blow in from the east with sustained winds of thirty miles per hour and gusts up to one hundred and ten. It acted like the *Santa Ana*, the Devil Wind, confined to the south. Embers flew half a mile from the flames onto calm forests and ignited, sometimes explosively. The tops of pine trees, the crowns, ignited and then the fire passed from tree top to tree top before the rest of the tree caught. These crown fires were too hot and hazardous for any firefighter. Tim and the other firebombers flew over huge sections of the inferno that were completely unapproachable from the ground and laid retardant strips along the flanks of the fire where they found them. Massive winds chased themselves in counter-clockwise gusts. By the end of the week, thirty four thousand acres were ablaze. They fought the fires for three solid weeks, stopping only to sleep and eat. Tim thought often what a difference the DC-10s or 747s would make. None had appeared from *Pinon*. He was sure the call had gone out. There must be more paperwork, more red tape, before these Super Tankers could fly to the rescue.

Finally, they wrestled the beast to the ground with what they had. On the very last day of flying, Tim watched a pilot die. He and another pilot were sent to a hot spot twenty miles to the southeast. There was a fire still burning in a ravine. It was a pretty typical situation, one they had all flown in many, many times. They picked their landmarks and their escape route, an easy shot into a wide open valley. Mike Appleby was flying the other S2V. He was lead and there were only two of them. Mike radioed that he would enter the bowl from the valley side of the ravine and make a steep turn once inside to line up and drop his load. The target would be obvious for the entire duration of the turn and the approach was short so gaining too much speed to drop his load was not an issue. Tim watched Mike fly in, make the steep turn, and level out for his drop. It was all perfectly routine. Mike pulled the trigger and red retardant began to fall away from the belly of the plane. Then a tinderbox below exploded like two freight trains colliding head on and the updraft sent retardant spiraling up into the air, coating the plane and whirling off into the sky. Within seconds, Mike had gone belly up and augured into the side of the ravine. The fireball was instant. Every pilot has heard of this kind of scenario. Every pilot prays they never see it. It was as if there had been a bomb in the ravine waiting for them. He pulled up, radio'd dispatch and made an arc back to the base. An accident team would be hurtling down on Mike and what was left of his plane soon enough.

The next day, he packed his bag again intending to head to his Dad's place. The door to his room swung open and one of the dispatchers appeared .

"Hey, you've got to hear this!" He gestured for Tim to follow him to dispatch in the front office.

A dozen pilots and firefighters were gathered around the radio, listening. Two teams had radio'd in from completely inert areas of the fire, large patches that had been contained days ago, to report that the trees were bursting into flame again because, it appeared, that the roots were still burning under the ground.

"What?" Tim whispered. How was that possible? There was little to no oxygen to burn with far enough into the soil.

"How far down?"

"Three feet… four feet…", the dispatcher answered.

This time he used his old Volvo to get to his Dad's place. He was shaken up. The tranquility of Lake Helen and the snow-capped peaks of Shasta and Lassen were absolutely necessary to him right now. When he got to *Pinon*, the first thing he was going to ask was where the hell had the VLATs been?

*****

It was an hour's drive north from the base in Redding to his Dad's place near Mt. Shasta. The smell of smoke still hung heavy in the air here. He rolled up his windows and turned on his radio. He sailed up I-5 past Big Bend on his right. As he drove, the spectacle of Mike plowing into the fire came into his mind unbidden and each time it did he chased it away, fearing the sight would hardwire itself somehow. He passed Dunsmuir Airport on the left and swung onto I-89. Lake Helen appeared on his left, such a beautiful lake against the white snow backdrop of Mt. Shasta. It was one of his favorite drives especially on a rare calm day when the lake became a mirror. Today was not that day. The sky was a bit white from horizon to horizon. He thought he must be looking at the remnants of the fire sixty miles south. Over his left shoulder he caught the glint of an aircraft. He looked up and spotted a DC-10 flying quite low, five to eight thousand feet only. Four white billowy trails spewed from wing ports, the same wing ports he had just inspected and approved, and laced out behind it. He thought it was a shame that if a DC-10 Firebomber had been in the vicinity it couldn't have joined the fire attack. Must be conducting more tests. He was sure it had been cleared for use, though. He'd been part of that himself.

He rounded the edge of the lake and past and turned onto the road to his father's place three miles further along. The dirt road was long and curved and dipped. Water ran during storms and changed the contours of the road, raising rock and revealing gullies. One had to pay attention not to high-center the car or blow a tire. Huck was waiting on the deck. Pheasant dawdling by the roadside scattered into the woods as he drove past. Tim, who was emotional for the first time in weeks, sprang up the steps and clung to his Dad, tears streaming down his face. His Dad patted his back and held tight.

"Well," was all he would say every once in a while. "Well."

Tim slept through the morning and half the afternoon. When he woke he found his father still sitting on the deck. He sat down beside him at a long redwood table. Huck pointed at the sky. Someone had laid down many long white trails of some sort of particulate since he'd been asleep. Some feathered out and were becoming sheer clouds. It was as if someone had spread a thin white blanket across the sky.

"Is this something to do with the fire, Dad?"

"No. It's coming from the damned planes. They were here before the fire."

"What, like the DC-10 I saw this morning? Thought he was laying down water... maybe a practice run."

"No, son. That's not water. It's an aerosol of some sort. I've never seen it before up here or anywhere else. The color reminds me of the boron we used to use but it's too fine a mist and it

hangs out in the atmosphere a whole lot longer. Can't think why anyone would be spraying

anything up here."

Tim was puzzled. If it wasn't water then what that pilot had done today was illegal. The law prohibits spraying any chemical of any kind over bodies of water – there were so many lakes

around here – unless the surrounding countryside is on fire.

"Look at this," Huck got up, went down the stairs and disappeared behind the house. Tim followed.

They walked about a hundred yards to where his Dad kept a dozen bee hives. His Dad pulled a drawer from the bottom of a hive and very dramatically dumped hundreds of dead bees onto the ground. He walked down the line of wooden hives and pulled a tray from beneath each one. Each tray was filled with dead bees.

The next morning the sky was blue again, or sort of. Blue was a generous description. If one tried really hard a little blue could be picked out from the white. Whatever had been laid across the heavens the day before Tim imagined would have floated to the ground overnight. Either some of it was still in the air, which demonstrated a phenomenal hang time, or they had sprayed more in the intervening hours.

He took his coffee out to the deck, heard Huck rousting chickens and ducks below. His Dad had made use of ample high space under the house by stocking the area with egg-laying creatures and a couple of goats. They were surrounded at night by a slightly electrified fence to keep black bears, skunks and raccoons away. In fact, Huck hung bacon on the fence every now and again to train the forest predators to stay away from the bacon-that-shocked-them. Tim heard the faintest drone of an engine in the sky. No one but a pilot would have heard anything. Above coming in from the south, what looked like the same unmarked plane began laying the same four trails across the sky. Within a minute the four were blending into one wide trail and fanning out across a portion of the sky. In an hour or two, this would look like a cloud – an unusual cloud – but a cloud, nonetheless. He watched until the aircraft disappeared over Mt. Shasta. Fifteen minutes later, to the background noise of his father doing dishes, another unmarked DC-10 came in from the west flying at a right angle to the plumes already there. This bird disappeared into the east, leaving a perfect 'X' in the sky above the trees. Each day the same planes flew the same patterns and laid down the same aerosol. One day there were crossed lines covering the sky, a grid. His father started to develop a dry cough. He wasn't ill; no fever or sore throat or aches. Just a dry cough, like something was irritating his throat.

"It's never been this bad," he said.

The last day there was no plane. However, by early afternoon, they were breathing some sort of yellow haze accompanied by the slightest stench of sulfur. There appeared to be a yellowish haze around the sun. His father coughed all morning, a dry cough. He said he'd been to the doctor about it, even been to the emergency room and sat in the waiting room filled with people whose only commonality had been that they couldn't stop coughing. No fever, no congestion, just coughing. There just didn't seem to be any reason for it other than the spraying.

"Huck," Tim asked, "haven't you called the town or the county to ask about this?"

"Sure," he replied. "They say no spraying is occurring. I'll show you something else, too."

He walked down to a white pine right on the road's edge and literally wiped the bark off with his hand like it was thick paint. The idea of the tree roots bursting into flame under the ground came to Tim's mind when he saw the devastated tree.

Esoterica: Life is Just a Bowl of Cherries...

The golden retriever, nearly white rather than golden, was bothering the old hound to death again. They started out as good friends, she and he. He, a two month old ball of the softest fluff nestled up against her old flanks. Playing with him had been easy then. She was bored and in dire need of companionship. The puppy, alas, grew as puppies will. He grew and grew and grew some more. In very short order, there was no fun in it at all. Christina often woke in the morning to the sound of high pitched yelping from the mud room where the dogs slept in the warmer months. The retriever had one game and it went something like this: *I am a skyscraper and I am falling on your head while I bite your hind end.*

Today she rose to rescue the old dog, somewhat resentful that Fancy wouldn't buck up and put the pup in his place. It was dark yet. It was the end of October and that's what happened, winter was drawing the shade down. Many mornings since the killing, she lay in bed waiting for the light and trying to imagine what being awake would feel like again when she finally reached the other side of this terrible, terrible thing. She was old enough to know that the only thing she knew was that she would live through this. People did that. What would that look like?

The yelping in the mudroom grew louder and more frenzied, punctuated with the happy growls of a male puppy who thought that the morning couldn't start with a more delicious game.

"That's relaxing," Otto grumbled from the other side of the bed, "like a fish tank in a doctor's office."

It was cold, even under the down comforter. The fire needed attention from someone. It was time to start letting Fancy sleep in the main part of the house again. She and Christina had an
understanding, one that Otto reluctantly ignored. The old hound would nuzzle Christina until she was barely awake on her side of the bed, Christina would lift the covers and the old girl would crawl under tucking herself up tight against Christina's legs. It was a completely legitimate definition of heaven for the two of them. By the time winter really settled in, Christina

would lift the covers in her sleep when Fancy started to yawn, so well-oiled would this warmth machine become.

There was also a newly delivered cord of wood to sort out. Piled in the driveway, if it wasn't stacked soon, the snow would come and the cold and then, sooner or later, fetching wood would also mean shoveling snow and chopping it out from under ice. It just wasn't worth it. That she would do today.

She drove Anya and David to school in her pajamas and a barn coat. Then she changed into knee high mud boots and a sweatshirt, donned old heavy leather gloves – with a hole in one from opening the top of the old cast iron Vigilant with them – and reported to the wood pile. Wood piles are unforgiving. The dogs sat staring at her out of the mud room window, longing to be outside.

While there definitely was no timetable for grief, grief definitely has a shelf life if it isn't yours. Even the bizarre and twisted details of this story held little interest for most of her friends at this point. She found herself keeping to herself more and more. That was okay for now. Again, she knew that would change eventually. Christina had met Big Grief before. Sooner or later it went on its way again, an unwelcome houseguest in someone else's life. She had agreed early on to help costume plays at both the middle school and the high school and she would keep her word. She was doing the one at the high school for Hank, to try to keep the one-act competition alive. Every year it threatened to go down for the count under the madness that turned out to be, for better or worse, the spring musical. A scant handful of students, like Hank, appreciated the opportunities the one-act competition gave them to develop. Besides, she hoped these projects would offer lots and lots of distractions so that time could just go right on ahead and flow by.

The house was an old green and yellow Queen Anne, circa 1890. There were three floors and a very cold, very austere basement. Outside, illogical twists and turns led to spaces just big enough for raspberries to go wild in, safe from harvest every year within their own brambly mess. Somehow, despite the drafts and the leaks, the old Vigilante managed to heat the whole thing respectably. There was a leak, a Grand Old Leak that started in the roof on the third floor, ran slightly downhill to the northeast corner and burrowed itself through to Anya's room on the second floor. From there it had recently broken through to the living room on the first floor. It was quite a feat of self-determination. They were relying on the impending snow season to plug up the hole and buy them time until the spring to have the roof fixed.

Halfway through the wood pile, she was startled by the dog's sudden explosive barking. There had been a hypnotic rhythm to what she was doing and her heart raced. She heard the mail box clank open and shut on the front porch and, though it didn't seem possible, the dog's yelping grew louder and more frenzied as the mailman made his way to the next house along the street. She pulled off the gloves and threw them on top of the remaining wood. The dogs stopped barking when she brought back several envelopes and leaned against the wood, sorting the mail. There was no hope now of a dangerous stranger to growl at. All was well again, unfortunately.

There was, among the other mail, a plain white envelope. It was hand-addressed in blue ink and there was no return address in the upper left hand corner. She thought the post office rejected mail like that these days. Inside was a copy of the barest bones of the police report made on the scene the day her mother died. She looked at the envelope again and checked the photocopied pages inside…no indication at all who had sent this. Until this moment, they had been told there was very little information and what there was, Christina had no right to see just yet. The report was short. There was a declaration of the fact that George Walters had run her mother down in the road and that her mother had subsequently died of her injuries. There was a description of the van. There was a list of the witnesses but they all went to church with her mother. She knew who the witnesses were. And that was it. A short, written account of what she already knew. Anger rose in her throat and took possession of her mind, so appalled, so disgusted, so left by the side of the road did she feel. Obviously, someone was trying. Someone had sent this to her although it appeared that perhaps they might not have been supposed to do it? This woman had a family, goddammit!

She went inside and sat down on the sofa, pulled her mother's laptop up onto her lap and signed on. A dog climbed up and flanked each side while she looked for the offices of the District Attorney. She was going to get to the bottom of some of this. If no one cared that there were people out here utterly broken over this death, if no one cared that this woman had a family, then why were they bothering with a legal case? Why try the man if the human damage didn't mean anything?

She found the main number for the district attorney at the county courthouse.

"Hello, courthouse."

"Hello, my name is Christina Galbraithe. I need to talk to someone who can give me some information about the court case against the man who killed my mother."

The best she could do was leave a message for the Victim's Advocate and wait for someone to get back to her. It was a step in the right direction to know such a thing existed.

She did hear back several weeks later. Her cell phone rang while she was in the costume loft at the high school. Thanksgiving had just come and gone, The Legend of Sleepy Hollow had gone up at the middle school. Someone had kicked the Headless Horseman costume under a chair right before curtain and so David, after letting Ichabod Crane hang in thin air on stage for some minutes, had thrown an old black pea coat over his head and finally done away with Ichabod, thus allowing the play to end.

"Mrs. Galbraithe?"

"That's me."

"This is Becky Tripp at the Victim's Advocate Office for the District Attorney."

She had to find a place to sit down. She sank onto a soft mound of prison tunics in a back corner. She had been waiting for a call just like this for four months. Here was someone who might actually know something. She hugged her knees to her chest. Seriously, what happened?

"I'm sorry it's taken us so long to reach out to you, Mrs. Galbraithe. I feel badly about it."

"Okay. Well, can you tell me about this case – this man? I literally know nothing."

"I don't have a lot of personal information about Mr. Walters… that's the DA's territory but I can fill you in on a few things."

"Okay."

"Well, for one thing he's been before a grand jury already and they recommended charging him with manslaughter."

"Wait, how is that possible? How has this man been in court again and I wasn't informed? How does this case continue to go on without the victim's family?"

"I'm not sure what's happening, I'm so sorry. You just seem to be out of the loop somehow but I promise you I will make sure you know what's going on from now on."

Christina buried her face in her knees, quiet sobs escaped her. She was buried among Steam Punk costumes from Richard III, some she had made herself for Hank a year or so back; jackets and black tulle and bronze-colored buttons. Hank's hung right in front of her where she sat. She took the jacket in her hands, buried her face in it. Presently, she forced herself back to the conversation.

"I'm sorry," she said. "You were saying?"

"That's quite alright, Mrs. Galbraithe, I understand," the woman cleared her throat.

"What about the results from the blood tests? Can you at least tell me what was in his system? Part of this is a DUI."

"Yes. I show that the reports were completely clean. There was nothing found in his system at all. No drugs, no alcohol."

"Nothing. Nothing? Not one thing? I was given to understand that he was completely incapacitatedat the scene. How could there be nothing in his blood stream?

"I don't understand either. The prosecutor might know more. Should I have her call you?"

"Yes. Do that."

She hung Hank's jacket back on its hanger, stared at it. It was black, covered with white braid and insignia carefully drawn on the cuffs with gold fabric paint. The front was a separate piece sewn on after she had painstakingly attached a hundred brass buttons by hand in the wee hours the night before dress rehearsal. Were they really going to say that he had killed her mother because he just wasn't paying attention? How were they supposed to live with that? Fuck all of it. She reached up and with one angry, wrenching yank, ripped the front piece off the jacket. At home, she pinned it to Hank's wall. She missed him and the outlines of their old lives, which now seemed simpler, terribly.

It was the terrible schism, the cleanly executed sword stroke that bifurcated her life that was the hardest to deal with. Half of her put one foot in front of the other, raised her children, helped out at school, fed the dogs, tried to smile. The other half tracked down the elusive event that had been, she was almost sure, her mother's murder. How does one body, one mind, one soul hold both reins of a horse dragging a wagon this broken? This was a big part of the reason she was withdrawing. She really couldn't keep the duality going. She had to solve one very big puzzle, put it to bed, and then take up the reins of her daily life again. That was the only choice.

What had her mother been working on for the Navy? Meteorology, atmospheric physics... she had studied it herself at one point. Weapons. It stood to reason that some of these would be atmospheric weapons. That, she thought, is why God made the internet.

Anya's group was performing a little known Arthur Miller work called The American Clock. It premiered in the middle of December, very soon, which was good because Anya was absolutely exhausted. It had been the most difficult of years, harder on the children but for less abstract reasons. For them it was a simple matter of Love Lost. Love obliterated in the street on the way to church. That wounded and made them tired.

Miller's work took place just as the Great Depression really got under way. There was big business, which seemed to be, as always, impervious to the tides of economic policy. There were the normal folks who either couldn't get or keep jobs, and who sold everything they owned bit by bit, even formed romantic relationships that might be economically advantageous. There was good music...*We're in the Money, Life is Just A Bowl of Cherries...* earthy humor, solitary and ordinary courage. By the last performance, the audience sat spell-bound and utterly caught up in the story, the story of today not yesterday, the story of what was happening to them now, the story of getting into their cars and driving home to their lives after the show. The students did not understand this silence. They thought they must have done a bad job that evening. They had not lived long enough to know they were telling their own parent's story.

Life is just a bowl of cherries, don't take it serious, it's too mysterious...

"Mommy, I'm so tired." Anya could not or would not get up for school. "My bones hurt today."

Anya's bones. She had complained about various degrees of pain for the last few years – not knowing how to describe the chronic, ever-present ache that travelled through her muscles and joints except to say that her bones hurt. Doing too much usually made it worse and then she had a hard time getting her limbs to move in the mornings. The doctors were at a complete loss. The only time Christina could remember Anya not being in pain recently was when she had surgery. She woke up, groggy from the anaesthetic and tears rolled down her face.

"What is it?" Christina had asked.

"My back doesn't hurt," the girl whispered, and wept for the relief until the medicine wore off and the pain crept back.

Christmas break was upon them. She assumed Anya would be able to cope again after a rest. Hank would be home from school in a few days, everybody got to sleep in, at least theoretically. Christina just wanted her ducklings all at home and around her. That's as much as she could do. She would not be sending Christmas greetings this year. There had never been a time when she hadn't been able to pull it together enough to save Christmas from whatever debacle was at hand; put it all aside for one Holy Moment. Not this year. The weather grew very cold, mid-winter cold, and Christina spent a lot of time drawn up to the wood burning stove, knitting. Most of the time she wasn't even sure what she was knitting but it helped ease her mind. David and Otto came home with the most perfect tree they had ever had. They put it up in the dining room as usual, to add light and sustenance to their meals. Hank hung the star on the top of the tree, honored for finally being home, noted for having been sorely missed.

On the first day of January, she heard a news report about an older fellow called Getz, a retired Rear Admiral, whose body had been found floating in Central Park. She was knitting something for Hank and so wasn't paying extremely close attention. It was a sad story, for sure. What a lovely holiday for his family, she thought. As the announcer went on, she straightened up and listened, put her handwork down and watched. There was a photo of him, jovial looking, with white hair, what there was left of it. Getz was a retired Rear Admiral, a Viet Nam veteran who saw distinguished service. He was employed at high levels at the Pentagon and was an advisor to three Presidents. He had an extremely high security clearance. The killing appeared at this moment to be random, they had yet no idea what happened or why. As a civilian working for the government, he was attached to several companies over the years seeking military contracts.

Over the next couple of days, Christina watched for news reports concerning this man. Just a few evenings later, she saw another report in which a very close friend of Getz' was interviewed, also a high level military official. He was calling the death a professional hit. Christina couldn't believe she was hearing this story, a story she knew in her gut paralleled her mother's story. Civilians working for the military can often find themselves in dangerous positions. She knew that. Why was an old man the target of an assassination? He was no head of state. His friend speculated that Getz was likely about to reveal some plan or information that someone – the government or the last firm for which he worked – did not want revealed.

"Police report that floorboards in his office had been pulled up but there is no indication as to why or whether Getz had done that himself. He was a specialist in biological and chemical warfare – had written a manual on the subject – as well as cyber-terrorism."

They heard the clank of the mailbox.

"I'll go, Mom!" David called from the foyer.

Otto must have remembered to dig the porch out, she thought. The mailman would not climb the stairs if there was snow on them and there was always snow on them right now. There were a couple of Christmas cards. One had an Australian postmark. Sydney, NSW. Bennie. Beautiful, summer, Sydney Christmas she supposed. She'd never been. Bennie and Christina were friends, though, bonded in some unknown but real way.

Dear Christina.

I know this holiday must be indescribably difficult. Call anytime.

Love, Bennie.

Bennie wrote novels, as well. They met working on a few committees, hung out in some discussion groups together. Christina sent an email.

Bennie,

I just can't do Christmas this year. I simply can't. I'll love my dogs, drink in Hank's face, kiss Anya, tickle David whether he likes it or not. Knit by the fire. That's all I can manage. It has to be enough.

Love, Christina

She caught herself, put a hand to her nose, sneezed. The retriever was startled awake, rose and laid a paw across her knee.

"Just a minute."

She sent the message, closed the laptop, and went to let the pup out into the snow. He loved it so much she often found him sound asleep on his back in a snow bank in the back yard.

The very next day, she and Anya were having breakfast when a report aired on cable news that five thousand birds had simply fallen dead from the sky. Blackbirds littered sidewalks and roads in the videotape of the scene in Arkansas.

"Mom," Anya asked, "what is going on? How do thousands of birds die at the same time?"

"Yeah, something's wrong there."

The news reporter went on to say that a few hours later twenty thousand fish had been found floating dead in a river twenty five miles from the bird incident. There was an interview with an Arkansas state fish and game official. He speculated that New Year's Eve revelers may have set off fireworks that literally scared the birds to death.

"Mom," Anya said. "Fireworks? Are they kidding?"

"I know," Christina sipped her coffee, "it's a pretty stupid reason to try to float. Five thousand birds don't simultaneously die and fall from the sky. Not via fireworks or anything else."

"Do you think it was some kind of weapon, Mom?"

Smart girl.

The same day a top military liaison to companies working on defense contracts has been found murdered, five thousand birds drop dead and fall from the sky. The same day someone says this guy must have known something he shouldn't have or maybe tried to blow the whistle, twenty thousand fish wash up on the shore of a nearby river. These incidents were related no matter what anyone said. A high-powered, well-connected chemical weapons guy knocked off… then mysterious death on a massive scale. Chemicals? Biological weapons, basically? Unfortunately, in Christina's mind, the idea of atmospheric weapons and people getting killed either by or because of them led her right back to her own mother. That scared the hell out of her.

The following night, one of the late night news programs promised a show covering both incidents: Getz' killing and the mysterious animal death. The program opened with video shot of the dead birds lying all over the sidewalks and roads. The voiceover was jarring.

Internet frenzy! Was Alex Getz murdered because he was about to reveal secret US military tests that had killed the birds?

Why bother with this? Why draw the connection for people so very directly and strongly when they probably weren't going there themselves? It was one of the strangest pre-emptive spins she had ever seen. She was fairly sure she would be one of the few people putting those two events together and even then those thoughts had barely bumped up against each other because the ramifications were horrifying. She and Anya had been scouring the internet for information about Getz and had yet to come across anything that overtly drew those things together. Was this a mistake? A message to others in positions to blow the whistle? What was this?

As the holiday went on, other reports of dead animals surfaced from around the world. They were varied: birds, fish, penguins. The only factor each incident had in common was the shockingly high numbers of casualties, each drawing farther and farther afield from the original incident. Christina wondered if some weapon was being tested worldwide or if this was being done deliberately to confuse the issue. Or maybe it was a battle of some sort, opposing sides firing salvos at each other, bringing down populations of animals to prove they could do it. No matter what, it was frightening.

According to an internet source, the German newspaper *Die Reflexion* reported that autopsies of the birds showed lungs and respiratory systems that had literally exploded, for lack of a better way to describe it. Those were some fireworks.

Then all of a sudden, probably thanks to the late night news, everyone was trying to put it all together online. Other television programs dedicated entire hour-long programs to smearing Getz, pointing to 'obvious' drinking and drug use. Hey, the guy was obviously hammered, they'd say. Then, just as suddenly, all the stories stopped... utter and complete silence, like none of it had ever happened.

Christina's intuition had been shoving her around since the moment her mother was run down in the road. There was a sinister element to be reckoned with here. She labored away for six months in shock, as it happened, then, just as she had known it would happen, random, seemingly unrelated pieces of the puzzle started to parachute into the chaos. This is how it was. This is how it would ever be. She and her mother: code and decoder ring, come to earth in the same box of corn flakes. Her mother – oblivious, self-serving, not wanting to think too much – was the slate, the glyph. She – hyper-observant, gifted at making ridiculous connections between things and events that meant nothing at all on their own but added up to everything when put together – would read what had been written there... and then decide what to do about it. There would undoubtedly be something to do about it. That was the problem.

When Otto came home from work that night, she was sitting on the sofa in the living room, staring out the window, waiting for him.

"What?" he said, sitting down beside her. "I have to write about this, Otto."

"Okay." He was puzzled, clearly, as to why she needed to make this declaration. She was always writing, it wasn't much of a surprise that she'd be writing about something as big and wretched as this.

"No, Otto. You don't understand. I'm writing about this – I don't really even know what 'this' is – because I believe my mother was murdered."

Another knowing. Great. "So, what does that mean exactly?"

"It means a couple of things," Christina said, "important things. First of all, it means there is some element of danger involved if I'm right. If whatever is going on is so inflammatory that a little old lady who couldn't even remember her own social security number anymore was a potential threat, then there is some serious risk here. So, I have to be very careful. I need to write on a computer that isn't actively connected to the Internet. Is that possible?"

"Sure, we can just disable the connection… keep your work on a thumb drive."

"A what?" How was Christina going to go up against the spooks who might have killed her mother if she didn't even know what a thumb drive was? No doubt they were operating on a practically extra-terrestrial level of technological expertise. Maybe that would be her ace in the hole. Maybe she would be able to do it because they wouldn't be looking for someone who operated just above caveman level, technologically speaking.

They won't even think to look all the way down here for me, I hope.

"Second," she said, "I don't even know what the problem was. I have to fish through her computer and that's going to hurt. I have to research. And I have to think of the best ways to stay safe up to and including sending pitches to the agents I know and getting the work published. There are about six places to find that your car brakes have been cut or there's poison in your apple pie in the scenario I just described. Mostly, though, I just have to pay attention because the story will come to me. It always does."

The news was done with Alex Getz. The news was done with dead birds falling from the sky. The journalists were disinterested now, or so it seemed. It was dropped like a hot potato. Buried by someone? Almost certainly, but no way to know for sure although she longed to be a fly on someone's wall, just the right person's wall. There were several good threads; she was prepared to yank all of them until she found out where they led. Getz, mysterious animal deaths, and her mother. Certainly these things gave her unique and meaty places to start.

End the beginning. Please.

She wondered if the people out there responsible for all this bloodshed would ever even be aware that she was out here? And if they were, would they care? She could put the whole thing together but, as of right now, she could only contribute one unique name to the scenario besides her mother's: Wolfgang von Marshall. It was a name that chipped away at her consciousness, the
atmospheric scientist, the brilliant physicist, the Naval Weapons specialist in plasmas who had worked most closely with her mother.

She opened her mother's old silver laptop. The finger pad was very worn and there was a slight depression on the surface. She didn't like doing this because her mother's name popped up every time the lid was pulled open and reminded one that the owner was dead. Still, she needed to take a look in case there was anything at all tucked away in there that would help her move forward. That's what kept happening, she became a nexus of currents – truths, facts, conjecture, hypotheses – that skewered her like thin wooden sticks, through her head, immobilizing her. It mattered not one bit anymore how much fuss her heart kicked up. That was just too bad; there was work to be done. She was not someone who liked to be immobilized. She found and opened a file marked 'editing work.' Her mother hadn't done any freelance editing for years, she didn't think. Certainly no government contracts. However, her mother was always trying to make money somehow. Her understanding, her perspective, on where she was in the world was always just a hair's breadth away from living on the streets. Those lenses through which she
viewed her position, that conclusion, was all so wrong. Still, she kept looking for a way to make
money no matter what.

Christina opened the file. There were two letters inside, both to local entities. One was a university-sponsored energy project. The other was a private contractor. They were both off-shore and had to do with, ostensibly, wind power and wave power. Two things occurred to Christina. First, she hoped the letters were drafts because they were not very good. It's possible that her mother knew contacting these people was the longest of shots and so had not put any effort into them. It was possible this was the best she could muster. Her mother did have lots of freelance experience working with and for companies looking to get government contracts in research and development off-shore. The bids usually went to Defense Advanced Research Projects Agency for funding. There wasn't a government agency with a darker, smellier side than DARPA, an agency that had started with the leftovers, cobbling together little projects no one else in the government wanted. Eventually they learned to build monsters, which in turn ate the rest of the defense industry, which set about trying to eat the rest of the world. The other thing that occurred to her was, would she have gone by unnoticed, just an old lady far-removed from the government work that had likely been her death sentence had she not sent up a flare like this? What if these companies were involved in some of the darker aspects of off-shore energy? She could only speculate that these letters may have drawn attention to her mother being nearby. She could only speculate because she couldn't prove anything. She wanted to be wrong because it was just too hard to imagine that her mother might have slipped by had it not been for her own avarice.

She started a little when a little white text window popped up on the lower right hand corner of her computer screen. It was a message from Bennie.

Hi, love. How are you?
I am decidedly unwell. Thanks for asking. How are you?
Oh, dear. What's up?
I'm stuck. It seems like I just can't move forward at all. My temper is short. Bad dreams. That kind of thing. I'm stuck, it sounds so pop psychology. Yuck.
Christina, have I ever told you about my Mom?
No.
I'm going to put you in touch with her. She has special gifts. She helps people get through things like this.
Sure, Bennie. I need someone, that's for sure.

Two days later, Christina had another instant message from someone called Adela. Adela wanted to know if Christina was a friend of her daughter, Beata, she called her. Christina had to think for a bit before she remembered that Bennie was Beata.

Yes, I'm a friend of your daughter's. She told me she was going to put us in touch with each other.

Christina, I know it sounds bizarre but I have a gift. I can sometimes talk to people in the spirit world. It may seem hard to believe but it's true.

I don't have any trouble believing that.

I asked to be given an idea where you are at right now in your feelings and the pain was so much I had to ask that it be taken away from me. However, I did have contact with your mother. She said something about a ring.

Yes, my daughter found a wide gold wedding band in my mother's things. I have no idea whose it was or where it came from. And now, we can't find it. It just vanished.

Yes, it was your mother's ring. That's just so you know it's her.

Is she alright? I mean I wonder often how it was at the accident scene. She must have been scared to death.

She says she didn't feel a thing.

That was exactly the way her mother would have said it.

She wants you to make things up with your father.

Now she wasn't so sure it was her mother.

I can't make things up with my Dad. He hasn't even acknowledged that my mother died. We haven't heard from him at all. And by the way, that is not a surprise. I'm disappointed in him but there's nothing my Dad can't ignore, believe me.

Well, just do your part. Tell him about me and see what happens.

Yeah, tell my Dad, a psychic in Australia says Mom wants me to make nice with you, Dad. Mmmm, no.

Christina talked to Adela several times a day over the next few weeks. She was a wonderful, warm, old angel, a refugee from Brazil, from

Copacabana. She and her husband had immigrated to Australia in search of a better life and, she was quick to say, they had found it.

> *Adela, I love you.*
> *I love you, too.*
> *How did you know you had this gift, which this was what you were supposed to do?*
> *When I was a little girl an angel appeared to me and I knew. I've always known. Your mother says she loves her family. She says she loved you the only way she knew how. She says she was raised a spoiled brat.*
> *That would be quite the admission from my mother, Adela. She wants to know if you will read to her.*
> *Sure.*

She did love Adela, very much. It was clear even across the tens of thousands of miles that Adela was able to give her love and her wisdom and her comfort to anyone, anywhere.

> *I wish could see angels.*
> *Your mother keeps talking about your writing, Christina. She is very proud of it.*

My writing, Christina thought. Utterly unappreciated I am but that just gives me tons of street credibility for if I could really make a living writing, that would make me a hack. This way, I'm a better person. All the best writers are total failures, right? She smiled. It was an old litany she trotted out whenever anyone said her writing was good. She would have liked to be making a living at it.

> *She wants you to put a photograph of her for some reason by the computer when you write. I don't understand this vision, really. And I see a photograph of her up when you read to her.*
> *These are very strange requests, Adela. They don't sit well with me. It makes me feel like she wants me and my writing all to herself. That would have been very like her in life.*

Well, sometimes I get my wires crossed. Also, I had a dream and I saw your mother bringing lots and lots of people with her. I don't know if those were relatives or what. Sometimes I get my wires crossed.

Shortly thereafter, on a bright morning, she received a call from Hank. It was unlike him to call in the middle of the day. He seemed energized, excited yet sort of penitent.

"Mom," he said, "last night I had a dream. I was having this conversation with a woman who looked like Grammy. I mean it looked like her but it wasn't her. She didn't sound like Grammy. She was nice and soft and kind. We talked for a long time. Then I woke up and lay on the floor and cried for a long time."

Thank you, Mom. He needed that.

Then finally, Christina worked up the courage. She knew her mother was waiting for this question anyway.

Ask my mother if her death had anything to do with her job.
Yes.

Christina had no idea what she was supposed to write but she knew it would become a story. There was a story banging on her door. It was left to her to invite it in, make it sit down and tell her what it wanted. At first she was very frightened of watchers and their bosses and what they might do about it if they didn't like the book she was writing. She might write about something that could get her killed and not even realize it. For a while, or maybe forever, this piece would be written on faith; faith that the other side knew what it was doing. She didn't even know yet whether the story was worth dying for. How many stories really were? They had killed her mother, though, and she wasn't about to let that go. She wasn't looking for a person; she was looking for a reason. She didn't talk about it except to Otto although she spent all her time thinking about it and researching it and so inserted another divider between herself and the outside world; one that she hoped was temporary.

She thought it would be good if other people had copies of the book as insurance. Then she realized if something happened that left it to other people to see the story got out into the open, then that meant she was dead. And when she realized this is what she was considering, she was scared all over again. After she calmed herself down, she would try to think who she should enlist. A friend in the United States might be too close. She had friends in Europe but much of the story was likely to be set in Europe. Then she remembered: Bennie. She would send a copy to Bennie in Sydney. She wasn't going to get any further away than that.

Just please stick a copy under your mattress, Bennie. Just in case.

Bennie agreed. It was good that someone knew what she was doing. It was like leaving a note when you went out so someone would know where you were in case something happened. Christina also wondered if it might be safer to approach a publisher down there. It was a small world but it might be harder to sit on the manuscript if it were being published on the other side of the world. She could be in danger herself if she made the wrong move. She knew the book could be intercepted and buried if she made the wrong move. It felt a little bit safer this way even if the idea that there was safe place was an illusion.

Bennie, when I'm done, can you do some research and see if you can discover which publishers down there might be open to a book like this?
Yes, I understand.

She tried so hard to remember what her mother worked on as a freelancer in Hawaii so many years ago. Then she found the entry on her mother's old resume: In February, 1993, the Defense Advanced Research Projects Agency (DARPA) awarded a grant for $5 million to the High Technology Development Corporation (HTDC), a State of Hawaii agency, to establish a National Defense Center of Excellence for Research in Ocean Sciences (CEROS). The grant supported 12 prime contractors working on 11 projects. Within the core, three projects produced algorithms or software products; three developed prototype systems; two produced models or design studies; two demonstrated proof-of-concept; one contract was cancelled before completion. After the projects were completed, DARPA required a written report documenting the research and development of each project. CEROS submitted the report to Congress in 1998.

Her mother had edited a report to Congress but Christina could remember nothing of it. The report itself, thankfully, was now in the public domain. She found it. There were twelve projects on the report. She could look those up, as well. That wouldn't take her very far, though, unless she could draw some connections to the projects her mother queried for work right before she died. And that, of course, didn't prove anything.

What am I looking for?

She typed her mother's name in a search engine then and, aside from obituaries, got a list of documents that she had worked on in London which were now available to the public; all except two. Written back-to-back in the summer of 1991, they were released and then removed shortly thereafter. That led Christina to type in the names of all the scientists she could remember her mother working with in London.

'Searching' Wolfgang von Marshall was like pulling the arm on a slot machine: it triggered a jackpot. He was listed as one of the Nazi scientists brought over under Project Paperclip. If she could believe what she was reading, not only was Lorna von Marshall still alive but incredibly so was Wolfgang, who would be in his late nineties by now. She even found an e-mail address for Wolfgang and tried sending a message.

The only later connections she could find at this point were between the University of Hawaii deep water programs, Pantheon's development in 1997 and 1998 of a stable drilling platform for ships and a research and teaching vessel called the Intrepid. It was currently stationed nearby in the Atlantic conducting long-term experiments. One of the ocean exploration outfits her mother had contacted before she died was called Intrepid Energy. She read that her mother's boss at National Defense Base for Research in Deep Sea Sciences (CEROS) had been the Assistant Director of the Office of Naval Research International Field Office. He was science advisor to the Joint Chiefs of Naval Operations and Science Advisor to the Commander in Chief of the Pacific Fleet. The biggest slice of the original Congressional money pie seemed to have gone to Pantheon, and their drilling platform for very, very deep drilling. Some days her research went so well, it was mind-boggling. She had come up with a lot this time.

She just wasn't sure how it all went together to make anything.

David appeared at the door. "Mom?"

"Yes, son," Christina answered.

"I don't feel good. Everything hurts. I feel exhausted, really sleepy. I don't want to go to school."

Great.

1997: Mo' Bettah No Can Get

There was more traffic on the Brooklyn Queens Expressway than there should have been at four a.m. during a hurricane. They even passed someone on a motorcycle.

"Jackass," Christina muttered under her breath.

"What, Mommy?" Hank asked from the backseat. He was the only one awake.

"Nothing, sweetheart."

An hour ago, they'd started on the Long Island Expressway then onto the BQE headed for Staten Island and then Newark Airport. The babies were sleeping. Hank was four, Anya was two, David was eight months old. Even if dawn broke, the light would be negligible. The rain pelted down mercilessly, pounding the windows and sliding off in sheets. Cars and weather. Christina, more intrepid than anyone she had known her entire life, found it impossible to explain what that combination did to her. And, for the last four years, it had only grown worse. Her younger brother had sealed himself in a running car in a garage he could no longer pay for, just before Hank arrived. Christina didn't talk about it. That was no doubt at the bottom of her problem with cars. In the water memory of her body, at that level of sentience, cars murdered people. Had not her beloved grandmother also died in a car? She would get out from under it someday, she promised herself that.

They were on their way to the Big Island because her mother was sick. She had just been diagnosed with multiple sclerosis. Otto was going to stay behind for now and work. Her mother was the only 'real' family she had left in her mind. The children were different. She meant that her mother was the last of the life with which she'd grown up for better or for worse. The same part of her that hated cars and weather needed to repel any threat to her mother. Christina... mother lioness to the whole wide world. It was a lot.

Whatever magical warrior properties could be rendered by

adopting that attitude they could never defeat the nightmare that was Los Angeles International Airport. Medusa to her Perseus, but before the good part. Nothing good happened there. She could get through San Francisco unscathed but never LAX. Still they had to make it to Newark alive and then take off; not a given right now.

"You're really going to drop us in front?" Christina asked as they pulled up at passenger drop-off.

"No money for parking, honey," Otto replied apologetically.

"Grrr...". Christina opened the umbrella stroller and settled David inside. "Anja grab one side. Hank grab the other side. Whatever you do, do not let go!"

They boarded alright then they sat on the tarmac in a very hot and humid aircraft for three hours waiting for a window in the hurricane. They took off, eventually, and just missed their connection at LAX because the airline rep who was supposed to meet her and help her get to the next aircraft never showed up. She yelled at the woman behind the counter until the airline got them a hotel room and then she shamed the local island airline into issuing new tickets for the next day when, in fact, they were going to make them buy new fares. Los Angeles and Christina. Perseus needed a sword and just one clean shot.

After London, her mother had rotated back to Dahlgren, Virginia, although she had not wanted to particularly. She did it anyway because it was an absolute guarantee of a job. Several of her co-workers came back at the same time or near enough to it including the von Marshalls. They were back in Alexandria but according to her mother stopped returning phone calls or e-mails. She was stationed at the Naval Surface Warfare Division this time when, at the age of sixty, she retired. She picked a spot on the Big Island, which was inexpensive because all of Hawaii, particularly the outer islands, were drowning in the leading edge of the coming recession. As a technical editor with her credentials, there was an unending supply of ad hoc military work to be had in Hawaii. Big, juicy, ripe defense contracts represented more than thirteen billion dollars a year in revenue for the state and there were countless testing facilities and bases dedicated to undersea warfare. All the local universities competed for the intellectual slice of the pie. The deep, blue harbors and roaring surf hid so much. What's more, these coastal defense 'farms' were nothing compared to what lay under the surface farther out to sea.

She bought a house on Old Volcano Road in Keaau just at the intersection where the road meandered up the mountain to the town of Volcano on one side or went straight on to Pahoa and the lava beds on the other. Active lava was never far away, streaming out from under the ocean just at the south shore, making the water steam and bubble. That took the pressure off the area around the caldera at the top of the road that led up to Volcano. The ground beneath your feet might turn to liquid fire and rush out from under you and pull you in, making ash from you, but fiery death would likely not come raining down from above. Her mother picked up a lot of editing work as soon as she got there and for the duration of her stay. In Virginia, her offices were concerned with submarine warfare and surface warfare. Naval warfare exclusively and endlessly. The trend here in Hawaii was toward deep sea endeavors and equipment that aided in that. There was a need for drilling equipment for use in deep sea platform research stations and the like. Sonar applications were big and weapons that barely acted as if they were under water were very popular. Many projects used the words 'sustainable' and 'energy.' Many projects had to do with surveillance. She mostly worked for an outfit called the Center for Excellence in Research in Oceanic Studies or with contractors trying to secure work with the same. CEROS was a division of Defense Advanced Research Projects Agency, sometimes jokingly referred to by civilians on the outside as the 'Department of Mad Scientists.'

"Wish that was funny," she would say.

Then she started to get dizzy while she worked in the yard and then when she drove, and she said, in a panic, she could hear her own blood rushing in her ears. It could have been anxiety. It could have been what happens when you have nothing to distract yourself with in the end and you can finally hear the beating of your own heart. Or it could have been something else. So she had a CT scan. Her doctor said he thought she had the beginnings of multiple sclerosis. So she called Christina just as soon as she left the doctor's office and Christina said they would be right there.

"Why is that necessary?" her mother had asked.

"Did you not just say for one thing that you get dizzy when you're driving? Are you going to stop driving?"

"No."

"Then I think we'll just stop by."

Her mother was excited to show off her house anyway. It was a very typical example of the houses in the area; mostly white with single wall construction and louvered hurricane windows. There was a giant avocado tree on one side, lemons in the back yard, a long-abandoned bomb shelter behind the carport and, the crowning glory, an enormous banyan tree in the front yard. A small Okinawan family lived next door. The elderly mother often appeared at the carport screen door bearing a plate of *Ondagi*, a deep-fried, sugary donut-like confection. There was a little oval Koi pond in the back courtyard and at night hundreds of frogs, excreting a deadly poison from their skin, gathered there and sang under the stars despite their somewhat tricky handicap.

The arrivals hall in Hilo was on the second floor of an open, light-filled, mostly-glass airport terminal. She had strapped as much carry-on luggage as she could to the back of the umbrella stroller. David sat in it but the counter-weight was dangerously close to pulling him over. Several commuters on the local flight from Honolulu to Hilo had become rather cross when three excited but tired children settled in behind them.

Her mother meandered happily on the floor below; they saw each other over the balcony. She waited, chatting away with someone – a friend or stranger – it made little difference anymore. If anything she was more open with strangers but these days she spoke to anyone close enough to listen.

Sighing, Christina pushed the elevator button. She had a vision, an image, as her mother looked up at them with an open, excited expression, talking and gesturing. She had an image that they were some sort of slides in her mother's slide show and her mother was down there narrating. This was one of her fundamental qualities: the idea of her family was delightful, a real conversation piece, a beautiful coffee table book. Same principle as talking to strangers… no strings. The actual reality of her family was a pain in the ass. The glass door slid open and Christina shoved all her things inside then threw herself against the closing door so that she could get her children in. She kept waiting for her mother to notice how burdened she was and rush forward to help but her mother was lost in her presentation. That was something that had never changed, she waited for her mother to notice but her mother was too lost in her own show. No one could ever argue it wasn't making her happy, though.

"My God, I have baby in one arm and a Volkswagen under the other. Come and help me!"

Her mother looked startled, as if she would never have thought of helping and hurried over, with the inevitable proviso.

"You realize, of course, I can't help much because of my arthritis...".

Yes, yes, yes... I realize you can't help me. That was one of the fundamental givens of her life.

Her mother drove, of course, although she wasn't really aware of the rocky relationship between Christina and cars yet. A young girl was there, at her mother's house, when they arrived.   She was cleaning. Her mother simply did not have the energy right now to do anything physical. They slid partitions closed and open around the house, as the set-up was based in the Japanese style, creating spaces for the children to have a room. Her mother was so proud of this house. The best part, as far as Christina was concerned, was a shower the size of an entire room. It had been at one time a traditional Japanese bath, complete with large Japanese tub and a shower. She had asked the previous owner to renovate it, make it nice and new and he had simply taken it out, making the entire room a giant shower. However, the next morning, Christina found that she could get inside with all the children. A shower for four and no babysitter needed. Like most mothers of young children, she had often gone days without being able to shower. No more. It was luxurious. Baby David sat on the tile splashing and laughing, crawled into and out of the shower stream.

"Just watch out when you go in there," her mother warned her, "that's where my cat keeps mice."

Mother lioness had arrived and set up camp. Why was this woman so ill? Christina realized in short order that her mother had herself on an enormously tight food budget so that she could continue to have travel money. It was the same thing every day, day in and day out: one cup of black coffee for breakfast with a banana and a bowl of oatmeal; a bowl of steamed rice for lunch or dinner… maybe a steamed vegetable. First of all, her mother was starving herself to death. She was doing this mostly because of a very distorted definition of 'needs' and, of course, that was fine, completely subjective, except that she was making herself sick because of it. Was she poor? No, she had plenty. She insisted that she was broke and Christina knew her mother believed it or at least obsessed about it to the point where she was compelled to get others to reassure her that she was fine.

Am I poor? Am I doing okay? Do I have enough money or is everything going to fall apart tomorrow? Do you think that person has more money than I do? Probably so. That's not fair. I deserve a lot of money. Do you think everyone wants to steal my money?

Christina was very used to this and the constant need for financial reassurance, this litany, which had been a huge part of the way her mother interacted with the world for Christina's entire life. As she got older, the litany seemed more childish and illogical. Now the obsession was becoming dangerous.

It wasn't very long at all before her mother tired of them, the noisy, messy reality, particularly of young children. Surfaces got sticky and there would be sand and toys on the floor with children in the house. There was noise in houses where children lived, spats broke out, unexpected fevers were spiked; sudden rashes appeared. There were *noises*.

She was working on a project for CEROS when they arrived. It was for a contractor who did not get the contract in the end. Then CEROS asked her to edit their yearly report to Congress; all the grant money had to be accounted for. Otto continued to work in New York on his own, a state of affairs for which he simply was not built. Toward September, Christina enrolled Hank in a preschool out in the jungle of the Pahoa District, the Malamalama Waldorf School, primarily because the constant action of a very bright four year old was likely to drive her mother to her wit's end. His four-year-old jungle companions had names like Mahatma and Orion. They made stone soup and oatmeal and played among the plants and animals. He grew very brown, happy and carefree.

Meanwhile, Christina cared for her mother from mid-July through mid-December, feeding her meat stews and eggs and trying to raise her precarious protein levels. Her mother did not like being told what to do although she did like to be catered to. The space Christina occupied between one thing and another was becoming impossible. The old woman labeled their visit, The Invasion.

Anya was too young for pre-school, although she desperately wanted to join her big brother. One morning she found the most exquisite pair of purple velvet high heeled pumps in her grandmother's closet and put them on. Color was always going to speak deeply to Anya. Christina took her daughter's hand and led her to the kitchen for her grandmother to see, making what she would come to understand was a fundamental error... she expected the same delighted and loving reaction her own grandmother would have given. Instead, Anja was greeted with sour disapproval and a miserly and selfish response.

Mine. Put them back. You've no right.

The shoes were, after all, her private property and she had never given her permission for anyone to put them on. Christina had no idea how a human adopted that kind of bristle in front of a tender-hearted four year old girl. Anya, big-hearted soul that she was, pretended not to notice. Christina was starting to understand how utterly and incurably self-absorbed this woman was, for who could resist the little doll with the big curls tromping about in purple high heels? Her mother did not like children. She really did not and yes, she had been a teacher, but the difference was there were students with whom her interaction was finite and who went home every day and came back clean and pressed as if they'd been to the laundry and, frankly, performed on command and stopped on command. Frankly, if the 'taking care of' was the only reward then she was not interested.

The chapter of her mother's life that was this time was written with words like 'alone.' 'Nothing to do.' 'Insular'. She was very social in certain circles, the ones she selected to be that way in, the people she could keep at arm's length. In her own home, she was often unnaturally territorial, especially with children. Her mental illness now stood out in bas relief. It came to the forefront because she was no longer inside a regimented world, endlessly busy or told what to do and when to do it. She became 'ill.' She became 'weak.' There was a neurotic little bus driver hidden within her that was now driving the 'bus' over curbs and up onto sidewalks and into mailboxes – metaphorically speaking, of course – the same demented bus driver who floored the gas pedal and stood on the brakes at frequent yet random intervals.

There just wasn't enough structure to keep everything in anymore. She rushed about picking up the bits and pieces that were falling out of the bus for a while until she gave up, lay down on the rattan sofa, turned on the History Channel and stayed there unless she was doing editing work for cash money. She tried to garden and take care of her lemon tree in particular, but that just wore her out. She often sat down outside, breathing heavily in the sun, listening to the relentless rushing of her blood and the constant pounding of her heart. The only creature she could bear to love right out in the open was her cat. Her cat required very little in the way of caring for.

She complained loudly that she wasn't making nearly as much per hour as she was worth – all the while she was nestled in a tropical bungalow in Hawaii, flying here and there among the other islands amid one of the most severely economically depressed areas of the entire country; one with a staggeringly high unemployment rate. Yes. Her mother's mental illness was in control.

Christina knew, like many children do, that there was someone in there who not only didn't mean for life to go the way it did: the verbal exchanges and the alienation but that someone wouldn't have recognized any of this as reasonable had it been presented to her in the form of another person. Someone she could see before her and ask, what the hell are you thinking? Then there was the mental illness itself. It was never happier than when it was pushing buttons, getting hysterical reactions, making everyone dance. It did not hear the beauty in a child's laugh or understand the contribution made in the day-to-day nurturing of another life. It wanted what it wanted for itself and it was unquenchable, voracious, sanctimonious and completely justified. Christina called it '*Me.*' *Me* is here today. *Me* wants what it wants and get the hell out of the way. *It's Mine, Me* would snarl. *Me* went along happily as long as *Me* felt it had lots of everyone's time. In Hawaii, *Me* was in full fly, wearing a crown and on top of the world. It was so easy for Christina to see the hostage underneath it all, the prisoner who could not get the cage door open.

Once her mother was feeling better, and it seemed like they'd be in Hilo for a while, it remained to make arrangements for Otto to join them. Christina decided she might as well take a couple of classes while she was waiting to find out what would happen next. No one really knew.

Her mother was incensed.

You are here to take care of ME," she snarled. "I hope you don't think I'm going to watch those kids while you're at class. You just find yourself a babysitter."

This same person would don a brilliantly colored muumuu and a wide brimmed straw hat and sit in a foursquare church every Sunday morning, fanning herself with the program and singing her heart out. Mostly she sang spirituals and when she was singing, she really believed them. There was a Spirit present. It was still *Me*, either lifting itself up to the heavens or, if the song reminded her of her lost son, feeling that pain all the way through her gut and down to her toes. It was also *Me* who lashed out on Thanksgiving, hitting and flailing at Christina because she wasn't getting her way about something. Otto moved the children out to the front porch but Christina could still see how horrified they were. Otto got mad that day and Otto never got mad. There was the briefest fiery flash in her mother's eyes when she realized she had managed to get a rise out of her son-in-law. It was only there for the smallest sliver of a second but Christina saw it. She knew *Me* quite well. The flash had been pure delight. When the family was finally able to leave the Big Island, when Otto had secured another position, it was a couple of years before they spoke to her mother again.

In the Wake of the Great White

All the way back to New Mexico, Tim mulled over the idea of VLATs spraying toxic chemicals unrestrained. They had to be toxic; they were putting people in the hospital. The idea that no matter who you called about it, the answer that no such thing was going on was the biggest clue that this was some sort of military operation – perhaps NASA or CIA or both – but perhaps higher and more clandestine than that. Everybody pretended it wasn't happening, despite all the visual evidence and the casualties. That meant people were scared. Too scared to talk about it. Why? He'd been in the military long enough and had a clearance high enough to know not to start raising hell the minute his boots hit the ground. If he approached it that way, he'd be in the dark forever. He would wait and watch and see if he could figure out what was going on just by reporting for work and doing his job. He was angry that his father's health was under attack but he also knew his Dad would never leave Lake Helen. Whatever the people were breathing up there would also inevitably end up in the soil and the water and that was very measurable. His Dad had done some testing of his own; Tim asked him to do a lot more while he was gone. His Dad had said that was already the plan. He knew some environmentalists and foresters and chemists in the area; northern California was lousy with environmental scientists. Results of those tests would tell them what they were working with and that might point to the how and the why of it. No one pretended they might like the answers that were coming.

In the meantime, he had a job to do. *Pinon* Airfield was situated on a plain in extreme northern New Mexico between two dormant volcanoes. The first thing Tim noticed when he got within visual range of *Pinon* was the sheer number of aircraft parked at the field. Cal Fire owned about fifty aircraft that serviced the entire state of California. *Pinon* was a tiny airport in the northern New Mexico mountain desert and he counted six DC -10s, three 747s, two Grummans, four S2Ts and two helicopters, a Super Huey and an Erikson Skycrane Helitanker. The DC-10s were a decade old. They hadn't been made in that long and went for at least five million each. 747s, again not the latest in the 747 line, still ran for about three hundred million each. The VLATs would have been appraised in the neighborhood of a billion dollars. Unless these planes were to be stationed across the entire United States, it was an obscene amount of firefighting airpower. It simply did not wash. Granted, Bluesky covered two states regularly – New Mexico and Colorado – and assisted in many fires elsewhere but this was a display of air power that had no connection to reality. The cost of the VLATs made all the fire attack planes together seem like a bargain. Apparently, though, *Pinon* had not been able to spare a single VLAT for the Bully Choop fire. Maybe the commander here had no authority at all over these planes. He would take that up with command at a later date. There might be a good reason. Maybe he just didn't know what it was yet, but he couldn't imagine what could have kept every single one of these birds grounded.

Keep your mouth shut and turn your radar on, Tim.

He set his Piper down despite being blown sideways a little in typical New Mexico ground turbulence and rolled to a stop. Landing a light aircraft (or a big one, for that matter) in New Mexico always spooked pilots a little at first. He would have to try to catch a ride with another pilot back to Redding to pick up his car and drive it back. This airport was so remote, most of the pilots stayed in the barracks on base. It seemed that most of them were single. They drove to Red River or just under an hour on their nights off to Taos to drink beer and play pool. Every once in a while they'd spend a few days in Santa Fe or Albuquerque. Tim thought he'd like to take a trip down to Los Alamos or maybe Socorro to see the Very Large Array. There would be someone to hang out with here – there always was. He planned to get up to Carson National Forest before it got too cold and see if there were any cutthroat trout left. Cutthroat were a beautiful, maddening and wily fish, and he loved catching them. It was just October. The leaves were starting to turn their full autumn shades. The hills were covered in low scrub pine and sage, *pinon* and other evergreens. The temperatures were still in the sixties, sometimes in the seventies. There might be some fishing left.

Out on the tarmac, the Huey started to scream. The thing about a Huey helicopter is that it does scream for a while until the rotors actually start to turn. It's disconcerting to listen to the pitch of the engine getting up to speed. The gale and the dirt and sand kicked up by the rotors hit Tim in the back as he headed for dispatch. Since all airports at which he had ever been stationed kept the tarmacs pristine and free from any debris that could affect flying, he was surprised. The wind and the desert, though, might just get away from them periodically. The barracks were behind the offices, briefing rooms, mess hall and gym. The dorms weren't really standard military, but more like dorms in a firehouse or a college with two men in a room. His new roommate was not at home when Tim went to stow his gear. He later discovered that his roommate was one of the Huey pilots.

He was hungry so he hit the mess hall, figuring that's where everyone would be anyway. There were a dozen pilots gathered there watching a football game, drinking coffee and soda, but on duty. He introduced himself. They had been waiting for him to arrive. They knew he was attached to the United States Forest Service in some way and had shaken out the VLATs. They were impressed.

"Hey," a big man with red hair and a light freckled complexion called from the far side of a table. "Come sit over here. I want to hear about those VLATs."

Tim wedged his way between tables and behind chairs and next to the wall and finally squeezed himself past bodies and boots and chairs to the other side. He grabbed a folding metal chair from where it leaned against the wall, snapped it open and sat down.

The red headed man stuck out his hand, "Phillip Yarmouth, welcome." He pumped Tim's hand firmly. Phillip Yarmouth looked like a big red bear.

"What do you fly?" Tim asked. It was always the first question any pilot asked another.

"The Huey. Call me Pip. Everybody does... or else." He grinned. "You? Aside from the big boys anyway?"

Short name for such a big guy, Tim thought.

"Grummans mostly. I've flown every fixed wing sitting out there right now." Sage-colored, scrubby pine trees obscured much of the view out the windows to his left. A picture window that ran the length of the room in front of them revealed the endless horizon under a gradually greying sky. A man walking a husky on a long lead appeared from the right. Tim watched the dog strain against the leather. A speck in the distance above the animal caught Tim's eye. He watched it move, it moved at maybe twenty thousand feet. It would never have been noticed except for the dog that caught his eye and then the thin trail of white it left in its wake. He waited for the trail to dissipate, waited for it to be a regular old garden variety contrail. Instead, it lingered behind the plane, had to be a hundred miles or more. No contrail this. He did not bring it to anyone else's attention. How long had this been going on now? He felt like a complete fool. He was up in the air all the time and had not noticed this. Or was it because he was trained to see contrails – condensation coming from aircraft exhaust – and had never lingered over the picture to see the difference? It was true that when he was flying he was usually busy dropping loads on a fire and there was a lot of smoke in the air. The emergency tended to be 'down' not 'up.' Certainly that's where all his attention was.

"You check in with Com yet?" Pip asked.

"Nope, what's the procedure? I met him briefly when I was here for the USFS but…".

"Well, I believe he's gone for the day. Report first thing, though."

"Got it." He squeezed back out of his seat and went to the kitchen for a cup of coffee. The galley was brand new. There was a cooking island, all the appliances were stainless steel, a dishwasher and a clean linoleum floor. Fresh coffee had been made.

When he returned to his seat he started the usual 'where you from?' round with the rest of the crew. Responses were varied as they always were: Denver, Phoenix, two from Chicago, Des Moines, Midland, Texas. Pip was from Klamath Falls, Oregon. It turned out that Pip was also his roommate. He was one of those guys who was tall enough that his feet hung off the end of the bed like Tim's did.

The next morning at zero-seven-hundred, Tim presented himself in the commander's office. Once you got past dispatch there was little difference between the commander's office and an office at a paper mill or insurance company. He sat behind a wide brown desk. The window behind him was covered with white levered blinds. The view out the window behind him was a row of parked cars; a couple of motorcycles. To be fair, there was an extraordinary computer set-up on his desk. To his right were a couple of grey filing cabinets. There were topographical maps all over the walls, photos of Unger standing beside a fighter jet or two in his younger days, and a fairly sophisticated ham radio set-up to his left. It squawked every once in a while. Unger reached over and turned the volume down. The commander of this airfield was one M.K. Unger. His first name was Mick but no one ever called him that. All the pilots on this airbase were ex-military and they would never call a commander of an airbase by some informal name. Tim found him to be quite stiff at first but by the end of the briefing had changed his mind to 'elusive.' He wasn't stiff. He was just like one of those people you run across in the military who has so many things to hide they've all but lost their ability to make conversation. He was so ordinary looking that it was extraordinary: five foot ten or so, thinning close cropped black hair, gold aviator-style glasses, a mustache, a button-down shortsleeved blue shirt. He might have weighed one hundred sixty five pounds. He wore a gold watch and a plain gold wedding band. He could have been an accountant anywhere is the United States. Yet, this man ran a very busy and very well-appointed privately-owned aerial firefighting company called Bluesky Airways with literally hundreds and hundreds of millions of dollars' worth of top-of-the-line aircraft parked just outside his window. Unger was such a picture of average and normal, he had to be CIA.

"Welcome aboard, Verzet!" Unger half-rose from his rolling chair and shook Tim's hand. "I've been looking forward to getting you back here and in the air. You know those VLATs inside and out. You're an exceptional firefighter and a top-notch military pilot. You have quite a bit to recommend you. For any mission."

"Thank you, Commander," Tim replied, gesturing toward the wooden chair on his side of the desk.

Unger nodded for him to sit. "I'm sure every other pilot here is just as capable if not more so."

"Well," Unger said, leaning back in his chair, "yes, they are all crackerjack pilots, that's for sure. That's the only kind we hire. Not everyone is rated on the big guys, though, and understands how the dispersal systems work on those rigs. It takes a special skill to make a ship that size maneuver. Besides you have close ties to the Forest Service and that is bound to come in handy. You married, Verzet?"

Tim laughed. "No, sir. Not yet anyway. Just me and my Dad." Unger studied Tim for a long ten seconds.

"All your paperwork done, Verzet?"

"Absolutely!"

"Very well. Welcome again. Check the duty roster in the day room for your schedule. You can go." Unger nodded, then turned to his computer and began typing. Tim stood up to go but stopped short.

"Oh, by the way, commander?" Unger stopped and looked up at him.

"What is with all the big birds just parked here? I thought they had homes."

"They do. They'll get there. Anything else?"

"No, sir." Tim turned and left, closing the door behind him.

Tim took a shortcut through dispatch to the day room. The rotations were posted on the wall, just as the commander had said. He ran his finger down the list until he saw his name. He was not 'on duty' for thirty-six more hours. He saw that Pip was off duty, as well. *Pinon* ran just like any other fire station; three days on, three days off. He went looking for Pip. He wanted to take advantage of the down time and the good weather to see about doing some fishing. He had a sleeping bag and a rod and reel stashed in the Piper. Pip had been here for a while and might just be able to shed some light on some of the anomalies if they got around to it during the lazy hours of watching your line bob in the water. He hoped his new roommate enjoyed those kinds of things. He spotted Pip out the window – or more specifically – Pip's legs, under the Huey on a rolling cart. The man did not seem to be able to stay away from his bird. Tim exited the building into the sunlight. The air blew gently today, not like it did in the spring here. New Mexico was notorious for springtime gales, day after irritating day. Tricky flying then. He stood beside the helicopter. Pip spoke from underneath.

"Can I help you?" the large machine made the voice seem farther away than it was.

"Hey, junkie," Tim said loudly, "what do you say we do something else for a day or so? I have the same rotation you do. Do you fish? I hear there may still be some cutthroat trout around here."

"Yeah, I fish. Are you prepared to be thoroughly humiliated because I happen to be really good at it."

"Sure. Shame me. Let's just get out of here before we have to go to work."

Tim leaned against the massive machine with both hands. He spotted a large blue Buick sedan making its way slowly through the gate. Pip rolled out from under his helicopter and lay there watching. He had been unaware of any pending new arrivals. The car pulled up outside the command building and two young men climbed out. Each had a duffle bag, slung immediately over the shoulder like any military man would carry it. They disappeared into the building.

"New recruits?" Tim asked.

"Got me. Us 'Ig-nints' aren't aware of anybody else coming." They watched as Unger reappeared with the two men. They got back into the car and drove the hundred yards to the area where the VLATs were parked. Unger led them up rolling stairs to one of the 747s and opened the hatch. All three men disappeared inside.

"Come on," Pip said, climbing off the flat dolly and brushing the dirt off his pants. "That happens. People come and go a little. Those birds are meant for other airports, it makes sense. Let's go find some trout."

They took Pip's truck. He had a two-man tent thrown behind the seats. That was all they'd need since they really just had a matter of hours of leisure, not days. There was a four-lane road, then a two-lane, then miles and miles of dirt road through lodge pole pines. The altitude was deceptive. The desert atmosphere made you think you must be at sea level when, in fact, you were almost always nearly a mile up. The composition of the forests reflected that. The ground here was clean and clear like it is in New Mexico, with a layer of soft pine needles on the ground. The Forest Service set controlled burns periodically to manage dangerous underbrush. Tim had seen a lot of firefighting work on private property, even out in the middle of nowhere, where underbrush collected dangerously and twig-like growth whipped back in your face if you moved within it.

"Hey, I think we should head up to El Rito Creek above Salvadore Canyon," Pip called over the radio and the wind roaring through the open windows. Pip had a thing for mariachi music, it seemed. Trumpets played high-pitched, staccato, utterly optimistic rhythms.

"You really are suckering me, aren't you, roomie? You know this area pretty well?"

Pip just grinned. "I was a hotshot supervisor up here for a while." Hotshots were twenty-person fire crews, mostly seasonal and dedicated to preventing and if necessary managing wildfires in the early stages. They were of the highest caliber training. They came upon an unexpected curve in the dirt road, Pip applied the brakes abruptly. A coffee can rolled out from under the seat. Tim retrieved it, pried open the plastic lid. He sniffed the greasy, gray contents.

"What is this?"

"Bacon grease! From the kitchen. Threw in some butter, too!" Pip grinned. He reached over and snapped open the glove box; pulled out a plastic bag filled with cornmeal. "I'm picky about my trout!"

He pulled off the dirt road at a tree tied with a plastic orange streamer. They were met by unmanned Forest Service backhoes. Luckily they could continue past this site a few miles. The state was digging up the creek for some reason and the water was cloudy and muddied up. Not much chance of catching fish there. At the end of the road, they parked the truck. They hiked along the river about a mile until they came to a fast-moving spot with a fallen tree across the river creating a bridge. They carefully shimmied out onto it over the river. Tim sat toward one bank of the river, Pip sat toward the other so as not to put too much weight on the center of the old log. The water raced madly over jumbled rocks below them. They baited their hooks with dragonfly lures and cast in downstream. The lures dipped below the surface immediately and were tugged down and away. They wanted to be very quiet so as not to spook the trout, notoriously crafty fish.

"Pip," Tim whispered. "I want to take one of those DC-10s back up. Want to go with me? I can get the Forest Service to make it happen… some kind of bogus test."

Pip chuckled. "Good luck. Can't get near 'em. We never fly those birds. Only the special crews have permission to do that."

"Why do you think that is, Pip?"

"Hell, you know why as well as I do. Special Ops of some kind. They'll be out of here soon, I hear."

"Where?"

"That I do not know, my friend," he said, reeling his line in and recasting it. "and I don't care. You shouldn't either if you know what's good for you. Hell, you know that same as I do."

By four o'clock, the sun was starting to dip below the tree line, as it will in the mountains, and they had four cutthroats nestled in grass in a fishing creel. They headed the mile back to their campsite. They had not pitched the tent yet but gone straight to the river. It was an easy set-up. Tim built a fire while Pip gutted and cleaned the fish. Within half an hour, the trout were rolled in cornmeal and frying in butter and bacon grease in a sizzling hot cast-iron pan. Tim lay back with his sleeping bag under his head. He really loved New Mexico. The sky was clear and blue and generally speaking you could see for miles, just standing in your own yard. Nothing to spoil your view. As he stared into the cloudless sky, a white trail appeared from nowhere. One minute it wasn't there, the next minute it was. It had to be an aircraft.

"Give me your binoculars, Pip."

He put the glasses to his eyes and adjusted the focus. They were powerful, military-grade binoculars. It was a 747. Unmarked. Blue and white. Under the circumstances, it really had to be the same ship he and Pip had watched strangers board before they left that morning. He dropped the binoculars to his chest.

"What's up?" Pip asked casually.

"Our bird. " Tim answered. He watched for a full five minutes as a hundred miles or more of white particulate was laid out and billowed across the sky as it fell ever so slowly. He did not remark upon this to Pip. On that, he had nothing to say. This was the point of departure, the point of silence. He felt somehow like an indigenous resident watching some encroachment, some invasion that had a taste of impossibility to it. He was not sure what it was… not sure, and he was careful not to provoke it quite yet. This brought on a silence, yet he continued to watch as long as there was light, not making a big deal of it with his new friend. The particulate dispersed until it was a much wider, gauzy white sheet-like 'cloud,' not particularly noticeable unless you happened to have watched the whole thing happen. It had such a hang time, he thought, and figured it would be the middle of the night before it hit the ground. What was going on up there? Do we need rain? The fire danger was low. This particular aircraft was flying at a lower altitude than most and the particulate plume it was disgorging was fat and white and huge.

"Give me those glasses, son," Pip said. He focused on the plane as it traveled. "I'm going to call DOT. That has to be a major fuel leak… the location is wrong… and they are way too low.
Something is just plain wrong up there."

Pip pulled his cell phone from his pocket. He dialed information and the operator immediately patched him through to the Department of Transportation emergency hotline. Tim could only hear Pip's side of the conversation, of course, but the steady stream of very trivial answers Pip was giving whoever was on the other end of the phone and the beet-red blotching on the back of his neck as he got more and more agitated indicated this conversation wasn't going well. Twice Pip interrupted with, would you please make a call to that jet? Twice the person on the other end doggedly stuck to a line of questioning. Pip finally gave up and hung up the phone. He looked stunned to say the least.

"I'm trying to save a goddamned crew! They had absolutely no interest in contacting that plane. That was the most infuriating five minutes of my life."

Maybe they keep a list of planes they should ignore, thought Tim. It seemed quite likely. A week later, Tim's cell phone rang at three in the morning. Pip grumbled, stuck a pillow over his head and rolled over. Tim tried to grab the offending phone but he inadvertently knocked it onto the floor.

He fished around blindly until he had it, opened it and spoke, "Hello?"

"Tim," it was his Dad. His voice was strained. Tim was immediately alarmed.

"Yeah, Dad. What's wrong?"

"It's Jeff. It's Jeff, Tim. He's died."

"Wait, what?!" Tim reached over and switched his bedside lamp on. "Dad, what are you talking about?"

Realizing something was very wrong, Pip sat up, wide awake.

"He's dead, son. I just got a call from somebody in Dallas. My name was in his address book or something and someone – a friend – was notifying everyone he could get hold of. There was no one to go and collect the body so they cremated him and buried him there. I wonder what his Dad would think of that? " Huck was barely able to hold this conversation, Tim could tell.

"Can you tell me what happened, Dad? Wait. I… I'm getting up," Tim swung his legs over the side of the bed, reached for his pants hanging over the back of a desk chair.

The voice was barely more than a whisper. "They said he killed himself."

"On my way, Dad. I have my cell phone if you need to call back. Really. I love you, Dad. I'm coming."

Tim switched off his phone and tucked it into his jeans. He pulled on a dirty T-shirt and a sweatshirt over that. It would be cold outside at this hour.

"Can I help?" Pip was wide awake now and sitting on the side of the bed.

"Christ," Tim said. "Look at me. My hands are shaking. My knees are shaking." He sat back down.

"That was my Dad. My brother's dead. Well, he wasn't really my brother, a foster kid. He was around all my life, in and out. My Dad tried to step in when he lost his family. I don't know what happened but I have to get home." He tried to stand again but his knees buckled.

"Hey, pardner. Sit down. Where are you headed again?" Pip scratched his head.

"Redding, California."

"I'll fly you out there. You are no shape right this second. Then you and your Dad can talk about this. Sound okay?"

"Seriously? You would do that?"

"Yes. It is oh-three-hundred. Let's get a flight plan filed and get ready and head out at dawn. OK?"

Pip had the controls of Tim's Piper. They flew away from the rising sun and into a purple and gold dawn.

"Hey, directly overhead!" Pip pointed up. Tim realized there was a DC-10 directly over them about ten thousand feet higher. As they watched, the pilot turned on four jet streams of particulate. They would have been worried but they were directly beneath and they both understood the stream was trailing behind them. The light made rainbows in the stream reminiscent of the rainbows in oily puddles on pavement. He had that feeling again, that feeling like watching an entity that may be friend or foe, ally or predator or both. It was akin to following a great white shark. Safe for the moment but that could change any time. It was closer than they had ever been to this phenomenon.

Just wait, Tim thought.

The silence grew too strained.

"Want to talk about this guy?" Pip asked.

Tim cleared his throat. He had been thinking about Jeff. Seemed like all you ever saw was the back of his head.

"He was a few years younger than me," Tim said, staring out the window. "His family was all gone. His Dad and my Dad flew together in the Air Force. He was in and out of jail for a while... into drugs. Then he just kind of showed up on Huck's doorstep... that's what everybody calls my Dad. Pretty soon Huck had him helping out around the property, taught him to fly and fix engines. Any kind of engine. Jeff learned to fly, got certified as a mechanic and got a job with one of the big guys. Haven't seen him in a while although Huck says he was just up home."

Once they landed in Redding, Tim sprinted for his car and headed for the mountain. He was calm now and ready to talk to Huck. Pip turned right around and flew the Piper back to *Pinon*. According to the newspaper story they found online, the Dallas coroner was sure that Jeff had committed suicide. They both knew that was a lie. They were both flabbergasted, in fact, that he had been found with a bottle of phenobarbital in his stomach.

"You know... and I know... that boy did not kill himself." His Dad said softly. "If he was going to go that route he'd have done it a long time ago, when things were really bad."

"Of course, I know that, Dad. We'll find out what happened."

"I know, son. I know what happened." He pulled an envelope from his coat pocket. It had been opened, was addressed to 'Huck" and mailed from Mt. Shasta, from Jeff. He must have stuck it in the mail when he was here. Tim opened the letter and read it sitting beside his Dad. It felt like he was talking to Jeff. It felt like Jeff was sitting right beside him. It felt like razors on his skin.

Dear Huck,

You will understand why I'm sending you this when you read it. I have some information that's important though I can't for the life of me figure out who to take it to. Maybe you can help me figure that out. I've been thinking about the chemicals being dumped on you up there since I came back to work. Now I seem to see it everywhere. You know the mechanics at the bottom of the barrel are the guys who work on the waste disposal systems, right? Nobody wants to work on the pumps, the tanks, or the pipes that are used to store waste from the lavatories. Only 2 or 3 mechanics in any airport will work on these waste systems but we have 'helping' arrangements with other airlines. Sometime or another we end up working on somebody else's plane.

One day last month, I was called out from our base to do that. The dispatcher couldn't tell me what the problem was, she just said get on out there and have a look. Turned out the problem was in the waste disposal system. I was pretty unhappy but I didn't have a choice, I had to fix it. When I got into the bay, I realized right away that something wasn't right. There were more tanks, more pumps and more pipes than there should have been. I just assumed that the system had been redesigned, it happens all the time. It was so obvious that all this extra piping and these tanks were not part of the waste disposal system. I had just realized this when another mechanic from my company showed up. It was one of the guys who usually works on these systems. I was happy to get out of there but on my way out, I asked him about the extra equipment. He told me to worry about my end of the plane and let him worry about his.

The next day, I was on the company computer looking up a wiring schematic. While I was there, I decided to look up the extra equipment I had seen. The manuals don't show any of it. That's just not possible, Huck. I even tied into the manufacturer files and found nothing. You know me. At that point I had to figure it out. The next week, we had 3 of our planes in the hanger for inspection. I had just finished my shift and I decided to see if I could find another system like the one from before. There were mechanics crawling all over the planes so I figured one more guy wouldn't attract any attention. Sure enough the plane I chose had the extra equipment. I began to trace the system of pipes, pumps and tanks. I found what looked like the control unit. It was a standard looking avionics control box but it had no markings. I could trace the control wires from the box to the pumps and valves but there were no control circuits coming into the unit. The only connection into the unit was a power connection to the aircraft's main powerbus. The system had 1 large and 2 smaller tanks. It was hard to tell, the compartment was cramped, but it looked like the large tank could hold maybe 50 gallons. The tanks were connected to a fill and drain valve just behind the drain valve for the waste system. When I looked for this connection under the plane, I found it hidden under the panel used to access the waste drain. I tried to trace the piping from the pumps. They lead to a network of small pipes that end in the trailing edges of the wings and horizontal stabilizers. If you look closely at the wings of these big airplanes, you'll see a set of wires about the size of your finger extending from the trailing edge of the wing surfaces, the static discharge wicks. You know they get rid of the static electric charge that builds up on a plane in flight, right? I discovered that the pipes from the mystery system lead to every 1 out of 3 of these static discharge wicks. These wicks had been hollowed out to allow whatever flows through these pipes to be discharged through the wicks and out into the clear blue sky. It was while I was on the wing that one of the managers spotted me. He ordered me out of the hanger saying no overtime had been approved.

The next day my GM called me in and suspended me pending getting some union guys in to investigate a claim that I had falsified paperwork. That night at home, I got a weird call. The voice said, "Now you know what happens to mechanics who poke around in things they shouldn't. Next time you work on systems that are not your concern, you'll lose your job." CLICK.

Huck, I don't know what they're spraying but I can tell you how *they're doing it. I figure they're using the 'honey trucks.' Those trucks empty the waste from the lavatories. The airports basically contract those jobs out and no one goes near those trucks. I mean, who wants to stand next to a truck full of shit? They can empty the waste tanks and fill those other tanks at the same time. They know the plane's flight path so the control unit is probably programmed to start spraying at a certain altitude or time in the air. The nozzles in the static wicks are so small nobody in the plane would see a thing. God help us all. Let me know what you think.*

Jeff

*****

Two days after Tim returned from Lake Helen, as promised, Unger asked him to report to his office. His excuse had been that his Dad was taken ill suddenly. There he explained that there was an offer on the table, a special project.

"Well, what's the offer?" Tim hedged.

"TDY to an airbase near the Gila National Wilderness along the border. Flying VLATs. The 747 in particular. The mission is NSA in concert with the Department of the Interior and your old buddies NASA. They want you for this."

Tim wrinkled his brow. "National Security? I'm a firefighter."

Unger shrugged. "Take it or leave it with the usual amount of information. You know they can't explain these things to every Tom, Dick and Harry. That's no way to run a secure operation. Pay is high. Really high. Sky's the limit."

"Legal?" Tim asked.

"Yeah. For a change." Unger laughed.

Tim knew that didn't mean anything. They all lied all the time from start to finish when it came to operations like this. He also knew it could easily be a situation he couldn't get out of once he was in. These things were kept so compartmentalized that Unger likely had no idea what was going on down there along the border and probably wasn't able to tell him more than a dribble of what was going on anyway. The guys flying the missions, like himself, would only know what they needed to know.

"NASA, huh? Do I get any time to think about it?"

"Do you need time to think about it?'

Tim was profoundly vulnerable and profoundly angry at the moment. "No, sir. I'm in."

He liked the jobs he'd done for NASA. He had essentially been with the Interior when he was a firefighter. Still, NASA could be just as dirty as any of the other agencies connected with defense. Most people had no idea that NASA was more defense and special ops – black ops – than space program and had been for a great long while. Tim badly wanted to get next to the rigged planes and the program that was so important that his brother had died because of it.

The next day he was piloting one of the 747s down fifteen hundred feet of runway with the two anonymous young men acting at First Officer and Navigator. Slim, short hair, aviator glasses and utterly nondescript in their appearance. Aloft they headed due south toward an airfield, Gila, which he had never been to and one he had not known existed.

The *Gila* Wilderness was still in New Mexico along the Mexican border. The base was somewhere down there. The border in this area was hilly and canyon-filled. People packed in and camped with their horses. Tim made absolutely no conversation at all with his fellow pilots and they none with him. They all slid effortlessly into covert operations mentality. Tim was dead-serious about this. His father's life was in jeopardy and his 'brother' was dead and it had everything to do with these converted aircraft. He had worked for the Forest Service and had vetted these planes for NASA.

They obviously had had their eye on him for some time. He would use the opportunity, knowing full well that once he was in he would likely not be able to get back out. He wouldn't live long anyway, if he did. Today, that was just fine with him. The list of questions sitting in his mind was short but profound: what is it they are spraying? Who is doing it? What is the objective? What's the set-up? How are they getting pilots, ex-military pilots, to go along with this? Whose neck could he get his hands around, how tight and for how long? If he looked at his own situation, since they had targeted him for recruitment, he would imagine most of the other pilots had similar stories. He was single, no real family, he was an ace pilot and used to TDY assignments with little or no information. At the moment he was deeply vulnerable and feeling reckless because of Jeff's death.

They would now tell him what they felt he needed to know and it might or might not be the truth. In reality, the story would be true enough that even if something told him it wasn't completely on the up-and-up, there would likely never be a loose thread to pull. These kinds of operations, like their purely military counterparts, were liberally sprinkled with soldiers from desperately poor backgrounds. They would make more money than they ever thought possible, they would be men who had never received any positive feedback or felt remotely competent or in control of anything until they joined the military. That made for ultra-loyal, ultra-compliant troops. There would also be a fair smattering of special ops pilots, CIA, and men with a mercenary streak; men without the burden of much conscience, just a few with more information than everyone else and knowledge of who is higher up the ladder... but just one rung. Need to know, after all. That was how the game was played and how masses of people could be manipulated within the realm of really filthy situations without their knowledge. It really was ridiculously easy.

As they approached the airfield and he was given permission to land, he realized he was looking at something in the neighborhood of forty five VLATs parked and ready to go. He was astonished although he did not show it. Who has the funding to keep that many planes in a stable? Some were all white, some were blue and white and there were a few smaller ones; red, gold, and white. One very special feature distinguished most of these planes from those he had left at *Pinon* – they had almost no windows. Tim had to turn his attention to landing his ship. He noted an empty space between two 747s and was directed to park himself there. Two planes stood alone, not part of the pack, bearing the insignia of National Express Package Delivery with Cargo painted in large letters on the side. Trucks ferried large bags and boxes between the planes and a warehouse. A dozen employees in brown and red uniforms worked at loading and unloading bags and boxes at either end.

There was no purpose for this as far as Tim could make out other than adding or subtracting items that would never have to go through customs or security. Primary rule of keeping everyone in the dark again. Compartmentalize everything. So few people had to really understand this operation for it to work. The employees handling packages here simply had to be well-paid and ignorant. They had to sign a confidentiality clause and if they were well-paid enough, they kept their mouths shut. One hundred highly placed people who really knew what was going on and pulled all the separate strings could literally keep a hundred thousand people or more moving to their tune. And if those hundred thousand were moved relatively well and with some care, millions could be manipulated. It was, as Tim knew, such an erroneous understanding of how people think and operate to assume too many people would have to know what's up before terrible acts could be committed. It just didn't work that way. If people judged what the secret ops people would do based on what they themselves would do, then they had completely lost the plot. Pilots did not know dispatch did not know ground crew. Ground crew had no idea what aircraft were involved in what action. Pilots getting instructions after a job was completed might get those instructions from the other side of the world, via satellite. The guy on the other side of the world had no idea who he was talking to and why. People are trained to operate within their compartments, their specialties, and leave other people to their specialties. And if they found anything out they wanted to report, who the hell were they going to tell?

He rolled to a stop into the empty space. They shut down the plane and disembarked. The other two fellows seemed to know what to do and headed into an office building. Tim followed them with his suitcase rolling behind him and a backpack slung over his shoulder. He was doing some fast math in his head as he walked.

Say $4 a gallon and a one gallon burn per second... something like 60 gallons a minute or 3,600 gallons an hour. If a 747 is up for five hours, it has used 18,000 gallons at a cost of $72,000. Times thirty? Over 2 million just in fuel every five hours. Just say one five hour shift for all ships 300 days a year for a total in fuel, conservatively, of 600 million a year. Who the hell is footing this bill?

They passed pallets stacked chest high with white bags. They resembled sandbags in their shape and size but Tim realized they were marked, 'Barium.' Well that was something. At least he could be pretty sure some of what was raining down on them was barium. It occurred to him at that moment that he was simply unable to do any research now. His every breath and step would be dogged and scrutinized. He would not be able to research the chemicals he might find. He would not be able to write to or telephone his father and get results of the testing they were doing. He was absolutely cut off. He was sure he would eventually find an opening, some sort of Achilles heel, however small. They reached the terminal, pulled open the glass doors.

The *Gila* (Hee-lah) National Wilderness was world renowned for fairly easy hiking access to spectacular canyon-lined trails, camping by horseback and secluded hot springs. It encompassed the *Gila* River. Marmosets sat on outcroppings and watched hikers as they made their way across cold crystal rivers. Silver City was the closest town to the *Gila* as well as to *Gila* Airfield – a part of what appeared to be a small network of out-of-the-way airports owned and operated by BlueSky Airways. Tim was provided an apartment as part of the hire-on contract just inside the town line.

Almost no one lived on base. Security was heavy and heavily-armed. When he arrived he was introduced to the dispatcher on duty and to someone he would come to understand was his 'handler.' His handler told him to stick to his job and stay out of everybody else's business, together with the fact that the only questions he was allowed to answer about what he did had to come from him. He signed a security agreement that prevented him from talking about the base, anything connected to the base, and anything he did for the company to anyone except his handler. Money was directly deposited into his account, two hundred fifty thousand a year in one lump sum. He imagined if he didn't mind his manners, the authorities would suddenly see that as drug money or something equally illegal and he would find himself in jail. He knew how these things worked. What he did find out in short order was that all the pilots carried side arms; 9mms and 45s for the most part. There was nothing written anywhere about it one way or the other. It was some unwritten, unspoken agreement and he knew that these weapons were for enemies within as well as without. As soon as he had a key to his apartment, he drove into Silver City and bought a Sig Sauer P226 9MM, which he kept loaded under his pillow or strapped to his back.

The temperature had climbed back up to eighty now that he was that much farther south. He could come and go into Mexico if he wanted to. He did not want to. He made everyone call him Flyer here as this was much more like a military base than Cal Fire or Bluesky. Everybody had a handle here. They were all ex-military and they were all hot-shots. *Gila* did not like to use any civilian personnel at all unless they had no choice or they were employed to handle packages. Military pilots knew how to follow orders without asking questions and shut the hell up. Flyer was not here to play. He was not here to find someone to hang out with. These men were lone wolves. They spoke to each other and only each other but the types of questions were different…the conversations were on the one hand more 'laid back,' but the ease was false. The exchanges were actually quite potent. The temperature, direction and outcome of these exchanges could turn on a dime. All the pilots were on edge. All the time.

He was expected to fly the planes, and fly them he did. The 747 covered the entire continental United States. His route was different every day and he did not know what it would be until he was airborne. He was never present during nor was he responsible for loading chemicals. Some days he was in control of pulling the trigger and some days he simply flew, knowing that the dumps were being managed remotely. He assumed the very, very small crews responsible for filling these tanks were the most highly paid, heavily pressured employees at the base. Again, someone loaded the trucks with chemicals, someone else drove the trucks to the base, someone else unloaded the chemicals, someone else filled the airplane reservoirs. Complete compartmentalization. Flyer had seen the inside of his planes now, completely stripped of seats and galleys and toilets. They were lined from stem to stern with barrels resembling beer kegs, row after row, silver with a gold cap, all attached by tubing to main lines. He had inspected the line system himself; he knew where it went. On any given day he could not have said what they contained. He was not privy to that information. If asked, he simply could not say. That's the way it was supposed to be.

Questions filled his mind: one, who was supplying these chemicals? What was the full list of chemicals being used? What about commercial airline pilots, who obviously had to know about these chemical dumps? The FAA would get information that military operations of some sort were on-going and advise both air traffic control and pilots but this had been going on long enough to cause serious questions to arise. All commercial airlines also hired ex-military pilots. Then it would boil down to scarce jobs and pilot's licenses and making a living for anyone who was thinking of making a fuss over airplanes dumping chemicals. It could also boil down to trumped up charges and being thrown in prison for a very open-ended period of time. These people were not kidding about any of this.

Then Flyer got lucky. One Sunday, there was a knock at his apartment door.

"Harry Gale," a man stood on the landing, extending his hand. "You Flyer Verzet?"

"Yeah," Tim shook the man's hand warily. "What can I do for you?"

"Well," Gale said, "apparently I'm your new roommate. Great handle, by the way. I was afraid I'd be bunking with 'Killer' or 'Mad Dog' or something. Very benign, 'Flyer.' Thank you."

He gestured toward the living room. In fact, he had a knapsack over his shoulder and a rolling suitcase behind him. Tim was puzzled. As far as he could make out there were no roommate situations in this company. That seemed contrary to all the evident security in place. That made him very suspicious. Still he stood aside so Gale could enter.

"Not much furniture," Gale said, setting down his bags.

"Right," Tim replied. "Listen I got no indication someone was coming. I need to call. You understand." The weight of the 9MM strapped to his back was reassuring.

Harry Gale nodded and sat down on the couch. "Of course, you do."

Tim dialed the dispatch and asked for the Commander-on-Duty; so far that was always the dispatcher. The story checked out although it was supposed to be temporary and Gale was placed with him because he was gone a lot.

"Make yourself at home," Tim said after he hung up. "You a pilot?"

Gale smiled. "Doctor. Pathology, gathering data."

Dr. Harry Gale. Tim knew he wasn't likely to get any more information out of him at this point... or ever... but his very existence confirmed one theory. Data is gathered when results are needed and results are needed after variables are manipulated in some way. Only an idiot would not understand there had to be biological effects from dousing the biosphere in barium and God-knows-what-else. Even if the project did not have experimentation in the official title, that it certainly was... at least in part.

Well, Harry, you'll have this place to yourself for the most part. I'm out of town mostly. Home maybe two days out of seven."

Harry laughed. "No such luck. I travel, too. I have offices in a few cities."

Sample testing, Tim thought. Yes, this had been a lucky day. Still, he knew that this guy could and probably was there to keep an eye on him, as well. If he was testing, if he was gathering data, Tim had to consider the idea that he would be a subject. At the moment, Tim was due to fly out the next morning. That was all he knew.

The next morning before dawn, he and his flight crew boarded their ship and were greeted within a few seconds by their handler. There was a man, called Thomas, although Tim wasn't banking that Thomas was his real name, who showed up periodically to chat with them and check on them. It was not the man who had met Tim and briefed him upon arrival at Gila. Thomas sat down in the cockpit and asked if things were going well, if they had anything to report. He asked each man a few questions privately in the hold. That one man, Tim assumed, was the only thing tying a larger unit together. It was the only way to provide some sort of direct conduit while making sure no one spent any real time with anyone else. Then they were headed toward Denver, and this time, whatever was being released into the atmosphere was being handled remotely. He assumed that happened when different mixes were ordered and perhaps the dispersal was switched off and on in some way. They never followed a flight path that allowed him to see where he had been. With the exception of the cockpit, there were no windows in this bird. This would be a short run. Sometimes when an airport was this close in terms of flight time, he would transfer to a different plane with a different crew and continue on another leg. Every seat in the cockpit changed crew member with every change of airplane. This particular day he and his crew would stay together overnight. Making friends was discouraged in this way. Too much potential for chit-chat. The only connection he could make was marking the cities and towns they passed over… the deserts of Las Cruces and Albuquerque; Santa Fe; Raton, nestled in its beautiful Pass; Pueblo, on the plains again; Colorado Springs, tight up against the Rockies, then Denver. The mountains were covered in snow as they always would be in November. They set her down at Denver International Airport with its ridiculous circus tent roof the size of a football field and then a silent crew came to escort them away from the airport. They weren't even allowed to hang around in case they might see something. His crew and another two crews were loaded onto a van and transported to condominiums in the hills above Golden. This is how it went. In the morning they would report to DIA, board a cold and dark 747, and be given instructions once they were airborne. In an industry in which there were no jobs and the few that came up were practically minimum wage jobs, every pilot working for Bluesky was happy to follow this procedure for a quarter of a million a year. He thought about the airline mechanics, as he always did when he disembarked and watched them go about their business, and now as they drove out of DIA and into Denver, thought of Jeff, thought of the honey trucks delivering death to some of the commercial flights, thought of the commercial pilots who watched death descend from another man's ship and couldn't say a thing. All of a sudden it was his own neck he wanted to get his hands around. He also knew Jeff would understand completely what he was doing. So would his Dad.

Tim threw himself onto the bed at the condo. It was a setting as luxurious as any other they were accustomed to having on the road. The rotations were many and a pilot did not often find himself in the same place overnight. There were fifty 747s flying spray routes in the continental US, so the permutations were endless. And every time he pulled the trigger he felt his grave was a foot deeper. There were international routes; he assumed he'd rotate in and out of those eventually.

The *Denver Post* sat outside the door so he had brought it in. He was not hungry so he took a shower then had a nap. When he woke, he glanced through the newspaper. The primary point of discussion was the economy, as always... the devaluation of the dollar, hints of real trouble in Greece. On the back page, he saw a story about the planetary summit being held on Okinawa. The gathering had taken up residence in a breathtaking reconstruction of *Shuri* Castle near Naha. The Reconciliation agreement the summit was working on covered a lot of territory and, according to the newspaper, would be in session for up to another year. There was a photograph of the castle next to the story.

He grabbed the remote from the night stand and switched on the television. The program was a local talk show. He dozed but then woke with a start when he realized he was listening to a
commercial starring his new roommate. Dr. Harry Gale was an expert in Respiratory Illness, at least that's what he was posing as, and asked the general public to step forward and call his office should they be experiencing asthma symptoms of unusual or increased intensity or any other unusual respiratory distress. He related it to pollution levels and Denver's notorious inversion situation. For better or worse, air got trapped at the base of the mountains and stayed there. He said he also had offices in LA, Boston and St. Louis. Very creative way to gather data, this was. Tim could be certain that medical experimentation was some sort of subsidiary of the spraying program.

The next time Tim saw Harry was three days later back at the condo. He was very unsure as to whether to mention the TV ads he had seen; decided against it. They were both in the kitchen; Tim getting water and Harry rooting around in the very bare refrigerator. Tim decided on a different approach; dragonfly lure to cutthroat trout. He started to cough. That would be something Dr. Harry Gale simply could not ignore, he hoped. Harry turned and looked at him, then turned back to the 'fridge. Tim coughed some more.

"Man!" he said. "Damned sore throat."

"What's up, pilot?" Gale was all business.

"Chronic cough. It just will not go away. Now I've had a sore throat off and on for a week or better. Hard to breathe at night, too. Know any doctors?" Tim smiled at his joke. "Maybe I could get some time off."

Harry stared silently at him for a few seconds. "Let me think about it."

A week later, Harry approached him in the dining hall at the airfield. "Let's sit together, eh, Flyer?"

Harry pat him on the back and half-pushed him toward a chair. Tim was not amused.

"What do you want?" Tim asked making sure a little irritation came through in the question.

Harry ignored the hint.

"Well, I have permission to look at that chronic cough for one thing. They want to make sure the pilots stay well and so they let me put together a program to re-do your physicals and then track any chronic illnesses. Since my specialty is respiratory you fall right into my area of expertise. So before you go up again, you, my friend, are getting the once over."

The next week was one long physical exam and then the following few weeks were routine flights interspersed with stress tests and CT scans of his lungs and sinuses and lots and lots of blood work. He had skin, hair, and urine samples taken. His kidneys and liver were examined with ultrasound. Vision and hearing were also tested and re-tested. Harry promised that these tests would then be performed monthly. All the pilots were undergoing these tests for the duration. The minute he said this, Tim knew he had to find a way to get access to some of the results. He also knew it would be next to impossible.

Tim had been at Gila long enough to see the non-cargo people – pilots, administrators, and dispatch – as falling into two general psych profiles. His roommate was a great example of the more dangerous type, the sociopath… people who are antisocial generally and tend to be aggressive or perverted or immoral. There is never any empathy, so never any sympathy and definitely no remorse. These are the medical experimenters of the world, the Joseph Mengeles. They usually hide it quite well and they made up the lion's share of captains of industry. Since they were often able to accumulate wealth and power, people admired these sick sods, when they really deserved it the least. What they really deserved was to be kept away from the rest of humanity.

The other types, in just as much abundance, were the narcissists.

They had huge issues with self-esteem and were utterly preoccupied with themselves. Again empathy and regret were not burdens they ever had to bear. These were the employees who followed orders without asking questions. Then there was the type – the category they probably filed him under – the man with nothing and no one, married to what authority figures thought of him and gave him in terms of approval or not.

During his next three days at 'home,' Tim drove into town every evening, alone, and had a solitary dinner at Chuck's Tavern. He didn't think any of the locals knew anything real about the airfield but there were sure to be lots and lots of rumors. He was bored with trying to get information without anyone suspecting what he was up to but he had no next move. Town would at least be a change of scenery. He sat at the bar, discussing the heat with a bartender, eating *chiles rellenos*. No matter what at least the food was good in this state. The third night, the door opened loudly as if someone had fallen into it, pushing it open as they fell. A man walked in who Tim recognized from the base. He was also alone, but unlike Tim it appeared he was more than a little drunk. He recognized Tim, as well, and made a line straight for the stool next to him.

"How're you doin'?" he wiped his face with his hand, turned and looked at Tim. "Don't I recognize you… from work?" He laughed as if the idea of what they did was work in the ordinary sense of the word was the funniest thing he'd ever heard. Tim narrowed his eyes and waited for the man to quiet down. He went back to eating his dinner without speaking.

"Hey, hey, hey…", the man said conspiratorially, leaning in toward Tim, "Sorry. I know we aren't supposed to talk about it. Never mind. But… shhhh… I'm a pilot, too." He looked Tim in the eye and winked. He grabbed a plastic-encased menu, propped up on a wooden beam in front of him, slapped it onto the bar and opened it. Apparently, they would be dining together.

"Tell you a secret, my friend," the drunken pilot began, "I… am moving over to the cargo side. What do you think of that?"

Tim shrugged. "Why should I care?" Sure you are. They're just going to let you walk out of piloting the poison machines.

"No reason. Except the pay is the same and I don't have to do anything lethal… you get me?"

Tim did not answer. No one working for Bluesky in his right mind would have followed up on that question.

"I'll tell you, it's going to be great. You know who squeezes their business through that little hangar, buddy? I'll tell you who. Anybody who uses mail and anybody who wants to get around the feds, that's who. Or INS. Governments, corporations, you name it."

The bartender stopped in from of the drunk. "You want food?"

"Yeah, I'll have the smothered burritos and a draft," he said. "Now where was I? Oh, yeah. Anybody who wants anything sent privately slips it into the regular mail or this cargo stuff at one of these airfields. Contracts for express mail, airmail, and overnight stuff to our own National Express Package because NEP always has connecting overnight aircraft. Bluesky picks up all these shipments from NEP. Hell, they're delivered here! You've seen the ships. They've got a freakin' office here! Bluesky and NEP sort all that stuff here. Makes sense if all you're doing is moving packages and mail. Makes sense if you want to add your own stuff to the shipments without anybody getting in your business…".

He ordered another shot loudly.

Perfect setup, right? What do you think they're smuggling? Go on," he tapped his temple
punctuating each point. Weapons? Drugs? Documents? People?" He burped loudly. "Who knows?"

"Sounds like a lot of back-scratching going on," Flyer sipped his beer.

Yeah, that's what I think, too. Special accounts, fronts, the whole nine yards. I'll tell you, my friend, I need me a black budget credit card." He seemed to think that was the second funniest thing he'd ever said and lay his head down on the bar and continued to guffaw. "Aw, this shit isn't new. They've been doing it for fifty years. Got a great, big network all over the world."

Tim stared at the drunken pilot. He was, had to be, suicidal. At the very least he was an idiot. Or he was a big, fat, noisy test sent to root out Tim's reliability. This is how you get shot and left in the desert. Tim was getting amazing information, perhaps, if it was legitimate, but just listening to him was going to get Tim shot. He was being backed into a corner. Just then a couple of women entered the bar; pretty, young. This guy was too drunk and too stupid not to fall for this right now. So Tim just stood back and let it happen, thankful for the 9MM strapped across his back. Test or not, he now had to do something about this guy or be part of a compromised crew. Nobody wanted to be part of that crew because everyone was automatically under suspicion and solutions to those situations could be permanent.

The drunk wandered off in the direction of the two women. Tim paid his check, picked up his jacket and walked outside into the late November night. Soon it would be December and he was going home to see his Dad. He had no idea how he was going to pull that off but he really needed to see Huck and Huck needed to see him. He had purchased an old Ford F50 truck from someone in town, not wanting to be bothered with getting his Volvo from Redding. He walked slowly to the vehicle under dim street lighting, listening to the gravel crunch under his shoes. It was finally cold enough down here to see your breath at night. He had a suppressor for his weapon under the driver's seat of his truck. He retrieved the silencer, took his 9MM from the back holster and lay it on the hood of the truck, waiting. It was not as if he had any choice at all. This man had completely compromised them all and, if Tim wanted to stay where he was or even move up to a position with more information and authority, there was only one thing he could do. There had been watchers in the bar, make no mistake. As far as he could tell, he had one option now.

Another hour and a half ticked by. He pulled his collar up around his neck and looked up at the sky. There were no true clouds in the heavens although the stars were dim, as if behind a film or gauzy sheet of some sort. He remembered the skies of his childhood, the glorious Milky Way Huck talked about, and wished someone had not thrown a blanket of chemical haze in front of them. It was not even in his memory, the last time he had seen the Milky Way against a resolute blue-black sky, surrounded by all the stars, stars that remained but could no longer be seen. The reality was if the skies were misted over in the wide open spaces of the New Mexican desert night, the skies were significantly dimmed.

Eventually the drunk reeled through the door of the bar and wove his way toward his own car, another truck. It was twenty yards away. Tim made no move, no sound until the man was in his cab then sprinted for the passenger side door, jerked it open, aimed and fired, almost silently. The drunk slumped over his steering wheel, engine running, radio on. Tim calmly walked back to his own car and drove off. Now he'd get promoted or shot himself. He felt he'd at least rooted out a second option this way.

Fool.

He wasn't sure which one of them he was talking to.

Dan Bleeth loved absolutely everything about his job. He was born to be a world-class scientist. He was so precise and so careful about anything he said or wrote that he literally repelled women. Academic laurels floated down on his head, piled high one upon the other, however, and that was just as good. He knew he was an ass, he knew he made people feel stupid. He did it on purpose and all the time and he loved it. He was associated with three universities in two countries at the very highest levels and was angling for another in France. He had graduated from McGill and was the head of the Physics and Chemistry Departments both there. He was a visiting scholar at MIT and Johns Hopkins and held PhDs from both those institutions. He taught doctoral candidates at all three universities even though he was possessed mind, body and soul by his favorite subject: geo-engineering.

Bleeth called it The Movement. Sometimes he referred to it as his whore. It was an addiction. As far as he was concerned, even though various manifestations of geo-engineering had been up and running worldwide beginning about the late 1950s, and despite the relentless increase in scope and intensity over all those years, geo-engineering did not yet 'exist' officially. There was no such thing because he himself had developed the definition and the programs out there did not match his expectations of The Movement. This is how Dr. Bleeth was able to tell any and all that there was no such thing, no such program, it simply did not exist. That was not going to stop the whore from making him a rich man, however. Bleeth, of course, was well aware that there were snippets and dribs and drabs of atmospheric experiments underway all the time; chemical and biological and electro-magnetic and nano-tech driven. He also knew that the little pieces added up to a big, global project well-funded by governments and private individuals. The corporations were using the military to enable them to do things they would not be able to do legally otherwise.

He was well aware that the science driving all this was dangerous as hell, reckless even, and he knew everyone else on the Committee had unsavory goals. They needed him to be the scientific face of the project when it was finally unveiled as they wanted it to be; they needed someone who could go toe-to-toe with any other scientist and bring them to their knees. Not only did he have his slice of the pie carved out but his was the only part of the whole business that would be defensible in the end. He was the master of the enormous amounts of CO_2 collected by trapping all emissions under the plasma blanket they were generating. In the end, he would be able to declare that he had saved the planet from global warming by harvesting the extra CO_2. He never had to admit... ever... that their program was doing an enormous amount of work heating the atmosphere up. In fact, his assistant was doing a doctoral thesis on selling geo-engineering to the public. He thought he might have to make a pass at that girl in the end.

Some poor schmuck at a university in New Jersey had, years ago, realized and worked out how to make fuel from CO_2 and nobody cared... or so the poor kid had thought. His work was noticed and carried on by others and then seized and hidden away by the Committee. In return for his compliance and hard work warding off a suspicious public, Bleeth was rewarded with the exclusive contract to produce and sell this CO_2 fuel. They thought the patent was still in play. They would do their level best to make sure it was.

He was six feet six inches tall and weighed one hundred eighty soaking wet. His face was very long and pallid, his hair thin and dark, his cheek bones angular, his nose razor sharp. His company was already up and running and registered offshore.

This day in November, he was in Manhattan at the very nondescript offices of Sceptre Corporation. Video conferences were the norm but at least once a month they got together and got the measure of each other. None of them nor those they represented were the least bit trustworthy. Who smelled like fear? Whose story didn't line up? What was going on in Washington? It was a rough if obnoxiously wealthy and powerful crew he was aligned with, like waltzing barefoot through fields of broken glass.

There was no elevator in the brownstone building. It was as

unremarkable as possible. There was more than ample security but no doorman; the security was not obvious. The meeting was held in a conference room on the fourth floor. There was a very large round table in a room. No one got very close to anyone else; they could all see each other at all times. Simple. The conversations were recorded then transcribed to keep everyone in line. Everybody got a copy.

Bleeth had made his way into this group via a speech to a small, exclusive audience at MIT nine years prior. Some of his colleagues in atmospheric physics were busy trying to locate what they referred to as the 'missing carbon sink,' but Bleeth knew exactly what was going on. Experimentation.

"Without getting into too much detail before your organizations have confirmed genuine interest and even commitment, I will just say I have a scientifically and economically sound method to convert CO_2 efficiently into something that we wouldn't need to spend all that money and energy to eliminate or, as current popular thinking suggests, bury it. We can recycle it. We take CO_2, water, sunlight and an appropriate catalyst and generate an alcoholic fuel."

He was playing with fire and he knew it. He also felt exceptionally confident that he offered them something they did not have: a public, credible scientific face. In this case, his brain would probably always save him. He understood so many things that they did not yet; this thing was so easy once a few key factors were known. Converting carbon dioxide into fuels is exactly what photosynthetic organisms – mostly plants – have been doing for billions of years, although their fuels tend to be simple carbohydrates, like sugars. Then we humans breathe the byproduct; oxygenated air. Bleeth was going to parlay this into a Nobel prize.

"If we blanket the planet in a plasma layer then more CO_2 is trapped and can be harvested ostensibly without taking what's needed for both plant life and, in the return on oxygen from plants, human life that is how we make money on this, how we control it," Secretary of Agriculture Bob Custer was speaking. "Getz, is there anything on that pending patent yet?"

Custer was an expert on patent acquisition having gained many for modified plant and animal types and for various insecticides. He had been the Managing Director of Sceptre Agriculture before being placed as the Secretary of Agriculture by the current Sceptre-friendly administration, and Sceptre had patents on seeds that resisted every single heavy metal being dumped onto the earth. Very soon theirs would be the only food that grew, that could grow. He also liaised with greedy cohorts at the FDA and Center for Disease Control, making sure they were busy looking at their fingernails when legislation needed to be passed or kept from passing.

Yeah, Bob," Getz answered. "The patent office insists it belongs to the university. That was their story last week and last month. I honestly don't see how it stops us from exploiting that process. Change a screw in the blueprints. Re-patent it… or don't. I just don't see it as a big detail."

He felt the slightest chill, a barely perceptible stirring in the room at his response. The Secretary held his gaze just a second too long. That was probably enough to get him killed right there. As soon as they moved to another subject he felt a wave of fear, near-panic, but could not show it. He had to be stone-faced. That had been a big mistake. He might have to make use of the transcripts he had of meetings of The Committee for the last five years to save himself after all. There wasn't a person in that room who did not badly want that patent for himself or his organization.

Rear Admiral Alex Getz, retired, was here as a liaison consultant for defense contracts with the Pentagon. He was a Navy man but he represented the Joint Chiefs – every military branch – in this room except his Navy. The Air Force had picked up the CO_2 project and continued to fund it until it turned into something usable so, in fact, the Air Force had as big a claim on the patent as the university did. That was another problem as far as these men were concerned. This technology represented trillions of dollars in profits over time. Conservatively speaking. Control was a non-negotiable.

Custer sat on Getz' left. Custer still talked about fraternities and the upcoming Dartmouth-Yale football game. He wore a crisply tailored black suit and tie with a squared off white handkerchief in the pocket. Seated to his right was commodities king, Georg Nero Pearle. Pearle talked about escaping from Eastern Europe and then going back there to exploit the business climate and the materialistically-starved population. Every program under development or implementation with the Commission's oversight was of deep interest to him. Many, many things could be accomplished by judicious use of the chemicals and other matter being sprayed into the atmosphere. The very least of these, the most mundane, was weather control. If a man made a fortune controlling commodities in one form or another, having control of the weather bent the odds a bit in one's favor. In fact, much of the funding for the airplanes had come from him. Half the fleet sitting at *Gila* and a few other airfields were his to begin with. Pearle had even devised a system of treating the weather itself as a commodity, in what amounted to making predictions then arranging to win. It was gambling, pure and simple. And he cheated. He had purchased millions of acres of agricultural land in every country. He was a majority stockholder in Sceptre Agriculture, a subsidiary of the research and development giant. His people developed and patented seeds resistant to all the chemicals falling out of the airplanes. And like every competent totalitarian, he had compartmentalized his companies such that almost no one knew why they were doing what they were doing or the global effects thereof. His dedicated teams were 'fighting global warming and climate change,' and gratified to do it. "Sustainability" was a very misunderstood word, pertaining to anything that could be sustained.

It took so little. Hence, in the near future, he would make billions on the crops he could grow when no one else could and billions trading 'weather' itself as a derivative. The NYSE was under massive scrutiny right now with the derivatives schemes that had all but wrecked the global economy. Chicago was a backwater in terms of stock trading and so far it was working well as a barely hidden economy. He took out huge insurance policies covering things like heavy rain or drought and made a fortune. This past summer he had insured one of his largest agricultural holdings against more than ten inches of rain and then he had proceeded to make the sky open up and flood. He insured crops heavily and then destroyed them from the air collecting huge sums. He had a very, very powerful and important partner in the insurance scheme… a partner that was not on this committee.

However, the biggest source of revenue and power related to Sceptre and the dousing of the planet had to do with the human population. Not only had they discovered that these chemicals created illnesses, they also suppressed the immune system. Pearle was the single largest pharmaceutical company in the west. It was a classic pharmaceutical business tactic of the late twentieth century: create the disease, then create the pill that cured it… or not. Custer was a great ally in this arena as he had control over the heads of the FDA as well as the CDC. Pearle himself was head of the World Health Organization.

Getz represented the Pentagon and most of the armed forces. The Navy was not here because it was fighting it out with the National Security Agency for domination in the intelligence game, even though that was the case. At least, as far as Getz could make out the Navy wasn't here. It wasn't possible to know how many layers enveloped each man at this table. What they showed was scary enough, thank you. The Air Force had publicly declared their intent to 'own the weather' as a combat tool. They made no bones about it and they knew every other super-power and not so super-power was trying to do the same thing.

Soon it would be like the clash of the titans, battles fought in the heavens with hurricanes and lightning storms, flash floods and tornadoes and earthquake engineering. It was that way now at times, though no one knew it outside the confidential arena. There were no longer any boundaries. There was no human decency. There was certainly utter disregard for the ecosystem of the planet and its human inhabitants. Getz was also present as an expert in biological and chemical warfare because the use of aerosols – as technically that's what the particulate being dispersed from the airplanes was – is fundamental to biological warfare.

The men gathered here under the umbrella of Sceptre Corporation had nothing less in mind than changing the face of the planet entirely and making sure they controlled it from here on in. It was a gamble of galactic proportions really. No one knew how habitable the future would be in the end.

Nero, as everyone referred to him, had actually calculated the remaining likely expanse of his life and made aggressive plans to shred the face of the planet, remake it with his own toys, and then if things didn't work out and the planet died, he likely would be dead first anyway. He did not think it would turn out that way. He was a gambler and this was worth the roll of the dice. The winner would enjoy nothing less than total control over the entire planet.

There was one video attendee. He lived in northern California and was well past the point of being able to travel by any means. It was remarkable that he was still alive and that he had almost all of his faculties but it did happen, particularly if one protected oneself from the aluminum and other substances in the atmosphere. He was always there, however, with an assistant by his side. The older he got the more he lapsed into German. It was Dr. Wolfgang von Marshall, emeritus of the atmospheric physics division of the German military, the United States military as well as Knell Labs, for whom he had worked and then become Director in 1997. He was, he knew, much more facile mentally than Daniel Bleeth but did not need to demonstrate it in the way that Bleeth did. Von Marshall's history was enough to cow a man like Bleeth and he knew it. The young American had command of English and youth, however, and soon enough the young stag would take on the old. It was inevitable. What Bleeth would never have, though, was the history. He would never understand even a little what it took to get here. Von Marshall's father had been a physics teacher in Germany in the twenties. Then had come the Reichstag and compulsory giving over of oneself... one's soul and mind and body... to totalitarianism. There had been the meat grinder of the war and the famine afterward. He had thought long and hard about which way to go when both Russia and the US were rounding up scientists. He felt that it would be better in America but there wasn't any real way to be sure and every day he worked for the military was dogged by security on both sides, after him, after him. No, Bleeth had no idea. He could not even look at the set of reptiles convened around this table and call them men. This was the Committee, however, carving up the world and its resources for itself using the technology Wolfgang had developed as a military scientist and then at Knell Labs.

Nero added the results of experimentation conducted by Von Marshall's colleague, Von Neuman. He was a kindred spirit despite the fact that they had never met. Von Neuman had perished at Los Alamos, a developer of the horror that was the Manhattan Project, slain by radiation even he had not understood. His ideas, though, had been brilliant. What had started with simple theories on painting the ice caps at the Antarctic to focus the sun and melt ice had been wedded to his own work in atmospherics and created patterns of atmospheric chemical application that melted ice in a way no one had ever considered possible. He knew Nero and the madmen he worked with who were not at the table were using his technology to uncover oil and even gold. They were pigs, all of them, he thought. Nothing ever really changes. And that Nero character? He did not think he had ever met such a ruthless psychopath even among the Nazis.

The only person absent was Mick Unger, who was exclusively responsible for the logistics of the fleet. He reported in twice a year at most. He had been given permission to purposely withhold the VLATs from states experiencing massive fires – fires which turned into uncontrollable conflagrations because the aluminum oxide nano-particles being layered onto and into every living thing on the surface, and seeping down into tree roots, were a near-unstoppable accelerant – until the states and the feds paid whatever he asked for to use the big planes and their retardant patented to put out these Monster Fires.

"We need that patent, Getz," Nero said again. "We need it now. That's starting to seem like a problem."

"I'll get it," Getz replied. "We, at this table, do not have problems."

You, my friend, have a problem, Nero thought.

Anya and David were both sick, all the time. Anya slept on the sofa near their bedroom and often could not make her body move until close to noon. The pain she had learned to live with over the prior two years had 'spiked.' She was trying hard to get to classes anyway. David was so tired all the time he had resorted to being homeschooled by Christina. Part of that had to be the trauma they had suffered over the summer. They – Christina and Otto – decided everybody got a 'pass' this year because of it. All weirdnesses considered, all bail-outs completely forgiven and justified. It was a one-year offer and it seemed necessary since none of them could refer back to the last time someone they loved had been run over in the road and killed and what the best way to get over that really was.

In the solitary hours when everyone else slept, Christina did her own research looking for threads that led to some of the atmospheric weapons being used today, either publicly or secretly, and maybe just maybe back to her mother's connections with the military. She began with the assumption that her mother had been killed because she had seen something she might remember in the context of all the animal deaths... deaths which were still going on around the planet months and months later but were receiving almost no press. She ran an internet search on 'atmospheric weapons.' There were many, many entries, unfortunately. She found reports on scalar weapons and electro-magnetic weapons and, closer to what she thought she was looking for, articles on biological and chemical weapons released into the atmosphere by means of aerosol spray. The majority of speculation was that the chemicals were being released via airplanes or weather balloons due to an avalanche of documented visual evidence worldwide. Some kind of toxic chemical released into the atmosphere in this way certainly would explain mass simultaneous animal die-offs. She read reports on Edward Teller the scientist after whom the psychotic film character of Dr. Strangelove was crafted because he was the first and most powerful proponent of this kind of project. She discovered sonic weapons, something the police in this country already have certainly; and poisonous aerosols being released in to the upper atmosphere ostensibly to reduce global warming but, as every expert not getting a paycheck for that effort pointed out, the logic behind the make-up of the compounds and the necessity of doing it was exceptionally poor. Scientists around the world had independently verified barium, aluminum, cadmium, arsenic and lead in these aerosol weapons among other components.

Eventually, Christina struck gold, informational gold. It was two o'clock in the morning, the first day of February. She had stumbled across a message delivered by a fellow calling himself 'Amistad.' He seemed to be saying that there was a vast network of people digging hard to find the truth of these matters – matters she had not even known existed until a month ago. He was Canadian, had a very slight French-Canadian accent, brown hair, a face of indeterminable age, and a pug nose. The only light in their bedroom was the glow of the laptop. Everyone else was asleep.

"This is a video announcement to citizens of every country and their leaders; to citizens in all walks of life. We must band together on a global level to investigate and fight against geo-engineering. I have created a group of networks and hyper- networks several thousand people strong and growing rapidly. We are focused and intelligent. We are not alone."

In Quebec City, it was also two a.m. He could smell the metal in the air. He was one in a thousand; someone who could literally smell what was floating down on them. It often made him ill. He lifted the front of his sweatshirt and sniffed. It reeked of sulfur. The nights were the worst as they filled the sky with white plumes and grid patterns all day and the particulates floated down on them all at night.

His name was Nikolai Louis and he was an artist and an activist and a father. He and his son, Hugo, lived in a flat in the center of the city where he took freelance work to pay the bills although he had a degree in biochemistry from Carnegie Mellon. He spent most of his time agitating, however, mostly on behalf of his son. Hugo was also becoming ill, anyone could see that. The chemical bath was constant and so much more harmful to the young whose immune systems were so vulnerable. Nikolai's muscles ached, especially at night. He heard a constant humming in the atmosphere, again something people were rarely able to hear. Some of the latest effects of chemical dumps were rumored to mimic heart attacks. He was also a single father, though; he simply could not 'get sick.' His head pounded, his throat was raw, and he coughed all night long. Still, he turned back to his webcam, cleared his throat and continued:

Chemtrails – which we will refer to from here on in as geo-engineering or aerosol engineering, which is very specific to what's been going on for years now – are having, we believe, a demonstrably negative effect on animals and plants. I personally have witnessed die-offs of entire colonies of beneficial bugs, ladybugs and the like. There have been unexplained continuous deaths of bats and bat colonies. Over 11,000 bats died in one incident in 2008. What naturally occurring phenomenon could possibly account for that? This year, Florida reported the simultaneous deaths of one million honeybees. I think we just got a report of millions more but I have to check. We have finally managed to inform huge numbers of people about the massive bee die-offs. The U.S. and U.K. both reported to have lost about one-third of their bee populations in 2008 alone.

Soils are becoming verifiably contaminated with very-high levels of aluminum. If aluminum levels elevate above 400ppm, numerous species of plants will die. Have you seen spots on your plants, your vegetables... a white powder covering leaves? Do not eat or even touch those plants! It is poison! Have you seen a structure resembling a spider web on your grass or trees in the morning? Those are chemicals.

Brown pelicans are dying in California. The cause is "a mystery" but they have found a "residue"on the feathers of the dying animals much like that on plants. Birds fall from the sky with no explanation at all – not one bird, mind you, but thousands of them drop dead. I have seen the sky raining dead, lifeless blackbirds. They seemed to just fall out of the sky. About one hundred were dead when they hit the ground.

Nikolai stopped to take a long drink of water, pushing pause. He took deep breaths and started again. There would be an antidote soon, there had to be.

We have this year received reports from California in the United States of the largest whale die-off on record. This is the single largest die-off event in terms of numbers, according to wildlife experts. Also, from California, hundreds of acres of crops are being damaged beyond repair... signs are small dots that appear to "burn" through leaves. These are not the result of beetles or any other kind of pest. Farmers are losing entire crops all across North America. Many other spontaneous, unprecedented, environmental problems are occurring and we believe we know what is causing this damage. We are in the process of making tests and then we will publish the findings for the general public. Then we will decide what legal action can be taken to stop this...what amounts to a mass poisoning... and punish those responsible. I am Nikolai Louis, Amistad to some, signing off for the week. Please contact me with any evidence or issues you may be party to. Bonne nuit.

Nikolai left his laptop open on the old kitchen table and walked over to the cot in thecorner. He let his son have the bedroom as he was generally up all hours of the night. Sleep was a thing that eluded him more and more since the chemical dumping had started. When he did sleep, he had nightmares. Whenever the airplanes left a covering thick enough, he actually felt the residue on his skin. It was ever-so-slightly hot and sticky. On such days the temperatures could shoot up twenty degrees or more. That was a very specific type of formula. It created a blanket, trapped heat, even generated it in some way, and burned the skin slightly. Two or three days later, the temperatures would return to normal and then a couple of days after that would come two days of rain to rinse the rest of the brutal mixture down onto their heads. It was hard for him to see this as anything short of an identifiable cycle. He had made a job out of collecting data on airplane sightings, heavy chemical occurrences, and reports of metal toxicity in the soil and in human subjects. He was a trained biochemist, after all. His database had grown enormous and he conducted mass letter-writing campaigns. It was useful to him to identify the percentage of the geo-engineering protesters willing to write letters or move on toward more visible protest. It was useful to see what world and local leaders had prepared as responses to their populations brave enough to ask. It was useful to collect the collectors of data.

Meanwhile, hundreds of miles to the south, Christina scrolled through all Nikolai's entries on his web site, reading everything he had collected about geo-engineering over the past six years or so. He spoke also of being able to smell and taste the chemicals as few could do and the illnesses he endured because of his sensitivity. His descriptions allied very closely with Anya's symptoms and now David seemed to be going down that road. There was a way to contact Nikolai. She could subscribe to his blog, contact him on Facebook – he seemed to be well represented within all the social media. She just needed to think about what to say. He hosted a group on Facebook, so she joined that. She did not sleep that night but rather read and researched, scrolling through posts from hundreds of people. She found there was a lot of public information already and was grateful as, real or imagined, it made her feel a little bit less like a target, a little bit less like she was the only one who knew. She was taken aback when she came across a very lengthy document issued by the Air Force and completely in the public domain for all to see called Weather as a Force Multiplier: Owning the Weather in 2025. The implications in the title alone were staggering. It was dawn, the sun rose accompanied by the soft hum of the printer and the delicate whoosh of sheets of paper as they appeared and stacked themselves. She made a pot of coffee, stoked the fire in the wood burning stove, let the dogs out and sat down to read. The first thing that stood out was one of the potential goals of controlling precipitation and how to weaken the enemy with it: precipitation denial. Induce drought. Deny fresh water. Access to water was a human right, she thought, mandated by the United Nations decades ago. Droughts were not something to be inflicted on one soldier or even a battalion or an army. Droughts were inflicted on entire segments of populations, including families, children, and the elderly. There was no honor in this kind of warfare. She put the document aside for later reading. There was only so much she could digest at a time. For now she just wanted to make contact with people who were informed and trying to do something about this… whatever it was.

"*Oui?*" a sleepy male voice was at the other end.

"Hello, Mr. Louis?"

He cleared his throat. "*Oui.*"

"My name is Christina Galbraithe, Mr. Louis. I hope I'm not disturbing you."

"No, I'm awake. How can I help you, Christina Galbraithe?"

"I am hoping to talk to you about these aerosol weapons. I see you have done years' worth of work in this field. And you are very public about it. People call them 'chemtrails.' I have reason to want to know as much as possible about these events."

"Well," he answered, "Christina Galbraithe, first things first. We try very hard not to call these things chemtrails although I understand that the public is in the habit of doing so and habits are hard to break. We refer to this phenomenon as geo-engineering or even aerosol weapons, but I prefer the first. We discovered fairly early on that the scientists we confront about this issue feel perfectly fine stating that there is no such thing as a chemtrail whereas they will not deny the existence of geo-engineering. So, I'm going to go ahead and save you some trouble on that front."

Already Christina knew she would learn much from this man.

"What are these phenomena you describe as the main focus of your protest group?"

"To put it simply, they are aerosols released into the atmosphere of this planet at varying altitudes, varying saturations, and with varying compositions of chemicals and metals. It is an absolutely undeniable fact that any or all of the additives will be heavy metals noxious to life… in fact deadly to life. Eventually they will make you sick and then they will kill you. Simple."

"Okay. Next obvious question… who is responsible for this?"

"Ah, Christina. That is the question, you are correct. There are many theories and frankly, the scientific and military communities world-wide are very well aware that they can no longer hide this program from the public. So some of these entities will soon start to bring the subject up themselves – it's already happening – and they will put forth a few 'humane' reasons both for doing it and for hiding it. We will have some concrete answers on that soon although these entities – the military, scientific groups – they are still very big, very difficult to really find out who specifically is accountable. As always it seems, half- truths get spun for the public. I have been following this for a decade and I can assure you that what they put into those aerosols – well, the best interests of humankind are not goals in this experiment." Nikolai was packing his son's lunch as he spoke. Hugo sat at the table eating oatmeal.

"Nikolai... may I call you Nikolai?"

"Yes, of course."

"My children are quite ill... my daughter over a period of time and my son rather abruptly. I see here that you describe symptoms of your own and they are remarkably similar to our case...particularly my daughter. You seem convinced that these symptoms are directly related to the aerosols. How did you come to that conclusion? I mean, some are ill and some are not yet I assume these chemicals are no respecters of person."

"Just so, Christina. Some are more sensitive than others. Children especially are displaying a rather alarming and snowballing set of maladies just within the last decade. This is no accident. I had my blood tested for heavy metals. Being asymptomatic does not mean one is not ill. You should do the same as I have with your own children. Labs are easily found on the internet."

"I will do that right away, thank you."

"And, Christina... if I can call you that... if you get these results, I wonder if you wouldn't mind sharing them with me? We are building a database to display trends and causes and effects. Should we ever be able to locate a source to accuse and hopefully prosecute, that kind of information will be critical. At the very least we can present these things to governments and maybe get laws passed to interrupt this spraying."

"Have you been able to get any leads in that regard other than just sort of large entities, as you said... like the military?"

"Yes, I think we have. In two weeks' time, I will be attending a yearly symposium... one of the talks will be on geo-engineering and, I think, some of the major players are bound to be there."

"Where? I would love to go, too, if it's possible. I need this information." Otto would have to take some time off and look after Anya and David. He would do it for her.

"Phoenix. Far from Quebec City. But it is necessary." Nikolai stopped to kiss Hugo on the forehead as the boy headed out the door for school. "If you make it there, I will look forward to meeting you. But I won't recognize you unless I see a photo of you. You will know me but I won't know you."

"If I can manage to arrange to go, I will scan a photo for you," she laughed.

Two weeks later she was aboard Delta flight 2706 bound for Phoenix. The Future Research for Social Service Conference covered five-days and included two events in which the subject was geo-engineering, with guest speaker, head of a distinguished panel, Daniel Bleeth, PhD. Three other scientists rounded out that particular offering. Christina had her laptop open on the flight and had located a couple of radio interviews by another expert, Charlie Shepard, out of California. She hoped to be able to listen to those at some point on the trip. Nikolai had been right. There was a broad, broad movement that concerned itself with what was quite obviously on-going 'secret' geo-engineering, referred to by some as aerosol crimes. The word 'secret' was profoundly ironic in that all one had to do was look up and pay the smallest amount of attention to see what was being done. Still, she had not known this was going on until her mother had been killed. She was not in a position to judge those who were still ignorant of the peril above them. As active as the movement was, the general attitude of the population toward this phenomenon and its attendant protest movement was that they were all crackpots. Big ones. That was the easy attitude and the options, Christina understood, were fairly horrible to contemplate.

At the baggage claim in Phoenix, Christina spotted Nikolai. He was holding up a sign with her name written on it in purple marker. She laughed. He had come separately and arrived an hour earlier. She rushed forward and shook his hand; he pulled her into his chest and hugged her affectionately. That fit with the general picture she had of him, one of a gentle but determined French-Canadian bear. He spent his life being an activist, after all, and generally speaking these are not people who do not care.

"Well!" Nikolai exclaimed. "Here we are in Arizona. And it's seventy degrees and it's February. How do you like that, Christina?"

"I like it just fine," Christina answered. "Let's go get the rental car and get to the hotel, okay?" She looked at her watch. "The seminars start in two hours."

"Yes, we can do that. There will be several people there to meet with, people just like you and me. In particular, I want you to meet a fellow from northern California. He's been doing a lot of testing of soils and water and plants and has a tremendous amount of data. He wants me to go back with him and have a look. Perhaps you can go, too, if you can spare a few extra days?"

The conference occupied the entire second floor of the Physics Wing at Arizona State University. The scheduled events for each day were posted on large easels strategically located outside classrooms and lecture halls. Generally, one had a choice between two symposiums at any given time. The symposium on geo-engineering was due to start in ten minutes; they had arrived just in time. There were still seats three rows back from the panel, four scientists already situated next to the podium. One fellow, a portly man with shaggy white hair and a beard, stood behind the podium as the images from a projector in the back of the room were tested behind him on a screen.

"Good morning," he said at last into a microphone on his collar. "I am Dr. Svenborg of Arizona State University and we are proud to host this conference today."

There was applause.

"We welcome all of you who have come to participate in the spirit, as the title of the conference suggests, and hear about brave new technologies, brave new trains of thought, aimed, hopefully at enhancing the health of our planet and everything living on her."

More applause.

"Our first speaker today is none other than Dr. Daniel Bleeth, professor extraordinaire at three leading universities and a highly-regarded expert in the newly burgeoning field of geo-engineering. You can and should have a look at his credentials, which are listed in the program. Without further ado, I give you Dan Bleeth!"

Through the applause, Christina heard Nikolai say, "Ah. 'The Tinman.' This is why I am here."

Bleeth began without introduction and spoke rather quickly, although he was very understandable. He used a very few chart images displayed on the screen behind him. He seemed to assume, and he was likely correct, that while he might not be speaking before other PhDs, he was speaking to a well-informed crowd. He began by defining geo-engineering.

"So, what is geo-engineering exactly?" he began his staccato, machine gun-like delivery. "It is the deliberate, large-scale intervention in or modification of the earth's environment."

And we don't see this as a problem already? Christina thought. Bleeth went on to talk about some of the more basic uses for geo-engineering, both of which had to do with global warming, although he did go so far as to say the two programs should not be connected in terms of research, which puzzled her. Surely all the research and applied solutions regarding global warming were intimately connected. How could it be otherwise?

"The main uses, we think, for geo-engineering would be to block solar penetration of the stratosphere thus cooling the planet and to remove excess CO_2 that already exists in the atmosphere. We have examples in history of how this would work; lots of written accounts of major volcanic explosions as a result of which tons of ash and debris filled the air and significantly lowered the surface temperature of the planet. So the idea of creating a blanket of sorts above us to block heat from the sun is not particularly far-fetched. The micro-particle, a nano-particle the size of a micron, which seems to best fit the bill would be sulphur. The other concept currently being considered is the idea of simply collecting up excess CO_2. Yes, trees perform that function and they should, and we should continue to make sure re-forestation goes on, but they do it slowly. And maybe slowly isn't going to fill the bill. We don't know because we are trying to create processes that would address future conditions. The reason nano-particles in the atmosphere may be a very good option is that this solution would be a quick solution. Let me stress here, though, that these notions are purely in the thought stage. Scientifically speaking though, it is true that one gram of sulphur can offset a ton of CO_2. Those are good odds, I think. But like I said, no one with any sense is talking about doing this now. We need to do the research first."

It was a stunning speech given how much measurable nano-particulate was actually being collected in the air, soil and water. If she thought about it though, she realized he wasn't lying. No one with any sense is doing this now. He never said it wasn't being done. Christina would be following this man carefully.

Bleeth ended his part of the symposium by announcing there would be another symposium, an ad hoc event, the last day of the conference since he had to fly back to Washington DC for a meeting. For today, he was very sorry but there would be no time for a question and answer period. Christina would certainly be there for the second meeting.

"Well," Nikolai said as he took her elbow on the way out of the hall, "that gives us a bit of free time. There will be a question and answer session after the ad hoc symposium and we will want to be here for that. Would you be able to go with me up to northern California in the meantime? There is a group of scientists who live up there and they have been taking samples of every type of surface: plants, animals, soil, water, people... I would like to discuss this. We would have to fly from here to Sacramento and then drive a bit."

"I have the time; it's set aside anyway for this conference. Let's book some tickets."

The flight gave Christina the time and opportunity to do two things she had been wanting to do: listen to a long radio interview by aerosol crime expert, Charlie Shepard, and ask Nikolai one question she had not asked yet.

"So, if you don't mind my asking, why 'Amistad?'"

"Because I am a prisoner. Amistad was an African forcibly removed from his free home and made a slave. I am made to breathe and eat and drink poison. Amistad ate whatever they deigned to throw at him, breathed the fetid air of the slave ships and prisons. I have to pay my taxes. Amistad was a commodity, or would have been, whose labor was used – the very moments or coin of his lifetime – to pad the pockets of the upper class. Those are my taxes, the coin of my labor. I have to obey laws. I have to eat food that I don't really think is even food anymore and drink water filled with acids and poisons that are deliberately added to the water supply to injure me. I have to do these things so that the people who don't have to do these things won't punish me by taking away my ability to move around freely. Doesn't that make me a slave? Amistad's story ended well because he actually found someone close to the founding fathers of the US to argue his case before a court which still embodied morals and ethics and knew the difference between right and wrong. The fire of those ideas was still burning in his mind and the mind of the country. Tell me, Christina... who will ride to our rescue? Who has the power to side with humanity and release the slaves? It seems there used to be places to go for help but I can no longer locate them."

Christina was silent. He was right, of course. The government had to know this was going on and was deliberately pretending it was not...or actively participating. Her mother had been killed over her potential knowledge of the subject... just on the off chance. She did not know what to say and Nikolai seemed to know there was no appropriate response to a statement so fundamental to their condition; he turned and looked out the window at the sky. She wondered how many hours he had spent watching the heavens. Her laptop was in the overhead luggage bin. She unbuckled her seatbelt, stood on tiptoe and awkwardly dug around in the recesses of her carryon until she felt its reassuring surface. Charlie Shepard's radio interview was downloaded and saved and waiting for her. She located it, made sure she had paper and pen, earphones, and started the recording.

"Barium, strontium, aluminum oxide... all routinely found in soil samples, snow samples, rain samples, plants and in human blood, as well," Charlie was saying. Aluminum oxide? There were a lot of chemicals listed she had not yet heard specifically. "There is an Air Force study from some time ago... readily accessible online to anyone who wants to look at it. These nanoparticles of aluminum are so small that it takes a while to demonstrate a toxicity. In the tested rats, what was affected was the ability of the immune system to employ white blood cells against intruders. Dramatically reduced. In other words the immune system is compromised – big time – leaving you susceptible to all kinds of bugs and diseases with little left to fight off sickness and bacteria. This aluminum oxide knocks down the ability of the immune system to go after toxins in the rat's body and theoretically this would also happen in humans. I mean, there's a reason they use lab rats to conduct medical experiments."

Christina had seen reports blatantly hidden in plain sight that originated with the military and flat out said these were the goals, to critically compromise human populations from the air for tactical advantage. Funny, she had always assumed they were talking about the'other guy.' Charlie was still talking.

"Toxicity in plants delays seed production, suppresses crop productivity by spraying it into the atmosphere and letting it settle out on the ground. All kinds of damage is done with this material and they know it – you can see it in the research. There are certainly benign goals or what seemed like benign goals in the beginning that maybe go back to the beginning of these kinds of programs. I know that aluminum oxide nanoparticles were added to jet fuel to enhance combustion efficiency and that worked out really well for what it was. Jet fuel burn times were increased forty percent by weight... that is to say the aluminum caused the heat to travel faster through the combustion but the payoff was that the reaction goes on forever. Not-so-benign kinds of reaction you get from aluminum oxide nanoparticles are, for example, when it soaks into vegetation such as trees all the way down through the root systems, and forest fires continue to burn underground when the root systems combust way after the visible fire has been put out. Oxygen is in the roots even in areas not exposed to the air at all and it ignites!"

How does a metal like that even in sub-micron sized particles... something that kills plants and causes runaway burn effects help to stop global warming? And if it makes us all sick what difference does the cooler planet make, assuming that's the outcome? She just didn't see any logic. There had to be other reasons, other agendas. The plane was touching down in Sacramento and she had been too absorbed in the radio interview to notice. They had not brought anything but carry-on bags and so were able to head straight for the car rental counter. Neither one of them had ever driven through northern California but the fates were with them and they made it out of the city with no trouble. The town of Mt. Shasta was a three-and-a-half-hour drive so Christina shut her eyes and slept while Nikolai drove. His dry, hacking cough returned and got progressively worse as they headed north. She awoke.

"Are you okay?" she asked.

"No. There was a heavy biologic taste and smell in the air. Now it's metallic. It's really heavy here and heavier the farther north we drive."

Christina thought for a moment. "What do you mean 'biologic?"

"The "iron" type of aerosol dump has been around for a while. I name it by its taste and odor, not because I know what it consists of. It tastes like iron... with other subtle things mixed in. There is, in my experience, a set of symptoms that goes along with that 'flavor,' I guess you could say. This has been the most commonly sprayed mixture that I have detected personally for a couple of years now. When I say things like that, people tell me I sound like a mad man. When someone has respiratory infection – or when they are about to get sick – their breath burns my sinuses and has a very unique odor. Weird, I know, but true. I just have a ridiculously sensitive sense of smell. It's no bonus to my life, believe me."

Christina was stunned.

"So, Nikolai, you're saying you encounter these odors and then you specifically have certain symptoms... you become ill or more ill?"

"Well, not just me, Christina. A lot of people become ill around me in predictable ways when I encounter those odors. These odors are, luckily for me, really unmistakable. There are a couple I have come across and then colds pop up like crazy and flu symptoms... sore throats... all of a sudden there's a bug going around. Children especially seem to get sick. I have not kept logs on this. I am just telling you my experience, for better or for worse."

They passed a road sign that read 'Mt. Shasta 2 miles.' She had managed to sleep for over three hours.

"Christina, can you take the directions from my knapsack... there in the front... and navigate for me? I have never been here before. I know we need to drive through the town and head toward the mountain. Not too far up the mountain road there will be signs for French Baum's place. He has several thousand acres with lots of water, ponds and such. He and his friend Isaac Masters have been conducting environmental sample tests for years on all the flora and the air and water. I believe they have a rather large vegetable garden, several acres worth, with which they have been able to see effects on food plants. Baum is a retired forester and Masters is an environmental scientist of some sort. There's another fellow up here, Huck something. I can't recall his last name at the moment. I thought Isaac would be at the conference but he was held up. He's a great cook, by the way. We must convince him to cook for us."

Indeed, a few miles north of the town of Mt. Shasta, a little way up a winding road, they spotted a sign, "French Creek Ranch." In smaller lettering beneath was inscribed the name French Baum. A left turn off the mountain road took them immediately to a gravel-covered road winding a bit down and around grass-covered hillocks and stands of oak, cedar and a few redwoods. The grass was yellow and dry and shorn short by a flock of twenty or so sheep grazing unconcerned by their noisy approach. In the distance, Mt. Shasta loomed, covered with snow that seemed a pristine white from their advantage. The day was a bit hazy but warm for mid-February. A large cabin appeared beyond a series of hills, two stories with an upper deck that ran the circumference of the house. White smoke escaped from two stone chimneys, one located on each end of the cabin. The smell of burning wood met them long before they saw the house. They pulled in beneath the deck and left the car, glad to be able to stand up and move around. Between planes and cars in the last few days, Christina was quite stiff.

"Hello, the house!" Nikolai called. Christina had not heard anyone use that phrase since she'd spent time in Ireland. Dogs began to bark above them, canine noses pushed their way through the rails of the deck above... one, two, then three. The barking became frantic. Firm footsteps hit the deck above them, making for the direction of the barking.

"Hey, quiet, you lot!" someone commanded over the din.

"French!" Nikolai cupped his hands around his mouth and called, then laughed.

Just then the sound of another vehicle on the road became apparent behind them. A very old, very beat-up Jeep Commando came around the corner, driven by an older man with short iron grey hair. He wore aviator-style sunglasses and a straw-colored cowboy hat. He waved at them briefly, parked and got out.

"Huck Verzet," he said, extending his hand toward Nikolai. "Pleasure."

The barking din above elevated itself to mimic an entire pack of hunting dogs on the scent.

We should go on up," Huck called out, "let them see who's here so they'll shut up."

He made for the door a few feet away and went in, Nikolai and

Christina right behind. They were standing in a small foyer. Above them, they heard a sliding glass door open and close.

"Hi, everyone," a man called. "I'm coming down, hang on."

A lean, fit man with thinning brown hair, perhaps in his forties, descended a staircase in front of them.

"Welcome to French Creek! Welcome." He shook hands with Christina and hugged Nikolai.

"Have you met Huck?"

This was French Baum. Nikolai had expected him to be at the first part of the conference but he had been detained by matters here at the ranch.

"Come on up on the deck."

There was a mountain range in the distance to the west, not visible from the road. To the immediate northeast was Mt. Shasta. French invited them to sit.

"How's the conference going so far?" he asked.

"We're off to a slow start. Just as well you waited because the Tinman had to race back to Washington for something. No question and answer period even. We'll make up for that at the end of the week," Nikolai answered. French chuckled.

"Right," Christina said, "I heard you call him that. What's that about?"

"I can answer that, Christina," French said. "We call him Tinman because mostly what's in the air and soil and water is an aluminum nanoparticle and nobody has been able to get Dan Bleeth to admit it, much less talk about it. It's the most ridiculous little game. If we don't admit it, it isn't happening. That's what my dog does when I take him to the vet, for God's sake... I can't see you so you can't see me."

They chatted for a few minutes, then Christina excused herself to find the guest room. She wanted to call home and check on everyone. Her room faced the western mountains and she could see both a huge garden and a pond from her window. She sat on the edge of the bed and pulled her cell phone from her pocket.

"Hello, mommy!" Anya answered her phone. "I miss you. What are you doing?"

"Hello, sweetie! How are you?"

"Pretty good. Wait, Daddy wants you... hold on."

"Hey," it was Otto, "how's it going out there? Seeing a little bit of the country?" He chuckled.

"Yes, of course. How are the kids?"

"The same. Up and down. Don't worry about it. I've got this, honey."

"Okay."

"So...". Otto sounded hesitant.

"What?" Christina knew something was coming.

He sighed. It was a sigh wrapped in a thin blanket of resignation. "Walters."

"Yeah?"

"Massive, massive stroke. Very sudden. Probably going to die shortly."

Christina had no words for a very long minute. Poor Otto. Over the years, he had been the bearer of some unutterably devastating news in their lives together.

"Well." Christina had to say something just to make sure she could still speak.

"Yeah." Otto said. "You'll call me?"

"Yeah."

She sat on this strange bed in this unknown house surrounded by people who, in reality, she barely knew. It seemed that her mother's killer would not be helping in the effort to get to the bottom of all this, whoever he was. She knew almost nothing about him. A stroke was certainly a 'price' to pay. But was this justice? She did not know. Thinking about Walters and the mystery surrounding him had a way of stopping her in her tracks, interfering with her ability to function or think. She was not at home where she at least had the option of crawling back into bed and pulling the blankets back over her head. Here, as long as she kept her wits about her, she had an opportunity to try to figure out what had happened from a much different angle. She could not dwell on this piece. Downstairs, the men were gathered in the foyer apparently waiting for her.

"All is well?" Nikolai asked.

"All is well," she replied. "What are we doing?"

"We are waiting for Isaac, who is just walking up the hill, and then we are going out to the vegetable garden to look at some things." Another man, fairly short and slender, had walked around the bend in the road in front of the cabin. He waved.

"Isaac," he said, shaking hands with Nikolai and Christina. "Right. Let's walk."

They set out: French Baum, Isaac Masters, Huck Verzet, Nikolai Louis, and Christina Galbraithe. It was to be a five mile loop including French's large vegetable garden, even though it was February and little grew aside from cold weather greens; a stop at French Creek to talk about the water runoff and the bacteria and little living things that should have been thriving there but were not; some of the oaks were inspected because they were dying at an alarming rate for no discernible reason; then they stopped at a rocky hillside overlooking a deep and beautiful valley. This part of northern California usually had snow this time of year but the weather had been warm... too warm. There was a fire pit there on the hillside amid the rocks and they would light a bonfire, put together some dinner and talk about the situation and the research that Huck and French had been conducting. Christina carried a pad and pen in her coat pocket.

French showed them how the pH level in the garden soil was way too high and showed them the records from ten years prior demonstrating it had been just right for growing food at that time. They used a powerful magnifying glass to see that there was little life left in the soil. Issac had water records showing that the level of aluminum oxide in water samples, even those up on Mt. Shasta, were quite literally tens of thousands of times higher than what was deemed safe by the government, as were levels of barium and strontium.

"The run-off," Isaac pointed out, "is practically a poison and it ends up as far south as L.A."

No matter how deep and insidious the attack on this land was, it was still a knock-out. French and Nikolai built a fire and stoked it until it roared into the deepening twilight. It would get down to about fifty degrees, making the hike back later a rather pleasant one. French pulled sausages out of his pack. They found long sticks and hung them between forked branches over the fire, turning them frequently. A large crow settled on a nearby branch and began to make a hopeful racket when he saw the food.

Huck Verzet had records on high lead and arsenic levels in the vegetation and water.

"You know astronomically high levels of any of these metals can make people act out, make them violent. We have been seeing a real spate of unusually violent behavior hereabouts. I can't draw a concrete correlation yet, but I'm working on it. Here…". he handed Christina a sheaf of clippings from the local newspapers describing spontaneous and nonsensical brawls. She looked at them and made notes of names and dates so she could look them up again when she was back home, then passed them on to Nikolai.

"So, stupid question probably but isn't there some sort of governing body… someone who watches these things?" Christina asked. "I mean, there has to be a law already in place that forbids this kind of activity."

The men chuckled, glanced at each other.

"Yes," French spoke up, "there are a lot of laws… most specifically some treaties, that forbid experimentation on humans without their express individual consent. Started right after World War II with the Nuremburg Treaty. That's what it's about for God's sake! There was a treaty the US signed in 1992 that says the same thing. Ever heard of the *Shuri Reconciliation*?

"Sure," Christina answered.

"It's been in session for two years now. It covers the same territory but this is the first agreement that uses the word "terraforming". That's deliberately changing the face of the planet. In the end, a hundred or more countries want a treaty that covers some of the more pressing global issues by focusing on the idea of individual human rights. Testing chemical weapons on entire populations is a very large human rights violation; a ban on terraforming of any kind without global or national authorization by popular mandate would cover just about every aspect of the program, whatever the program actually is."

"Well, wait. If there are treaties in place, what's the deal?"

"War Powers Acts," Huck spoke up. "We enact these special war powers exceptions when there's a war on that allows them to go around all the treaties. Then we 'forget' to undo them."

"The *Shuri* people need evidence. Real, hard evidence and testimony because if not this is never going to specifically make it into any document."

There was a lot to consider, especially for Christina for whom this data was new. As they walked back to the cabin, she noted dead trees dotting their way. The men had said there was no real reason for it other than the high levels of aluminum oxide found in every sample from every dead tree. This metal nanoparticle was not consistent with life. It just wasn't. Yet it was everywhere… tons of it. Why?

The next day, she and Nikolai needed to head back to Sacramento to catch their return flight to Phoenix. This time French Baum was coming with them. They had been invited to stop by Huck's place. His trees were in worse shape than French's.

"Good morning," Huck called out. He was standing by the road near the same tree he had shown his son. Under his arm, he had tucked a manila envelope which he handed to Christina. Inside the envelope were articles that Huck has collected for the last year and a half. Some journalists had written about thick heavy metal concentrations around Redding and maybe a correlation with the high rates of violence among children.

"Miles and miles away from any industry and yet we are measuring crazy levels of chemicals," he said quietly. "They can only be coming from one place because of their even distribution over acreage. From the sky. So why here? Why this place in particular or a place like this? I'll tell you what I think. We're between two mountain ranges and in the heaviest watershed area outside Hoover Dam. Water. People drink this water, bathe in it, cook with it… it's used in agriculture. Lots and lots of it gets back into the water cycle because there is so much here, it's such a huge watershed. And the ocean isn't that far away, that's a big driver of the water cycle. That is the only thing different here than any other place in particular."

They thanked Huck, who told them to take the envelope with them. He had made copies of everything. Back inside the car, French said quietly, "Huck lost a boy recently… a foster son, not really his blood son, but he loved him anyway. He thinks it had everything to do with this program. So do I."

"Listen, Nikolai," Christina said, pushing away thoughts of her mother and the man who killed her lying in some hospital bed incapacitated, "I want to take a small detour on the way." She smiled at him, a little nervously.

"For what reason?" Nikolai asked.

"Between here and Sacramento... a little to the west... is a place called Knell Labs."

French guffawed in the back seat. Nikolai pulled the car to the side and stopped, turning to face

Christina.

"Yes, I know this place. It is a very, very bad place. Why on earth would you want to go there? Everything that happens within twenty miles of that lab is filmed and monitored. We already have so much potential trouble."

"There is a scientist there who I think has a lot to do with this program, Nikolai. I might be able to get in to see him because he worked with my mother. I know him. He's still alive although he's in his nineties. How dangerous could that be?"

Nikolai turned and looked at French as if to ask, what do we do? It was nearly irresistible to thinkone of the scientists who concocted this mess might be available to the three of them and that they were so close. French shrugged but looked ever so slightly alarmed. Whatever happened he had to continue to live nearby.

"Alright, if you really want to do this," Nikolai said finally. "Do you have an address?"

The diversion would take them forty-five minutes out of their way. Just as they left the highway, they spotted Knell Labs. There was a very small sign by the front gate surrounded by very large signs warning the public to stay away. Several uniformed security guards were stationed outside the gate, which was a sliding fence of sorts about twelve feet high. The lab looked for all the world like a small prison. Barbed wire lined the top of the twelve foot fence that spanned the perimeter of the compound. From the road, the buildings appeared to be made of cinder block painted white. There were many long, rectangular buildings with thin slit-like windows sitting high in the walls near the roofs. One square building was clearly the main office. It looked decidedly ordinary and sat in the curve of a circular drive. They were afraid to slow down. Security cameras were in evidence everywhere. They were even afraid to look but they did. Ten minutes later they slid into the small town adjacent to the lab; many of the people living here would certainly be connected to it in some way. The lab was a primary extension of the Department of Defense and as such was dangerous, secret and often lethal.

They passed a very small elementary school. A handful of children gathered around the swing set. The town was small, riddled with tree-lined cul-de-sacs, lace-curtained windows and mini-vans. At the very center of one particular cul-de-sac sat 42 Playa Encantada. This was to the best of Christina's knowledge the home of the Lorna and Wolfgang von Marshall. Nikolai parked on the curb in front of the house. It was a very unassuming house, perhaps a two bedroom bungalow. The giveaways were various sculptures placed in the front yard among the trees and bushes. There was a grape arbor on the side of the house, painted white. It was warm.

"Well, there you are," Nikolai said. Someone needed to contribute the forward propelling moment and it came from him.

"Go on."

Christina took a few deep, slow breaths. There was simply nothing extraordinary about the town, the street or the little house. Yet she was quite certain that one of the fathers of aerosol experimentation on the general human population resided right there. She walked past strategically placed ceramic and wooden faces placed in tree branches and behind bushes. She started when she realized she had just placed her foot on a face that was acting as a path stone. The path continued without any more people staring up at her until she stood before the front door, where she rang the bell. There was no movement from within. She waited, then rang the bell again. She waited. She knocked on the door, loudly. No one responded to her presence, to her having shown up to remind people that her mother had existed. She wanted to see Lorna's face as the door swung open and her realizing it was Christina. These two probably had no idea her mother was dead but Christina would be more than happy to catch them up.

"So what would you have asked him anyway, Christina?" Nikolai asked her once she was back in the car.

"For one thing, I would have asked, Wolfgang von Marshall, why the hell are birds dropping dead and falling out of the sky by the hundreds and thousands? If I could get that answer, I bet I could answer fifty other questions." She pushed her hair away from her face. "Forget it; let's just get out of here. We have a plane to catch, right? Thanks for doing this for me, guys. It was worth a shot."

They made their way slowly and silently back to the highway and turned for Sacramento. There was little traffic, and in that way they had been fortunate. The hills were rolling and gentle. As they crested a particularly high ridge, French spoke.

"Do you hear that?" He turned toward the sound, growing louder. It was behind them. It sounded like an army of snow ploughs; it was so loud and mechanical.

"What the hell?" French sat riveted to whatever he could see out the back window of the car.

Nikolai adjusted his rear view mirror so he could see what French saw. Christina twisted in her seat, craning her head back. A Blackhawk helicopter appeared over the crest of the hill behind them flying straight at them at extremely low altitude. It continued to fly straight at them, avoiding them at the very last possible moment by pulling up. Christina screamed. French unbuckled his seatbelt, got on his knees and tried to look up above the car through the back
window.

"Shit!"

He sat back down fast and buckled his belt. There was a loud roaring all around the car, like a mechanical hurricane. Through the back window a Blackhawk helicopter hovered ten or fifteen yards off the pavement following them very closely again. The torrential draft generated by the rotors made it hard for Nikolai to keep the car on the road. They could literally see the pilots – two of them – staring at them behind very dark sunglasses. There were no markings on the craft, no livery of any kind, it was simply black. The pilot's helmets were black, their sunglasses were black, their jumpsuits were black.

"Drive!" yelled French.

Another helicopter appeared overhead and settled in beside them on the passenger's side. It appeared they were being escorted, or menaced, or both by two Blackhawks. They pulled their shirts up over their mouths and noses to keep from choking on the fumes. They drove this way for three miles or more when the helicopters finally veered off and returned to whatever hell they had emerged from. No cars had appeared behind them or coming toward them. A few minutes after the Blackhawks peeled off and flew away, they passed a road block. California Highway Patrol had stopped traffic, probably without even being sure why. No one pursued them, which was very odd. They just drove away and no one had seen what they had seen.

They drove another ten miles in shocked and pale silence, afraid to stop or even slow the car down. Every once in a while French turned and searched the horizon behind them. Eventually, they found themselves in another small town and Nikolai felt he might be able to safely stop for a moment. He had to. He couldn't keep going. As soon as he did, Christina opened the passenger door and vomited all over the sidewalk. Presently, she wiped her mouth with her sleeve and sat back up inside the car.

"What the hell was that?" she asked. They were still shaking. She kept the car door open and one foot on the pavement as if creating a getaway path. It was a nonsensical proposition but it kept her from being sick again.

"That," French answered a little too loudly, "is what we get for randomly sticking our noses into Knell Labs territory. A very aggressive warning. Certainly Nikolai and I are not unknown to them and now I'd venture you're right on their radar now, as well. In fact, you probably just leap-frogged right over us on the curiosity scale. Congratulations."

They managed to make their flight back to Phoenix, despite the harassment from two Blackhawk helicopters by all but sleepwalking through the car rental return and through security. After they were safely aboard the plane, it occurred to Christina that the powers behind her mother's death could make it very difficult to get through the simplest security on the way home. She could not dwell on that without panic rising from her gut. It was the same bile she fought back when it first began to dawn on her that not only had her mother been murdered but that she would almost without question have to do something about it. The poison in the sky left little choice for anyone. That town near Mt. Shasta, as gentle and ordinary as it was intended to seem, was an illusion of the highest order. Unseen eyes watched every move, weapons were ready to be drawn and used at any moment and when they appeared they would seem to come from nowhere. Yet children laughed and played at the elementary school nestled in an unpretentious small town in rural northern California; people shopped at the market and took their kids out for ice cream and went to the movies in that dangerous little town, as well.

They had one very important symposium to attend in Phoenix and then they were all going home. French would have to make the same drive back to his property and he was damned worried about it. He would be alone that time. Still, there was nothing to be done about it. Nevertheless, the three of them joined a hundred others in the same room they had been in on the previous Friday and the same panel sat on the stage, including what Christina had come to understand was their main adversary in the working scientific community, Dr. Daniel Bleeth. He was dressed much the same as he had been on Monday, a look of resignation on his face. He seemed prepared to bolt directly after the last question was answered.

This symposium was strictly a question and answer opportunity, based they hoped on the previous lecture. French Baum raised his hand and stood when Bleeth acknowledged him,

Dr. Bleeth, my name is French Baum and I'm an environmental scientist and rancher from northern California. I have personally done random sample testing within a one hundred square mile area, or participated as a partner in that sampling, and we have discovered something on the order of sixty times the so-called actionable level of aluminum oxide in water... in snow samples...in vegetation and trees and soil. What is your opinion of the effects on the planet and its inhabitants of levels of aluminum that high?"

French stood and, looked Bleeth in the eye.

Bleeth very nonchalantly delivered his answer.

"As of yet there are no studies that have been published regarding alumina and how that affects the health of living things. Obviously we need to do that. So far we have no data on that and the effects will be demonstrated over time... if any. It's sort of like borrowing your grandchildren's future, there is no real immediate moral dilemma."

"Well, with all due respect, Dr. Bleeth, that sounds an awful lot like experimenting on groups of people without their consent."

The room was still.

"So, let me get this straight. You're saying that something like the order of sixty tons of aluminium oxide nanoparticles in the atmosphere and water and soil have zero ill effects when merely one thousand nanoparticles per billion requires federal intervention? " French pressed the issue.

Bleeth blanched. His colleagues shifted a bit, uneasily.

"Let me be very clear here. I said we have published no findings on alumina in the biosphere. Obviously we need to do studies on that."

'We' have not published studies on the biological effects of tons of aluminum oxide in the atmosphere, which subsequently floats down and infiltrates land, vegetation, water and human beings. That was a true statement. It did not mean there were not studies out there, done by the top organizations both military and civilian. It just meant that Bleeth, the king of dancing on the head of a pin, the Tinman, could say he had not done any himself. Actually what he said was he had not published any. This was such a dangerous man.

The Good Soldier

Patton had said something like "three minutes' worth of yeas or nays...". Tim didn't remember the exact quote although he had certainly heard Huck say it on many occasions. General Patton stated categorically that a man's military career was the product of three-minute's worth of nays and yeas.

His path was set and history was changed. It was a game Tim himself played, a game he knew to be fundamentally true. It was a statement that could probably describe most people's lives. He tried to add it all up at night when sleep eluded him, as it almost always did. He tried to add up the yeas and nays of his own three minutes. It helped him dig through the detritus of his life, the truly unimportant stuff, which at this point felt like most of it, and figure out how he came to be where he was. It would also help him, as an ex-military man, to explain himself in sixty seconds or less should he ever have to. He absolutely hoped he would have to do that.

Just after shooting the drunken pilot at the bar, he had calmly climbed into his truck and driven back to the base. He had not gone back to his apartment but driven straight to dispatch. The dispatcher, who was very surprised to see him, had let him in the front gate after the guards had called. He told them one of the pilots had experienced an 'accident' and he was here to report it. Lights went on immediately all over the ground floor level of the office building, as it seemed as if he had woken some people up. It was a moment to work on honing his life down to those three minutes, which kept him calm as it seemed like a good idea to practice that in the seconds before all hell broke loose.

To his great happiness, all hell did not break loose. This was not that kind of an operation. One man shot up in a bar, a pilot and a drunken pilot at that, was not a particular cause for concern. The only concern, and Tim knew this to be true, was what the poor sap had said to Tim, to the bartender and the girls sent from Bluesky – as Tim was sure they had been – when whatever rat in the bar let them know there was a problem. That accidental information exchange could earn him a bullet in the temple, no questions asked, depending on their habits. His handler walked in accompanied by an old familiar face, Mick Unger. Unger let a smile creep across his face.

"Hi, Tim!" Unger's smile was wide and aggressive. It did not hold up on both ends at once, one side caved with every sharp intake of breath and realigned when he exhaled. "You had a busy night, I hear."

He picked up a straight backed wooden chair, turned it back towards Tim. He set his right foot on the chair and leaned on his knee elbows crossed. Even in the wee hours he was still wearing a light blue, short-sleeved dress shirt and tie. His sunglasses rested in a case in his pocket. His pants were crisply creased black dress pants, his shoes polished black and tied with dress laces. Tim had seen this posture countless times. It was supposed to exude a simple, let's get to the bottom of things attitude. It was the 'understanding vice-principal' pose, calculated to elicit teary-eyed confessions from thirteen year olds. Yet Unger's smile continued to fail, it fell – he pushed it back into place. It fell; he pushed it back into place.

"Sure did," Tim replied in his best attempt at neutral. "Not nearly as busy as it could have been. Just as soon as things got ramped up I walked out the door. Then I removed the problem from my immediate area. Seemed like the thing to do since I have no intention of being pegged as part of a problem." He wanted to ask Unger what the hell he was doing at *Gila* Airfield but now was just not the time.

"That's what we heard, as well, Tim,' Unger remarked. He seemed unsure still. Naturally. "Our information is exactly what you've been saying. How come, though, you decided to clean up your immediate area? What was the stink?"

"Blabbering about how things run, one thing and another, sir." This was the most dangerous moment. He had to admit that the drunk had been laying out Operations details, right or wrong. The bartender had heard them and was probably in their employ. The two girls had come in later but surely the drunken pilot had not been able to resist. Impressing a beautiful woman just greases the already booze-soaked wheels. The bartender – or someone nearby – would have relayed exactly what was said so there was no point in lying. Tim had not heard much. He had made sure of that. He was also fairly sure the two girls were casualties, even if they did work exclusively for the company. The drunk would have revealed far too much to them to let them stay alive. He would check into it next time he was in town. A car accident, likely. The girls would not have survived the evening.

Unger stared at Tim for a while, as he did sometimes. He turned and looked at Tim's handler, who had found a spot behind a remote desk in the corner of the room, sat moving a toothpick around in his mouth. The man shrugged.

"Good work tonight, Tim. Exactly the right thing to do. Go on home, shake it off. I want to see you first thing. Tomorrow's a busy day around here and you just got invited to the party." He stood up, replaced the chair crisply, turned and left. Tim's handler struggled a bit to catch up. And then Tim was alone, under fluorescent lights in the slightly green-tinged, Naugahyde-filled office at two o'clock in the morning. He was not sure what had actually been decided. He was not sure if he would walk out the door and take a bullet or meet with an accident on the way home. He had no choice but to drive that mile. Three minutes of yeas or nays. He could certainly add this moment to the top of his list. He ran what he had on his list as he walked, very purposefully and evenly out the double glass doors of the office building and headed for his truck.

Reach for it. Push the button. Door open, nothing happened. Get in. Turn the key. Nothing happened. Okay. Put the car in reverse and slam on the brakes. The brakes work...for now.

Tim talked himself through every step on the way home, surviving each one. There were no menacing headlights in his rear view mirror on the way home. He climbed the stairs and turned the key in the lock of his apartment, with his gun out and ready. Both hands on the stock, the muzzle pointing at the ground but ready to swing up at the slightest movement or sound, he cleared the apartment room by room, checking behind every door and under his bed. He shut and locked his front door.

His roommate was out of town, as he usually was, he thought, but was due back the next day sometime. He lay down on his bed, fully clothed with his firearm at his side, chair propped against his bedroom door, wedged right under the doorknob. Then he got up, pushed his bed right up under the door so that if anyone tried to open the door he'd feel it plus the door would be blocked by his bed. The only thing he would not survive was if someone fired repeatedly through the door. He wouldn't survive that anyway unless he hid in the closet. This angle gave him a straight shot at the window. He lay down, gun on his stomach, and watched the window until the sun rose. He realized that his reaction was very twentieth century, very instinctual, very military 101, and he realized he lived in a Rat Cage built just for company 'assets.' They could probably gas him right where he lay without hurting so much as a cockroach in the adjacent kitchen. He also knew they were almost certainly watching him and he didn't care. This is where his reflexes had led him. And, frankly, he was prepared for the local police to swoop down on him. His reflexes and experience as a human being in this country screamed that they would soon be there to demand justice. His intellect told him that the company had eliminated such possibilities altogether.

"Flyyyy-yeeeeerrr!!!"

He had closed his eyes without realizing it. He shot upright, both hands on the handle of his gun.

"Hey, you home?"

It was his roommate, Harry. It was morning. The clock read 7:11 and the desert sky was a faint pink streaked with purple out his window. He rubbed his face and grimaced. He needed to pee. He needed to shave. Rising stiffly, he pushed his bed back to where it belonged, noisily as he was bone tired and very uncomfortable. He threw open his door as if to say, shoot me. Screw it, just go ahead and shoot me. His roommate laughed.

"Calm the hell down, man."

Tim gave Harry a filthy look and headed for the bathroom, weapon in hand, gun arm hanging at the ready. Harry laughed. He seemed to have some understanding of the situation, perhaps having been called to dispatch upon his arrival at the airfield. He spoke to Tim through the closed door of the bathroom.

"You have moved much, much higher up the food chain, Cap'n." Tim could hear Harry rooting around in the refrigerator. It was the first thing he did each and every time he entered the apartment, a ridiculously fruitless habit, since, for security purposes, neither one of them ever kept anything in the refrigerator. Food and drink could be so easily tampered with. Tim zipped his jeans back up and flushed. The fact that Harry did this so often, in fact, and was part of the 'medical' team was the very reason Tim had nothing to do with anything edible or drinkable in the apartment.

"Seriously, Harry," he barked softly, "why the hell do you even look in there?"

He turned the faucets on, longing for the comforting feel of hot water on his face, lather and a razor's edge. He was going to stop and shave, to calm himself.

"Habit. Maybe I'm clearing the fridge. Did you ever think of that?" His eyes sparkled. Harry was clearly excited at the turn of events.

"How am I higher up the food chain?"

Tim scraped the last of the night's stubble off his face, dried his face roughly. He walked past Harry to his bedroom, opened a dresser drawer and started pulling out fresh clothing, which he threw on the bed. He reached into his closet for a clean shirt.

"You just are. Priceless, brilliant move last night, my friend." Harry leaned against the doorframe watching Tim pull on his shirt. Tim grunted. Harry gave up and sat on the sofa in the living room while Tim changed his clothes. Suddenly, the playful mood was over, like a switch had been flipped, and he seemed to have orders for Tim. He was responsible for thismoment, this left turn, in some way.

"We are to report to the field in thirty minutes. You have a couple of things to deal with today. Unger will give you your orders. At four p.m., you report to me, at the lab. We have to get you a Class A Health Upgrade. You just became a helluva lot more valuable to the company." He grinned again. "In fact, if I were you, I'd check my bank account."

When he finished dressing, Tim left the condo and drove back to the airfield. The guards let him in and he reported to dispatch as if it were any other day. The dispatcher from last night had been replaced by a woman working the day shift. She stood and escorted Tim back out the door to an idling sedan manned by a driver Tim did not recognize.

"Mr. Unger is waiting for you out at the test range, Mr. Verzet." She turned and went back to the building.

Tim climbed in and shut the door. His life from now on would be a series of never-ending moments in which he calculated the odds of being killed. If he remained inside this organization and he wanted to stay alive he knew that had better not change. His driver drove away from dispatch, away from the primary airfield and the stable of airplanes parked there, into the desert. Within five minutes, he had spotted the building he assumed was the test range facility. His mind wandered to photographs he'd seen from the White Sands range, buildings that seemed no more than Quonset huts, to protect human beings from the madness of nuclear bomb tests.

What kind of stupid monkeys are we?

Just on the other side of the building he could see there was a small bank of enormous C-dishes, very reminiscent of the Very Large Array in Socorro. One GWEN tower, bristling from top to bottom with metal antennae, reached into the sky on the near-side of the building. It may have been one hundred feet high. The sedan slid to a stop in front of the long, boxcar-shaped two-story building. It was mostly windows and he saw perhaps fifty or more technicians inside, all wearing white lab coats, together with a handful of people wearing civilian clothes. He got out, headed for a double-glass door into the only building within visual range. Unger appeared as soon as Tim stepped inside the building and pulled him aside.

"Verzet, again, good job last night. Now let's move on. Have a seat."

Tim sat down in one of the two chairs in a very small room, too small for a desk. Unger stood, arms folded across his chest.

"I've moved you up to Handler status for now. It's a 100% pay grade advance, if you get me. That math is pretty easy. You have thirty three-man flight teams you are responsible for. That does not mean morning meetings. We are not in the Air Force. It means you appear when your teams least expect it and check in with them. It means you invest some time in getting to know each man so hopefully you can be aware before someone heads off to a bar and starts to sing. It means you are kept far more apprised of impending tech changes, one of which we are getting ready to roll out right now. That is why we are meeting out here at the test range. Any questions?"

"No, sir."

"Great. I see the big bus out there bringing everyone else."

They stood up. Out of the window, Tim could just see reddish dust rising on the horizon. It looked like a larger vehicle, perhaps a bus. He followed Unger out into the main room and up a short flight of stairs. The second level afforded a panoramic view of the surrounding field and nearly-empty desert. Twenty or so tech specialists were there, standing or moving around the room, modulating equipment, speaking into headsets. They all wore knee-length white lab coats with one word across the left breast: Pantheon. Apparently Pantheon ran the research and development portion of this project. He had seen three logos now: Bluesky, National Express Package Delivery, and now Pantheon, a very, very big fish indeed among Great Big Fish. Just about the biggest.

Twenty people left the bus and joined Unger, Tim and the various technical personnel on the top floor. A man with a Pantheon emblazoned white coat stepped in front of the group to speak.

"Okay, why are we here today? We have an experimental delivery system to roll out. You'll see it outside on the tarmac at the far end of the runway. This is the new titanium-covered aircraft, reminiscent of a 747, equipped with the dispersal systems you are all used to. It is sitting right next to an ordinary-looking DC-10-30 type aircraft, also new, also state-of-the-art and then some, and now one of our stable. This DC-10-30 type we call the Plato and it's an expensive bird, I'm sure you can guess... just about a billion each. However, when we have a population who is finally starting to look up, it's good if when they do, their monitoring equipment cannot 'see' the ship as easily. Russians have been using the titanium tech on their subs for years; it makes the subs invisible to magnetic tracking systems. You may or may not know that only works under water. The titanium comes from Russia actually. So," he went on in a clipped tone, "why titanium? It is infinity lighter, more malleable in a way and makes a more maneuverable ship. The Proteus we call her. The other one, the Plato, is essentially invisible to radar. Today we cannot demonstrate the 'invisibility' of our Plato, but we can at least demo the visibility of the crew inside. That is the reverse proposition. At this level, you have all been or are being cleared of ordinary bioaccumulation. Below your level and out into the general population, once the body conditions itself to this bioaccumulation of our product, a product which can, in fact, be detected through titanium... I can see those wheels turning in the pilot's head here... a unique electronically reactive particulate signature is created that we can detect absolutely anywhere; and soon even several hundred feet under the ground."

There was a low murmuring in the room.

"Hang on before you start that. The Plato alongside the Proteus is also a new animal. It's skin is an alloy, a carbon composite, with almost no radar cross-section. The carbon fiber composites are actually lighter than the titanium and stronger. The demonstration goals today are twofold. Can we make the plane 'invisible' while keeping the people 'visible,' and traceable should we want to do so. It's also crucial that our next generation fleet becomes highly maneuverable and develops a much lower profile in terms of cost."

At this point, Unger stepped up.

"Besides which, pilots, imagine what a difference the light materials will make in flight. Everybody has to train on these. At least one of you has long experience shaking out new systems."

Tim had an uneasy feeling he would be pulled to shake out the new plane. It would be nearly impossible to do so not knowing how it would be used. There would be no joy in it this time. Even an audience as jaded and paranoid as this one could not help letting out a few stunned noises. There was a major escalation in the level of technology here, and also a brilliant opportunity to fly a new bird. The tech turned to a bank of screens set up in a row along a table that ran the length of the window facing the runway. All the machines were on, looked very much like the same radar the FAA uses to track airplanes although their display was 3D. There was the outline of one plane, not two. They assumed it was the Proteus; they could see because they had been led to believe that's what would happen. The most interesting thing to them about this display was that they could see three figures, dots that were suggestions of shapes, inside the cabin of the Plato. The tech flipped a switch and the names and locations of each slender suggestion of a human blip were displayed on the lower right of each screen.

"You'll have to just believe me when I say it works that way on anyone who has not had a Class A Health Upgrade," the tech said. "Keep watching, gentlemen."

Outside, the Proteus began to taxi down the runway. Despite its length, the runway was just long enough to get a Proteus airborne, so the pilot punched it. The bird screamed as it gained speed just this side of too fast. It all but managed to lift off before it ran out of tarmac. The screen registered as it normally would, or nearly, and certainly there was nothing suggestive of an innovative airplane in flight. The tech pushed several buttons and there on the screen were three of the same human 'suggestions' moving across the screen seemingly flying on their own although the titanium registered intermittently.

"Obviously this is remote detection at its finest and is really meant to be used in other ways. This was simply a convenient way to demonstrate. We have the plasma backdrop produced in the sky thanks to decades' worth of efforts, research and practical application. The plasma is now stable and maintained in the atmosphere by our dispersal systems. This background chemistry combined with satellite tracking and generally a handheld tracker, or as in this case, means we are able to complete the pinpoint through the console and pick out the targets we want. In real life scenarios the subjects won't be that compliant. Anything else I might tell you would land me and you, as well, in very hot water indeed but there you have it. We'll be shaking the planes out for our purposes in a few months' time."

Later Tim met Harry in the lab back at the dispatch building. Harry ushered him in, led him to a sink and handed him a beaker of purple liquid.

"Swish and spit," he said.

"This tastes like grape juice," Tim said.

"Yeah, go figure. Do that, fifteen seconds at a time, every five minutes or so for a while. I need you to come here every day and do this unless you are out of town."

"Why? What am I doing here?" Harry grinned, almost gleefully.

"Just do what I tell you to, pilot. I need to douse the lights, turn on an overhead black light." He reached over and flipped the switches, one up one down. "Continue to swish and spit, please."

Tim did what he was told. When he spit out the mouthful of grape juice, he realized he was seeing bits of something come out of his mouth and hit the sink. They looked like fibers. There were hundreds of them, some small, some large, some clumped together. Stuck among the fibers were what looked to be little black seeds... at least he hoped they were seeds. Then he realized that some of the fibers were moving just a little.

"What the hell are those?" he screamed.

"Those are just the little friends who help us conduct experiments on the unwashed masses. Over time, based on bioaccumulation, these critters combine with every person on the planet – their cellular individuality – to create a radio signature as unique as a thumbprint so we can track anyone anywhere at any time. You saw that in action today, I believe. Look in the mirror over here. They exit the body via the gum line at the root of the tooth given the right stimulus."

He moved Tim a bit to the right. His irises, the space around his pupil, gleamed fluorescent. That should not have been so.

"That is the way to judge how cleaned out you are," Harry said. "We need to go for zero fluorescence." He patted Tim on the back brusquely.

"How much of that is in me?" Tim was hyperventilating a little.

"Get a grip. We're going to clean you out. It takes a few months but it's pretty simple. Do this every day, a few times a day. Take this liquid clay mixture every day in the morning on an empty stomach. Drink pure water only from now on. We have a distiller on site. And, last but not least, I'm giving you pills. One a day, every day. See me every month for a new bottle. Over time, your system will clean itself out although you may get some skin lesions should some of the little fellas try to exit that way. Just let me know if that happens." He smiled the smile of a science-crazy twelve-year old who's just gotten a chemistry set for Christmas. "But, listen, if you want to stay 'clean' you have to take these pills. Do you understand, pilot?"

A tried and true way of keeping hostages, Tim realized. This was the old 'take the antidote so the poison didn't get you' scenario. He was enraged to think his Dad and everyone he knew was loaded with these things. He needed to find out what they did and find out he would. Additionally, he now had five hundred thousand dollars in the bank. Despite the fact that the dollar was tanking so fast, he was really looking at about one fifth of that in terms of real monetary value, a flick of a petulant wrist from the right person and he would be in jail for having enormous sums of money for which he could not account. Perhaps there would be a convenient backstory that had to do with money laundering or drugs. There would certainly be no jury trial. Legislation was on the verge of being passed that would allow anyone to hold him indefinitely without a trial. He was a pilot dumping biologicals onto the general population. They would hang him.

When he had drained the cup he was given, he turned to leave.

"One more thing," Harry said, "this is brown paper wrapper stuff. We are trying to get the stuff we save for the Team off the store shelves. No access for the general public, obviously. Until we do that this is all 'eyes-only.' Understand?"

Tim would be kept healthy but he was far more trapped than he had been two days ago. Sometimes the trap is ignorance, sometimes the trap is knowledge. He stepped into the small, white room they called a commissary at *Gila* in the dispatch building. He just wanted something in his stomach. On the one hand, he felt sick wondering what was crawling around in his body. On the other hand, he really didn't want an empty stomach. He chose milk. Two little cartons of milk and a handful of crackers. He found a table by a window hoping something would distract him. It had been a terrifying day.

He now knew the word 'bioaccumulation.' Bioaccumulation – saturation – things 'checked in' but they didn't 'check out.' He was ashamed to admit that he was exuberant, shockingly relieved that he was one of the few getting what Harry referred to as a 'health upgrade.' He knew he should feel badly – did feel badly – that everyone wasn't being healed. He hoped that by doing this he'd end up in a position to at least help eliminate the poison. That was the best anyone could hope for; that and never knowing what was crawling around in their bodies.

As far as encountering the special planes were concerned, any military man was accustomed to the idea of stealth technology. Aside from the actual cost of the thing, the phenomenon had been almost boring. It was the remote sensing of human beings that captured everyone's attention. Then Dr. Harry had shown him the internal mechanism by which humanity had been 'tagged.' That was a staggering breech of integrity, ethics; God knows how many treaties, and the simple sovereignty of the individual. It was enough. He couldn't think about it anymore. Three minutes of yeas or nays and the course of history is set or changed.

Someone had left an LA Times on a table near the door. He retrieved it and sat, thumbing through the pages, sipping milk. He stopped to skim an article on page two, Queen Elizabeth on a royal tour of Canada. Economics tended to take page one and half of every other page these days. Inflation was out of control; the dollar was still in a steep slide here and abroad causing riots everywhere. A black and white photograph of a Japanese building on page eleven caught his attention; an update on the *Shuri* Reconciliation. The document itself, a treaty, was nearing completion. A few countries had last-minute arguments or evidence of infractions that should, they felt, affect the language of the document. Such cases had to be argued or even tried in a court of law eventually. There was a panel overseeing the project, the members of which did their level best not to allow the legal cases to bog down the effort itself. The *Shuri* Reconciliation caught his eye every time he came across some mention of it. The point was human rights; the atmosphere, like water, was a huge part of what Tim hoped would lead to recognition of, and an absolute injunction against, the practice of terraforming without express consent of each signatory country.

If only they knew. I could sure as hell show them some terraforming.

Tim couldn't think of a bigger stab at redemption than taking a truckload of evidence relating to this madman program of which he was now one of the major hostages and dropping it into the courtyard of *Shuri* Castle on Okinawa. Let someone else, some group of diplomats or magistrates, look at this filth, this disaster, for a change. He would pull out his sixty-second explanation and hopefully receive amnesty and forgiveness for turning them all in. Then he would walk away and spend the rest of his life trying to make sense of what had happened. It was an achingly exquisite wish that fled when he realized a DC-10 mule was landing. The noise and vibration pulled him out of the dream and back into the nightmare, making him feel like he had landed on his back, the wind knocked out of him.

He decided to go back to his apartment and sleep. He stood up, folded the newspaper and dropped it on a table for someone else. He glanced out the window at the crew from the DC-10 making their way now toward dispatch. The third man in line was a foot taller than the rest and was wearing aviator-style sunglasses. His red hair reflected the sun like a mirror on fire and he sported a red beard. It was Phillip Yarmouth. It had to be a dream, an hallucination brought on by the yearning to be back at the point of rethinking this ridiculous, life-ending decision. He stood there and watched the crew get closer and closer. It was, indeed, Pip Yarmouth. Tim didn't hurry to dispatch to greet his old buddy. Danger lurked behind every interaction there and he would not compromise Pip.

When he thought about it he realized that, of course, Pip would end up here. He would never have been able to stop watching the sky once he started, especially after that phone call he'd made trying to save that crew. He would need to follow Tim. Here he was. Tim would almost have to hide from him until he could figure out how to proceed.

Big, red sight-for-sore-eyes bear. Stupid, stupid bear. Thank God you're here.

Before he went home, he stopped in at the local mall and bought clothes. Every kind of clothing he could think of. It would look like he was on a bit of a spending spree now that he had so much money in the bank. They would see him as relieved and happy. That would confirm their categorization of him as someone who was motivated by money. When he climbed the stairs, he had six giant shopping bags filled with clothing: pants, shirts, sweaters, ties, silk handkerchiefs, shoes. He had previously done nothing at all normal or mundane and every day since the Bully Choop fire broke out. He threw his bags on the living room sofa and retrieved a metal file jacket, the one they used when they were going through any kind of security check to help block unwanted eyes. He sat down on the couch, turned on the television, and began writing on a yellow legal pad already in the folder. He stopped periodically and rifled through his new clothes. He needed to make it seem he was being as normal as it was humanly possible to be. He did this for about an hour intending to bore anyone watching into losing just the slightest bit of concentration. He plucked the silks from a bag, left a yellow silk handkerchief in his hand, admiring it. He kept it and the clipboard when he rose to change the television channel. He still had the silk in his hand when he sat back down; slipped it inside the file folder onto the yellow pad. He wrote just a simple sentence on the silk. "*Not safe.*" He then carefully and methodically packed up and folded all his clothing, folded the hanky and put it in the pocket of the pants he was already wearing. Then he put all his clothes away in chests of drawers and closets. He returned to the couch with just the clothes he was wearing. He purposefully flipped through the TV channels again, lay down on the couch, slipped one hand inside his pants pocket and spent an hour tediously rolling up the hanky with four fingers until it was about the size of a bullet. It was an old trick, any World War II buff would know it, but it worked. It was a piece of silk. It made no noise. It became incredibly small and so was easy to pass. He could keep it until he spotted Pip again. Then he would pass it to him and hope for the best. The one thing he knew was he had to find some way to communicate. He would use this with Huck when he visited home, as well. The process of getting two words onto a surface he could transport without getting shot had taken about two and a half hours and cost him twelve hundred dollars at the mall. He would get better at it.

Tim awoke at two a.m. His sheets were soaked although he was shivering, clammy and cold rather than feverish. The triangle described from his Adam's apple to each side of his collar bone burned, screamed in pain. He coughed, bringing up clear phlegm. He coughed and then he coughed some more. The affected 'triangle' hurt every time he coughed.

"Ow," he rasped. "What the hell…?"

He was ill, obviously, and it reminded him of the bronchitis he'd had as a teenager, swift and debilitating. However, had it been that, his phlegm would have taken on several shades of green and yellow by now. He felt so sick he wanted to weep. He vacillated between wanting to weep and hearing the phrase, get it out, go through his mind. Every exhale was accompanied by a deep, sharp cracking sound. He struggled to his feet, made his way to Harry's bedroom door.

"Jesus," Harry said, "let's get you back to the lab."

By the time they arrived, Tim was also experiencing random stabbing pains in his muscles and joints, and completely spontaneous but truly excruciating muscle spasms.

"Concentrate on keeping those muscles relaxed," Harry cautioned him. "I'm going to give you a megadose of potassium."

"Lay down here," Harry pointed toward a small, dark room that contained two cots. It reminded Tim of the nurses' office at elementary school. He fell on one of the cots, half pulled a blanket over himself and moaned.

"Where did you live before you came to New Mexico?" Harry asked. "You're not dying but this is serious detox."

"Redding, California," Tim replied.

"Yeah, that explains it. Heavy dump site, lots of respiratory stuff there."

Tim thought of Huck and his relentless cough.

"I'm going to give you some activated charcoal, too" he said handing Tim tablets and a cup of water," then push some glutathione, some B12... tomorrow we'll start mega doses of niacin. All good stuff for a quick scrub at the cellular level. This'll last twenty-four hours at most. I'll leave liters of water by the bed. Drink all of it."

He left the small room where Tim lay in agony, snapped off the light in the lab. Twenty-four hours later, Tim was able to go back to work. When he was back on his feet, he started his new routine of stopping by the lab for his grape juice mouthwash and his pill then on to Unger to get instructions regarding 'handling' his first crew. Handlers were not given lists of their charges as a security precaution. On the day they were placed aboard an aircraft and sent to a crew somewhere else, a crew that was not expecting them. He wondered, in fact, if once all thirty crews had been evaluated he would be assigned a new 'set' of crews.

The dispatcher directed Tim to board a DC-10 bound for Des Moines. He was not to communicate with the crew but rather sat in a 'jump seat' in the cargo bay facing rows and rows of metal barrels attached to piping and tubes directed down and, he knew, out. There was another handler on this flight. Again, they did not acknowledge each other as this was strictly forbidden within the context of performing their jobs. Their focus was on the crew at the other end of the line and only on the crew. At Des Moines, he easily located the blue and white 747 he was looking for, the ship with no livery or markings of any kind and no windows aside from the cockpit. He boarded and rapped on the cockpit door twice. The navigation officer swung the door open. It was Pip. Tim could not believe his luck, for good or ill. He reached into his pockets, palmed the yellow silk handkerchief, and introduced himself, sticking out hand. Pip grabbed it, felt the little bundle and took it.

"Gentleman, I'm your checkpoint for today. Permission to come aboard?"

He shook the hand of the co-pilot and then the pilot. No one looked particularly perturbed. This was a very frequent event although he doubted all the handlers asked the same questions. It would be too easy to memorize an acceptable response.

"Mind if we get back to pre-flight?" the pilot asked. His name was Leon. Tim thought he caught the faintest whiff of contempt in Leon's tone.

Not at all." Tim took a seat, waiting for the crew to get airborne. He would take them one by one to the back of the plane and ask a few simple questions prescribed by his superior and get a read. A report would be made to Unger, as it turned out. He would save the pilot for last, his instincts telling him this was the tougher psychology, the one who would be a little inscrutable. Pip could go first.

"Mr. Yarmouth, can I borrow you for a few minutes in the cargo area?" Tim asked once they were well on their way.

"Certainly," Pip replied. He stood and followed Tim to the rear of the plane.

They sat. Tim looked at Pip and ever so slightly shook his head. Pip understood.

"So, they send me with a set of questions every once in a while. You probably already know that."

"First eval actually," Pip replied nonchalantly.

"Oh! Okay, then. First topic. Let's talk about your health. How is everything? We want to make sure the integrity of the ship is top-notch. Nothing getting in here during dispersal."

"Not that I can detect. I'm still healthy," Pip knit his brows. "I've had a long upper-respiratory thing but that was checked out at the lab. Otherwise, no complaints."

Unger, of course, knew that they knew each other and they would have to openly admit that but that meant they had to be ten times more careful. Just be normal. Pip was taking his cues from Tim.

"Good to see you again, Pip," Tim said, standing. They shook hands. "Could you send the co-pilot out?"

His note to Pip was supposed to indicate the level of camaraderie they could display, which should be almost none in this case. Avoiding each other, though, under Unger's watchful eye, would be just as suspicious.

The co-pilot was Josh. He was blond, fairly young, thin and wiry. He pinched off each step like he was marching in formation.

"What branch, Josh?" Tim smiled.

"Air Force." Josh sat stone-faced.

"Permission to speculate, pilot." Tim said, looking into his eyes. "Seriously."

Josh was suspicious but if this was an order, it was an order.

"First off, have you since your last check-in been given any reason to believe you are being monitored by any entity outside the company?"

Josh thought seriously for a moment. "No."

"Josh, again, some wide latitude with this question but the only recipient of the answer is me…understand?"

Josh nodded.

"What is your level of contribution?"

Again, Josh had to think, evaluate the question.

Tim assumed motives were under scrutiny here. Perhaps Josh didn't seem to be quite as turned on by paycheck as they wanted him to be.

"Why are you here, Josh!"

"Protection. Solar flares. Radiation. Protecting the grid from the same."

The problem with an answer like that was that you could never be sure. It might be the truth; it might be what the pilot considered to be the safest response under the circumstances.

Leon appeared next. He carried himself with a bit of a swagger. Tim did not imagine this man had ever had a self-conscious moment. He smiled. This was another character from his book of military types: smooth, slick, ingratiating, completely out for himself. Leon would assume Tim was an idiot for thinking he had what it took to evaluate someone like himself.

Tim asked the same questions. Then suddenly he barked, "Why are you here!"

"Money." Leon smiled again, a grin confident that he was in the position he was in because he was the best. "… and power."

"Elaborate, pilot."

"I feel very powerful. Let's cut the bullshit, okay? Much more powerful than those saps down on the ground, right… because I am part of a secret program. I don't know what the hell I'm spraying… it just makes me feel like God and I love it. Yeah, it's probably hurting people but if they cared they'd stop us. Actually…I'd like to see 'em try because I'd like to see for real how powerful I am."

"Thanks, Leon," Tim said, "that'll be all. You look fit. Have a good flight."

Jesus, what a nut case. How many of those have I got?

Thirty minutes later he was boarding a flight in Chicago for *Gila*. The only thing he wanted to do now was get to his Dad, for so many reasons. Huck was dying from what he was breathing and did not know it. Huck knew he'd been transferred, he knew Tim had asked for the transfer, but he had not been able to contact his Dad for almost two months. He would take a few days and go home between Thanksgiving and Christmas. He just had to approach Unger and find out how to make that happen. Maybe he got ride along and do a check-in with a crew and stay over. He would go home and leave one hell of a long hanky message, as well. He might be losing his biological radio signature but he knew they could watch and listen to him no matter where he was.

The Book

"Mom!" David called to her through old windows shut up tight against the winter's day when she got out of the car.

The dry desert warmth of Arizona and the unusually languid mildness of northern California were behind her now. A foot of snow had finally found its way onto village streets, only the second snow of the winter. The air temperature hovered below zero for weeks at a time even so Christina was glad to be home. Now she would gather information on George Walters; this absurd enigma revolved around one crippled old man who could barely read or write, the actor who had precipitated the event and whose place in all of it was still a complete mystery.

Most of all, it was time to sit down and make sense of the notes that would eventually comprise her book. It would trace the evolution of her mother's involvement with entities attached to the atmospheric weapons programs, for better or worse. In so doing, she would travel back to times when they were together and relive the good and the bad. There was not a moment between them surely that had not built the long staircase leading to this task. Many months had come and gone. She was where she was because of her mother's death. She had no expectation at all of putting a name to one specific human hand responsible for the tragedy. It no longer mattered. She was doing what she was meant to do. She needed to figure out who Walters was simply because he was the other local player. He might hold clues, he might not. Right now he lay unmoving in a rehabilitation hospital, unable to recognize anyone, barely able to speak. This she knew. Otto had told her so and that the coma had lifted a bit.

What she brought back with her today that Walters had no conscious part in, at least no part in what she now knew and would say publicly, was the imperative. The air had to be reclaimed, the sun reclaimed, the water cleaned and the soil healed. They were in the ironic position of having to terraform their own planet for themselves, of making it a place hospitable to human life again. Some 'force' had shaken out a nice thick blanket of poison between the surface of the earth and the outer atmosphere without asking or explaining. Evil? Greed? Psychosis? Which of these was responsible? This certainly was not about a crime against her mother in particular anymore. She sat down with her notes and used what she could use, did what she was trained to do, to sound an alarm. She did this with no real hope for the future over and above a general hope and belief that the answers would come, if not to her then to someone else.

That evening, after she had worked for several hours and then got around to emptying her bag, she sat in front of the television and watched an interview with the wife of Rear Admiral Alexander Getz, the man who she instantly remembered had been found dead in a lake in Central Park, the man who had been linked to the thousands of dying birds. Getz' wife spoke, a few months on from the immediate paralysis of his violent death, while video of her husband's funeral was shown.

"I was beginning to get mad because he was supposed to be home for New Year's Eve, and then we were going to Hartford for my sister's anniversary party. I tried his cell phone, of course, but he didn't call back. Even though that wasn't unusual... he would get so sucked into what he was doing or what was around him... well, by the weekend I was pretty angry. They found his sister when they couldn't get hold of me. I got on the train by myself on Friday. His sister called but I didn't get back to her until Saturday morning."

Then the camera focused on her, clearly still in some level of shock, and Alex Getz' son, Alex, Jr.

"She called me back the next day and said, 'I have to see you right away. I have to tell you something about Alex.' "

The camera located Alex, Jr. alone, while his mother continued to speak and remember those horrible, awful hours once again. The expression on the son's face reached down into Christina's gut-level empathy. She could read his inner dialogue, see the expected refusal to meet the eyes of the interviewer while his mother told the story, or the eye of the camera; he was trying not to scream, my father was assassinated! He wasn't robbed, he wasn't demented or drunk or any of those things. It was clearly a 'hit' that went right back to his job. Yes, Christina recognized the taut lines of his face, the struggle to remain placid, the struggle to keep it to himself in case he ever wanted to do anything about it.

The wife continued.

"So his sister arrived and took me away from the party right away and said, "He's dead. Alex is dead.""

It was the son's turn to speak.

"It was like a book or a movie in slow motion or something. I've been dealing with the unsolved issues and the criminal investigation. It's all-consuming, it has the ability to blow one's emotional stuff out of the water. For a while you actually spend time thinking about what you might do – even now – to make it come out differently. Of course, it's done, but it takes a while to get that."

The unanswered questions. The case they never quite solve. Christina knew, these things are more than just unfinished crossword puzzles. They're pieces of people held hostage until the end of time, pieces of Alex Getz's son, pieces of Christina. It should have been so simple. Yet the closer she got to what would have ordinarily been such a simple affair, a logical answer to a logical cause-and effect question, the more there seemed to be forces repelling her, pushing back harder than she pushed. In the end, she would push just a bit harder and a bit longer and she would be in, make no mistake. Otto sat beside her on the couch and put his arm around her. He was a good foot taller than she was so she fit neatly in the right angle under his shoulder.

"So," he asked, "good trip?"

"Yes," she replied wearily, closing her eyes, "if good trip means getting a lot of information that scares the holy hell out of you but also meeting some people who are working as hard as you are and taking the same risks. Then, yeah, good trip."

"Remember the good old days," he said, "when 'good trip' was a nice beach and lots of food with garlic and cheese?"

Christina laughed. She did not mention the helicopters that chased them away from Wolfgang von Marshall and would not. She suspected those moments could start to add up and she would be keeping more and more from him.

"I suppose you ought to catch me up now," she said. "Thanks for holding down the fort. Did you get any work done?"

"No. Yes. Maybe. Does it matter?"

"Okay. What about Walters. Any more information?"

"He managed to postpone the sentencing just after you left. Said the whole thing was his doctor's fault. Then he had a massive stroke… for all intents and purposes he's completely incapacitated now, physically and mentally. The prosecutor's office said his family feels that even after the months of physical therapy his doctors have planned it would just be too hard on him to attend a sentencing."

Christina had no idea at all how to feel about that. Would it be hard on him to be sentenced for running her mother over in the street and killing her? Well, tough shit. That was her immediate reaction. She did not say anything.

"Have we heard from the attorney about the discovery? He should have it by now. The prosecutor said it was an easy matter of filing a motion to get a look at it… have a judge rule on it. I want to know what was going on medically at the time. I want to know why that man was behind the wheel of a car." Christina rubbed her eyes. "It's so frustrating to have an attorney who's pretty much not in a hurry at all about things that are life and death to us."

Otto handed her a fairly thick manila envelope. It was addressed to her. The return address was her attorney's. She looked at it; let it fall to her lap. Finally.

"Thank God," she patted Otto on the hand, sighing. "You know what, though? It's enough tonight to know it's here. I'm going to open it in the morning when the kids are at school."

Anya and David were situated, Christina was at her desk, stirring her coffee and staring at the manila envelope. Despite her resolution to wait until morning, she had not slept well. The packet was fairly thick; it had some weight when she hefted it. It waited there, silently. The thing had a lot of work to do, whatever was inside had to make up for months and months of void, emptiness, nothing. She slid the flap open with her finger, pulled out a sheaf of paper. Inside was a long motor vehicle record.

Walters had been hitting things and people for some time, it seemed. Eventually, the state demanded he be examined and cleared by a doctor before he could have a license to drive a car. She searched through the documents looking for the date of the last clearance exam. If some physician had either just turned the man loose on the streets or failed to report his condition, then she would want to talk to them, and that would likely be in court. According to these records, the last court-ordered checkup took place years prior to the accident that killed her mother. Yet there were multiple traffic citations since then on his record. Then she looked to see who his doctor of record was at the time of her mother's death. The medical information dropped off to nothing after the last clearance exam. There were no records at all from then until now. Here was a man who, by all accounts, was so medically infirm that every expert he came into contact with after the accident until this very day had assumed he was under the influence of something. They all thought they were looking at a man who was high as a kite. He must have had medical attention in the last four years for his diabetes and whatever it was keeping him on oxygen, if for no other reason. Christina sent her attorney an email, who agreed there were significant medical records missing. He said he would try to get them for her.

You tell me nothing's wrong here! Tell me this is all on the up-and-up, go ahead!

She was happy that Hank was home for winter break. The children often took her thoughts away from this sad tangled mess. She could hear him in his room, right above hers, hopping around and shouting dialogue. It was completely normal as he was studying acting. God knows why he was hopping around and shouting dialogue but it was an assignment, no doubt. Every so often he retreated to home, told no one he was back in town, and caught up on work. He loved the city but also needed trees and shoreline and wilderness every so often. Acting homework was a little disconcerting, though, until one got used to it. She was glad to see him, glad to be able to softly open his bedroom door in the mornings and see him sleeping in his bed. She knew those days were swiftly coming to a close.

Two days after asking for the missing information, she received a message from her attorney informing her that he had decided those records were not necessary to the case and he would not be pursuing them; it wasn't cost effective. Christina was absolutely stunned. She called Otto.

"That's absurd," he said. "How can your attorney of all people say that his medical supervision at the time your mother was killed isn't relevant to the case? Does the court have those records? The prosecutor? I'm starting to think we need a new attorney."

Christina agreed. She had a right to see those documents and, cost effective or not, she deserved answers. She deserved to understand exactly the circumstances in place on that Sunday in July. She did some research and located the best firm in the state. She contacted the senior partner who put her in touch with someone who specialized in these kinds of cases.

"Mrs. Galbraithe, you should have those records by now," he assured her, "This is just ridiculous. And there is a time constraint. Let me look into it for you."

She felt better. It seemed like a fresh pair of eyes would be a good thing for this part of things. Five days later, the man had not only not gotten back to her but would not return her calls. Two attorneys scared off getting the last few years of medical records and a perpetrator who blamed his doctor and then suffered a massive stroke. Nothing suspicious there.

It was time now to put every other thought aside, every emotion, as best she could and look at the facts. First, no one was questioning George Walter's medical state. There had been a time, she'd been assured, when he had sufficient control of his faculties to understand that he should not be behind the wheel of a car yet he had chosen to continue to drive. As he became less and less able to make any kind of a decision, he continued to 'decide,' with the help of physicians and the state, that he was okay to drive. One scenario, the simplest scenario, was that George Walters had killed her mother because he had deliberately chosen to stay behind the wheel of a car. That would be exceptionally difficult to live with but it was a very simple conclusion to draw based on straightforward events.

Christina then had to add other things she knew to be true. Yes, Walters was as physically disabled as it was possible to be and still be walking around. However, there was a long list of incongruities. She had never been able to get a police report until one had anonymously been sent to her house. She had never received a single phone call from the village police, despite the fact that it was a very small town and one would have expected to hear something from the cops, some of whom she knew quite well. The silence had been deafening. Now the last several years of his medical records were missing or unavailable. Walters himself blamed the accident on his doctor. Her own attorney had done a complete turnaround and refused to try to get the records. He was one of two attorneys to be scared away from getting those documents. Going back to the beginning, she had almost been run off the road herself while driving her mother's car. Now the one man who might be able to provide the missing pieces had suffered a massive stroke and was even more completely incapacitated. These things simply did not happen around a straight forward traffic accident involving a pedestrian. They simply did not.

Another possibility, no matter how preposterous, was that the man had been too ill to drive and too mentally incapacitated to make the proper decision – although the grand jury had most definitely not seen it that way – and the doctor taking care of him had just seen him on all his 'good, competent' days, if there were any, and the people who had been responsible for sending her the records relating to her mother's death had all just forgotten to do so, and his medical records up to the point her mother died really weren't relevant to the case after all nor was it really something Christina was entitled to know. Could the situation really be that absurd? If it was a simple case of a lonely old man having access to a van and turning himself loose on the street, then what the hell was all the secrecy about?

Over and above all of that, she was still determined to find out why her mother's organ donation had been refused because she lived in England during the 1990s. There was nothing on the level about this case. Not one thing.

Christina turned her attention back to what did make sense. On the occasions when they were all together, at home, in the big drafty green and yellow house, there was always Supper. The children stayed home when they could have been out with friends and hovered near the kitchen. With Hank at college and everyone busy making plans, 'Supper' became a special moment sometimes set aside. Soon Anya would be off as well, to Toronto to study art. David was not looking forward to being the only one at home. This far north in March the winter cold was still firmly settled in. The stove burned wood around the clock, as it did in the deep winter, and even the long-haired cat slept beneath it on the red brick hearth.

The children would circle the kitchen, singly at first then all at once, flying into the dining room and back again, testing the air for readiness. Then they would spin off in different directions, to the telephone, computer, homework or pets. 'Supper' rose through the house, filling rooms entirely, such that they returned more frequently until the food was finally released from the kitchen. Anya was on Otto's right. David was on Christina's right. Hank sat between Otto and David. Thus it had always been. Glowing beeswax tapers would bisect the table from Otto to Christina... usually.

"Damn," Christina said softly, peering into the dining room closet. "Hank, can you please drive over to St. Demetrius for candles?"

St. Demetrius was the Greek Orthodox Church half a mile away. The church used beeswax and only beeswax inside the sanctuary because they, like Christina, believed beeswax was of a higher spirituality, never having touched the ground, a thing of the air. It was suspended between heaven and earth.

These were their rituals, the clothespins that kept their lives properly pegged in place. Hank certainly counted on them being right where he left them. Christina now counted on them when everything disintegrated. The children would all know how to make something simple and beautiful, she hoped, upon which to build their homes. Even the blessing they said had been theirs since David was in kindergarten:

Earth who gives to us this food,
Sun who makes it ripe and good,
Dearest Earth and dearest Sun,
We'll not forget what you have done.

Hank headed to the church. Christina was always sorry when she couldn't go herself. She loved to stand in the sanctuary, gazing up at the ceiling, turning in the space toward one icon after the other, each more beautiful than the last. She adored the small gold-flecked framed icons lining the hallways. The sanctuary paintings were a result of a father and son team, who had been sent for from Greece. This was their life's work. They had arrived and spent much time in each sanctuary until the spirit living there spoke to them and they knew what to paint. Then scaffolding went up and from there they transferred their vision from dreams to breathtaking reality. Hank returned with four beautiful tapers. Up they went onto the table to restore light to their supper.

Somewhere between the carrots and the apple cake, Hank told them about the homeless man and the big stack of money.

"I was walking around the city one day, like I do, and I had just come up the stairs of the 14th Street subway station to Union Square. I heard somebody just screaming their heads off. Then I realized it was a homeless man – really as filthy as any homeless guy I'd ever seen. He took this stack of something – money – out from under his coat and he threw it on the ground and just started jumping up and down on it screaming about how bad money is. I don't know if it was real or fake. Doesn't matter, I guess."

"What did you do then?" asked Anya.

"I took a picture with my cell phone when he wasn't looking and sent it to myself. I do that a lot when I'm wandering around on the weekends – text myself about what I see. I'll write it all down someday."

"Well, Dad and I are getting ready for Anime Boston," Anya said. Otto always chaperoned this huge comic art convention for the school and ended up spending Easter weekend in Boston every year with Anya and fifty-eight thousand of her closest friends. Anya always sewed costumes, and planned and schemed over months in advance. There was nothing that existed on the planet that did not fall under the category of art for Anya.

"Dad wants to go as the 'Crimson Chin' but we can't figure out how to make the chin we sculpted out of Styrofoam stay on his face."

Otto was such a good sport and he really did enjoy going down there, thankfully. Next year, David would go, too. Christina thought she would go visit Hank in the city that particular weekend.

I wonder if there's still such a thing as an Easter parade in Manhattan? she thought.

"Mama," David asked, "what did you do on your trip?"

"Went to a symposium on…", she sighed, "what amounts to terraforming, I suppose."

"What's that," he asked around a mouthful of apple cake. The golden retriever hovered under the table, always close to David, where crumbs and bits of food were more likely to find their way down to the dog area.

"I believe the strictest definition is changing – deliberately and deeply – very, very big parts of an entire planet's overall environment."

"Why would you want to do that?" Hank asked.

"I think the idea and the word came into being when we started to think seriously about changing other planets to become habitable." Otto answered.

"So, Mom," Anya laughed, "are you joining the space program?"

"No." Christina had to tell them something. "I am looking into the reality that there is overwhelming evidence that someone or some agency is terraforming the earth – right now – and has been for a while."

"What?" Hank put down his fork. "Why?"

"Well, there are lots of theories. I think soon, since so many people are asking the same question, they – whoever they is – will have to say something about the why. It will be very interesting to see who their spokesman turns out to be and I'm sure they will say they have to do it to save us from something. Let's take a look at the possibilities. What was the purpose of terraforming again?"

David spoke. "To make a planet okay for humans to live on."

"Fair enough," said Christina. "And the program includes modification of the land where we grow our food, the water we drink, and the air we breathe. If we adjusted things properly, maybe we could live on a planet hostile to life, like Mars. Or Venus. Right? Even if you agree that our planet somehow needs all of that changed – and that is a monumentally big if – there are a couple of things to think about. First of all, seems like what you'd want is to remove the things that hurt humans and other life forms, since we already have the things that promote a healthy life in abundance, yes?"

They all agreed.

"Well, the evidence proves that just the opposite is true. Many, many things that are deadly to humans and other life forms are actually being dumped into the environment... and I don't mean CO2, guys. I mean other far more deadly poisons."

She had not anticipated getting this far into the situation but they were there now and she had to try to figure out how much they deserved to know without scaring the hell out of them. Kids shouldn't have to make decisions about how they live based on fear. Otto had not tried to intervene.

"Second of all, everything else being equal, what is the one thing we have that Mars and Venus don't have? Think, guys."

"Us." David said firmly.

"Yes. Life. All kinds of life. We have a planet tailor-made for human beings and animals and plants. I have to wonder if it's possible to terraform a planet when there are billions of living things depending on what's already there and not affect the life forms pretty dramatically? I don't think it is. I thought it was the standard party line that the natural setup was a very delicate balance we had to try to avoid upsetting at all costs."

Silence settled in at the dining room table.

"It's a lot to think about," Otto said finally.

Christina found as time went by that the very few people she confided some of this in, well, a fairly high percentage of them just flat-out didn't believe her. Not necessarily about the intent behind her mother's death or even the lack of intent behind it. She trusted what her mother had told her almost a year ago. What they didn't believe was all of it, any of it. It took a while but eventually they let it slip somehow...

"Are you just saying that or is it really true?" Military involvement? Not our guys. Governments laying down blankets of poison? Well there has to be a good reason, surely." People literally thought she was just 'saying stuff.' When the realization came that people did not see what was right in front of them, even people who knew her well, she thoroughly understood some of the reasons the human race was in so much trouble. Granted, there were things – critical things – that were veiled, not completely known, enveloped in gray. She desperately hoped to help yank everything out into the light. Her job was to go forward with that and it didn't make a snowball's difference in hell who believed her... or didn't.

This is what she was doing and by God in heaven she would finish it. Thankfully, Otto believed in her absolutely. She couldn't begin to imagine what would happen around her when the book came out... if the book came out.

A few days after Hank went back to school, Christina called the prosecutor's office to try to arrange an appointment. She wanted to know if she herself had the right to access Walters' medical records. That was such a big, stupid, missing piece. The woman who answered the phone was the person Christina had spoken to before.

"Yes, how strange that you should call. I was just getting ready to call you! Walters' attorney was just here asking if you had ever received the medical records you've been looking for."

Christina lost her breath. What?

"No, actually, I haven't. No matter how many times I ask my attorney to get them, especially since we have a motion granted by a judge that gives us access, he ignores me or stalls or says it isn't worth our time looking at them... I guess he feels there's no money in it. I don't really care. I just want to know who was medically responsible for this guy when he ran over my mother. I think anyone would want to know that."

She did not add that another attorney had been profoundly interested in the information and then had just disappeared.

"This is crazy," she said. "Of course you would want to know that. Let me dig around and call you back, okay?"

The next day, the prosecutor's office called back and said they would get the records for her. She could come and look at them with the prosecutor at her convenience. It was the first break in the case for Christina and it had been such a long time coming. She would go as soon as possible. She would get distracted by something bigger.

Otto answered the phone. She could hear him talking in the kitchen.

"It's Bennie," he called.

"Good morning or whatever it is there," said Christina when she took the phone.

"Hello," that unmistakable Australian accent with an underlying Latin current. "Christina, have you seen the news? Are you aware what's happening in Japan?"

"No, we haven't. What's going on?"

"A monstrous earthquake, I'm afraid, followed by an even more monstrous tsunami."

"Oh, gosh," Christina said quietly.

"Well, the worst part is that a nuclear power plant with four reactors in failing... right on the sea."

"Good God," Christina replied.

"I know," Bennie said. "The radiation has to be accounted for. Those reactors are leaking. It will spread all around the planet, I think."

"Where is it headed?"

"Across the Pacific, I'm afraid... your direction." There was silence.

"I can't stand anymore, Bennie. I'm going to think about moving my children."

"Come to Australia!"

"Seriously... we are a big noisy bunch, you know," Christina laughed.

"The more the merrier," Bennie said. "Tell me, how is the book coming along? That's really why I called. I've been thinking a lot about it... and you."

"Just really getting my teeth into it."

"Keep me posted, alright?" They chatted a few more minutes, then said goodbye.

The morning of March 11th, there were special bulletins on every channel and internet site. An earthquake had pummeled Japan – almost a magnitude 9.0 in the Richter scale – followed by an unbelievably destructive tsunami. The entire family watched, Hank on the phone from New York, as news programs allowed the world to see the terrible power and finality of the unstoppable sea coursing over cities and farmland, deep inland. The video showed jumbo jets floating out to sea. It was a wrathful thing.

Then reports came in, just as Bennie had said, that one of Japan's nuclear power plants, a plant with four reactors, was in deep trouble due to either the tsunami or the earthquake or both. Christina felt like she was living through Armageddon. Eight months ago her mother had been run over and killed. She had spent the intervening time discovering what appeared to be a plan to poison the planet. Now the world, or at least the northern hemisphere for now, was in danger from vast amounts of leaking radiation. So many souls washed out to sea or killed by debris, the Pacific Ocean filled with airplanes and jet fuel and cars and houses. How could a year have added up like this?

Later news started to trickle out about the meltdown at the nuclear plant. Otto was more nervous about this event, which was immediate and critical, than the long painful slog since the accident.

"There will be radiation heading around the northern hemisphere from this, Christina," he said quietly.

"Otto," Christina said as they watched the water sweep so much of Japan's east coast into the sea, "we need to talk about moving the children to a safer place, if there is one anywhere anymore."

He said nothing but waited for her to speak.

"What about Australia?" she asked. "Bennie is there."

"We could plan a visit... a scouting expedition. It'll have to be at Christmas."

Meanwhile, Christina made an appointment to visit with the prosecutor in a few weeks' time. She continued to make notes on the timeline of her mother's work with the military for the book and allowed herself, at first tentatively and cautiously, to travel back within her memory of their own history to some happy moments and some exceptionally unhappy moments. In a separate notebook she wrote events as they happened now, in real time. Things had happened, yes, they were crucial but things were still happening. The story was unfolding before her. She didn't want to lose track of the now while she investigated the past. The morning she spoke to Bennie she began.

She set the wide-brimmed red straw hat atop short, iron-grey curls...

It was time to get it all down.

*****

After much deliberation, the countries participating in the formulation of the Shuri Treaty decided to go all the way back to the Nuremberg Code, which had been developed after World War II. The other document they were launching from was the Universal Declaration of Human Rights, again from just after World War II. They intended to add the best of every human rights treaty formulated since then because every concern, war, experimentation, withholding of basic life necessities, biological and chemical warfare, all of it boiled down to whether or not humans had a right to say no. The head of this endeavor felt the 21st century could not start with a better gesture. She also meant to bring enforceability into play. That was the key. That was the rub. They spent two years collecting data and evidence and debating in committee about what should be included and what penalties might occur to those who didn't comply. It was not apparent that there was anything big enough, something directly dangerous to everyone on the planet, some treachery that might just force global consensus.

The statement caught Christina's attention. She was listening to Charlie Shepard on the radio again, this time discussing something going on in Japan referred to as the *Shuri* Reconciliation.

"The very first sentence of the Nuremberg Code reads: The voluntary consent of the human subject is absolutely essential. What else really needs to be said?"

"So, Charlie, let's get this straight," the female host was saying, *"you feel that geo-engineering in the atmosphere amounts to human experimentation?"*

"Yes, I do. There are dozens of chemicals and biologics falling on the global population every day. What is known about people and these substances is very bad news for humans indeed. This phenomenon has to either fall under biological and chemical warfare or experimentation, or both. The test population is almost completely unaware and did not consent even as a group much less as individuals."

Christina wrote the man's name down, Charlie Shepard. This was someone she had to meet, another person in the trenches she needed to know. She picked up the phone and called the show but they were through taking callers. The fellow who answered their phone said contact information for Charlie Shepard would be noted on the show's web site. As soon as she hung up, she got Shepard's e-mail address off the web site and sent a note. Then she called Nikolai.

"What is this *Shuri* Reconciliation thing in Japan?" Christina asked. "Are you aware of it?"

"Oh, absolutely," Nikolai said. "It is going to be a treaty, really, a new one; the first global treaty attempt in this century. We have some really good experience now with failed treaties…human temptations and tendencies…what changes and what never seems to. It's been a project for a long time with international support from religious leaders and secular activists and the legal community. I think the turning point was getting sponsorship from a woman who was a Japanese princess, a member of the royal family, until she married. The head of the panel is a Buddhist leader and she is the former princess's spiritual advisor. I believe the Buddhist is a Swede. There are a handful of others from around the world."

"This is really an exciting possibility to bring our data and case to global attention, to people who have some way of raising the stuff going on in the sky to the level of war crimes. What do you think? How could we get their attention?" Christina asked.

"I read recently," Nikolai replied, "that there will soon be a period of calls for papers and input and such. In July, I think. That's the opportunity to try to get some attention."

The idea of putting together a team to go to Japan and present evidence on atmospheric geoengineering under their observation scared the hell out of Christina for so many reasons. It seemed like an enormous amount of data might have to be boiled down but there was a team in California unofficially working on this already. She needed to talk to Charlie Shepard. She wondered if he might want to participate. He was so accustomed to speaking about this already and he seemed to know the woman… her name was Choshin Soderholm… at least fairly well. Someone would have to have the guts to stand up in an international arena and be the face of the resistance. She was honestly hoping it wouldn't have to be her.

"This is Charlie," Charlie Shepard had sent Christina his phone number. The area code placed him just north of San Francisco. California again.

"Charlie, hi! This is Christina Galbraithe."

"Hello, Christina. I see you managed to find me. What can I do for you?"

"Charlie, I'm really involved in the movement to track down the source of toxic chemicals in the atmosphere and trying to figure out where they're coming from."

"Good. Always glad to know more and more people are paying attention."

"That would have been enough for me to call... I've heard several of your radio interviews on the subject. However, I heard you talk about the Shuri Reconciliation a few days ago and I really want to talk about that in conjunction with the toxic sky. That's my shorthand for it anyway."

"Toxic sky. Short and sweet and sums it up. That's the other half of the coin, Christina. What do we do about it? I'd be happy to talk about the Shuri document because I have a lot of hope for that effort. I have to walk out the door, though, right now. I'm flying to Boston for another interview."

"I live near Boston," Christina replied. "What if I meet you there and we can talk? I could buy lunch or dinner or...?"

"I'll tell you what. Come down to the studio and you can hang out while I give the interview. We can chat there. Sound good?"

"I can do that." After Charlie had given her the name and address of the studio, Christina hung up. He was scheduled to appear at two o'clock the next afternoon. The guards at the front desk would have her name.

That night she dreamt of her mother.

She was dressed for work, wearing an overcoat and nice flats. The setting could have been Virginia or England, either one; cloudy, rainy, a little cold and gloomy. Christina looked long and hard at the woman walking into the office building. At this time, she was perhaps in her mid-fifties. So hard to say now. She entered what was clearly her work space – at least in the dream – although there were cabinets and a sink along one wall. She sat at a long table rather than a desk, and pulled a yellow legal pad from her briefcase. She wrote the word 'Classified' across the top of the blank yellow paper, very clearly. She was writing a letter. As clear as the word classified appeared, Christina had a hard time reading the name of the recipient... Stavros... Stamos... .The 'S' was the only thing she could be sure of.

Christina then watched her mother pull out a bag of caramels,

Brach's Caramels, carefully and thoughtfully unwrap them, and eat them one by one as she wrote. She found that hard to understand since her mother had extensive bridgework and would never have eaten anything like that. It was going to get even stranger rather quickly as she took out a pack of cigarettes and lighted one. Her mother was a singer. She would never have smoked. Yet tobacco smoke curled around her head and filled the little room. Her mother sat at the table smoking, eating caramels and writing this classified letter on a yellow legal pad. The caramels and the cigarettes had to be a clue. Everything in the dream was a clue. What did they mean?

Dark green liquid began to flow across the table and then down to the floor. Soon it was flowing down the walls. Her mother scooped some up in her hands. Cupped in her hands the liquid had an oily sheen although what was running across the floor and down the walls looked thicker, the consistency of anti-freeze. Then it was coming out of the taps at the sink in the room. It seemed to be seeping into the entire building. Suddenly her mother was coughing, having difficulty breathing.

She looked at Christina and said, "I tried to stop it."

She had not dreamt of her mother until now nor did she know what to 'do' with the dream for the moment, other than hold it in her mind until something came along that helped her make sense of it.

Christina took the train to Boston at six the next morning. She then boarded the subway to Copley Square and walked a mile to the radio station where Charlie was being interviewed. As promised, the guard in the lobby had her name on his list and she was allowed to ascend to the studio on the tenth floor. It was a small radio station, alive for a mere three hours each day, with interviews from activists across the country. Sometimes they were phone interviews, sometimes guests travelled in. Charlie saw her through the small window in the door, pushed it open and let her in.

"Good morning, Christina!" he said warmly. "Did you have a good trip down?"

"I did, thank you." She stuck her hand out to the other man in the room and shook it. He was conducting the interview.

"Hi, I'm Cliff," he said. "Have a seat."

"How was your trip, Charlie?" Christina asked. She was a bit nervous, hoping to fade into the background when the interview began.

"Okay, I guess for a commercial flight."

"Do you usually travel some other way?"

"I used to fly myself. I'm a pilot. When I started going public with this stuff, that became dangerous. Light aircraft are far too easy to sabotage and it happens all the time. So I generally fly the biggest airline carrier I can find, say a prayer, and hope for the best."

People involved in this could talk very casually about their lives being in danger.

"About ready, Charlie," Cliff said.

Charlie sat, donned a pair of headphones and motioned for Christina to sit on a stool across from him. The host of the show introduced Charlie and gave some of his credits, including all the research work he had done relative to geo-engineering in the last decade and thanked him for his outspoken campaign to educate the public.

"Today I don't want to just talk about what we already know is going on in the sky... literally millions of people around the world are talking about it and documenting it, calling and writing politicians and even bringing lawsuits. Suffolk County on Long Island is in the midst of a tenacious battle to get the air over their heads clean. We can all do this, of course, and many communities are bringing these suits since it's against the law to pollute the sky without the consent of the citizenry. That stuff is really important. Take your well-being and the well-being of your children into your own hands. One thing I want to talk about between now and July... which is about three months from now... is the convocation, because that's what it really is, of concerned citizens from around the world working on the first international treaty of the 21st century. They call it the *Shuri* Reconciliation. And, you know, Cliff, I know the woman who is spearheading this movement pretty well. Her name is Choshin Soderholm."

"Choshin," Cliff chimed in, "that's an unusual name."

"Yes, it's Buddhist. I'm not an expert but I believe they are given these names when they take on a spiritual mantle within their Buddhist community. It would be fantastic to get a chance to ask her these questions directly on the show at some point. Anyway, the Soderholm is Swedish because Choshin is a Swede. She grew up in Stockholm and immigrated to the U.S. in about 1970. And there are a few others from around the world, a priest, a civil rights attorney and war crimes judge, a teacher from Argentina, doctors from Japan and Botswana... they've been working on hammering out a human rights treaty for a few years. They were able to connect with the Japanese government and arrange for their sponsorship because one of those doctors used to be a member of the imperial family of Japan."

"Really," Cliff replied. "Interesting. So that was a great connection to people who might be able to arrange this movement or treaty in such a way that it got international attention and recognition? The thing about a conference like this, though, is it almost makes me feel as if we've covered this ground to death. What's hopeful about this new treaty?"

"Good question, Cliff. I believe what we have going for us in the 21st century is exactly that. We don't have to waste any more time on deciding what a human right is. We just did that for a hundred years – at least. Then we tested all our suppositions through all the means that bring the question of human rights to the surface; war, invasion, totalitarianism, fascism, famine, disease, empire building, scientific testing for its own sake. Questions of individual sovereignty have been hashed out. Discussion revolving around children and those unable to protect themselves, help themselves or even speak for themselves raged through the last century. We've done this work, the list is exhaustive. Whether there are entities out there who give a damn about these things or just see them as speed bumps in their path is neither here nor there in the sense that the work has been done. The sort of self-imposed mission of the *Shuri* panel has been to take those definitions and the international treaties that were forged in the 20th century and reconcile those absolutes with 21st century crimes against humanity."

"I know you've said the panel is sort of opening up the discussion to the world public this coming July. Where is that taking place, Charlie?"

"At the site the treaty is being named after, *Shuri* Castle on the island of Okinawa. Everyone on the panel has been in residence near there for two years. The government has kindly given them permission to hold this world conference there for two weeks in July. I intend to be there."

Christina sat spellbound. She knew the audio recording of this interview would be available online so she wasn't taking notes but she also knew that first and foremost she had to be part of this movement. Second, this meeting in July would become part of the book, part of her mother's story. It had to. In one year's time, Christina would have been led down a path that started in a crosswalk in a seaside village in northern New England to a medieval Japanese castle on the island of Okinawa. That was one hell of a trip.

The Sun Thief

Georg Pearle Nero planted himself on the marbled terrace behind the mammoth main building of Chateau de Geier and surveyed the meticulously sculptured and manicured grounds that ceased abruptly but unmistakably at the knife-edge of a very large private game reserve. This was a mandatory stop for Nero en route to his own estate on Lake Maggiore in Italy. There were things that were to be spoken of in person. Every mode of communication around them was stringently and obsessively secured for privacy. They were never worried that their conversations were recorded or marked down in any way but it was a matter of custom to decide some things face-to-face.

There were so few intimates in their circle.

The quick issue today was that of Committee member Rear Admiral Alexander Getz. They had known almost from the beginning, of course, that Getz was playing both sides. As long as he proved useful, that was neither here nor there. Everybody they knew played every angle. It was, in their minds, the only intelligent course of action. Getz had negotiated and secured countless profitable contracts between the Committee and the United States over the years.

De Geier wrote the checks that funded the Pentagon because the U.S. was flat broke. His family had written many large checks to underwrite the United States government since the Great Depression; the depression of the 20th century at any rate. It appeared that another was just over the horizon and with luck it would encompass the globe. At least one of their militarized programs, one of the most important, was on the verge of moving into a mass testing phase and it was imperative that it do so. Getz would, they knew, never allow this to happen. He had reached the end, the line was drawn. He would try to stop them. This asset must be retired. Because the topic was this particular program, however, and now the Committee called for permanently retiring an instrument one step removed from the Joint Chiefs, dispensation had to be obtained. Nero went to Lord de Geier who proceeded up a very, very short chain to a committee of two. 'Dispensation' would require one brief telephone call but that was a telephone number Nero would never have.

"Nero, my friend," a voice called out from the house and Carroll de Geier emerged, tan, white hair windblown. "To what do I owe this extreme pleasure?"

He glided forward and the men clasped hands without affection. "Good afternoon, Carroll," Nero replied. "Good to see you, of course."

"Sit?" de Geier motioned to a sofa on the far end of the terrace.

They made their way there and sat, as far apart as they could manage without creating an obvious space; each man turned toward the other and observed, striking an air of alert casualness. For Nero the casual tone was a charade. No one was casual around this man. Nero became aggravated when he realized he was either going to have to sit with his back to the door or not look at his conversation partner. Having his back to the door was far less dangerous than insulting Lord Carroll de Geier.

"Now," said de Geier, "we can chat. Would you care for something?"

"Thank you, no. Not just now."

"Very well. In which direction are you traveling?" "Milan."

"Lovely," de Geier was done with the pleasantries. "What is on your mind, Nero?"

"Getz." "Oh, yes?"

"That instrument has outlived its usefulness" "I see."

"You will confirm for me?" "Depend on it." De Geier smiled.

And that was the end of Alex Getz. Nero stood, as he was needed in Milan, and took his leave. De Geier had no interest at all in knowing anything more about Getz. There were forces within the Pentagon that could retire him and there were resources within Sceptre that handled this sort of thing. It mattered not at all how it happened. Getz was a thing, to be used then discarded. De Geier's son, Rupert, passed Nero in the foyer.

"Have you seen father?"

"Yes, Rupert... on the veranda." Nero slipped through the front door to a waiting Rolls.

It was disconcerting that Rupert de Geier had not exchanged

pleasantries with him today. He knew that Rupert and his brother, Solomon, were disgusted with the in-fighting between himself and Cordham. The tussle, the revelations, the legalities were all providing an unnecessary glimpse into everyone's lives. Nero's driver had not even stopped the engine, condensation billowed from the tailpipe.

The sound of gravel sliding recklessly under car wheels came to Rupert as he turned and went to locate his father. Rupert stepped out into the sunshine of the English countryside. His father still sat on the chaise, now with a large gin. His father was certainly no idiot and, obviously, Rupert had to broach the subject of Nero. To the Families, people like Nero and Cordham were nothing more than human resources. As far as Rupert was concerned, they weren't even that. Those two were merely Rottweilers at their respective gates. One Rottweiler guarded the gate marked "Food." The other guarded the gate marked "Information." The Family plan for the 21st century could be reduced to three imperatives: control food, control information, develop the means to punish with violence. Elementary. Guaranteed to completely secure any outstanding human assets. The Rottweilers were not Family; they were not one of the other Families. Perhaps they should be set on each other to tear each other apart. One savage might emerge triumphant or they might just tear each other to shreds. Either way it would be a fine spectacle and settle a problem. Perhaps, in fact, it had been arranged just like that. He would never know. Even his father might not be privy to that particular information.

Most of the time, the de Geier's lived in Mayfair in the City of London. However, life at Mayfair was supremely ordered and rigid, almost fascist in its merciless rules. Rupert's grandfather had seen to that. Dozens of servants helped the Family rise and dress and valets outlined the day's duties. His father's valet was also his personal secretary and a highly skilled bodyguard who commanded a salary in the millions of pounds. When the Family became weary or needed to regroup, they came out here to Chateau de Geier where things were a bit less structured albeit still quite formal. After three centuries of living just this way, they hardly knew any other way to behave. That is why so many of the young ones took to drinking and partying as heavily as they could for as long as they could... usually just after leaving their ancestral university of the *Institut d'Études Politiques de*

Paris. It was the only way any of them could put aside who they were and what was expected of them for a moment before the door to the cage swung shut behind them forever. In fact, Rupert's older brother, Sebastian had hung himself the day before he was supposed to start working for their father, take over the Lisbon office. Weakness. It was better to get rid of that genetic stock. He had only his younger brother, Solomon, to deal with now. Solomon had done the partying bit for six gloriously debauched years. The whole world expected Rupert to take over for his father and for Solomon to die in a fiery crash of some sort. Then all of a sudden he stopped... like he had turned off a switch. He was a devastating business competitor for others and for Rupert. Solomon was brilliant. Solomon would have to be dealt with.

"Father." Rupert used the word as a greeting.

"Rupert," Carroll replied.

Rupert sat on the sofa in the same spot Nero had vacated a few minutes earlier.

"That one really brings to mind this mess he's made with Cordham. I'm seeing our name... your face... on the nightly news in Britain, for God's sake. Those two have brought so much attention to themselves. The so-called alternative news is digging relentlessly. Trying to catch that thread is like chasing a firefly. God-damned internet. Nero and Cordham make me wonder if we've opened a hole just out of reach in the dyke. We really must get our grip back on the press."

Lord de Geier stared into his empty crystal tumbler.

"Perhaps. One of those idiots is going to win their little squabble and the masses will periodically raise their heads and look around them. If for some reason they muster the energy to form themselves into something annoying, then they will simply have to learn. It has always been so, Rupert. This fight over the food bowl in the kennel changes nothing."

"Hmmm," Rupert replied, gazing off at the forest's edge. "There are so goddamned many of them."

"For the moment. Our whip is perception. We invest in perception, nothing else, although the perception of wealth or poverty is a great driver. We decide what has value and the whole world accommodates itself, like water to a vase. If I said horse shit was the new currency, then inside a week, people would be scrambling to buy as much horse shit as they could get their hands on. So in a small way, yes, I agree that the public brawl between Nero and Cordham is draining our perception account slightly. However, the public are so used to being molded in this way that the remediation will be easy, a relief to them," Lord de Geier said. "Even now, they look to us to tell them what to think about it. The herds don't like to have to work things out. It makes them supremely uncomfortable."

Three centuries prior, Chateau de Geier had been a simple hunting lodge. Queen Anne had been on the throne and had ceded the territory to the very first Lord de Geier as a reward for his loyalty. After seventeen pregnancies the unattractive Anne had yet to produce a child who lived past the age of eleven and was always within a hair's breadth of being deposed. She also developed a rather disgusting gout, according to the first Lord de Geier's written recollections, was grossly overweight and difficult to look at. The de Geiers had remained loyal nevertheless and Anne had knighted the first de Geier. At any rate, the de Geiers all preferred to be here except Solomon who preferred to be in every business capitol on the globe, preferably all at once. The rumors as to his whereabouts were endless. He wanted it that way. It made him seem omnipotent.

There was an oil portrait of the boys, just about half life-sized, that hung in the foyer of their mother's suite. They all carried the gene that resulted in red hair, their faces were pale and a bit freckled. The flame red would fade to a dim memory soon enough when all the color fled early on and the hair turned white. It had done so with their father. Eldest Sebastian sat on a brilliantly brocaded Louis XIV chaise, lanky legs crossed casually, easy posture belying his intense unease with his lot in life. Those who were dissatisfied at this level had few options, especially the eldest male, who was expected to slaughter every other comer and take his place at the top of the pyramid.

Every once in a while the most anemic hint of conscience would leak into the gene pool. It was a horrifying accident when it surfaced, a decent impulse looking for air, looking for sunlight. It was their very definition of insanity kept locked in an upstairs attic, but it usually took care of itself as it had in the case of Sebastian. No one knew if he had designs on some other life or career. He probably had not known himself, had not allowed himself to think there might be another side to this ancestral coin. He would only have known to the depths of his soul his choicelessness. His father had played a round of golf just after hearing of Sebastian's death.

Middle son Rupert sat next to Sebastian on the same chaise. He was a bit livelier in features, had his mother's mouth and cheekbones. It was always a motivator for the younger males to chase the elder. Unlike, for example, within the context of a royal family, any male could best the others and take the whole empire for himself. Rupert found that possibility, even probability, to be intoxicating. He was driven mad by it. Empathy and conscience were not burdens anyone in the Family carried, especially Rupert. The ability to objectify had been bred into this line like some sort of indestructible rapier blade. It was no longer an ability, in fact, because 'abilities' can be used or not, as the bearer decides. It was now fixed, like a form of sociopathy. Tell a de Geier to pick a coin up off a table without using their hands, one would have more luck.

Standing behind them both, at the time the portrait was commissioned only sixteen years old, was Solomon de Geier. He was a full four years younger than Rupert and seven years younger than Sebastian. His concerns were tennis, ponies, university and girls. He was no threat to anyone except himself.

The sons were very young and Carroll de Geier was very old, forty-eight years between himself and Sebastian. That was absolutely intentional. By the time the young bucks sorted themselves and each other out, de Geier would probably be dead. It was certainly possible that whoever emerged triumphant would try to take the Old Stag down before then but he did not think it would turn out that way. Setting his sons upon each other freed him to look after the empire they were sparring over. Generally speaking, all the offspring of the Families were fiercely protective of their rights of precedence but they had been trained to finagle concessions for themselves at every turn. It was an inevitable consequence of a terrifically small gene pool. Periodically the father had to slap one of them back down. When they were old enough, he let them do it to each other.

The next evening was Lord Carroll de Geier's eighty-second birthday. His wife, Elspeth, would be there. Social functions were her primary task. Of late, likely due to his advancing years, de Geier had begun to treat his wife more like a human and less like a piece of the furniture. She was quite accustomed to that environment, as she came from one of the other Families... the Sylver-Jones Family. Lady Elspeth de Geier was also considerably younger than her husband, not yet sixty. She maintained a permanent and exclusive staff to cater parties such as this one, all thoroughly vetted and handsomely paid, all having signed confidentiality agreements, all living under open threats of death. Lady de Geier had no grandchildren yet. That was becoming a deficiency. Rupert was thirty-four and if he, like his father, waited another fourteen years to start a family that would be very boring indeed. Elspeth thought, though, that Solomon was going to take Rupert. She looked forward to that. She despised Rupert. She despised all of them really, wished she had borne a daughter or two. The priorities were completely different with girls.

Yes, there would be a party the next night. All of the important Family players would be there – some of the most ruthless men in the world and their immediate families – including Solomon de Geier who was due to arrive for the weekend. The catering team of fifty would soon start preparations for a gathering of only about twenty-five people and would be long gone before the guests arrived. Ordinarily, the Families preferred to convene on the back lawn but it was December and a bit too cool at the moment. Dinner would be served in the Great Hall. The Great Hall was mirrored on all sides such that anyone caught with their back momentarily turned could see who was behind them. The dining arrangement was a great horseshoe table at which all diners faced the entryway. This elite cadre interacted with the household staff and occasionally Lady Elspeth but that was it. They caught glimpses of the rest of the Family at times. They would not have any idea who else attended any function at the estate. No connections or patterns could be derived from the information these employees gained over time.

Solomon arrived at the estate at eight-thirty in the evening. He was not alone. There was a woman with him, a woman from outside the established Family gene pool, as he had chosen to add some fresh genetic stock to a line he considered to be all but enfeebled due to in-breeding. She was Lady Helen Lippincott, a tall leggy brunette a good two inches taller than he. She was a Scot. Solomon intended to marry her and he intended to make the announcement, completely unexpectedly, tonight at his father's party. He was not asking anyone's leave to do this thing. He was just doing it.

Solomon had spent the last three years traveling, working and studying Family interests and history and, based on the brutal fact that most of the world's currencies were either tanking or about to, he was by God going to make his move. The same breeding which has forced a kind of sociopathic emotional structure upon this circle of tyrants had, by association, also created a baseline arrogance that, in his opinion, was now a pathology and might just end the Family's hold on the world.

They were met at the door by a butler, who, if he was shocked to see a stranger enter with Solomon did not display it in the slightest. He took Lady Helen's wrap and Solomon's great coat and handed them to a second servant. Solomon had a folded newspaper tucked under an arm, which he declined to relinquish. The butler led the pair toward the large opening in the Great Hall. There were half a dozen steps up onto the large floor of the Hall. This was not a customary arrangement but they felt it was an advantage to be up rather than down relative to whomever might be entering the room. There were two doors leading out of the Great Hall and into the bowels of the house on each wall as a safety precaution. Solomon took Helen's arm and led her up the stairs behind the butler, who stopped and announced them. The room became suddenly and deathly still. Five seconds later, Lady Elspeth swung into socialite mode, refusing to allow the situation to deteriorate in the moment. She breezed across the floor, long skirt catching the breeze as she walked, making her seem more like a thing on the air than a matriarch. She extended her hand to Lady Helen first.

"Oh, my!" she exclaimed softly. "Solomon has brought us a wonderful surprise. Welcome, my dear. Do come in."

"Lady Elspeth de Geier," Solomon stopped, "meet Lady Helen Lippincott."

She turned to her son and kissed his cheek, stopping for the merest second to fix his eyes with hers. He knew he had broken one of the cardinal rules of the Families. He had brought a stranger into a group gathering without permission. Lady Helen did not seem to have any idea what had just happened.

"Let's all be seated, shall we… now Solomon and his friend have arrived?" Carroll de Geier tried to gain control of the situation. Lord Sylver-Jones was clearly ready to strangle Solomon. It was not possible to meet his gaze at the moment; it was so filled with violence. It was a bit early to dine but everyone in the room, save Lady Helen, understood two things: face must be saved and the evening must be gone through and end as soon as possible so that Solomon's unbelievable violation could be dealt with.

As for himself, Rupert de Geier was delighted. What an end this would be to his only rival: what a brilliant act of self-immolation this was. Rupert no longer had to worry about Solomon. Solomon might not actually live through this, although deactivating an immediate Family member was exceptionally rare. It had only happened twice in three centuries and no one was exactly sure who had done what in either instance.

As soon as all the guests were seated and wine was poured, Solomon, who had placed the folded newspaper by his side upon the white linen, stood and spoke.

"Friends and Family," he said distinctly, "can I ask for a moment's attention?"

The Lords de Geier and Sylvester-Jones were immediately and dangerously fixed on Solomon where he stood. He looked down, beaming at the poor, clueless woman at his side.

"I have to take advantage of this moment – since we are all so rarely gathered together like this. And I beg my father's pardon for stealing a bit of birthday thunder but hopefully when he becomes aware of the reason, all will be forgiven," Solomon went on. "I'd just like to say simply that the exquisite Lady Helen and I are officially betrothed. I have asked and she has agreed. I am the luckiest man in the world tonight."

There were a few, inescapable sharp gasps around the table. Carroll de Geier threw down his napkin. Lady Helen looked a bit surprised as if this reaction was something of a shock. Engagements were happy news. They certainly didn't know her enough to dislike her; they didn't know her at all. She looked back up at Solomon, alarmed. Solomon continued, unperturbed. If anything he was enlivened by the reaction – any reaction from this crowd was almost impossible to elicit. They had been too well trained in facades. He snapped open the newspaper he had brought to the table. It was *The*

Evening Coronet, the single most read daily newspaper in all of England, even if it was acknowledged by all as a rag. There, on the front page, was a full-page color photograph of Solomon and Helen and a caption reading Solomon de Geier to marry Scotswoman! It was all over England already. Again, Rupert de Geier felt vindicated, although he was absolutely furious about this particular ploy. The press was slipping from their control in some very key ways. The Coronet was owned by none other than Richard Cordham, the publishing magnate currently feuding with Nero Pearle. Cordham was a dead man.

The evening spun itself out, eventually ending with a magnificent birthday cake being wheeled in for Lord de Geier. It was a gesture more than anything as only the children ate cake and there weren't that many of them in attendance. De Geier had no grandchildren yet, but there were small ones among the Sylver-Jones clan. Lord de Geier cut the cake to enthusiastic applause, his wife by his side. Rupert stood on one side of the hall, Solomon and Lady Helen stood on the other. The other attendees exchanged cursory pleasantries with Solomon but for the most part stayed well away. No one wanted to be mistaken as having been part of this. Eventually, Lady Elspeth brought two slices of the cake herself, waved off the servants, to Solomon and his new fiancée. Helen took hers, despite the fact that she would never have eaten it under other circumstances.

Elspeth smiled broadly, "Solomon, now perhaps I'll have the grandchild I'm longing for. That would make me so happy."

"Maybe you will, mother," answered Solomon. Provided nothing completely unacceptable could be discovered about this girl and her family, his mother could be persuaded and she had just communicated how and why. Lady Helen laughed softly. She was only twenty years old. She did not understand yet that everything she wanted could well hinge on just how fast she could become pregnant.

In the end, the night got itself finished and Solomon sent Helen up to their rooms without him. He knew his father would want to speak to him and he was anxious to speak to his father. He was exhilarated rather than fearful. De Geier men always won and so fear wasn't really something they had to contend with. There was really nothing to lose and everything to gain. Rupert passed by Solomon and Lord de Geier, leaving the Great Hall.

He slapped Solomon on the shoulder and laughed outright.

"My God," he snorted, "really. Great to see you. Really." He continued to laugh loudly as he climbed the stairs. He honestly could not imagine what the scene between Solomon and his father would be like.

The Great Hall was cleared. Carroll de Geier walked with measured steps to the large door on each side of the massive entrance and half-swung, half-pushed them shut, one after the other. He was slow and deliberate, allowing his rage to build yet containing and focusing it on this whelp, his youngest son, who had dared what almost none had ever dared before. It was critical at this point to win, even if it were by the slimmest of margins. Solomon waited. He allowed the old man to approach knowing full well what would likely happen. Carroll was not his prime target. He knew he could bulldoze that playing field in short order and he needed his father to save face, to believe he was still running the family. Solomon intended to paint with bold strokes and, if they were discovered and the blame could be fixed, someone would hang. Until such time as his father died, his father made a very convenient and deserving scapegoat. Carroll landed a stinging slap on Solomon's face, a brutal slap really, his father's ring cutting his lip badly. His head whipped to the side, right brow hitting the mirrored wall behind him, opening another jagged gash in his face. Blood poured from both wounds. Solomon strangled the fury rising in his throat and choked it back down. Strangely, Carroll had not expected retaliation. That would have been bad form indeed, a loss of emotion indicating deep weakness in his son. He knew that would not happen. Almost certainly, Solomon would simply stand there and within moments, despite his obvious injuries, cold calm would overtake him. That was the only possible reaction.

Carroll stood before his son, the one who had performed this ridiculously reckless stunt, and, straightening his cuffs, began. He was in no way prepared for this conversation.

"Explain yourself immediately," he snarled quietly.

"You're not an imbecile, father," Solomon replied through broken lips, "… yet. What do you think such a thing means?"

"That you have lost your mind."

"I've spent three years in every major office we have worldwide, old man. You are weak…impotent… lazy… and our house will fall if someone does not decide to once again wield the sword."

A direct challenge. Truthfully, Carroll had not expected it. He was too old, too close to the grave. He did not reply or demonstrate any emotion. He let the challenge play out. Often strategies were gained in this way, lifted from another man's audacity.

"I'll marry whom I please, Father, and bring some new blood into this sickly family line," Solomon continued. "It's really that simple. I could have eloped, of course, but I want a very public and extravagant celebration of my willfulness… my ascendancy. I want everyone to see that I am the heir apparent. "

"Why do you think I cannot stop this, Solomon?"

"You will need to save face, for one. You will also not want to lose a part of your business that you've spent decades building… although for the life of me I can't see what is so intriguing about it. We have atmospheric technology so powerful we can clean the planet of all its vermin and own the whole thing. All ours. They're all parasites anyway and it's just time but no one has the stomach for it. Instead, you mess about with these stupid insurance scams and the genetic modification of foods and all of that. What is the purpose of the façade at this point? My God how boring. Why not just eliminate two-thirds of the population through some enhanced epidemic and be done with it, you stupid, stupid man?"

Finally, Carroll was taken aback. Solomon was going to turn him over to hang for the family business.

"At any rate, I can sell you to the highest bidder along with Nero Pearle and the insurance scams, created droughts and famines, foods that are so altered our bodies practically turn themselves inside out to get rid of the stuff… and I will. Let us not forget, Father," Solomon snarled, "you and your partners have overplayed your hand; you've panicked, run too fast. The currency is worthless in every country on the planet. Gold reserves are utterly beyond our reach now. Have you seen the eastern bloc countries use their currency for firewood? It's the Age of the Pirate again. I will build enough infrastructure to hit the restart button and clean this goddamned planet up once and for all."

"Clearly you don't know everything." Carroll retorted. "Solomon, we have enemies. They are powerful and they are spread across the globe and there is more than a good chance they would exterminate the few of us long before whatever we could initiate to be rid of them was finished."

"Oh, for God's sake. I understand that. I simply do not believe it after fifty or sixty years of putting the infrastructure to eliminate most of them into place. And think about it! Does it even matter at this point? The dice have to be rolled and they have to be rolled now."

Rupert James de Geier could not remember a happier, more satisfied moment... not even when they had found Sebastian's lifeless body. Sebastian had never been a threat. The Sylver-Jones contingent had gone quickly, without ceremony, understanding there was blood on the floor and it had to be wiped up. It had to be handled completely so no one ever thought of trying such a thing again.

Rupert had seen the last of them through the front door and turned for the grand staircase. His suite lay up the left side and down an endless hall. He passed his mother suites along the way, rapped on the door, pushed it open curtly. She sat on a sofa before a blazing fire cradling a champagne. It was their House Label, shipped from France. She looked up at him, eyes dull despite the events of the evening. She hated him and he knew it. He did not bother to say goodnight. Nothing could dampen the effect of the evening for him. His father would take care of Solomon and, if he lived through it, his younger brother would never regain anyone's trust. How he hoped Solomon had to live the balance of his life watching Rupert lead this empire. Solomon, his children and his children's children would become untouchables. Rupert would see to that.

In his rooms, in a very secure safe, he kept a recent purchase, worth one million pounds. It was a bottle of *Henri IV Cognac Dudognon Heritage*, mixed by the descendants of Henry IV since 1776; each batch aged in a barrel for a century. He pulled the bottle out carefully. It was dipped in twenty-four carat gold, the bottle covered with sixty-five hundred diamonds. The barrel it had been decanted from was filled with this liquid in 1899. The vessel appeared to be filled with light and tonight was exactly the right night to release its contents. He had been saving it for the moment he destroyed his younger brother and the moment was here. He had not had to lift a finger. His valet rapped lightly on the door and entered with a tray on which sat a large warmed brandy snifter. Rupert opened the bottle and poured a precious ounce into the snifter. The valet withdrew to the bathroom and turned the water on in a cavernous sunken tub. His bath was hand carved from Swedish green marble, one of the hardest and most beautifully veined stones on earth.

Rupert sipped from the warmed vessel, felt the wonderfully delicate smoke on his tongue followed by an indescribably tender burn teasing his soft palate and then throat. He set the glass down with regret and began to undress. Likely he would not sleep tonight, he was too excited, too exhilarated. However, he wanted a bath. He wanted more of this cognac. He wanted blood. They lived in such bloodless times, it was a shame. Bloodletting amounted to moving a chess piece and then noting the casualties on a spreadsheet. The first Lord de Geier had drawn his opponent's life force regularly and eagerly; far more interesting than trying to suck the vital economic life force out of a person or a company or a nation. That took time. The cognac warmed his body, inflamed a need to conquer, to win. He had triumphed tonight, no matter what happened.

Beside the tub, he dropped his robe and stepped into the water. Three steps led down to a bench along the back wall of the pool. He lay an arm on each side of the marble behind his head, allowing his head to fall back, looking at the chandelier above him. Mist drifted lightly down on him from an arrangement in the ceiling. Half a minute later, he realized he could not lift his head back up, could not move his arms, could not even blink. He had wanted his cognac, thought to reach for it, and realized he could not. He appeared to be paralyzed. His respiration appeared to be slowing. He had been drugged, poisoned, a paralytic… conscious but unable to move, muscles shutting down as the elementary synapses right at the muscles were blocked. It was probably curare, a drug that smacked of ancient squabbles and dusty historical assassinations and blood feuds. No question that the cognac had been pristine, unopened from the time it had been originally sealed a decade ago. The glass? The bath water? The mist? Inwardly he was panicking. His mind raced. It was not his valet's habit to return after drawing the bath. There were panic buttons everywhere, even voice activated systems, but he could do nothing. Terror was a thing of the mind not the limbs and it filled every part of his being. He could feel, he just couldn't move.

He heard a soft padding behind him, someone walking on the thick rug toward the bath. He was desperate to speak, unable to. Hands appeared over his head in the mist, holding each side of a large silver ice bucket. There was a sound from inside, a sloshing, perhaps? The hands told him nothing. He could not see the face, the arms, the clothing. The bucket was being tipped slowly and carefully over, the contents started to spill, just a bit... then more... then water began to pour in a slim, steady stream from the container. His panic was excruciating as it had no place to play itself out. Small cylindrical, torpedo-shaped objects fell haphazardly into the tub around him making small splashes. There could have been a hundred of the creatures, white, four or five inches in length, no other distinct markings that he saw as they tumbled into the water before him. Then the hands and the bucket simply went away, withdrew as if they had not been, the door closing softly a moment later behind him.

His attention was torn back to the bath water, now boiling around him. The torpedo-like fish attached themselves to his skin with teeth and span and rolled, effectively ripping away chunks of flesh and muscle and drilling holes into his body cavity. He could not cry out in pain. The holes got deeper and deeper until he could actually feel a fish grab something in his belly and spin. The pain was indescribable. Most of the fish had found their way inside within a minute or so. His respiratory system shut down, then and there, and he lost consciousness. The water his body lay in turned red in a matter of seconds, he was being eaten that fast, from the inside out. This was the little Amazonian catfish, one of the *candiru*, which drilled into a body and ate all soft tissue, leaving only the skin and bones. Anyone looking casually at a corpse killed in this fashion might literally assume the holes in the body were bullet holes, they were that clean, unless there happened to be a multitude of them.

The mist was heavy in the woods the next morning. Giant oaks covered with hoar frost lined the edge of the lawn and guarded the entrance to the forest. Lord and Lady de Geier stood there, just this side of the wildness with half a dozen servants. There were footprints and tracks in the frost.

Someone had rung the house before dawn, an event followed very shortly by a knocking on the door by half a dozen local police. They were, they said, preparing to walk across the grounds down to the edge of the wood. It seemed a local fellow walking his dogs had come across a body. It seemed the body was almost certainly Rupert de Geier. He was unclothed. He lay just inside the woods, covered by a thin layer of frost, filled with surgically-clean holes the size of large bullets. There was no blood on the ground or the body. The coroner's office was on the scene very quickly. When they lifted the body onto a stretcher, it was apparent there was nothing inside. Bones and skin; that was all that was left. All soft tissue had disappeared; he had been scraped clean. Lady de Geier, wrapped in a long coat over her night things, a shawl around her head, looked down upon the corpse of her middle son and felt nothing. She caught the eye of the fellow leading the investigation briefly, revealed nothing, then turned and walked slowly back to the house through the hoar frost.

*****

Tuesday, December 24th. The Beltway, Washington D.C. Alex Getz had a meeting with the Secretary of the Army. Then he was having lunch with Lieutenant General Toby Morrow. Morrow was attached to the Air Force and firmly entrenched within the command structure that was actually able to give orders, which meant if you climbed his ladder in short order you would bump up against the Secretary of Defense and then the President. Toby Morrow had access, up, down and across – laterally and on the down through the troops. Morrow was convinced that the open conduit 'down' was every bit as important, maybe more important, that access up. Getz agreed with him.

The only person who understood the Military Industrial Congressional Complex better than Morrow was Getz, who had a slight advantage on Congressional 'ins' due in great part to his time at the Naval Academy. Morrow had worked for decades within the context of the Planning, Programming and Budgeting System, the hopelessly tangled mess that provided 'justification' for defense spending and lots of places to hide for those whose entire reason for living seemed to be to get fat, pork-laden defense contracts for corrupt technology firms. He was a deep-cover disciple of a group of retired military giants, men of sound conscience, experience and brilliance, who were attempting to identify, define and release to the public, practical evidence of the insane labyrinth that was the 21st century Pentagon and the psychopaths running it. There were many such as Toby Morrow within the labyrinth, doing an excellent job of working the system for the bad guys while building a launch pad for the good guys. These Getz referred to as the White Hats and they were biding their time. Between the two of them, no one was out of reach. Toby Morrow also happened to be Getz's handler.

The toothless Joint Chiefs; fangs pulled long ago in terms of command no matter how powerful their titles made them sound. One didn't need powerful canines to do business. They were deeply involved in defense contracting so in terms of sheer pork barrel politics, they were still mighty. Getz had immediate access to all of them and they each had hands deep in several pies. After the meeting with Hap LeBlanc, Getz and Morrow were headed to Hell Point in Annapolis for some crab cakes. They knew they were being followed, watched and recorded. They gave orders all the time for others to come under just such surveillance. In order to meet more often without arousing suspicion they had cultivated a decade-long history of traveling the Washington DC and Chesapeake Bay area in search of the perfect crab cake. They managed to meet once a month, sometimes more. Since both handled some of the same defense contracting entities, this sort of discussion was to be expected and constituted the lion's share of doing business within their group. Morrow was army, Getz was navy – it made sense that they would put their heads together on many contract points. They were old friends, as well.

Before he could meet with Toby Morrow, Getz had to deal with LeBlanc. 'Hap' LeBlanc was Secretary of the Army and had been for eight years. He was a civilian, in fact, who cultivated a wartime nickname with a backstory – one he loved to trot out – that was ninety percent fiction. His offices were in the Pentagon. A caricature of a civil service career man, the worst kept secret in the Pentagon was that Hap LeBlanc had his eye on the Presidency. The best shot he had at that job was to make a run for it during war-time. Perpetuating an atmosphere of red alert and immediate threat was job one for LeBlanc.

Getz had the highest acknowledged security clearance possible and so drove his car past the MPs at the guard gate with a fairly cursory check-in and parked. The topic today would be Co-Operations and Strategic/Tactics (COAST). Getz' specialty over the last decade was countering cyber-terrorism which meant he was a genius at understanding and implementing computer tactics against an adversary. COAST was a program of advanced technology developed to detect and locate very specific weapon signatures making strikes against them very on-target and reducing collateral damage significantly.

Whatever that means, this week, Getz thought.

That had appealed to Congress. Minimizing civilian casualties while continuing to ramp up defense spending; in their eyes it was win-win. Because he was a genius within this technological realm, he was, to his everlasting regret, expected to mount counter-terrorist strategies that went way beyond responding to what was already out there. 'They' said it was proactive, just like 'their' wars. The real trouble was, there was hardly anything 'out there.' Most of it was a fiction... a grossly exaggerated, over-blown fiction designed to keep the MICC in business. The fish tale was that more sophisticated technology was needed by the second when in fact it just wasn't. The American public had bought said fish tale, hook, line and sinker as a response to the atmosphere of artificially generated fear the country had been breathing for ten years or more. That conduit, the structure that allowed ridiculously dangerous and reckless war machinery to be built... the structure that had provided for the seemingly bottomless bankruptcy of the United States in great part was today the least of his worries.

Sceptre had the COAST contract. That meant he was the prime liaison. Too much was politicized, spun to fit whatever the administration's agenda du jour was, the agenda itself often being a plan generated and sent up to the White House by the MICC. The all-encompassing definition of 'threat' made true definition of a threat or target impossible. One cannot defend from an enemy one cannot define or identify clearly. Protection isn't possible. Everything that moved was politicized, militarized and 'pre-emptive.' The inevitable slippery slope was to surrender to the avalanche and define everything and everybody – every situation – as a threat and, subsequently, a target. Everyone was an enemy until they could prove otherwise. At this point in time, that meant all of the above were mandated to be 'handled' by COAST operations within every arm of the military and local police forces. Sceptre had the nation under its heel, at long last. Of course, the opposite was possible: the citizenry could snap out of the trance, come to its senses. No one Getz worked for was hoping for that, except Morrow.

Policies based on profit caused the whole kit and caboodle to hurtle down that slippery slope and were gaining inhuman speed, taking everything in its path with it. On the one hand, the people with their hands on the reins liked things that went 'boom.' They were like children who never wanted the fireworks to end... explosion upon explosion upon explosion. Those same people often sold themselves to the highest bidding defense contractors, who did not necessarily enjoy the 'boom' but more the ring of the cash register. And the people with their hands on the people with the reins wrote the checks. They underwrote the entire process since the United States no longer had the cash to do so. In this way they could co-opt the infrastructure and do whatever they pleased for ends they did not have to reveal or justify. Day-to-day 'special ops' could be made so complex that even the brightest minds were kept too busy to spot the real machinery in motion. Nero was a maze maker. Sceptre was a representative of those, as well. In fact, three-quarters of these people running the show were not even U.S. citizens. Getz hated that.

Nero and the creeps he works for, thought Getz.

Most of them the American public never heard of; they were not who anyone thought they were outside the pinnacle levels at the Pentagon and some particularly observant and intelligent fellows such as Morrow. The truly frightening part was that even they had people they worked for and God knows who they were.

Getz stopped at the desk of LeBlanc's secretary.

"Rear Admiral Alexander Getz," he announced himself as was the custom although he was expected. The young officer rose, opened the door and announced Getz. Getz walk past him and the door shut swiftly.

"Alex." Hap Leblanc rose from behind his formidable desk, came around and shook hands. He was a man who had gone to flesh, Getz' mother would have said. Short and thick. Probably always needed to watch his weight but hardly ever did. His desk was built for a much more imposing figure. Getz assumed there was a very adjustable chair back there, ratcheted up full height. He always reminded Getz of the bald, mustachioed Monopoly character with the cigar in his mouth, short with black tie, tails and a top hat. He was the fellow with wads of cash falling out of his cash-stuffed pockets. He chuckled every time it occurred to him.

LeBlanc gestured for Alex to sit.

"How goes it at Sceptre, Rear Admiral?" LeBlanc was only really interested in this enormous entity which housed half a dozen of their most lucrative contracts.

"It goes," Alex replied, choosing his words carefully. This was not going to be an easy meeting. "As of right now, my assignment is to finesse the on-board aircraft flight planner such that data…tremendous amounts of data… can be incorporated into a flight plan to pinpoint target locations. I have no problem either strategically or professionally completing that assignment."

LeBlanc did not respond. It was clear Getz had more to say and it probably wasn't going to be anything he wanted to hear. Goddamned Sceptre. They had to run their own agendas all the time. They gave themselves the green light. The Joint Chiefs were informed later as to some of what Sceptre was doing as a courtesy but they had no control over it. The Secretary of Agriculture, a far more powerful position than anyone would have guessed, was the conduit to the White House and that was usually about food, farmland, and weather. The Joint Chiefs were filled in as much as they had to be on weaponry of all kinds and security programs. Filled in. Not asked, filled in. Sceptre was capable of putting him in the White House, though, and that was all he cared about so he played ball. On the face of it, he was supposed to shut down any operation that crossed a line code-named *Molly*. That was coming, LeBlanc knew that. He would never shut down any Sceptre project. He knew that, too. Men like Getz wouldn't work for him unless they believed there was a limit somewhere. A big part of what LeBlanc did was create ever more sophisticated mazes; keep the mice running round and round, keep them busy with work that seemed crucial, while Sceptre rolled out its top echelon programs. He did not like using men like Getz in this way. They were too valuable. The problem was they could never be completely turned. Now Getz was privy to information that could shut down too much, deeply black programs that operated over and above the executive and military level. He was too close, had no real fear, and was too powerful. He would have to be removed.

"There's a problem," LeBlanc was forced to respond finally.

"Yes, we are at Molly, sir," Getz did not waver.

"You know that has to be justified, Getz," Le Blanc responded crossly.

"Sceptre is on the verge of integrating several of their biological warfare programs with their microwave weapon program. Not a problem in theory. However as of January 1, massive tests will be conducted globally on living animal populations. I do not believe that massive tests on localized human populations are far behind, probably within the boundaries of current war zones but not necessarily. We're in a zone where the targeted population doesn't much matter nor does the near blatant public experimentation. The very short-term goal is also to calibrate these two programs with the advanced human tracking program based on both micro-chipping and the bioaccumulation of nano-particles released over the decades. Both of those long-term experiments will now be shaken out. Once that is accomplished, they will have a weapon that can eradicate large populations or hone down to a single individual and that is the line we agreed cannot be crossed. Worse than that, we will have a totally controllable species on this planet: human beings. It's pretty clear the 'sides' are Sceptre on the one hand and everyone else on the planet on the other. They will be in total biological control."

Le Blanc was silent for a long minute.

"We need to cross the t's here, Getz. When is your next committee meeting?"

"December 28th."

"We'll pull you in at that point."

The real tragedy is that he thinks there's something we can do to stop it, thought LeBlanc.

"Toby Morrow," the voice on the other end said.

"Toby, Alex Getz here." Alex dialed as he pulled out of the parking lot. "Don't bother leaving the farm today, buddy. It's Christmas Eve, for God's sake. I'm going to drive down there and we can check in with each other. Then I need to go home while I still have a wife waiting for me."

He laughed. The traffic was heavy with people leaving for the Christmas holiday.

"Sure, Alex," Toby replied a little hesitantly. "If that's how you want to do it, that's fine with me. I expect I'll be out in the barn when you get here."

An hour later, Getz pulled onto the long dirt drive that idled by pastures belonging to ToMorrow Stables near Culpeper, Virginia. Toby Morrow and his family owned a couple dozen thoroughbreds, bred them and kept them for stud purposes. They were primarily Arabians but he did keep a couple of Norwegian Fjord horses, thickly muscled blond ponies with reckless blood and manes that stood straight up like scrub brushes. Getz loved all horse breeds but he was fascinated by the Fjords. The Virginia hill country seemed a sleeping and ancient giant, asleep so long as to be outside the memory of mankind. It fairly breathed if you sat still long enough and watched. The trees were so thick on the hillsides anything could hide behind them. In the winter, air settled into the valleys and you could swear it was blue. Right now there was no snow on the ground but that would change in the next day or so.

Sure enough, the barn doors were thrown wide open. He saw Toby, a wiry fellow with dark hair just this side of a crew cut, pushing a full wheelbarrow. He wore coveralls and a turtleneck against the cold air. Muck boots up to his knees were covered in mud and straw. Getz honked his horn as he passed the barn. Toby looked up and waved. The trees that lined the road inside the white wooden fence that stretched for half a mile from the road to the house were bare but the grass retained a fair amount of green due to the lucky geography of the Chesapeake Bay area and the moisture that stayed year-round.

Getz climbed out of his car and doubled back to the barn area, opened the fence and went in, wishing he'd worn boots. The mud was wet in the corral and seeped over the tops of his shoes. He found Toby in the barn, brushing a Fjord.

"Ah, you're a brave man, Toby Morrow, to get in there with that hellion."

Toby laughed.

"He loves me, don't you, Deke?" He continued to brush the horse. Getz leaned on the front of the stall.

"So why the hell did you come out here?" Toby asked pointedly. "How am I ever going to get my crab cakes now?"

"We are at *Molly*, my friend," Getz said soberly. "It's a meltdown."

Morrow stopped brushing the horse and left the stall, making sure the gate was latched firmly. He headed for a small tractor which pulled a wagon stacked high with hay bales.

"Come on," he said to Getz, sitting down and starting the engine. He drove slowly enough for Getz to walk along side. Morrow asked for the same report Getz had given LeBlanc. They talked as they drove the perimeter of the first pasture dropping hay bales as they went, horses following closely behind until the hay bales were kicked off the wagon one by one. He stopped his little tractor mid-field and leaned across the steering wheel.

"The biggest problem we have is Sceptre's Super User status. I don't even know who the hell rescinds that because I don't know how a corporation or research firm or whatever they are even gets that capability."

Sceptre was classified as a Central Controller with Super User privileges. That meant they could override any existing order to any part of the Department of Defense, NORAD, the Air Force and the FAA. No matter what might be going on, Sceptre could step in and change the ballgame in any way they wanted to at any time. Sceptre employees were able to produce credentials to get into any facility or attend any meeting that were better than the National Security Administration could produce themselves. They often did that, presenting themselves under false names at meetings to which they were not invited nor had any business attending, and then were untraceable. People spent years trying to find out who the 'two men' had been who were at their top-secret meeting uninvited. Super User status meant that any time anyone tried to shut Sceptre down they would be over-ridden by Sceptre themselves.

"I'm meeting with them on the 28th," Getz said. "Then I'm out... supposedly."

"You feeling confident they'll extricate you?"

"It's the only way I'm letting myself feel."

They stood in terrible silence in the field, horses scattered randomly in the pasture munching on hay bales. A scant handful of snowflakes drifted down around their shoulders.

"You just send the word down the line," Getz said, as he turned to leave. "Send the word that meltdown is under way. I expect the troops to save us. God help us if they don't have the balls for the job."

Getz made his way back to his car and drove away, drove home to his wife and son for a few hours before he had to be in New York.

Molly

Thanksgiving became a memory. Christmas slipped by. Finally, toward the end of January, Tim Verzet was able to get two precious days away to visit Huck and Lake Helen. Two pristine, uninterrupted days. To pass the down time while he waited for his escape, he surreptitiously prepared a silk message for his father. Short. To the point. Filled with hints about what to watch and where to watch for it in the coming months. He waited at *Gila*.

In the far north of California, in the elevated portions, he found deep snow. He had come to associate the desert, fair or not, with the avarice of some, the malevolence of others. Here in the northern mountains, snow drifted almost straight down unencumbered and clung to his wool cap. He had come to believe that there was almost no such thing as natural weather anymore but here, he pushed that knowledge away with all the strength he could muster. The moon was full; not the Snow Moon of February, but the Wolf Moon of January. It lay behind the clouds but the faint outline could not be ignored. It was there. The myths attached to the moon, those that touched the very folk soul of humanity, helped him grasp the personal relationship he had with time, the seasons and with storms. That Tim found reassuring. It was a goddamned birthright. They could not yet do anything about the regular rhythm of the moon. It lay beyond their reach.

Up the road, Huck waited for his son to catch up, resting comfortably on his skis and breathing thick clouds from his nostrils like a horse being breezed on a racetrack on a cold morning. Tim was so relieved that Huck still had it in him to cross country ski at night, one of their favorite quiet pastimes. Huck said it wasn't always the case with his diminished breathing and he never did it alone. This was a special occasion and, after all, it was only midnight.

The silk Huck had taken from his son, both amused and alarmed by the old war trick, guided his conversations with his son. He understood that Tim was wrapped up in something as a result of which he would be very closely monitored at all times. They were on the rutted road that wound uninterrupted past Huck's cabin. It was a solitary, strenuous, concentration-intensive pastime; like Huck, like Tim. Words from Tim's message kept coming to Huck as he sliced softly through the snow; dangerous work, biological weapons, global population, *Shuri*, Okinawa. One word terrified him; bioaccumulation. It was exactly the science-backed legal case he and his friends had spent years building. That data was available to anyone who could stop the genocide. The *Shuri* Reconciliation was as compelling to Huck as it was to Tim. Now his son, his only child, was right in the middle of enemy territory. Huck hoped that a lifetime of teaching and Tim's experience in the belly of the beast as an ace fire bomber would keep him alive although he didn't know how a man escaped the clutches of something like this. On the other hand, Huck was old enough and experienced enough himself to know that a solitary human could rise above anything; anything at all. These thoughts anchored themselves in the insistently falling snow on the mountain under the Wolf moon, the pale light of which would inevitably break through the clouds and shed light on the dark night. Several owls lived around Huck's place. One made itself known in the night, deeper in the woods.

They pulled up together at the top of a hill to rest. Huck started to cough violently in the cold, moist air. He kept coughing, bent over slightly. Tim waited.

"Dad, I'm sorry," he said when the coughing spasm finally passed. Huck wiped his glove across his mouth.

"Well, son, the damage was done long before any of us knew what was happening," he replied. "All any of us can do now is try. I'm proud of you, Tim. This'll likely cost you plenty. It's an honourable sacrifice. I can live with it."

"I love you, Huck."

"Love you, too, boy."

They stood together at the crest of the hill in the drifting snow, which was now tapering to nothing. There was the smallest sliver of a break in the clouds above them, allowing the moon to pierce the night. Five minutes later, they quietly turned for home.

He and Pip took jump seats on the same flight back to *Gila*. Pip had been visiting his parents farther north in Klamath Falls. One was almost never completely 'out' for long. A day or two at best and then never truly unmonitored. The scrutiny was intense and relentless. Tim slipped Pip the same silk he'd slipped his Dad. He wanted Pip to be ready, at all times. He didn't know for what but just wanted him to stay prepared. He wondered if there was any way at all he could request that Pip help him shake out the new airplanes. Probably not but he might risk a try. He knew something big had to happen, this could not continue, someone would have to try something desperate to throw a spanner in the works. He knew it would have to be him. He did not have any real idea what it would be.

It was the mighty spring wind season in New Mexico, the wind an icy cold terrorist. It presaged the coming warmth but was just this side of not worth living through. The bigger planes didn't react too badly but it was hell on earth for a small plane. Sand and dirt flew unrestrained, like a weapon. Windshields pitted under the barrage of tiny little pebbles. Toothbrushes were carried everywhere because inevitably, if a person was outside for any length of time, grit built up on one's teeth. The maddening dichotomy was that one needed to be bundled up against the cheese-grater wind while all the time the sun beat down from above, a cruel joke, the wind allowing no real heat to reach the skin's surface. The winds generally lasted the entire month of March, sometimes into April. Temperatures climbed quickly at that point, and in the end the sun always prevailed. Lizards sunned themselves on rocks, roadrunners raced across highways while the sun returned to rightfully claim dominion of the heavens.

What they thought would be the new DC-10-30 and the new 747 had turned out to be the Pantheon Plato and Proteus, and they were finally scheduled for flight tests in June, with pilot training beginning in July. Tim was lead pilot for the project because he had shaken out the 747s and DC-10s in the first wave and was, strangely, allowed to make a request or two for flight crews. He named Pip as a first officer or navigation officer and Pip was duly added to the roster of twelve. In the end they would all be able to train the large stable of pilots on these new craft. The real difference for the pilots was in the handling.

Technicians on the ground worked out all the algorithms for chemical dispersal and fueling. Many pilots had volunteered for these tests.

Tim tended to want to pick those who hung back, not sure why. Maybe he imagined somehow they were less 'okay' with what they were all doing and those were the people with whom he wanted to associate. Eventually he realized that despite the extreme paranoia this outfit usually operated in, the test crews had to be able to develop some sort of history with each other and with the planes in order to properly test these aircraft. The last thing this company wanted was for a chemically-laden plane to go down out of their reach, and so it was worth it to allow working relationships ensuring sound aircraft that had previously been forbidden for the sake of secrecy. It had happened only once, in the Balkans somewhere a plane went down, and the United States government had immediately frozen all the assets of the helpless little country involved, demanding immediate return of their aircraft. Tim had no doubt the US would have gone to extreme measures, including blatant attack or even a declaration of war, to get that plane back.

The co-pilot Joshua, who volunteered and was selected by Tim as Pip had been, continued to hang onto the idea that the sun was scheduled to release unheard of amounts of solar radiation over the next two years. Worst case scenario was that the world's infrastructure would crash and it would take not months but years to restore order. Very bad things would happen in the meantime. Josh was convinced that the atmosphere was being transformed to try to deflect or mediate this radiation in some way. Having been given the green light by Tim to talk about this once, Josh took every opportunity to continue the conversation. Tim supposed all that was at least partially true. It was how these people operated... just enough truth to confuse the issue. Many men flew these missions strictly for the money. Some flew because they rose high in the military and came from backgrounds in which they did not receive praise or experience success or competence. At a certain level, these men just followed orders no matter what. No questions asked. Success was how fast and well one could execute an order. Tim was still convinced, however, that the pilots were the key to ending this insanity, the Achilles heel of the program.

Tim and Pip got the game of slipping each other silk messages down to a science. They were almost completely sure no one had picked up on it. In order to legitimize their friendship within the confines of this very tricky environment they sought Unger out whenever he was present at the base and shared meals with him. They were the only two pilots out of *Pinon*. It made some sense. Also, Tim was aware that, for whatever reason, Unger wanted Bluesky's ties to the United States Forest Service renewed. Tim had years of experience working for that department under his belt. Unger had remarked on it once, bookmarked it for later, it was that important. As far as living arrangements went, Pip lived on the other side of town in another building... a building Tim had not even known was theirs.

The idea of the *Shuri* Reconciliation became more and more the object of Tim's waking thoughts. So far it was the only life raft he'd managed to locate. He knew so much. If only he could get there. If only he could bring evidence; evidence in the form of the plane itself, fully loaded with chemicals if possible and some sort of medical evidence. Harry the 'doctor' might also need to make a 'visit' to Okinawa. Tim had no idea how to make that happen either.

June 1. The sun had beaten back the spring winds. It was time to learn the new aircraft. Tim was to report to Unger for a briefing. There were two other men in attendance neither of whom Tim had ever seen before. Introductions were not made. Unger began.

"The new Pantheon Plato was designed and is being produced by the Skunkworks at Pantheon. That's all you really need to know about that. Obviously you are pilots... you realize these planes fly. Pantheon has determined that these birds fly and they have been flown here to us. Pantheon people are right here on the premises to help us local yokels determine how they fly fully loaded and to watch us learn to fly them well enough to teach the rest of us hillbillies here how to fly them. Strike that. Pantheon is all over the place here so that's no secret. They tend to piss me off. They are the only ones who have their hands on our aircraft. These aircraft take a while to produce but since we're not hauling passengers for a profit and we have a fleet in place we don't have to be in a hurry to manufacture airplanes until we're sure these are what we want. They're doing it this way because that's how we want it done no matter how it's been done in the past. This ain't the past, this is now and we call the shots. Hopefully everybody's got that by now."

Tim started to write things down.

"No notes, men, unless it's actual operating or flying specs. Thanks."

Tim closed his notebook.

"If we wanted to outsource electrical and other systems, we could literally throw one of these together in four days. We aren't about to do that, obviously. At least, not yet. The entire aircraft is made of carbon composite fibers. You know as professionals that these planes are now about four times stronger than steel and much, much lighter. They're going to look different to you, too. Carbon composites can be reduced to just a few panels put together and they adapt more easily to curve changes. More continuous curves are part of the stealth aspect of these new aircraft as shape angles are often the most noticeable hotspot for reflecting radar energy. Between the new composite and the curve changes, the carbon constructed Pantheon has almost no radar cross section. The turbines were still an issue. Spinning steel attracts a lot of radar attention, as you know. That issue has been dealt with in two ways. First, we've put large cone-shaped inlet gratings over each inlet. That leaves the final problem of the heat signature of the exhaust. We've borrowed the idea of infrared jammers – the same countermeasures as on Air Force One – mounted above the exhaust cone and wired back to the Auxilliary Power Unit in the tail section. The bay is also much bigger. It's been reconfigured to hold about twenty percent more 'product.' Most of the systems that rely on hydraulics have been replaced by electronics. The computer is much, much faster. It can handle turbulence you'd never believe it could handle. The adjustments are so extensive you may not even know there is any turbulence out there. It'll take the plane through one helluva storm. In fact, gentlemen, putting this one airplane together has cost us eight hundred thousand plus hours on a supercomputer and upwards of forty-five billion. Luckily we were able to reuse most of that crunching to produce the titanium Proteus, as well. Although we are going to shake that bird out for our own purposes, most of our goals with that one are still need-to-know and you guys do not need to know."

Tim knew that the titanium was still going to show up on radar so stealth was obviously not the purpose of the bigger one.

"The cabin and the cockpit really have not changed. The difference in flying, if any, is going to be in the weight and the curve changes to the frame. We don't know if the extra cargo combined with the lighter, shapelier frame will cause flight problems. The computer says it might. Let's see."

The Flight was scheduled for the very next morning. Pip was his co-pilot and Josh the navigator. They met for breakfast in the commissary. Tim arrived first and grabbed the morning newspaper. He had found over the months it would likely be his only real chance for news. The front page of the L.A. Times reported that the publishing magnate, Sir Cecil Cordham, after having been found guilty on several counts of fraud and bribing public officials, had been found dead. There was a photograph of the famous Solomon de Geier and his new wife, Helen, standing on the balcony of their family flat in Mayfair waving to the crowd. There were some rather unhappy people standing around them.

Seriously red hair on that guy.

Baseball. Weather. He was always looking for mention of progress from the *Shuri* panel on Okinawa. There was not much today, just a reminder that there was a call for papers and the open forums were still scheduled to begin on July 1. They would last the entire month. The economic news was catastrophic. Tim wondered if the U.S. dollar would soon be valueless. It might as well be now. In real terms, each dollar was now worth about twenty-five cents… on a good day. The really surprising thing was that most people still seemed unaware of that or able to ignore it. The stock markets were on a roller coaster no one seemed to be able to stop. Pip and Josh walked in together.

"Sports page?" Tim asked. Pip was an absolute baseball fanatic.

"Yeah," Pip was between his first and second cup of coffee. "Hang on."

He walked off to find more coffee. Josh was alert, cheerful, ready to go… as usual. Tim thought it would be nice, just sometimes, to be convinced of the sanctity of one's mission here. Sadly, he never envisioned Josh as being among the pilots who finally refused to do this work. He was a top-notch flyer, though, and deserved to be part of this team. There were four teams of three each. Each team would take each plane up six times and then write up reports which Tim would then bring to Unger and Unger would pass up the line to Pantheon. Pantheon personnel were always here watching anyway and this would be no different.

They climbed in to the cold, dark cockpit with more excitement than Tim had felt since he started at *Gila* several months ago. Good pilots lived to try new forms of aircraft even if they felt guilty about it.

June 24th. Memphis, Tennessee. The pilot Leon Gore sat upright in the hotel bed in the dark, smoking cigarette after cigarette, the fresh one lit from the glowing embers of the last one. His roommate had abandoned the room and bunked with another aircrew because the smoke, the stench and the nervous energy were overpowering. *Fuck you, tiny little man.*

The cash. Leon was thinking about the cash, his brain grinding in ever smaller, more tightly wound circles. His brain was screaming. He had two million dollars in the bank. As of this morning, that money was worth a quarter of that. His stocks had plummeted over the last month. He had lost millions there. There was no end to the economic death spiral in sight, no matter what anyone said. The economy was bleeding out. He was not stupid even if most of the rest of the country was. He was about to lose it all. The power was no longer enough on its own. He had become very fond of all the zeros on his bank statement.

His t-shirt stunk. He had not changed clothes or showered for several days. He had flown his schedule, reluctantly. His body was present and that was about all. He was supposed to fly back to *Gila* this morning. Then he had a few days off. He did not think he could survive a few days off, no purpose, no job, nothing for his body to do. He would surrender completely to his madness. *What difference will that make?*

He sat up on his bed in the pitch black. The clock read five a.m. It would be light soon. As agitated as he had been in the weeks leading up to this morning, he had crossed some sort of Rubicon through the long, long night. He felt as if he had crawled uphill toward the mountain pass on his belly, using only his hands to pull himself along. Now at the top, he saw the valley below and a dangerous calm descended on him. He knew a place near here. They did not know he knew, but he did. They were watched but there was no guard outside his door. He'd be picked up at seven and taken back to the airport for a flight back to *Gila*. He would drop the balance of his load on the way over the St. Louis metropolitan area. It would linger there until night-time when the usual inversion would push it down, down, down toward the earth and the wind would have spread it out thin, a nice thin blanket of soft kill wafting down upon the sleeping citizenry of Missouri. Nano-particles slipped easily into every space between fabric fibers, window seals, lots of open windows in June in Missouri anyway. The poisons would settle on the grass and the trees, the flowers and the water. Colorless, odorless, all but weightless. Easy dousing.

Leon saw the sky beginning to change color ever so slightly. His fellow airmen would be stirring. He rose quickly and stepped into dirty blue jeans; pulled a shirt on over his t-shirt. His tennis shoes were good enough for this mission. He slid his wallet into his back pocket and ran a comb through his hair. Then he slipped out the doorway silently and was down the hall and outside in a matter of seconds.

The Manly Chemical Mixing Company plant was three blocks east and one block north from his hotel. It was an easy matter to walk there. Despite the darkness, birds were already singing in the trees. He couldn't see them, he was walking too fast anyway, but he thought he would have liked to this once. He passed a very large tree of a kind he could never have identified. The branches and leaves formed a globe, a sphere thickly hidden by thousands of green leaves. It sounded as if hundreds of birds were inside, just waking up, shaking the morning awake. He kept walking. By his estimation, it was about his last twenty minutes on this earth. Whereas he had barely been able to contain himself at the knowledge of how profoundly he had been cheated out of what was coming to him, he was now just this side of serene knowing what sort of sword he could lay at their throats. He would draw it cleanly and deeply across their throats and blood would be spilled, make no mistake.

The plant was dark, locked, quiet.

Great, he thought, no third shift here. Money troubles, perhaps?

He doubted it. There was a tremendous amount of money to be made mixing made-to-order chemicals. He walked around the brick building once, located a window propped open ever so slightly yet low enough for him to jump up, grab the lip and pull it down. It was already ajar. He would be very surprised if opening that window now caused an alarm to sound. He grabbed the window, frosted white to prevent people from seeing inside, and hung his whole weight from it. It groaned under the stress and finally one side broke away and swung down. He had an angle at least to try to get in. He found he could reach the inner sill now with his hand. He pulled, leveraging his feet against the side of the building. Although his feet slid off under his weight it was enough to get his chest up over the lip and halfway into the warehouse. For a warehouse it was at this part of the building. It was a plant, he knew that. Here orders were filled for chemical mixtures to be transported to the Bluesky aircraft, wherever the aircraft might be. Large tractor trailers took the chemicals to sites where their liquid cargo was off-loaded into honey trucks. The honey trucks carried the poison to waiting airplanes under the guise of draining the toilets. It was ridiculously easy. Back at *Gila*, some specialty mixtures were created, he knew, when the barium was added to the mix. There were many times when barium was dispersed all by itself. It took such a low level of observation over time to see these things but even they, the pilots, were thoroughly trained to mind their own business and stick to their own job. Besides, nobody really wanted to die because of what they knew.

He threw his right leg over the sill and dropped, his left leg stretching unnaturally until it popped over the window's edge and he dropped to the cement floor. He waited. Sometimes there were dogs in these warehouses. Not tonight. He smiled, the same slow grin that always crept over his face during a special ops mission. It was that feeling he was going to win.

He walked purposefully through the warehouse creating leaks in any way he could. He strained to open large red valves on giant vats of liquid methane. The sides of these vats were marked '9000 gal.' The noxious liquid ran toward the center of the warehouse, which was indeed built with a slope toward the center along which sat half a dozen drains. He found tarps over pallets holding stacked five gallon buckets of a custom powdered blend of some sort, yanked them off and lay them across the drains. The trick worked wonderfully well. Very little methane went down the drain, most of it stayed above and floated, spreading outward rapidly. Next he wanted the office, somewhere he could make a regular phone call… somewhere he could see the door and aim his weapon at it while he talked. He spotted the office he knew must be there and headed for it. Anytime he spotted a methane valve, he stopped and struggled to open it. Most of them he managed to turn. He did not yet want to mix chemicals because he did not yet want to be overpowered by some bizarre and deadly gas. He had something to say. Just before he entered the office area, he made a mental note of a 12,000 gallon tank with black lettering on it, "potassium hydroxide." He saw petroleum distillates, hydrochloric acid, benzene and lithium salts. Some of these, he knew, required only a drop or two of water to ignite and blow the roof off this plant. The fire would burn for days.

He quickly picked the lock on the office door, sat down at the desk inside, placed his pistol in front of him, then rifled through the drawers for a phone book to get the phone number of a local television station. Keeping his finger on the number, he cradled the headset on his right shoulder and dialed. It was five twenty a.m. The call went straight to the newsroom.

"KRTD newsroom," a sleepy voice answered.

"I need to speak to someone who can put me on the air. It's an emergency."

"What?" The voice came alive a bit. "On the air?"

"Yes, you stupid deaf bastard. I've barricaded myself inside a building which I intend to blow up and I want some air time."

"Very funny. You know you can get into real trouble for this."

"I'm completely serious." Leon's voice was ice cold.

"Hang on." Leon must have sounded plausible or at least worth checking out because the overnight news director was the next person on the line. They were required to call the police in situations like this anyway and keep the kook on the line as long as possible. They had all been trained for this.

"Hello, this is Ed Hillary," the voice sounded much older, more mature. "What is it that you want?"

"I am holed up in the Manley plant... which I intend to destroy unless I get some air time," Leon said.

"Um, okay, I have to get the station manager in the loop here. Stay on the line."

And the cops, Leon thought. Go ahead. It'll be more spectacular that way. As soon as the locals put me on the air, the national news will pick it up.

"The morning show is on, mister... uh...". The night news manager was back on the phone. "Who are you?"

"Leon Gore is the name."

"Okay, Mr. Gore. You can have some time... a direct live feed. But you know we had to call the cops, right?"

"I'm counting on it. Do you have a piece of paper and something to write with?"

"Sure."

"Well, write down these numbers. These are the numbers to access my bank account. I want someone to have a look at it before I go on the air and all hell breaks loose. Can you do that?"

"Okay, but why?"

"I have two million dollars in that account for no good, traceable reason. I think we should all start there, don't you?"

"Jesus."

The sirens began to wail in the distance. By now the liquid he had released would be seeping out of the building under the large warehouse doors. That should be enough to keep local law enforcement at bay.

"Hello, Leon Gore. This is Charles Foster and you are on the air. Mr. Gore, am I correct in my information that you are inside the Manly Chemical Mixing Plant here in Memphis?"

"Yes. That is good information. I don't want you to ask me questions, Foster. That will waste what little time I have left. I hope you're recording this... you want to be, I promise you. I work for an outfit called Bluesky Air. I am a pilot, one of hundreds. We fly airplanes worldwide that are spreading toxic chemicals – lethal poisonous chemicals – in the atmosphere around the clock, seven days a week. We never stop. Aluminum, barium, arsenic, lithium, you name it. We're dumping it on the population. I get paid a lot of money to do that. Except the economy has crashed... idiots. The dollar is worthless. I just want someone to understand that I sold my soul to the devil for money – mass murder – for nothing. Nothing at all."

"Excuse me, Mr. Gore, but why? Why would any company want to do something like that? And how come nobody knows about it?"

"Why? I don't know why. Sick bastards with too much money.

Ask them. And plenty of people know about it. They dress it up… call it geo-engineering… and the dumbasses think, oh, the smarty scientists must know what they're doing! Or give them a super-secret save the people mission but it's top-secret so shhhhh… Christ every kid in the world will fall for that one… or they're like me and the feeling of dumping poisons on sleeping people makes them feel powerful. Really addictively powerful. It's one hell of a buzz, man."

He heard fire engine sirens. Several of them and they were close. A helicopter whirred overhead.

"Good. I hear all the emergency stooges outside," he said into the phone. "I want witnesses. Anybody check my bank account yet?"

The anchor listened to his producer answer that question in his earpiece, touching his ear.

"Yes. At first we verified two million. Now they show no record of your ever having had a bank account, Mr. Gore."

Leon smiled. "Remember that. That's important. People will show up soon and tell you to shut me up. You won't have a choice. Try not to let them do it."

There were two men from the government, in fact, at the station now. They had just arrived, displayed impeccable credentials to the head of the station, now on the premises, shaken from his sleep by a true emergency. Leon could talk but they reserved the right to shut him down at any time. And, no, they did not want to talk to him. They just wanted to know what he was going to try to say… for now.

In New Mexico, the handlers were called into Unger's office at the test site. There were only six of them at the airfield. The rest were spread across the country working. This guy had walked out of the hotel and holed up three short blocks away in a chemical mixing plant. He had known about this plant and right where to go. How? That was something they could not figure out.

"Who the hell is it?" Unger growled.

"Leon Gore," someone spoke from the back of the room. "Calls himself 'the Bull.'

"Handler?"

"Mine," Tim said. This would be the end of him anyway. It was time to go. Pip was still on board the Plato. Tim had been paged to come to the building fast. How the hell had Leon known about this chemical mixing plant? Tim certainly hadn't but you can be sure they'd blame him.

On the large television monitor overhead they watched the fast-moving emergency situation in Memphis; the local cops and SWAT team arrived, rescue vehicles were everywhere. The news anchor reported that the madman was on the phone, then he was talking to Memphis, then the nation as the national news companies picked up the story. The local station stream was patched into the smaller computers all over the second floor at Gila. The Manly Chemical Mixing Plant was located in a heavily congested area of a Memphis suburb. The area was being evacuated as rapidly as possible.

Aerial photos showed pools of chemical escaping the plant building, firefighters running, jumping away from it. The chemical river engulfed the undercarriage area of a fire engine completely. He had engineered a chemical deluge. The news team reported methane and other deadly chemicals kept in tanks on-site, mixed to the specific orders of purchasers. No other information was forthcoming from the owners.

The local authorities had little choice for the moment other than to let Leon talk. It was so fast. Within thirty seconds of having reached the local news station by telephone, he was insisting he speak directly to the audience... through the local press only. As soon as the word Bluesky was mentioned, the national news outlets claimed to have lost the feed. The little local telecast chugged forward... until the government emissaries asked them to cut the audio due to national security interests. The video scenes were frightening enough. The local police were evacuating the immediate area as fast as they could. Without warning, fire shot along the surface of the chemical river from within the plant itself and raced along the entirety of the liquid outside. The underbelly of the fire engine was ablaze instantly. Five seconds later, the entire ground mixture exploded violently, sending thick black smoke roiling into the air. The concussion was felt miles away.

Unger was on the telephone throughout the newscast. He put the phone to his chest and grabbed the radio transmitter to dispatch.

"Get on the radio and land every plane. They are to make for the nearest Bluesky base and land. Period. No questions asked. I want everyone down inside an hour."

The dispatcher now tasked with a series of unbelievably complicated arrangements, Unger returned to the very important person on the other line. No name had been used. By the time the plant exploded, Tim had already made his way back to the waiting Plato. No order had been given to cut the engine and the aircraft was parked at one end of the tarmac as it was next up for running tests. Tim and Pip had run through a flight at five a.m. off the central coast of California in the Proteus. They had just finished pre-flight inspection of the Plato and the three huge engines were spooling up.

The counter measures on this bird were otherworldly. Each engine had a circular shroud that wrapped around the engine nacelles, with a gap in between for drawing in ambient air while in flight. The carbon composite structure tapered back and completely enclosed the exhaust nozzle, then flared out into a horizontal shape reminiscent of a flattened out funnel. It more or less employed the same exhaust diffusion concept of the F-117A Night Hawk stealth fighter, mixing cooler passing air with a flattened out exhaust stream to dramatically reduce the engine's infrared signature. The first time Tim saw these modifications, he chuckled because they fell under the category he called Buck Rogers aviation. The number two engine, blended into the plane's vertical stabilizer was the weirdest looking of the three.

Tim forced himself to lope casually over to the crew chief beneath the port wing, who was standing near one of the engines, waiting for his signal. Tim's automatic response was to cup his hands over his ears as he approached the plane to protect them from the deafening whine of the engines, even though they were merely idling. He caught the chief's attention, who then leaned in to hear despite his headsets, mindful of the COM cable still plugged into the bird's belly.

"Chief, there's some kind of emergency!" Tim shouted over the engines. "We need to get this bird airborne on the double!" His face was right up against the chief's headphone, so he could hear what was said. The crew chief nodded and gave him a thumbs-up.

"Once I'm aboard, move the rolling staircase and pull the chocks right away! We need to book!"

The chief's expression made it obvious that he understood the urgency of the situation. He waved an informal salute at Tim, saying, "I'm on it!" His direct link to the aircraft over the COM line had prevented the chief from picking up the order to ground all flights.

Tim bounded up the rolling staircase, turned and pivoted the door into the hatch opening, latched and locked it into the fuselage. Then he stepped quickly around to his left, through the galley and latrine area and grabbed his headset as he took the pilot's seat. He stepped over the center console and throttle sector to take his seat, irritated that this awkward maneuver was one more incidental that slowed him down. Pip glanced over his left shoulder from his clipboard and checklist, and did a double take, as he caught sight of Tim's grave expression, and quick, deliberate movement.

"Go," Tim said, trying valiantly to repeat the mantra Huck taught him... it's not an emergency, it's a job. It's not an emergency, it's a job.

"What?" Pip said, lifting his headset away from his ears, thinking he had misunderstood.

"I said go. This is it."

Tim prepared to taxi, adjusted the rudder pedals and grabbed the steering wheel on the left console. He knew he would have to push take-off procedures to dangerous limits. They had to get into the air. He leaned to his left impatiently, watching from the pilot's side window as the Chief rolled the staircase away to a safe distance as fast as he could. Tim was relieved to see the chocks were already pulled away from beneath the huge aircraft's tires, and his COM line was pulled. He pushed the throttles on the engines, harder than usual and immediately felt the bulk of the massive aircraft lurch forward, compressing its giant undercarriage, its massive weight shifting.

As it began rolling, he cranked the steering wheel to guide her into his launch position at the end of the main runway. He held the brakes for a few seconds, advanced the throttles as the engines quickly spooled up, and then released them once Pip indicated that everything looked good according to his instruments in the all-glass cockpit. The rollout was hard, fast, and they were airborne.

During their rollout, they saw technicians on the second floor of the test site building running to the windows, waving their arms. Tim and Pip did not know it, of course, but Unger had just grounded the entire fleet.

Luckily, they had been scheduled for take-off at that time anyway. Unfortunately the runway ran right past the area Unger had gathered with the other handlers. Pip cycled the landing gear as soon as the weight was off the main struts. The plane looked like it had gone from a rollout to a hover as the gear disappeared, immediately boosting their airspeed as this parasitic drag disappeared into the smooth ventral surfaces of the plane. Tim pulled back on the steering yoke and put her into a steep climb.

Unger was incredulous.

"Goddamn it!" Unger shouted as the Plato climbed away. "I said all planes down. Who the hell is that?"

"That would be Verzet and Yarmouth, sir. They were scheduled to take that bird up right at this time," a technician shouted from down the line.

Unger picked up the dispatch microphone again. "Get that bird down! Now!"

"Trying, sir. No response, sir," came the reply.

"What heading, Captain?" Pip asked. Resigned now to the situation, he was fairly calm. For now, he just needed to know which way they were going.

"Turn northwest on a heading of 280. Keep her at 2000 feet AGL. I think we'll have to fly this first leg VFR and use the terrain to mask our flight path as best we can. We will probably have to hug the ground if they send anyone after us. This big, black mother will stick out like a sore thumb in the middle of a clear, morning sky, low observables or not," Tim fumed.

"Verzet doesn't seem to want to come down," Unger snarled. "Somebody here who can get the Proteus up?"

"Sir," a handler responded, "we're grounded."

"This isn't a mule, this ship. It won't be recognized as part of our fleet or belonging to us in any way. The Plato is out of visual now and it cannot be spotted on radar, we made damned sure of that. Somebody has to catch it... somebody we bloody well can see... and stay right on its tail. I'd like to keep this in the family if possible. I'm sure you understand."

"Yes, sir," the handler replied. "Josh and his crew are here. They were rotating to the Proteus when this started. They are aboard and the pre-flight procedures are complete save for the fact that the bird has not been refueled yet. It was supposed to be a very short flight."

"I don't give a shit! Get that aircraft in the air. Now!" He ran down the stairs to dispatch.

"Get me patched through to the Plato," he said. The radio crackled to life.

"Bluesky 10 Heavy, this is base, copy?" A vein in Unger's forehead pulsed. "I say again, do you copy?" Unger leaned forward, craning his neck to look downfield. The Proteus was in its rollout.

Silence.

"Verzet!" Unger barked into the radio. "Bad things are going to happen unless you respond."

The Proteus passed dispatch, sailing off the runway with graceful ease. Josh was being conservative on the launch to save fuel. It banked slightly to the left as it climbed out. Josh anticipated Tim's flight path based on what was left of his exhaust stream.

"We've got another bird chasing you right now. Bring that aircraft back unless you want to get hurt... or maybe you want other people to get hurt."

A long moment passed. Unger thought Tim would refuse to respond.

"Uh... that's a negative, sir."

"Damn it, bring that airplane back!"

"Nope...sir."

"What do you intend to do with my very expensive aircraft, pilot?"

"Fly it away, sir. Steal it. Abscond with it."

"Where to?"

Sounds of laughter burst through the radio.

In the moment, it hadn't occurred to Tim or Pip that the all-titanium Proteus was lighter and faster than a regular 747. In fact, it was about twenty percent faster than the stealthy all-carbon composite Plato with all the drag that the added 'low-observables' technology brought to its airframe. Suddenly, from the upper right corner of their windscreen, Tim and Pip saw Josh in the Proteus in a banking dive, flash across their flight path. Purely on reflex, Tim clenched the steering yoke in his hands and rolled the Plato into the bigger plane's point of origin, the composite airframe groaning under the strain, arriving in the airspace the Proteus had just vacated. The wake turbulence caused by the wing vortices of the bigger aircraft caused the Plato to shudder. The whole cockpit lurched violently as they struggled to steady themselves.

"Shit!" Pip whispered. "Are they serious?"

"Thank God we're in an all-carbon composite airframe. Those tip vortices could have snapped the wing off of any other aircraft," Tim observed as the vibrations and wing flutter subsided. "With all the flight stabilization software they built into this baby, we could probably fly through a damn hurricane! In some respects, we have an edge, even though we're slower. I'm almost positive…".

Tim watched the Proteus circling back around behind them to the port building airspeed, then glanced over at Pip. He was as white as a sheet. Tim looked back to Josh and the other aircraft, and watched him level out above the desert floor. He began to climb out again for what would probably be another pass.

"Time to take her down on the deck," Tim suggested. "He can't dive on us if we're as low as he can fly."

"I was hoping you'd say that," Pip laughed nervously, as Tim pushed the yoke forward. Tim glanced over at Pip again; they laughed as their eyes met. The negative G-force during the wings-level descent reminded Tim of the roller coaster rides he had taken as a kid with Huck. He loved that falling sensation. It had spawned his interest in flight and the chance to experience it practically whenever he wanted to. It also made him laugh to think of how his weapons systems operators bugged him about it when he flew fighters in the military, because along with the fact that every particle of dust would become airborne in the cockpit under negative G's, most of his support officers would lose their breakfast too. Flyer had a reputation as a one-man "vomit comet".

Tim brought the Plato down to 200 feet and leveled her off. This close to the deck, every thermal or updraft created a bump for an ordinary aircraft. In a fighter plane, this kind of sortie would have felt a lot like four-wheeling through the desert. But the Composite Plato was remarkably smooth.

This new strategy forced Josh to adapt, and they found themselves flying into Monument Valley with its spectacular mesas and rock formations. Josh leveled out and mirrored Tim's course. He gradually came along side off Tim's starboard wingtip. He could see Josh in silhouette through the windscreen of the Proteus.

"Josh," Tim spoke quietly into the radio microphone. "Go home. Turn around, Josh. I know how much fuel is in the bird you're flying. I'm the last pilot who had her up. That was this morning. There was no refueling yet."

The radio crackled back. It was Josh.

"Tim," he said, "I have to do this. I have my orders. You turn around then you won't be killing me and my crew."

"Son of a bitch," Pip said between clenched teeth. "Why the hell did they send that kid after us?"

Josh, who had been staring intently across the sky in hope of some response from Tim that told him he would back down, was shaken when he heard a female voice in his headset. It was the terrain obstacle warning system. A mildly urgent female voice said, *"Terrain warning! Pull up! Terrain warning; pull up!"* The Proteus was headed straight into the mesa. Josh pulled back hard on the yoke. The ship began to shudder as the wing neared a stall. He cleared the huge formation – barely – banked slightly to the right leveling the wings, then looked back to where Tim had been.

"Sneaky son-of-a-bitch," Josh muttered.

They were deep into Arizona. Flagstaff was coming into view, three hundred miles and only half an hour behind them. Zero eight hundred. Tim knew the limits of Josh's piloting capabilities. He would offer Josh one more opportunity to set his plane down. Then, if he refused, he had to shake him. That meant he had to take him on the ride of his life, straight through the Grand Canyon. If he survived that, he'd still be out of fuel. He would have to land somewhere because the only thing worse than losing the Plato would be crashing the Proteus in the open desert, for God and the world to see.

"Why don't you just let him chase us in a straight line until he runs dry?" Pip asked.

"He's faster than us. He can keep after us with that cut-off maneuver until someone makes a mistake and maybe we all get killed. Frankly, straight out over the Pacific? I don't want a zealot on my wing all the way out until he splashes into the drink, thanks."

Tim's expression was grim as he hit his mic button again.

"Josh. Final warning. Abort your pursuit. Veer off. Do it now!"

"No can do, Tim."

Tim looked at Pip, shook his head. He banked back to the north, heading directly for the eastern terminus of the canyon, about sixty miles northwest. They'd be there in a few minutes.

"Ready, Pip?"

"Hell, no." he replied, the color draining from his face. "But here we are."

In fact the altimeter suddenly registered an AGL, altitude from ground level, gain of seven thousand feet as they crossed the south rim of the canyon which had just abruptly plunged those thousands of feet toward the Little Colorado River below. As Tim dove in a banked left turn into the spectacular depth of the canyon, he heard Josh talking to base and Unger, who was by now seething.

"Sir, Bluesky Proteus Heavy, request permission to orbit Grand Canyon until Verzet climbs out. There's not a lot of room down there for two jumbo jets...".

"Son, let me be very clear... I do not give... a... shit... how you do it, but you stay right on Verzet's ass and maintain visual contact without fail. Do you read me loud and clear? Over."

"Five by five, sir... Uh... Maintain visual." Josh replied resolutely. Then he rolled the Proteus into a graceful left handed bank to follow Tim down into the depths of the Grand Canyon.

That morning at Nellis Air Force base just east of Las Vegas, fighter pilots Captain Steve Fitzgerald and Major Jamie Steiner were drinking coffee in the ready room next to Base Operations with two other pilots. The four of them comprised Razorback Flight, their code name if they were activated in an emergency. The shift had just started when the alert status buzzer shattered the morning silence. Everyone in the building stopped cold. Where there had been many conversations, there was now utter silence in anticipation of immediate orders. Over the metallic-sounding PA system, a voice from the North American Defense Command (NORAD) facility deep within Cheyenne Mountain near Colorado Springs broke in. The audio signal crackled as the airman on the other end cleared his throat.

"Attention: Standby for a NORAD-authorized TCAM... this is a Covered Wagon Alert. Repeat: this is a NORAD-authorized Threat Condition Alerting Message. Covered Wagon. This is not a drill...".

Fitzgerald looked across the table at his Flight Leader, Steiner. 'Covered Wagon' meant there was an unknown aircraft approaching or inside U.S. airspace. They were both wondering if this was a legitimate terrorist attack on the United States. Their eyes met the other pilots' in their group; they rose as one and headed for Base Operations. The specialists working there were in high gear. A major handed them each of them a printout. The only way to assess a threat was to get 'eyes on it' or receive an IFF – Interrogation-friend or foe – transmission. That was Razorback's job.

"Looks like NORAD has picked up a threat originating in New Mexico and its headed our way. Moving through Monument Valley right now. They're scrambling flights out of Luke and Edwards also to box them in. So this will be a two-ship flight. Fitzgerald, Steiner... you two are picking this one up. Intel's coming in moment-to-moment. We'll have specifics by the time you launch...".

"Good hunting!" said the other two pilots and returned to their table in the next room. Steiner and Fitzgerald trotted to the pilot's locker room and grabbed their helmets, G-suits and sidearms. They raced to a waiting transport.

"I was looking forward to that coffee," Fitzgerald joked.

A real live air-to-air intercept to a pilot was like a ticket to Disneyland would be to a kid. It was the culmination of years of dedicated training and there were few rides in the world as exhilarating as an F-16, loaded for bear, in 'full after-burner.' The transport would take them to the Alert Barn where four fully-armed F-16 Vipers waited, four abreast, each in its individual bay. The hangar doors in front and behind were already up, the ground crew scurried about the aircraft pulling pins on the weapons and other gear preparing for flight. Weapons systems mechanics sat in each cockpit running preliminary checks on weapons and avionics. Fitzgerald and Steiner spent the ride suiting up. The crew chief was just pulling the last pins.

"Good morning, sir," the crew chief saluted. "Your Viper is ready to roll, all systems one hundred percent."

"Thank you, Sarg," Steiner replied, smiling faintly. He liked his crew to know they were truly appreciated, especially if he did not come back. The nature of the threat was still a complete unknown. Steiner did a quick walk around, climbed the ladder hanging off the canopy sill and lowered himself into the cockpit. He was surrounded by a complex array of switches, dials, and instruments on several electronic display screens. They buckled themselves in with assistance from the crew chiefs, plugged in their G-suits, COM lines and gave the thumbs up.

Major Steiner keyed his mic, ship-to-ship. "Ready to roll?"

"That's an affirmative," came the reply. "Let's get this show on the road."

"Nellis Tower," Steiner said, "Razorback Flight, One and Two, ready to roll."

"Control – copy that, Razorback One. The pattern is cleared. Taxi when ready."

The heavily laden aircraft rolled forward, following the lines painted down the centerline of the taxiway. As the engines began to roar, the nose gear of each Viper compressed under the thrust of the jet engines. The landscape behind the two aircraft became a swirling, translucent cloud of dust as the exhaust blast of the F-16s carried away anything that wasn't cemented to the ground. Steiner alerted the tower:

"Nellis Tower, Razorback flight ready to launch. Over."

"Razorback flight, you are cleared for take-off. God speed, gentlemen."

Once in the air, Nellis directed them to climb to 15,000 feet on a vector of 160, heading roughly toward Flagstaff.

"Razorback Flight... Nellis Control... uh, that Covered Wagon appears to be an unidentified two ship heavy, originating out of southern New Mexico... headed through Monument Valley towards Flagstaff at the moment, no known destination. NSA is concerned if there's a target, it's Vegas. IFF signature and radar return on one aircraft only... looks like a Boeing 747... uh, supposedly government contractor... NORAD saying 747-type aircraft in pursuit of another jumbo jet... but we have no read on that one at all. No radar, no IFF or IR. If it's real, it's real special... speculation only but there was a chem plant explosion this morning in Tennessee."

"Razorback One copy."

"Razorback Flight, you will be taking up a pattern north of the Grand Canyon. The interceptors out of Luke... another Viper two ship... Navajo flight... will bring up the southern flank and Edwards is launching two more to cover the west end of the kill zone...".

There was a brief pause, the controller still had an open mic. He was questioning someone offline.

"Are you kidding me? Terrain masking?" He came back full volume.

"Razorback, we're being told that these two heavy aircraft are flying low – under 500 feet through Monument Valley. Looks like knap-of-the-earth... a terrain masking profile...".

He broke off again to listen to low voices in the background.

"Oh...", he said, then returned. "Are you sure? Are... you... sure...? Copy that."

"Razorback, this is Nellis Control again. Pilots, we have a Molly situation here. Repeat. This is *Molly,* Razorback."

Steiner and Fitzgerald looked at each other across the airspace. 'Molly' was code for stand down. Pilots truly in the know like they were knew this was an order from the Pentagon, from Lt. General Toby Morrow, to stand down and allow this ship to leave. If this was a true Molly, all the base commanders, including the CO at NORAD would be facing house arrest or worse if they did not comply with the order to stand down. NORAD was accustomed to taking orders from the Secretary of Defense only. The commanders would be apoplectic that their scramble orders had been aborted by someone in the Pentagon.

Tim found a spot about five hundred feet from the canyon wall on the updraft side and tried to stay there despite having Josh on his tail. In a canyon with sheer rock walls thousands of feet high, the proximity warning system went nuts. Smack in the middle was where shear knocked things around. He knew there were Flight-Free zones below fourteen thousand five hundred feet to keep noise away from the tourists. That was the safest place to take a couple of very large renegade planes…if there was a safe place. The tourists were just going to have to duck. It's not like they wouldn't see them coming after all and the noise would not kill anyone.

"Shut that thing up!" Tim barked at Pip to disable the terrain enunciator.

He had enough to worry about without the warnings going off constantly. The G-forces generated when the big plane dove suddenly and banked at high speeds were enough to contend with. Josh would be having the same problems. Pip flipped a switch. Despite the width of the canyon, the minute Josh was sucked down behind him in the Proteus, Tim re-evaluated his immediate goal. There was an almost certain chance they'd all be killed. These airplanes were just too damned big for the canyon. He made a decision.

"Pip," he said, "I'm just going to fly and I'm going to pull some maneuvers Josh can't pull in that whale. Sorry."

Pip thought for a moment. "Okay. It was his choice. We have got to get out of here."

Tim dropped altitude quickly causing negative G-forces to work on everything in the cockpit that wasn't nailed down. Clipboards went flying. Empty coffee cups from the morning run hit the ceiling. Pip's legs flew up.

"God, I hate negative G," Pip said when they leveled out briefly.

Tim had no idea whether Josh knew anything about the Grand Canyon or even mountain and canyon flying. Tim was a firebomber. Terrain like this was his bread and butter. If Josh had any sense, he would not take the Proteus up this particular alley. He came right after Tim.

"Damn it," Tim said.

He'd been hoping Josh would disobey orders but knew he would not. Such a stupid thing to die for. Tim pulled up and banked left. He'd performed the maneuver a thousand times in a fire. Josh did not have the time or the maneuverability to react in the same way and so flew his bird right into a sheer canyon wall. Inside the Proteus, the nose impacted the wall of the canyon causing the cockpit and front end to accordion like tissue paper. The floor ruptured down the middle and the gleaming silver kegs tore themselves loose. Simultaneously, chemicals filled the belly of the plane and the engines burst into flames. The explosion caused the Plato to shudder violently. Tim climbed above the rim of the canyon moments before it became too narrow for him as well. It was not a space where there were likely to be people. He hugged the ground again until he was clear of the area. He and Pip did not speak again until they got a visual on the sea.

As soon as they saw the white-capped surf rolling against the Pacific shore, they climbed to 28,000 feet then up using the aluminum oxide fuel injection thrusters to save fuel. Typically, the Plato climbed near the service ceiling on jet power, then engaged the thruster. There was enough fuel to maintain thrust for three minutes. But in those three minutes, Plato went from 28,000 to 70,000 feet. Then they leveled out.

Get a weather report, will you? No one's catching us up here," Tim said. They had both performed this maneuver half a dozen times in this aircraft but the thrill had not worn off.

"Typhoon warning in the Philippines... Class Two. 37-62 mph winds within the next twenty-four hours," Pip replied after a moment. "Doesn't sound too bad."

They had about ten hours left to fly.

"Let's take shifts, okay?" Tim suggested. "You first. Get a few hours, pilot."

Two hours later, the radio came alive. Tim and Pip looked at each other, puzzled.

"Ah," Pip smacked his forehead, "satellite. Same principle as the space station. That would take orders from the very top."

"Gentleman," a voice crackled into their headsets.

They were silent. This voice would have to give itself a name before it got any kind of audio from the Plato.

"Gentlemen, this is Georg Nero Wolfe... and that is my airplane."

Tim's eyes went very wide and Pip shook his head in disbelief.

"Did I just hear that?" Pip asked.

Tim shrugged.

"Bring my aircraft back, Verzet. You, too, Yarmouth."

Tim flipped the mic switch. "No, thanks."

"Verzet, you can turn the Plato around or you can land in the middle of a typhoon. There is a nasty one building over the Philippines right now... could hit Okinawa right about the time you want to not run out of gas."

Pip's head whipped around. "What?"

"They could probably do that, yes." How did they know about Okinawa? "Well, where do you want it to land then?" he answered. "China? Japan? India? Moscow? Take your pick. I can get there without running out of gas."

"Very well. I will sink that plane, mark my words." The radio went dead.

"Wow," Pip sat up, straightened his headset. "What do you think?"

"They can or they can't. It'll happen or it won't. I survived the bottom of the Grand Canyon and I'm up cruising at 70,000 feet right now. I guess we can slide through some rain in this bird. The on-board computer is supposed to be able to handle a hurricane," Tim yawned, although he was a little worried. "I believe it."

"Thanks," Pip said wryly, "that little dance was very comforting."

Eight hours later, they had to descend. They were running out of fuel, finally. At 28,000 feet, it became clear Nero Wolfe was a man of his word. There was a Class Two approaching Okinawa. They would slice through the leading edge but would be on the ground before the typhoon hit, if it actually did. Winds were forty miles per hour at 28,000 feet but did not seem to increase below that. It seemed that Nero's aircraft had outrun Nero's storm. Still, in any other plane it would have been a ridiculously bumpy and fairly risky landing.

"Hell," laughed Pip, "I'd like to see 'em land this thing in New Mexico in March. Now that's a problem."

The Hologram

Dearest Christina;

I've thought long and hard about you and your situation and your book. I woke up this morning with the very clear sense that I ought to have nothing whatsoever to do with it. I can't help you. Further, I am well known here in Australia and I have a reputation to protect. As to Christmas-time, I will be gone. Travelling and promoting my own book. So sorry.

Bennie

When she showed the note to Otto he said, "Well, I guess it's a damned good thing we hadn't bought any tickets yet."

May was giving way to June. Christina had been working on her book for a few months now. Otto set up a small dining table for her to use as a desk by the picture window in their bedroom. It was generally strewn with communications from Charlie Shepard, her own research printouts, and various drafts she had worked on, was working on or planned to work on. There were usually the odd set of child's mittens in some stage of being knit, scattered photos, flowers in a vase, and remnants of half-eaten meals. The walls in front of her desk were covered with tacked-up poster board she used to write details, timelines and questions and a thousand other things she might forget. From her seat in front of the computer, she looked out over the front veranda and onto the street. She had marked the change of the seasons through its frame this year.

Some secret mission this is, she thought. You can see what I'm doing through the window.

She was typing, in fact, that day. Every dog being walked down the street passed by her window causing her mismatched pair of dogs to howl. Their elderly postman, long past the age of retirement, trudged up the front steps with the mail every day at noon and dropped the mail into the box a few feet away from where she sat. Bennie's note, in a crisp white linen envelope, had been the only piece of mail today. It was more than enough.

Christina could think of a hundred immediate reasons to be afraid but Bennie had no real experience of what was going on at all several thousand miles away other than the knowledge that Christina had reason to believe her mother had been murdered. Bennie was frightened in a nameless sort of way, almost as much for her status as anything else. Despite the curt tone of the message, it seemed Bennie had panicked. While the abandonment of a friend she was counting on did sting, no question about that, she was quietly aware that she had to stick with those who were already brave enough to be part of yanking this filth into the light, where it could be seen and dealt with. There were so many out there occupied with this task... Christina was simply joining them. This treachery against humanity could not stand the light of day. She wondered if people would be so afraid if they believed that. At the moment, it did not matter what anyone else was doing; there was work to be done.

Her plan had been to secure the manuscript with someone trustworthy on the other side of the world but fear had found its way there, it seemed, as fear often does. She had always thought of Bennie as a brave soul. That had been her best shot. Now believing more than ever that the more people had the book and its contents in their hands, the safer she and her family might be, she decided to aggressively push the story into the open. It was a tough decision, a scary proposition. That would mean braving the privacy-free realm of e-mail for one thing. Charlie Shepard had warned her right up front that his e-mails and phone calls – all his communications and actions – were monitored constantly and that every once in a while someone he knew would be subject to some sort of in-your-face intimidation; what kind and how much depended on the subject at hand. She knew this was a risk. From the moment her mother died and she opened her mother's laptop and started to think about what might have happened, she had assumed her communications were monitored, as well. She thought, only half joking, that there were more people monitoring others in this country now than people actually being monitored. Having someone try to run her off the road in her mother's car just a few weeks after the accident only served to boldly underline her suspicions. Christina knew that if she was going to throw herself out into the open she needed to move as fast as possible and email was the fastest way to do that. The biggest problem was that the book wasn't finished and so she would be vulnerable for a while yet.

Nevertheless, she sat down and wrote a pitch for the book. That night she sent out nearly two hundred emails to various literary agents, some she knew but most she didn't, and a couple of messages to independent publishers whom she thought might just have the guts to take on the story. Then she went back to work.

And she kept writing as she had been; day after day, month after month, alone in a corner of her bedroom. She cared for her children, of course; the ones most clearly manifesting the effects of the poisoned environment, although summer seemed to have brought a slight reprieve. The cold, the shut houses, all seemed to heighten the symptoms. Everything else dropped by the wayside for the time being. Dishes stacked themselves into precarious towers by the sink, laundry piled higher and higher on the bed in the spare room, the idle vacuum cleaner collected a layer of thick dust. The front garden lay under a pile of very old and wet fall leaves when ordinarily hundreds of bean plants would be sprouting there. This is how it would stay until the story was told.

That was the book, though. Only half of the equation. The other half was the tantalizing opportunity on Okinawa. Christina and Charlie and Nikolai. The more she thought about it, the more certain she was that they should form the core of a group intent on being at the open sessions of the *Shuri* Reconciliation Panel in July. Charlie and Nikolai had yet to meet face-to-face. She also wanted to enlist the California contingent for the trip. Their documentation was priceless, hard-won, and they deserved to be given a voice. No matter what the constellation of people forming the embassy to *Shuri* Castle, they had about three weeks to create a plan; not much time at all. Once they were all there, they would have their first opportunity to plead their case before the panel and they would pray they'd get onto the list for the longer hearing. Christina and Nikolai would be traveling the greatest distance and Nikolai said he had no funds for the trip. They had to decide what to do about that. Nikolai had to be there. He had been in the forefront of the battle for years.

"Never heard of him," Charlie told her on the phone. "I'm going to check in with Cliff and see if he knows who Nikolai is. I know you keep mentioning him and the guys up at Shasta have mentioned him. Why don't I know this guy?"

She sent copies of her work in progress to Charlie but not via e-mail. Charlie would question, challenge, confirm... all the things she wanted a reader to do. She was deeply grateful for another set of eyes; someone well-versed in the reality of the situation. She was grateful that she knew someone with the courage. There was some difficulty in deciding how to get the chapters to him under the circumstances. She varied her form of delivery as much as possible. Her least favourite choice was her local post office. She just had a bad feeling about it. E-mail she would save for desperation. Then, of course, there were all the days... fewer and fewer as time went by... when she simply wondered if she had slipped into true paranoia. She knew, intellectually, that she had not. It was good to question, though, she reassured herself. It meant she was still being rational. It would have been more worrisome to ignore what was happening.

Then the day arrived when she had to turn off her computer, set aside plans for traveling to Okinawa, and meet with the prosecutor to go over George Walter's medical records. Months and months of blind alleys and people pretending they were either deaf or didn't understand English when she asked about them had finally ended with a plea to the prosecution. Otto drove with her to the County Court House thirty minutes south. They were ushered to the second floor. An assistant gave Christina a large folder filled with discovery evidence and a quiet room to sit in. The assistant instructed Christina to call her in the next room if she had any questions.

"Well, I know there are a couple of things I want to ask the prosecutor already," Christina said.

"Oh, so sorry," the assistant replied. "The prosecutor isn't here today. She had to attend a meeting in another town. We can make another appointment if you want to talk to her. She said she wasn't sure if you were coming or not."

Otto and Christina looked at each other.

"What are you talking about? We had an appointment. Why would I not be here?"

"Well, she just wasn't sure." The assistant smiled a charming smile and went back to her room.

"Okay, well," said Christina quietly, "let's have a look." That made no sense at all.

She scanned each page; accident reports, lists of witnesses, accounts of police officers... even the bill from the ambulance service. Finally she found a list of the medicines he was on at the time. There were a dozen, including aspirin and a multi-vitamin. It was the kind of list one would expect an old man to produce, with one exception. The blood tests conducted in Boston revealed an extra drug in his system. She had been told well over a year ago that there was absolutely nothing in his system. It was a central nervous system depressant.

She forged on through the folder; page after page of motor accidents, a long history of hitting things and people. She knew all of this. In the end of the folder, she found the same two assessment reports she had already seen, a few years apart and that was it. This folder ended in the same place the other discovery folder did. There was no medical record of any kind on or near the date Walters had run her mother down. She pushed away from the table and went to find the assistant.

"Sorry to bother you," Christina said, "but there are no medical records here. We came to see those records, as you all know, that so far we have not been able to get."

"Oh, dear," the assistant replied. "Let me make a call, see if I can get hold of the prosecutor."

The reality was that Christina had half-expected this to be the case. Those records, as important as they were to her and to Walter's state when he was driving his van that day, were going to stay hidden. She knew that there was something in those records, perhaps a name that was protected. The question was why?

The young woman returned. "Yes, the prosecutor says they didn't need to know any of that to prove the case."

"So, you're saying, in effect, that his health care at the time, any additions to his treatment or omissions of treatment that really could have contributed to my mother's death just weren't worth finding out about? What if there's a doctor out there who seriously contributed to Walter's ability to operate a car that day? Shouldn't we know about that? The primary question in this entire case is, why was this guy behind the wheel of a car when he was so clearly almost completely medically incapacitated?"

"Well, that would likely be a civil matter, not a criminal matter." The assistant smiled.

Christina rubbed her forehead, trying hard as she could not to cry. "How would we go about getting that information?"

"Well, his attorney would have to get his signature on a release for his records."

"You mean the man lying in a bed after his massive stroke who doesn't even know his own name? That guy? His own attorney didn't even think that might be material information?"

The assistant gave Christina a smile even broader than the one before.

"Yes."

If she tells me to have nice day, I swear to God I'm going to slap her.

Did that drug further interfere with Walter's abilities that day? They would likely never know. It also occurred to her that maybe the reason attorneys kept backing away from the case is that they knew, without telling her and putting her out of her misery, that they would never gain access to this information before the statute of limitations ran out. Likely Walters would have to be declared incompetent in a court and then whoever became his power of attorney would have to sign a release. That would take a long time. Longer than she had. So now she had three possibilities as to why attorneys were turning their backs on this vital part of the mystery: one, they were scared; two, they didn't see any money in it; or three, they knew they could never get the records in time to do anything about it. Maybe, all three. Not one of them had ended her suffering over the long months by saying these things to her in plain English.

Otto was irate. Once they were in the car he let loose.

"I cannot believe they are seriously telling us that the last five years of his medical history are irrelevant when his physical ability to drive a car is the question here. Should he have been behind the wheel of a car, that's the question. I think we may need to go up the line here and fast."

"Yep," Christina agreed. She knew Walters would never see the inside of that courtroom and she knew that she might never see the pertinent records she had a right to see but she could by God start raising hell about how this had played out and see if she could shake any crooks out of the trees. That she could do.

She went back to work; it was what she could do. Two days later, she heard shouts and laughter from the driveway. She set her reading glasses on the desk and went to see what was going on. Otto and the children were erecting her beloved hoop greenhouses. Despite the fact that all the seeds should be in the ground and percolating right along by now, her husband had seen that she did not have it in her to direct any attention to this summer tradition but he knew that she would need them desperately as the weeks went by. He noticed her standing in the window and cuffed David on the shoulder. Anya and David looked up from turning earth in the little bean garden, smiled broadly and waved.

"Hi, Mom!" they yelled together.

"We're putting in some veg, honey," Otto hollered.

Christina smiled and waved back. She would be so glad to find little sprouts in the ground in a few days. The insistence of these seedlings on living was an important act of defiance.

"Mom!" Anya called. "I need to go to the library for my project." Christina had been sitting at her computer for hours. She could use a break. Burying herself in the book for a couple of days had evened things out and taken her mind off the unfinished business of the state's legal case. Ultimately she knew that was the blessing and the problem. She had not had to look squarely at this man, decide what to accuse him of and how he should pay for it. On the other hand, the state operated with absolutely no regard for the victim or her family. It was purely a question of which law the man had broken and what was the customary penalty for breaking it. There could be little more than a crippled sort of healing for those left behind with so many unanswered questions.

"I can drop you two off," Otto said. He already had car keys in his hand. "I'm on my way to the office for a bit."

They drove the mile to the little brick and white painted wood library in front of the elementary school. It sat on a trim acre of green grass near the highway entrance and exit. Otto let them out of the van at the double doors in the front and pulled back into traffic. The school year was coming to a close. Anya had one more project to finish. Christina wanted to get out of the house, this was the perfect excuse. Here she could sit and read a copy of the New York Times Sunday edition in a sun-soaked reading room, a quiet warm place by the tall window, while Anya did her research.

An hour and a half later, Anya returned with an armload of books. "Come on, Mom," she said. "Let's wait outside for Dad."

Sure enough they could see Otto approaching the exit ramp from their vantage point in the reading room. They made their way out through the 'New Fiction' section and past the check-out counter. As Christina was pushing the door open, there was a tremendous screeching of brakes followed by a loud crash. She and Anya looked at each other, wide-eyed and raced outside.

Several people were running across the grass ahead of them. Otto's van had plowed into a parked truck. It was large, white, with 'Rick's Appliances' painted on the side. Luckily no one had been in it. The air bag had deployed and Otto looked very shaken up. Christina ran to the driver's side door and pulled it open.

"Oh my God," she said, "what happened? Are you okay?"

"Daddy!" Anya was right behind her.

"The steering failed," Otto shook his head, not quite believing what he was saying. "Thank God I was coming down the off-ramp and slowing down anyway. Jesus Christ! The steering failed."

The next morning, their mechanic said it appeared a bolt had simply 'fallen out' of the steering column. Christina did not think the bolt had jimmied its way loose over time and just happened to fall out at such a vulnerable and dangerous time in their lives. However, she did not make the connection out loud for her husband or her daughter. A few days later their Subaru was vandalized in their driveway, all of the compartments and doors left wide open, she realized, when she left the house to drive David to school.

Later the same day she got a message from Charlie letting her know that a friend of his, interested in the same topics the book covered, had been cornered and threatened. All this was a result of her sending the pitch out into the world. Just the pitch. This simply could not be a coincidence. Going public had prompted a rash of intimidation. She felt roughed up for a while. She was jerked back to that moment when she stood beside her mother's tangled, broken body in the emergency room. That was the whole idea. These things were meant to remind her of that scene but the thought process that went along with the idea of quitting because it was too dangerous was territory she had covered very early on... in great detail... in the autumn after her mother had been killed. If the atmospheric poisoning was allowed to continue they were all going to die anyway. There was little point in not trying.

Christina was more convinced than ever that she needed to make sure as many people as would accept the book had copies of it and she needed to make sure that she said that plainly, over the phone and in e-mail where the spooks would hear her. So she did. The intimidation had failed. All was quiet until a package of chapters en route to Charlie disappeared. It finally reappeared in her mailbox, manila envelope slit open in several places.

The book was a novelized version of what had happened, liberally sprinkled with concrete and provable facts. Names had been changed to offer what little protection she could offer. Nevertheless, she was obviously hitting a nerve in there somewhere. She didn't know where and she didn't care where; she was just telling the story as it happened. If it captured people's imagination just enough to make them look up, things might start to change. That would be good enough.

In the end, though, it's just a freaking story, for God's sake.

"Hello, Christina here," her cell phone had chimed.

She was sitting at her desk again, just back from beating back violently red raspberry vines, more like thorny whips than bushes, and from turning earth in the side garden. She knew the plants and the soil in which they were growing were poisoned. Distilling enough pure water to use on a garden the size she wanted was simply not possible at the moment. She could, however, experiment with ways to remediate the soils. She'd been reading about this – it was happening all over the world usually right under the noses of people who had no idea anything was amiss. They saw the unexplained white powdery substance on their broad-leafed plants and the mysterious spider-web formations in the grass and trees in the morning and scratched their heads but let it go at that.

I wonder how many near-Armageddons have occurred, what other sorts of life or death crises had slipped by most people's notice just in the last century?

She had to believe there was an 'after all this stops' moment coming when they would need to be ready to help the earth start to heal. Any other scenario was simply impossible to contemplate. Besides it helped her stay sane as she recounted on paper the ridiculous story she was living.

"Hi, Christina," the voice on the other end sounded far way, "French Baum here."

"French! Of course you would call… I've been out among the plants this morning. You got my note about coordinating the trip to Okinawa…?"

"I did. We're all going. Forming a posse, I guess. A bunch of old scientists with lots of evidence to present. Things are actually getting worse here."

"Worse? What do you mean?"

"Remember there was some talk when you were out here about a documentable steady rise in violence in this area? We had another night of insanity last night. This stuff doesn't just happen, Christina. It's not like people are robbing stores because they're hungry… things like that. This is brutal, senseless, random stuff. We've been working on trying to document it alongside our environmental sampling. We're pretty sure we'll be able to indicate a relationship."

"What happened?" she asked.

"I'm going to fax you the article. I've been talking about this all day. The county sheriff is a friend of mine. Everybody is so shaken up… I want to use my energy right now to talk about the trip. I want to focus on what's good." He sighed heavily.

"Okay, French." She could hear the shaking in his breath.

"Should we meet in San Francisco and fly over together or try to meet at Naha?" he asked. "I understand there's some rough weather heading north from the Philippines... it may turn into a typhoon. I hope we don't get caught in that."

"I heard that, too. It's just unpredictable out there right now. I'm thinking we should each carry all the information and spread out a little. Take a few different flights. Life doesn't seem to mean anything to these people. Charlie says he has a house for us. It belongs to Choshin Soderholm's Japanese friend, the one who was a member of the royal family until she got married. It's at the base of the hill that leads up to *Shuri* Castle. I'm pretty sure we're in great shape once we get there. Um... I need you to talk to the guys for me, though."

"What about?" he asked.

"Nikolai and his son. They haven't got the funds to do this and he deserves to be there. Can we pool our money for this... chip in?"

"I imagine they'll be happy to do that. I'll let you know."

"Great," she said softly. "And, French? I'm really sorry about what's happening out there. I really am."

"Thanks, Christina. Let's just stop it." He hung up.

From his house in Carmel, Charlie Shepard, having just put down the phone, shook his head in disbelief. He knew the Fire Chief in the little town where the massacre had happened. Such a rampage; such bloodthirsty violence in northern California coming to a boil in one little area between Redding and Mt. Shasta. It had been going on for a few years and had escalated noticeably in the last year or two. Charlie knew this area was a thick dumping spot for airborne chemicals. Granted, there were sites like that all over the country. Thanks to ordinary people keeping diaries, taking photos, taking readings and comparing notes they were starting to identify a few of them. The seacoast of Maine was another one. The aircraft came in off the Atlantic and dropped their payloads where winds then swept them far inland. Residents didn't seem to be violent there; the area was just saturated. There was more evidence of illness in northern New England, like Anya and David. More unexplainable suicides in tiny, little areas. The bitter truth was, though, that the entire country was drowning in toxins.

French Baum lived up near Mt. Shasta. Shepard knew French pretty well. They were both deeply involved in the geo-engineering mystery. He would give French a call later. This morning, though, he was waiting for something else; a call from a friend in the FBI. He wanted information on one Nikolai Louis. There was a problem there, he could feel it. Cliff, the fellow with the radio program, had heard of Nikolai but, despite repeated attempts to get him on the show, had never been able to get him to return his calls. If anyone could dig something up on Nikolai 'Amistad' Louis, it would be this guy.

Charlie got lucky, as he knew he would. There was a sloppily hidden resume that included a security ranking... a dead giveaway. This guy was supposed to be an artist and an activist. On the other end of the phone, his FBI contact laughed.

"This guy's an asset for sure," he said. "Don't get too close, man."

Charlie had the resume faxed to him. Nikolai Louis had started out in special forces in the military and maintained an 'enhanced security' clearance. He had a degree in biochemistry. His job history actually listed the CIA, NSA, Interpol and the Royal Canadian Mounted Police, the National Research Council of Canada – NRC, the Canadian Security Intelligence Service – CSIS, the US Department of Health and Human Services... the list was damning. He'd been a consultant for several major universities, mostly in the United States, on social data collection. It was right there for anyone to see but you had to have a reason. Interpol, for Christ's sake. Nikolai Louis was listed as co-author of a scientific paper on Information Extraction in the Global Human Genetic Inventory, a twenty-five year old project that was nothing less than an ambitious and exhaustive database effort on every human being on the planet, initiated and funded by the U.S. government. He was a mole, a spy, an expert collector and collator of information. He had spent a decade collecting names, locations and contact information of people around the globe who vehemently opposed geo-engineering. He conducted surveys to try to establish which among those long lists of opponents were most likely to be active and vocal and to what extent. Welcome to the social media.

Most of the private companies listed on this resume had primary functions of data mining and intelligence which then went to the military, police and health institutions. He was an expert in and had spent a large portion of his career networking databases for those agencies.

The next thing Charlie did was sign on to Nikolai's web site. He could see, as he scrolled back through the weeks and the months, requests by Nikolai for lab results from anyone who had themselves evaluated for heavy metals and other toxins. He conducted polls as to what natural detoxification regimes were working for people or not working. He had created a database with names and contact details in the thousands. Nikolai was a shill, a fake, a hologram set up to mimic the world people thought they lived in; make them feel empowered to fight for a cause they believed in. He was a decoy, as well. He kept them all busy talking to each other. It was a con, plain and simple. Its façade however was a group of dedicated activists trying to unearth the true purpose of this global project. It was the double-edged sword of the social media. Without this 'mining,' there would not be a network spanning the globe keeping each other in vital information.

Charlie leaned back in his chair; put his hands behind his head. What now? He had never met this guy. That had to change. They'd be on Okinawa together. What an espionage coup that would be for Nikolai Louis. An operator for whomever he was ultimately working at the very heart of the resistance at potentially the most important moment in the resistance. Charlie would not tell anyone else. This guy would pick up on it right away and disappear. He would wait until they were all on Okinawa and force him to testify. Nikolai Louis had mountains of data, much of it medical, all collated to be useful. He would testify or else.

Christina pulled the fax from French Baum off her machine. She sat at her desk, watching half a dozen teenaged boys skateboard in the street. A truck slowed and honked at the boys, wanting around. French had written a little note in the margin around the article: Another day of carnage here yesterday. This article is from just south of here, where the chemical fallout has had the highest impact on the landscape. I'll let you read the rest.

Yesterday, police responded to a 911 call from a man reporting that three men, who lived together, were engaged in a spectacularly violent argument. Two of the men were stabbed repeatedly. The assailant continued his bloody rampage down the street, butchering an elderly neighbor and attacking a maintenance worker sitting in his truck. The truck driver tried to flee, crashed into another parked vehicle and the assailant set both vehicles on fire. Sheriff's deputies were unable to free anyone from the burning vehicles. No motive is known for the assaults.

Huck had spoken at times, she remembered, about the steady increase in senseless violence in his area and a youth population that seemed unnaturally aggressive and constantly agitated. Christina left her work, left the computer and retreated to the garden once more. When she felt overwhelmed by the damage, the fear, the disbelief – the contemplation of what sort of mind puts together a program of poison like this – she disappeared into one of the hoop tunnel greenhouses, as Otto had known she would. In early June in northern New England it was bone-warming to have an atmosphere resembling Bermuda providing the sun had beat down on the white plastic all day. In other years, when she set the hoop houses up and started to turn the earth over, the worms were still hibernating. Today she had early June crops pushing up through the loamy soil: spinach, kale, lettuce, carrots, peas, radishes. She crawled into the smallest greenhouse and began to pull out tiny weeds. Her heart swelled unexpectedly when she heard the dove in the elm tree. This lone dove appeared every year, all by itself. When the summer sun was hot and high it often walked around the driveway, completely unconcerned about the coming and going of the residents of the house. In fact, the first time it appeared, Christina thought he must have been injured he did so much walking and refused to be startled. The sound of a dove cooing plaintively reminded her of Hawaii, as there was always a dove cooing in the trees somewhere there. It might have been the proximity to the seashore that brought them although she hardly thought of doves as shore birds.

They – Nikolai, Charlie, Isaac, Huck, French and Christina – planned to leave on St. John's Eve and spend the last few days of June in Naha. There was talk of a typhoon developing but it could just as easily head out to sea. Charlie knew Choshin Soderholm, for one thing, and wanted to meet with her, discuss the document and bring her an idea of the issue at hand... if she would allow it. This strategy might very well offend her sense of fair play. They probably had firm rules in place already.

At the moment, Christina's group was trying their best to determine what sort of testimony would be the most effective. As far as they could make out, they would initially have five minutes to pose an argument as to why they should have a place at the longer hearing. Many groups wanted the attention of the panel. The public testimony was allotted two weeks. Then the panel would adjourn to finish crafting a document that was largely already in place. What would happen after their bit was included in the treaty? No one knew. It was all they could think to do and so they poured all their hopes and energy into it.

They converged in San Francisco. Nikolai, his son, Hugo, and Christina rendezvoused with Charlie and, each of them armed with full and complete copies of the evidence they were taking with them, they boarded an All Nippon Airways flight together. They weren't taking any chances. French, Huck, and Isaac Masters travelled as a group aboard China Air. Charlie could not decide whether it was more important to stay with Christina and Nikolai on the flight or make a third team with one of the other guys on another airline. It wasn't that he felt Christina was in any danger. It was that Nikolai himself was a piece of evidence, a major one, which needed to be watched and kept in pocket on principle. One plane would take the team of California-based scientists and their quantitative environmental data to Shuri. The other would take this government agent who had collected the personal data, lab results and metals levels and health information through taking polls: to what lengths would they go to stop geo-engineering, where are they located, how well are they organized, what are they thinking, what might they be getting ready to do? Shepard had found that Nikolai had a separate unconnected site discussing methods of data collection research and use.

Charlie decided to stay with Nikolai because that man had to be forced to tell even a small part of what he knew, he could not be allowed to bolt if he sensed something was going
wrong. He was too valuable. It might help that Hugo was along, it might not. If Nikolai decided to return to Canada after the conference, and he couldn't think why he would want to do that, Charlie would advise that no one be on the same plane as Nikolai. The best way to handle the confrontation might occur to him on the flight. Beyond that he would not think. The storm they were worried about had touched the eastern edge of the Japanese islands then changed its mind, turned and blew out to sea.

The aircraft approached the island from the north and so skirted brown and green cliffs, narrow beaches, and ever more transparent lagoons until they made their approach Naha Airport. The sea was a bit rough still, the only evidence that a giant storm had passed by here. Instrumental Japanese music wafted vaguely from the aircraft sound system, in the background, barely audible above the muffled noise of the jets. They sat, the four of them, in the two rows nearest the wing. The metallic squeal of the flaps complaining as they opened startled them they were so captured by the view of Okinawa as they circled it. The runway began just at the ocean's edge and one moment the plane was sailing over water, the next it kissed the asphalt. The bumping of the touchdown was so jarring, so abrupt, it startled Nikolai's son, who cried out.

"Regardez! Nous atterrissons!"

They were, indeed, bumping along a somewhat rough tarmac. The attendant must have been giving instructions in Japanese for a while but it wasn't until the aircraft was rolling along the runway that they were jarred back into the task at hand and realized that someone was speaking. Okinawa from the air was a deeply colored patchwork of terraced hills with fields of sugar cane and rice. Christina later read that the farmers also grew pineapple, tobacco and, on the smaller outlying islands, peanuts. There were centers of dense, modern human activity fenced in by lush jungle and abundant agriculture.

They disembarked then met the other group twenty minutes later at the baggage carousel. Walking was tough as they had been on the aircraft for many long hours and they were stiff. Together again, they made their way through customs. Then they took two taxis to their hotel. They would spend one night in a hotel, and then be taken to the little house set aside for them. Hugo begged to go to the beaches he'd spotted as soon as their bags were in their rooms. It was unbearably hot, unusually so, as the heat was a remnant of the storm.

"I'll tell you what, my friend," Charlie said, "what if you guys go to the beach right away before we all get really busy tomorrow. You up for it, Nikolai?"

"Sure," Nikolai said, "that's okay with me. I'm dying."

"I think the old men will stay here and take a nap in the air conditioning, if you don't mind," Isaac said, chuckling wearily.

Christina had a room to herself. Charlie was bunking with Nikolai and Hugo. The 'old men' were sharing a third room. Their hotel was situated on *Kokusai Dori*, Kokusai Street. It was the main artery, the busiest street in Naha, a city of well over three hundred thousand. There was a tremendous amount of traffic, both car and bicycle, and fish-filled canals divided the city. They sat in the shadow of *Shuri* Castle no matter where they were in Naha. The mighty fortress of the old Ryukyu Dynasty would be closed to the public for a fortnight while the panel entertained testimony from all over the world. The majestic location had been arranged to infuse the effort with a ceremonial, diplomatic air. Then the panel would adjourn to write the *Shuri* Reconciliation, a Human Rights Treaty and the first international human rights effort of the twenty-first century. It would be presented to the Japanese government first, which had already promised to support the treaty internationally.

Christina and Charlie ducked into the passageway beneath an elevated monorail; the train whooshed past as they walked below. The city pace was frenetic, although the taller buildings generally were not more than half a dozen stories high and there weren't that many of them. There were, however, many, many low-slung houses with Chinese-style red tiled roofs down narrow alley-like streets. The sounds of people riding bicycles filled the air. They passed two grocery stores, a seductive-looking chain ice-cream outlet which called to them like a Siren in the heat, a fern bar style restaurant and two well-appointed book stores. The sound of a loud, happy crowd drifted toward them from further on somewhere. They kept walking and eventually realized it was coming from a baseball field, filled to capacity even in the unbearable humidity of the afternoon.

Fifteen minutes later, they approached one of the narrow alleys situated between a vegetable stand on one corner and a noodle shop on the other. The aroma of dried fish was pungent. Two hundred yards up the road, narrowing to a winding path, the jumble of small shops ended abruptly as did the steady onslaught of people who had been rushing down the lane and back out into the city. Just where the path ended in a sharp left, a small house stood surrounded by a high but plain wood fence. Charlie pushed the gate open and they stepped into a small, well-tended garden. Several pair of shoes rested by the gate but the path between sunflowers and hibiscus on one side and tomatoes and carrots on the other was made of loose gravel so they kept their sandals on.

Christina felt there was something mildly miraculous about a house this serenely beautiful tucked away, unassailed, within the mad dash of the large city. A small bronze bell hung beside the wooden red-painted door. Charlie pulled the bell twice. A moment later, they heard quiet footsteps within. The *shoji*-style door of wood and glass slid open and a tall man stood before them leaning on a cane. He was thin, wore spectacles and kept his thinning hair shoulder length.

"*Buenos tardes,*" he said, clasping Charlie's hand. It was a surprise to hear Spanish in this setting.

"*Buenos tardes,*" Charlie returned. "You must be *Señor* Maldonado." The man nodded once, almost a slight bow.

"*Señor* Shepard?"

"*Sí.* This is Christina Galbraithe."

"*Encantado,*" he said clasping both her hands, as well.

He beckoned them silently to follow him through a short empty passage. Christina could just make out softly murmuring voices behind a closed screen door.

"Kindly remove your shoes," he said.

They slid their sandals off and left them in the hallway. Maldonado stopped before a screen door on his right. He slid it open gently with the fingers of his right hand revealing a room just large enough for a gleaming, low cherry wood table. Six people sat around it on *zabutan,* flat pillows on the floor. Charlie recognized Choshin Soderholm, smile wide, hair shorn so short as to be almost completely gone. It was impossible to determine what color it had been. Half-moon reading glasses rested on her nose, secured around her neck by a string. Her face was round, her countenance relaxed.

"Charlie Shepard. Christina Galbraithe. Join us, please," she waved them in. "Come! Come!"

Christina followed Charlie into the room. They sat on the two waiting *zabutan* at the table, Maldonado returning to his place, his cane tucked away under the table. Every place was now occupied. Behind Choshin, a reed mat hung over a door, swaying in the light breeze. The sliding door was open as the temperature was around ninety-five degrees, with the humidity to match, and closed houses in such heat turned into pressure cookers. Okinawa was the only island in the Japanese archipelago entirely in the subtropical zone.

"My friend," Choshin said warmly, as Charlie sat down. "Would you like something to drink?"

"God, yes. I'd love a beer."

She rose, stiffly, all of her sixty years in her limbs. "Oh, hey, don't get up," Charlie said. "I can get it."

"Listen, you. I'm fine. I am proficient in yoga and in being old. I'm stiff because I'm too old to stop eating sweets and the sugar settles in my joints. You'll notice, though, that you did not hear any joints crack?" She laughed softly. "You are lucky! You missed the storm."

"We heard. Didn't see much evidence of damage."

"No, we were also lucky. Christina?" Choshin stopped directly across the table and looked down at her through her bifocals.

"Whatever Charlie is having is fine," she said. She was a bit intimidated by this woman who had spent her entire life as an activist and spiritual leader and was now shepherding such a critical mission. Fearlessly, she supposed. Christina wanted to make a good impression.

Choshin returned quickly with two cans of Orion beer on a tray, beads of condensation trickling down the sides of the aluminum. She had a glass in each pocket of her shirt which she set firmly on the table before them and poured while she talked.

"You met Maldonado at the door," she said.

"Yes," replied Christina.

"He comes from Venezuela, does our Maldonado."

"She likes my last name," Señor Maldonado said, grinning. "She never calls me Arturo. Please don't feel you have to call me Maldonado, as well."

"Maldonado... Maldo-NA-do." Choshin let the name roll off her tongue in a Latin accent. "It's like watching a bullfight or a flamenco just to say it. Don't you think?"

"Venezuela!" Charlie said, accepting his beer from Choshin. "Beautiful, rugged country. Very independent, as well. Doing a lot to stand up for itself against the imperialists, yes?"

Arturo smiled.

"Why, yes." He said. "We are fighters; that is certain. I have been living in Spain for several years, though."

Choshin bent at the knees and eased herself back down to her mat. "Christina," Choshin asked, "how far have you journeyed to be here with us?"

"Oh," Christina sipped her beer, "northern New England... in the United States. I flew out of Boston."

"Lovely," Choshin returned, "I spent many happy years in Cambridge. Are you far from there?"

"Not really. About two hours' drive."

Christina knew that Choshin had come from Sweden, above the Arctic Circle actually, as a teenager. Charlie had already filled Christina in on some basic details about her; he and Choshin knew each other well as he had been her houseguest many times. She settled in Brooklyn on her own in 1967, taking classes at night and working in an automat – a kind of a cafeteria – during the day. Eventually she was credentialed to teach elementary school. She lived on Lincoln Street in Park Slope decades before the area was reclaimed as a neighborhood. Her landlord there was a Buddhist fellow from Thailand. She and he had occupied the front stoop discussing Buddha and the Dalai Lama and life and the nature of good and evil... many things... for hours in the evenings when it was too hot to be indoors. In 1970, it was helpful to have a cause with which to sort oneself out as a young person. There had not been, it seemed, quite as much distortion between a person and an event then as there was currently.

"Who else?" Choshin asked. "Well, this is Father Francis Sullivan." She nodded to the small elderly man sitting to her right. He was very slight with unruly wisps of white hair on his head. She leaned over conspiratorially, whispered very audibly.

"He's a Catholic. Shhh...".

"Call me Frank," he said in an Irish brogue, "everybody does."

"Frank lives in retirement in Hawaii," Choshin had settled full force into the introductions at this point. "He is a friend to this other handsome fellow to his right at the table, Professor Theo van Hal. He teaches history and sociology at *Chaminade* University. More Catholics."

"Good Lord, Choshin, stop it," Dr. van Hal said. He stuck out his hand, slightly to the right of Christina's, and suddenly she was aware he did not see well. "Father Frank here helps me get around and such as my eyesight is failing me. Just a couple of old hermits. The sultry South Pacific is wasted on us, I suppose." He laughed softly.

"How do you do?" Christina said.

"Then on around the table, we have Polo. Polo Matambo is a physician from Botswana. He runs the Scottish Livingstone Hospital and founded a group called Physicians for Human Rights in Africa. They have groups across the entire continent, I believe. His hospital has very graciously given him an extended leave to be with us."

Christine and Charlie nodded, shook hands. Dr. Matambo appeared to be suffering as much as they were in the heat and humidity, which surprised Christina. Equatorial Africa surely was much hotter and more humid. He was a younger man, with a very dark complexion and a bit doughy. He was also missing quite a bit of hair on top. He seemed serious and uncomfortable, and maybe even grim. Well, there's a lot to be grim about, Christina thought. And they are engaged in a grim business right now.

"Polo comes from the very precipice of the Kalahari Desert," Choshin volunteered. "The abundance of water here is something of a shock to his system, I think."

"And at the end we present our Canadian, Philip Ford, a civil rights attorney from Vancouver," Choshin continued. "His name makes him sound very prep school, I've always thought, but he's more than half Inuit. The Inuit are a people I find intriguing to say the least."

"Yes, I've heard of you," Christina said. Ford handled mostly impossible, dangerous, very public civil rights cases.

"Sir, it's an honor," offered Charlie.

"And then, last but never least, my dearest friend Mai Arikaki, a local doctor and a beautifully willing conduit to the Japanese government. She and her family live on one of the smaller islands. It is their bungalow in which you will be staying as of tomorrow. It happens to be two lanes over and a bit further up the hill. Another one familiar with the Boston area,

Christina. She went to medical school in Cambridge. That's where we met."

"Thank you so much," Christina said. "We are so grateful to have a quiet place to be together and prepare."

"Not at all," Mai bowed slightly.

They shared a meal of *soki soba*, noodles in a rich broth with slices of pork and ginger bobbing in meat broth, a bit of poached whitefish and tea. Choshin and Mai both sprinkled hot red pepper liberally on their noodles. For dessert there were blood oranges and plenty of talk.

"Arturo," Christina said as she peeled an orange, "how is it you have come to be part of this panel?"

"Ah," he replied, pushing his glasses a bit farther up the bridge of his nose, "I was a school teacher in Venezuela. Though I now make my home in Spain, I am also a member of a teachers' collective of activists that struggles to bring the idea of South America's existence into the minds of the inhabitants of the northern hemisphere. We also acknowledge that most of our continent is going from completely agrarian and rural to shocking encounters with most of what's taking the world into an abyss. We haven't much experience with anything in between and that, we feel, is in our favor. The pure 'wrongness' is very apparent to us."

"Do you feel that makes the people sitting ducks of a sort?" Charlie asked.

"No more so than anyone else, actually. Is it better to have no knowledge of an evil and then meet it unexpectedly or to have been trained from birth to accept the evil as a benefit and then have to rip the blinders off? Maybe you even go out looking for it because you've been taught it's to be desired? It would be hard to say any of us are not, how did you put it... sitting ducks? I mean to say exceptionally vulnerable." Maldonado smiled.

One by one, the panel members took their leave. They each had an important part to play in the coming weeks, the climax of two years' work. Finally, it was just Choshin at the table with Charlie and Christina. The sun must have been setting as the air had cooled ever so slightly. Shadows lengthened in the garden. Choshin disappeared briefly to make sure everyone was settled.

"And finally Charlie," she said as she sat back down at the table.

"what is it you'd like to talk about?"

Charlie smiled as he looked at his empty bowl, toying with his chopsticks. It seemed he might not know where to start.

"Let's walk in the little garden, shall we? Christina?" Choshin swung her legs out from under the table. Charlie stood quickly and helped her up despite her protests. She pushed aside the mat between the room and the garden and they followed her through the door.

"Choshin," Charlie said quietly, "I am here with a delegation as you know. As to why I wanted to see you and the panel ahead of time, it's somewhat unclear to me, as well. I wanted to know who they were. Our information, our presentation is so critical... so immediate... that we cannot waste that five minutes on anything that doesn't convey the message."

Choshin let his words rest for a moment.

"But you knew I would not consent to actually hear anything ahead of time. That would be political lobbying," she said.

"Yes," Charlie replied. "I suppose I would have been disappointed if you had. I just wanted some concept of who we were addressing."

"Knowing you, Charlie," Choshin offered, "I can imagine you've gathered a wealth of important information today. On another note, what about getting you from the hotel to the house up the lane tomorrow? Mai will meet you and make sure you are all settled. Can you find your way back here early in the morning? Get a taxi and give them this address."

She slipped a piece of folded paper into his hand.

"Yes, we'll be here at eight o'clock? Will that do? And then the preliminary presentations are in four days' time, right?"

"Yes. It's very good to see you," she reached up and kissed Charlie on the cheek. "And lovely to meet you, too, Christina."

As promised, the next morning the six members of the contingent along with Nikolai's son, Hugo, arrived at the address provided by Choshin. They were indeed some distance closer to the castle. It was the home of Dr. Mai Arikaki and her family when they were in Naha. Often they were in residence on one of the outer islands where Mai practiced medicine. This was a two-storey home, replete with the red clay tiles on the roof. Once inside, greeted by Mai, they were met with a combination of Chinese and Japanese influences with a few western conveniences tucked in as a reminder of Mai's days studying medicine at Harvard Medical School. There were four long rectangular 'sections' to the house, with a hallway encircling the house on three sides on the outside, the exception being the side closest to the street. Along the inside wall of the rectangle was another hallway running the length of all four sections. Nestled into a large space in the center of all of that, open to the air, was a garden. It was one of the most beautiful and practical designs Christina had ever seen. On exiting any room, one became immediately aware of the garden in the open courtyard in the center of the house or, if one was in the outer hallway, the world outside the house. One had only to push aside the shoji to the inner courtyard or gaze out the wall-to-wall windows lining the outer hallway. Shoes were left at the door and exchanged for slippers. The floors were covered here, as they had been at Choshin's residence, in *tatami* mats. They were buoyant and comfortable under the feet. To the immediate right was a narrow staircase leading to the sleeping rooms on the second floor. Beyond on the right lay a dining room, with a table made of what appeared to be a black lacquered material. On the left there was a small room with a brazier in the center, surrounded by neatly organized sitting pillows. Christina imagined a tea ceremony taking place there. There was a 'sitting room' of sorts with short, wide, cushioned benches which led to an utterly western-style living room complete with sofas and loveseats. Mai directed them here when they arrived. Their bags were left in the foyer. Mai's two sons were with her.

"I thought Hugo might like people his own age to 'hang out' with?" she said pointedly using some American slang she thought might attract Hugo's attention. "These two are headed back to Kumejima with their father later this afternoon. Snorkeling, fishing, television… we have it all out there."

Hugo looked up at his father expectantly.

"I am sure that will be fine, Hugo. But you'll have to put together a knapsack for a few days," Nikolai said, smiling, "thank you so much, Dr. Arikaki. I can't imagine this here will be any fun for Hugo."

"Good, it's settled. Hugo," she said, "the trip out is on a ferry. It takes about four hours."

The sleeping arrangements were exactly as they had been in the hotel. Beds in this home were traditional futons, meaning several layers of thick pads covered with blankets and folded and tucked away in the day. Christina imagined that the kitchen would be the most westernized room in the house only to find that it was the most traditional.

"That is due to my husband's heritage here on Okinawa," Mai explained. "We have a Buddhist shrine here, obviously, out of respect for my beliefs. The garden is very formally Japanese, a nod to my former position within the Imperial household. On Okinawa, the kitchen is the center of the house as well as a woman's power and not in a demeaning, Western way at all. Kitchen goddesses, yes, but the women rule the islands and this is their throne room within the social context, if you will. Okinawa has a very strong animistic culture with females leading society and nothing has been able to push that aside. I quite like it... but then, why wouldn't I? The situation has none of the negative American connotations."

There was, she said, an ancient animism, older even than Shintoism that had never been dislodged. Happily it was a matriarchal spirituality, with *Noro* of old – the seers and priestesses of the Ryukyu Dynasty – and now, Uta. Uta were the women shamans of Okinawa.

"My mother-in-law is an *Uta,* a sort of combination of a shaman and a psychologist and maybe a little bit priestess. She is very influential here, as are all the Uta," Mai explained. "They often become *Uta* as the result of some sort of unexpected mental collapse or intense emotional crisis. *Uta* is what lies on the otherside of this sort of personal implosion. Mysticism."

They carried their bags upstairs to their respective sleeping rooms. Christina seemed to have the master bedroom. Tucked away in a corner was a butsudan, a Buddhist altar. It appeared to be a gold and black lacquered cabinet that could be closed if desired. Aside from a small statue of the Buddha, there was a black and white photo of a seated elderly man, some pieces of paper with Japanese characters written on them in black ink, a few flowers, a very small wooden box wrapped with silk ribbon and a delicate plate of thin crackers. A small glazed porcelain incense burner rested there with the ashes of incense, the scent still lingering in the room. Below this shelf of precious items, there were drawers of black with tortoise shell inlays. Christina could only assume this was a piece that Mai had brought from the imperial residences. She wondered if the presence of a photograph was some nod to Shintoism but wasn't sure.

As soon as Hugo was on his way, Christina would call a meeting. They needed to sit down and talk about what she and Charlie had learned sharing a meal with Choshin and the other panel members. They needed to formulate a strategy based on who the panel was, what the purpose of the Reconciliation was, and the evidence they had with them. They had a few days left. The preliminary testimony would begin Tuesday morning, the first of July.

Hugo appeared with a stuffed knapsack on his back.

"*Papa*," he said, "*pouvez-vous m'aider?*" Hugo did not often use his English, especially when he was simply speaking with Nikolai.

"*Oui*," Nikolai replied. He got behind his son and pushed the unruly contents of the knapsack a bit farther in and strained with the clasp. The flap burst open twice causing Hugo and Nikolai to laugh. It stayed closed after a third try.

"*Au revoir, Papa!*" Hugo walked out the door and down the path on his own adventure for the weekend. Christina thought she might actually prefer his journey, perhaps trade places.

As she slid the door shut, Christina called to the others. "Hey, you lot! Let's get to work."

She had a yellow legal pad and a pen but left her copy of the data in her room. The data belonged essentially to those who had collected it. She had a copy for safekeeping and that's all. Huck, Isaac and French appeared. Nikolai was already there, his several manila folders wrapped with sturdy rubber bands in his knapsack. He found a place on a sofa and started to unpack them. Charlie had several folders as did the others. Suddenly, Christina started to wonder why she was there, perhaps she wasn't needed.

Cut it out, she thought, you're just scared.

She was there on behalf of her children. She was there as a representative for her mother and everyone else who may have died because they knew about this program in some small way. She was there because she was supposed to be there.

Charlie opened the meeting.

"Christina and I spent some time with the panel informally last night, as you know. That was an incredible stroke of luck. We obviously did not talk about the hearings or anything specific about the reason we're here but we met the panel and that will go a long way toward deciding what to emphasize in the short time we have on Tuesday."

"Why don't you go down the list, Charlie," Isaac asked, "we can make notes. See what lines up?"

"Sure. Great idea. I'll start with the panel members and work up to the leader, Choshin Soderholm."

Everyone in the room began to take notes.

"Stop me if you want to add anything or if I forget something, Christina?"

She nodded.

"Let's start with the fellow from Botswana. Some of this is research I did last night because we needed the blanks filled in. First of all, Botswana is a stable country unlike so many others surrounding it. I'm sure they'd like to keep it that way. Dr. Polo Matambo is a fairly young guy who runs the Scottish Livingstone Hospital in Molopolole. That's characterized as Botswana's largest village... interesting terminology. Over 63,000 residents yet they still refer to it as a village. That's a mindset. The hospital's modern so the village probably is, too, mostly but they also call it the Gateway to the Kalahari Desert. Water is a big deal to this guy for every reason you can think of. Drinking, sanitation, growing food. So he's going to be thinking of the health aspects, the biological research, and the precious, precious water being made unusable or toxic. He's also going to know about drought big-time. These so-called geo-engineering people manipulate the weather, causing floods and droughts we think for insurance payoffs. That's going to hit home with Dr. Matambo right out of the gate."

"So we'll need a combination of water and soil data, agricultural data and health data for him. Until we have proof about the insurance thing... which is right around the corner, we're looking at the Chicago Stock Exchange for that evidence... we may have to leave that out or end with a theory. Just say the word drought, suggest we are looking into the claim that entities are manipulating rain and crops for insurance payoffs," Nikolai offered.

"You have the collection of blood toxicity studies, right?" Huck asked.

"Yes." Nikolai replied.

"Next is Arturo Maldonado, a teacher from Venezuela...although we need to stick a pin in that insurance payoff thing for the attorney in the bunch. Anyway, Maldonado is part of a South American activists' group composed of teachers but he's also active in Spain. The effects of these chemicals on thought processes and on the children will be a big deal for him. Also he's Venezuelan and those people pride themselves on being self-determined. Most of South America is uninhabited and unspoiled. They are hyper-aware of those international locusts who want to savage their resources with no thought for the future. The data that's coming along on birth defects and on increased levels of aggression in the youth population... French and Huck? How is that going?"

"We are only starting to put that together but it's very obvious. It should be straightforward. We can work on that over the next couple of days together?" French looked questioningly at Huck.

"Yes," Huck said. "We can handle that."

"So we might as well get to the attorney in the group, Philip Ford. This guy has a big presence online. He is a fairly well-known civil rights attorney in Vancouver, British Columbia. He has Inuit ancestry although I'm not sure how that plays into this situation specifically. He is fearless when it comes to taking on dangerous cases and that plays really well into this situation. Our position is that geoengineering chemical dumps are medical experimentation on human beings. So that needs to be addressed and pains need to be taken to point out that this would break several international human rights treaties going back to the Nuremberg Code or before. Also access to fresh, clean, healthy water is a human right according to the United Nations, isn't it? Access to safe water is a fundamental human need and therefore a basic human right. That's a quote from the ex-UN Secretary General, Kofi Annan. This water is toxic. Weather manipulation as a great big insurance scam would be of interest to a legal mind which goes right back to safe water as a human right and not a commodity. There's no substitute and it can't be done without."

Charlie paused.

"I guess I'll take that one," he said.

"There is another doctor in the bunch," Christina continued. "I've been thinking about her, Dr. Arikaki. She will have all of the same medical concerns that Matambo has. She is the only one I think who has a family so the effect on children will be a high priority. I would like to suggest that deceptive governance, given her background, her awareness of a ruling class and a conquered nation, and the price tag of totalitarian agendas might strike a note for her. There's a world domination theme here and a genocide theme. I think that should be touched on even if it's just in terms of philosophy."

"Can you do that then, Christina?" Nikolai asked.

"Sure. I know what it's like to watch children get sick, just like you do, Nikolai."

"That should appeal to the professor in the group, too," said Charlie. "Theo van Hal. Professor of History and Sociology at Chaminade University in Hawaii. He's Dutch, likely his parents were caught under Hitler based on his age. Medical experimentation and totalitarian governments are something he will know about. Chaminade is a Jesuit institution."

"Well, what would that have to do with the price of tea in China?" Isaac asked.

"Don't know," Charlie replied. "just throwing it out there. He is likely to be a very principled man for better or worse. Then we come to the two religious leaders here. One is Father Francis Sullivan, Frank. He is in his eighties, I'm sure. Lives in Hawaii now and takes care of van Hal, who can't see. I guess I should have mentioned that. Frank was a priest in a town in County Cork, plain and simple. Also ran the county astronomy club so the fact that you can't tell the moon from a moon pie anymore with the thick plasma in the sky really will matter to this guy. That is a real loss in many ways... scientifically, aesthetically, academically. He will be interested in that and all else and certainly the idea of evil. This will be a man who has met evil and shaken hands with it; a man who has spent some time trying to understand the nature of good and evil... would you mind taking that on, Nikolai?"

Nikolai looked surprised.

"I don't mind but I'm not sure why I would be the best choice."

"Just a feeling I have," Charlie said.

"That leaves one person. Choshin Soderholm, the leader of this effort. The generator of this effort. She will be interested in evaluating the treaties in place since World War II, I'll bet, and saying very specifically who didn't abide and in what ways. She or Ford will anyway. Choshin is very interested in the spirituality of the planet as a whole. She understands evil, I think, as a darkness... in a very old spiritual way... and wants to bring everything into the light. If it can stand the light of day...she will be looking for ways to honor the sovereignty of each human being and their connection to their God, whatever that might be. So medically experimenting on or changing people's ability to think or make decisions is an absolute affront to their free will. I know Choshin. She just thinks it's time for humanity to grow the hell up and find better things to do."

"If you can't help them, at least don't hurt them?" Christina said.

"Yes, the Dalai Lama." Nikolai replied. "and, of course, first do no harm... the physicians in the group will have that in mind."

"Okay," Charlie rubbed his hands together, "I think we have it all in front of us. We have a couple of days. Anything else?"

"Yeah," French said. "We need an order of speaking and who's saying what when and for how long...".

"Well, we have five minutes. Why doesn't the California contingent take two minutes, I'll take a minute and Nikolai can take a minute?"

"What about me?" Christina asked.

"You are going to lead off. Take the first minute, make the first impression."

"What? Why?"

"Because you brought us here, Christina. We're following you."

Christina sat in the courtyard the night before the *Shuri* Reconciliation public hearings commenced.

The crickets were still scraping away in the garden even at midnight. It was a sound she associated with evening, just after supper. Mai's garden was established around three upright stones representing the Buddha and two companions. It was not really meant to be 'in' but rather 'seen.' A stone bench rested just on the side toward the house for that purpose. The outer boundaries were comprised of maple trees standing like royal sentinels. In the autumn they were crowned in a magnificent orange-red. Upon a three foot rock formation clung an ironwood tree, bent and curled until it resembled a discus thrower from an ancient Greek frieze. A stream raced over rocks somewhere in the garden but could not be seen from the bench and that was likely on purpose. It was meant to be heard, stimulating an image within the mind. Christina rested. In a few short hours she would be at the *Shuri* Castle standing before the international panel putting together the first human rights document of the twenty-first century. It was just a few days short of the first anniversary of her mother's death. The broken body of one old woman on a crosswalk had become the catalyst, the furious gale that had blown her ship here. She was so fortunate to have the family she did, and Otto. Most of her friends would never have understood the violently beautiful transformation that had occurred upon her mother's death. And that was fine. It didn't matter. She knew.

She had not heard him coming. Nikolai sat down beside her. He leaned forward, arms on knees, silent for a time.

"All is well?" he asked finally.

"Thinking about the morning and what I'm going to say. Thinking about the hundreds of mornings that have led to tomorrow. You?"

"As always, thinking of my son."

"How do you feel? Anything particularly different about the air here?" He had not mentioned any illness since they arrived. Perhaps the breezes over the small island kept things moving.

"Only at night. The convection effect, you know, when it all comes settling down. But even then, the breezes blow for the most part. The truly hot season when there is little air... it's like that on some islands... that may bring a different situation. We won't be here to find out."

She listened to the mad cricket song.

"The day I left home, the sky was filled with chemical trails... dozens. Some days a dozen planes are in the air streaking and criss-crossing the sky. How is it no one on the ground sees?'

"My belief is that it's largely due to the chemicals themselves. They are a sedative in a way... I know barium is."

"I want my children well, Nikolai. No one should be able to take one's health away just because they can. No one should want to."

"That is my over-riding goal at the moment, too, although it seems selfish to say so. Whatever it takes."

"I never told you that I'm here because my mother was killed, did I? I suspect she was killed by the people she used to work for in defense... she was attached to some of the Operation Paperclip scientists who developed much of this atmospheric poison," Christina wasn't sure why she had never told Nikolai that. Something had held her back.

"My God, no!" Nikolai replied. "You never said. For which agency did she work?"

"Never mind," Christina put her head in her hands, "I don't want to talk about it. I have to think about the morning. I think I'm ready. It's just so important. How about you?"

"I think I am also ready," Nikolai said. "I know it will be hard to sleep tonight but you should try. I'm going up."

"Of course." Christina said. She followed him into the house and up the stairs.

In the small bare tea room, which was the room directly behind Christina's bench, Charlie Shepard waited and listened, just in case. He was profoundly relieved she had not started divulging information about her mother at this point. He was profoundly relieved Nikolai had proved only to be dangerous in terms of information gathering. They were almost 'at the station' now. He had a surprise for all of them in the morning and that is when Nikolai Louis could get out of hand. However, Hugo was in pocket four hours away. That would be some sort of leverage for, no matter what Nikolai was doing as an undercover asset, Charlie was certain that he did love his son. Also, they were on a very small island thousands and thousands of miles from North America. He was as vulnerable as they could get him. Chances were he'd be caught off-guard.

Charlie had not slept and doubted if any of them had. At six a.m., he called them into the dining room. He had put tea, fruit, bread and cheese on the table. At each place, there lay a manila folder.

Each manila folder had someone's name on it, which is how he maneuvered Nikolai into the center between himself – nearest the outside door and French Baum on the other side nearest the rest of the interior.

Christina was directly across the table from Nikolai with Isaac on one side and Huck on the other. Once they were seated at the low table it would be very difficult for Nikolai to bolt. Under each of their names on the folders, he had written 'Do Not Open.' It was already nearing eighty degrees already and the sun was unobstructed. The interior rooms were cooler and a little dark, as intended.

One by one, they ambled into the dining room, a bit bleary-eyed but filled with anticipation on the day for which they'd been waiting, mostly without knowing for what.

"More homework?" grumbled Isaac.

"Probably the most important thing we've seen for the future… but hey, let's get some food in our stomachs," Charlie actually managed a laugh. "We shouldn't face this on an empty stomach."

"What is it, seriously?" Christina was in no mood for surprises. She was struggling to stay calm about the presentation.

"It's fine," Charlie replied. "Just eat. It may not be new information to a couple of us anyway. Just want to make sure we all know everything we need to before we hit the official part of this project."

They were too tired to argue. The bread and cheese were already sliced… Charlie had not wanted any silverware, particularly knives, on the table with them. Hot tea might be an issue but Nikolai could only hit one of them with it before he'd be down and he would know that. Charlie would have been willing to bet that anywhere Nikolai Louis was he had an exit strategy. Most great assets did and he had to admit, this guy was one of the best. They could only do their best. Twenty minutes later, they were done. They were eating because it was a good idea, but it was a
chore. Little conversation had passed between them as they were all exceptionally nervous.

"Okay, hang on," Charlie said, "French, you're closest. Will you go put the kettle back on… take the teapot with you?"

As they ate, Charlie realized the tea pot had a handle and, should he so desire, Nikolai could clock several of them in the head with it and be out the door before they got him under control. Two minutes later, French was back with them, legs under the table.

"Alright. What's in this folder is pretty important. We need to be very alert to this situation. Go ahead and open it, if you would, one page at a time until I say so. Okay?"

Charlie tried to convey the seriousness of his instruction. Racing ahead would be a problem. There was a note to each of them on the first page, except in Nikolai's packet and Charlie's packet. In Charlie's packet there was a technical diagram with which he hoped to distract Nikolai for just the few seconds it would take the rest to read his note.

It is one of God's imponderables as to why there is almost always a Judas among the faithful. However, this will work to our great advantage. That is a promise. Everyone stay here. Everyone be ready.

Five seconds later, Charlie spoke.

"Okay, everybody, let's have a look together."

Inside the manila folder was a copy of Nikolai Louis' resume. Written at the top was a note from Charlie pointing out that Nikolai was listed as working or having worked for most of the top security and espionage agencies in the English-speaking world. In fact, there were only three pages, each with a summary from Charlie at the top.

"Stay calm," Charlie suggested quietly. "Let's not talk for a second."

Nikolai adopted a relaxed tension, Charlie could feel it. He closed his folder carefully while the others continued to read. Huck's face turned a shade of red so dark it was nearly purple. Christina felt the ground go out from under her although she hadn't moved.

"You don't really believe this, do you, Christina?" Nikolai asked. He would appeal to her first, the one he knew to be the most compassionate. "I am ill beyond reason and my son is ill. Why would I work for the people making us so very ill?"

"That's a great question, Nikolai," Charlie replied for Christina, who was speechless. "Why work for the people making you and your son sick? Do they have a way to make you healthy? Some way to provide immunity? Certainly that's an old theory out there and the tactic is ancient. I mean, we're all breathing the same air."

"I deny this completely," Nikolai said.

"I thought you were an artist…", she whispered.

Nikolai looked across the suddenly vast black table at her stonily.

He refused to speak for some time despite questions. Charlie let them talk for a minute.

"You son-of-a-bitch!"

"I could kill you right now."

"Which agency are you feeding this to in particular? Somebody has to be acting as a clearing house for this information."

Charlie held up his hand.

"Enough. Look, it is what it is. We have to make a five minute presentation in one hour. My strong suggestion is that Christina open the bit, like she was always going to, and then Nikolai spend the balance of time making a full confession and talking about the mountain of data he has collected over the last decade. Then the boys from California can wrap up... unless we manage to create a ruckus in which case we have to throw ourselves on the mercy of the panel and Okinawa prefecture," Charlie said, a wry smile stealing across his face.

Nikolai looked surprised then started to sputter. "What? Why in God's name would I do that?"

"What other choice do you have? I'll out you right there in front of God and everybody if you don't do it yourself. Maybe you'll end up in custody then or maybe the trolls in the audience... and we know they will be there... will just put a bullet through your head because you're blown and they don't want you talking. So go ahead and talk. Then I'll ask for protection. Or you could just run, let me blow your cover and try to stay alive back in Canada. Your son is safe, for now. You know you'll both be in jeopardy in about an hour. You can try to control the damage or panic. Which will it be?"

"Is there are cure?" Christina demanded.

"Christina, we'll get there," Charlie said.

"No, asshole, is there a cure? Because if there is you'd goddamned well better tell me about it!"

The testimony would take place in the hall the Ryukyu emperors used to reserve for greeting those from Japan, the south hall. There was a north hall, which had been reserved for meeting with Chinese emissaries. It was half the size of the Great Hall but filled to capacity. A few television networks were in attendance, mostly from non-English-speaking countries. Choshin Soderholm and her fellows entered the room from a side door and stood behind a long table. The six other panel members seated themselves on either side of her. There was a microphone before each panel member. Choshin remained standing and addressed the sizeable crowd.

"Welcome to this day and thank you for joining us on this auspicious occasion. How can it be otherwise when so many have come so far to continue such critical work? We have now almost a century under our collective belts, a century of experience with various human rights documents, for better and for worse. We know what works and we know what would work if only we used such to govern our actions. Yes, we must, I think, hearken back to the time just after the Second World War and the development of the Nuremburg Code. It is an excellent document. All human rights treaties seem to come to life as a result of unbearable atrocities committed; one against another, one state against another state and so on. So in a very real way, each is written in blood and that requires deep respect. We should also recall an older document, The Covenant of the League of Nations – as far as I know the first attempt at ensuring human rights of the 20th century – short-circuited unfortunately by the U.S. President Wilson on the basis of advice, perhaps given with other agendas in mind, by his advisor Colonel Edward House. Nevertheless, we have tried and failed; tried and failed. A treaty, unfortunately, cannot force the human heart to be or stay as it should.

What has a century of human rights work given us then? We have substantively defined over and over what a human right is. These answers don't change much. We can take these foundational truths and apply them to current misdeeds, the current state of affairs. We know more from our failures almost than our successes and can view a situation anywhere in the world and perhaps have an inkling as to which aspect of humanity is being denied and what we might do about it. We cannot turn men's hearts with treaties but we can save our fellows from blatant abuse with treaties provided enough of us are willing to abide by them.

My wish for us and for everyone we share this world with is that we can continue to refine and forge ahead in our understandings until such time as each of us or each nation might say, no, we cannot cross that line. We have all agreed that is too far. As those here today know, we are hearing preliminary requests for longer hearings later. Please don't think if you are not granted a longer hearing that your wishes will not be included in the body of the document. Rest assured that they will. We simply feel it is imperative at a time like this to get a good read on what is happening around us now. Some issues require a more lengthy time in the sun, as it were. So, let's get on with it, shall we?

Quickly, because they are listed in the program to which everyone has access, I want to introduce Father Francis Sullivan, Dr. Theo van Hal and Arturo Maldonado to my right. On my left we find the Honorable Philip Ford, Dr. Polo Matambo and Dr. Mai Arikaki. No more hesitation! To work! We call the first, the group from...", she glanced at the notes on the table before her, "... California, the United States, led by Christina Galbraithe."

They were first so not only would she open for her group but apparently for the entire conference. That did not bother her at this point because she was angry, so angry, and she would fill her minute with blood and passion.

"Madame Chairman, thank you. We are a group of six today. Five of our members have spent a decade patiently watching, collecting data, making real-time observations and collating such into a voluminous piece of evidence that an atrocity is being committed upon all living things of this planet so pervading, so severely toxic, and so secret as to only be characterized as a kind of genocide, perhaps a chemical warfare, certainly a mass medical experiment. I, Christina Galbraithe, am for my part here on behalf of a woman whom I believe was killed for having been somewhat involved with those who developed this program of genocide. She is surely one of many. I am here also because my children are ill and are not recovering, I believe, as a result of biological experimentation being conducted within the earth's atmosphere. This is personal for me. It led me to several people who have known there was murder in the skies and have sought to both pull this atrocity out into the light of day and accumulate so much quantitative evidence as to make it impossible to deny. We also have something of an enhanced presentation following mine. It can do nothing other than validate the scurrilous nature of what we are bringing to the panel today. Thank you for hearing us. I concede the balance of my time to my fellow, Nikolai Louis of Ontario, Canada."

Standing before the seven at the *Shuri* Reconciliation open hearings, Nikolai Louis went through the eye of the needle. He did it for the same reason people do anything excruciating... because he had no choice at all, it was this or be turned over to the authorities. Long before he went back to Canada or anywhere in North America his bosses were going to know his cover was blown and that people knew what he and they were doing so they would kill him. If he didn't get shot right where he stood – which was a possibility, even a probability because there would certainly be trolls in this crowd – he might stand a chance of waiting out the legal process on this. He also did it for his son. It might be that together they could disappear. The people he worked for would never now give him the detoxification regime and the antidote to the chemical poisoning but if the whole thing came out into the light he might be able to get healing for his son.

"My passport says my name is Nikolai Louis." He held up his passport, opened to his photo page. "My birth name is John Clayfell and I was born in Nebraska. I am a U.S. citizen in the employ of the Secretary of the Agriculture, as I have been for every Secretary of Ag for the last twenty years, and for the Sceptre Corporation. My sole purpose for the last two decades has been espionage against my own kind in the form of intense gathering of private intelligence about them and their activities."

The people gathered in the hall began to murmur.

"Can we maintain a respectful silence, please," Choshin said clearly. "Go on, Mr. Clayfell, if you please."

"There exists a massive privatized and militarized program in place using weapons of mass destruction, deployed within the atmosphere globally. It is a medical research program, a biological and chemical warfare program, unacknowledged by those in power and unknown to the majority of the citizenry. In effect, it has become a program of genocide. I would like the opportunity for myself and my panel to present our absolute evidence within the jurisdiction of Okinawa and to the honorable panel gathered here for this purpose. I believe time is of the essence as I am perfectly sure once this is known, that I am here and prepared to testify, that

I and likely my entire group, will be in the gravest possible danger. Therefore, we would like to request sanctuary."

As Nikolai spoke his accent faded until he might have been someone speaking to a P.T.A. somewhere in the Great Plains of America. They were instantly taken into protective custody by the Okinawan police who shepherded them quickly into another room in the south wing. Within twenty minutes reporters from all over the world appeared at Shuri Castle, most from the smaller, less controlled news agencies or from non-English speaking countries. China, Japan, Indonesia, India, Russia, some European agencies... the Swiss, the Greeks. The only English speaking news agency on hand immediately was from New Zealand. A contingent from Canadian National Security appeared as if by magic, as if by some strange chance they had already been in the room, begging a moment of the panel's time.

"With all due respect, Madame Chairman, the Canadian government would like to request an immediate private meeting with the panel." A man from Canadian Embassy Security pushed his way to the podium where just a few minutes ago Nikolai had become John Clayfell. Three others stood in the doorway to the hall.

"You can have your private meeting, sir," Choshin responded, "at the end of the day's testimony. We have people from all over the world who have come here at great cost to themselves...sometimes at great personal peril, as well... and I have some idea what you want to discuss. It is by no means an emergency. It is also highly unlikely that the panel will change anything based on that discussion. We will hear petitions as scheduled."

The hall was filled with noise despite their best efforts to regain control of the hearing. A certain amount of processing out loud was going to have to occur before they could get back to business. The proceeding was being televised to the countries represented, something the panel appreciated deeply. Choshin stood and reined in everyone's attention briefly if somewhat tenuously.

"We will adjourn for ten minutes strictly in the interest of sorting this out to the point where we can get back to work. If you are waiting to speak, please forgive this brief interruption but I do think it will be in your best interest anyway. Maybe you won't have to shout to be heard." She and her panel rose and exited through the door by which they had come.

The man from Canadian Security began to protest but, perhaps because of the amount of attention being drawn to the incident already, he did not. He stepped away and returned to his colleagues although they did not leave the hall. They spent the ten minutes' recess with their heads together, murmuring, oblivious it seemed to the roll of video cameras around them.

Meanwhile, Christina's group had been escorted to a room in the castle itself. Video feeds were set up in many places throughout the buildings of Shuri. Small knots of people stood around each, watching intently. They had not realized the event would be televised but they were glad.

"I want to talk to you," Christina said to Nikolai/John. "I'm going to watch the proceedings first though. I don't trust myself at the moment."

Nikolai ignored her, turned his attention to the television screen in their room. She was the very least of his problems now. The panel was coming back in. Choshin asked for quiet.

"I have been informed that we have another unusual presentation," she took her reading glasses off her nose and cleaned them with a cloth.

She seemed concerned, troubled. She was both encouraged and frightened that the conference had started off in this way because it meant things were actually as bad as she thought they were, maybe much worse, but theoretically it also meant worldwide attention. She was awed by the courage on display, as well. It would require this kind of courage to turn the ship around for the coming century and for the future of humanity at all on this planet. Perhaps all of those who had died to bring them to this point would not have died in vain.

"We're going to have to hear this testimony via the television feed as it has been deemed very unsafe for this particular group to appear here in public," she added. "Quiet!"

*****

The Plato finally came to a full stop despite the gale and the blinding rain. Thank God for the ship's computer, Tim thought. I may just kiss the tarmac when we get out of here. I really want to kiss whoever upgraded that system.

"Whooo!!" Pip screamed, beating his chest. "Hard core!"

He started to laugh hysterically, the manic laugh of someone who is far beyond exhausted and stunned to be alive. They were whisked off to an abandoned military base at Onna Point about twenty-five miles from Naha under blankets in the back of a jeep. First it had been occupied by the Air Force then Marines; now it appeared to be completely abandoned. They were met and guarded by a mixed volunteer group of Ryukyu-trained Okinawan police and elite Marines, with ForeCon insignia. Tim knew there had been a battalion of these soldiers stationed on Okinawa, the 5th, but he was sure they were defunct. The soldiers were silent except to give basic directions. Tim and Pip were pleased to see Okinawan police, unhappy to see elite Marines. They were not sure which side the soldiers would be on or where their orders were coming from. However, if it turned out they had these soldiers' backing then the tide had turned. Period. Okinawa was virtually an all-Marine island.

A man appeared, carrying himself with palpable self-control and order, clearly an official from the Okinawan police. He intercepted Tim and Pip seconds after they entered the building. Despite his distinctly Okinawan features, he spoke with a firm American accent and asked them to call him 'Salty.' The pilots weren't in any position to ask questions about anything. They were just grateful they weren't in jail yet. The trail of military people who had paved the way for them to land this bird on Okinawa was the most miraculous thing they'd ever seen, like Moses parting the Red Sea. They had expected to have to run from stealth fighters and be shot down over the Pacific. Instead, someone had made sure they got away.

"So, you men...", Salty sat and began to question them in a neutral, matter-of-fact way, "are you military?"

"Ex-military," Tim replied. "We work for a private company at this time. A private airline called Bluesky. They have a base out in the middle of nowhere along the border between New Mexico and old Mexico. This is their bird."

"Anybody going to come looking for this piece of equipment?"

"I expect a lot of people are sweating blood right now but I don't think anyone will step forward to claim it, no. I don't know if the U.S. government can get involved under the circumstances, at least not publicly. She was put together and designed at Pantheon stateside. That's a private corporation. I don't know myself where the buck stops or where the orders to design originated. I will say I did have a pretty nasty radio conversation over the middle of the ocean last night with an obscenely wealthy industrialist," Tim laughed.

"Oh, yes?" Salty continued. "Just who would that have been?"

"Nero Pearle."

"Nero Pearle got on the radio with you? Why?"

"Said he wanted his plane back," Pip volunteered.

Salty was silent for a moment.

"Noted," he said. "Next question: why Okinawa, boys?"

"The *Shuri* proceedings. That aircraft is hard evidence, a big, fat smoking gun, of... God...it's a weapon of mass destruction, it's a chemical weapon, a biological weapon, evidence that medical experiments are being conducted on humans on a global scale... it's everything." Tim ticked the reasons off, one finger at a time.

"Acknowledged. Let's say I boarded that aircraft right now. What am I looking for?"

"A big belly filled with canisters containing lethal chemicals. A dispersal system rigged through the wings. You'll find that the system is such that one chemical can be dispersed or a combination of any number of them. Chemicals that have no business being in the sky, at all, ever, for any reason other than out-and-out warfare. Even then, I believe that kind of warfare is outlawed."

"Okay," Salty shrugged, "and so I have an aircraft filled with chemicals. Prove it's being dumped on people. Maybe they're just being transported. Maybe it's some kind of global dry cleaning empire...".

Tim understood what Salty was doing. Any number of half-baked excuses could be thrown at them from Pantheon or the US government or Nero Pearle. Unless they had everything nailed down, they'd have to give the aircraft back and Tim and Pip with it.

"I intend to testify that Pip here and I did a lot of dumping. We're going to confess and we're going to give you names and dates and the location of the primary airfield. We're going to tell you what to look for and you can do it right here. Okinawa is no exception. Take random samples all over Japan. Water, soil, vegetation, and air. Compare the levels with the rise of respiratory illness, Alzheimer's, any autoimmune response disease that's skyrocketed over the last ten years. There have to be records of soil and water and air samples from a decade ago, two decades ago, with which you can make comparisons. Ask for volunteers among your people or just the police force to have their blood tested for heavy metals."

Salty sat quietly, listening to Tim and Pip. He had been told to receive these two and their aircraft and to protect them and the aircraft at all costs. That validated what they were saying. Now if the US government started to raise holy hell about it, he'd be utterly convinced.

"Hungry?" he asked finally.

"Oh, yeah," Pip answered wearily.

"Let's get you to your bunks and then we'll bring some food in. In case you didn't notice, this base is abandoned. Shut down for a while. Used to be Air Force, then Marines. Now it's nothing, a ghost town, so we use it for special occasions," he smiled.

He led them through hallways lined with swinging fluorescent lights. They squeaked rhythmically as they swung a bit. The gale was moving some air inside, as well. The wall and ceiling paint was pale, peeling badly, and the rooms reeked of decay and mildew. The humidity of the tropics quickly laid claim to any structure left unattended by man even for a moment. They arrived at a room with two sets of bunk beds and a lamp and table. There was a television set
on top of a three-drawer chest.

"Stow it here, men. The latrine is right next door and it works. I am responsible for your safety until further notice. That means you don't eat or drink anything I haven't handed you personally. It means you don't do anything or go anywhere unless I am with you myself. There are a dozen of us here at the moment; we are as highly skilled as it gets. You are never to be alone. You know we'll be moving a lot. The detail with you will always be small but highly… efficient… so we don't broadcast anything unusual.

Understood?"

"Yes, sir," Tim said. "Something you should be aware of, though."

"What's that?" Salty asked.

"They can track us. They will always know where we are."

"Explain."

"Yeah, explain," Pip chimed in.

"Bioaccumulation. That stuff they've been dropping on us from the skies? Nano-particles that can be tracked. It's been going on so long that our bodies are accustomed to it and have sort of bonded with it creating a very unique signature for each person. In fact, inside the aircraft is the only place we might have a chance. Okinawa is small. That bird has a zero radar profile but it's no longer moving. They'll have a visual on her soon unless she's in a hangar."

In fact, at that moment two men in police uniforms appeared to guard the door into their room. Two Marines were stationed outside the window on watch in the driving rain, despite the fact that the opening was three-quarters of the way up the wall and louvered. There would be men patrolling the grounds as well.

"I see," Salty was taken aback. "I've got to get orders on this. Hang tight. I'll get food."

As soon as the door was shut, Pip opened up. "What the hell are you talking about, man?"

"It's true, Pip. It's not just us. It's everybody. A human surveillance and control project. Don't ask me why they care about 'chipping' every human on the planet. Seems like a waste of time and money to me. I can't tell you any more than that because I don't know any more than that. I'm sorry."

"Well, we're by God going to do something about that," Pip muttered.

Ten minutes later, Salty returned with a tray of sandwiches, fruit and coffee. He set the tray on one of the lower bunks.

"Look men," he said, folding his arms, "I spoke to my superiors. The idea that you can be found no matter what we do with you creates a serious challenge. The first consideration is, naturally, what's more important... the hard evidence or your confession? We simply can't say one of those is obviously the winner here. So a tech team is coming in. We'll wait. They'd be here already except for the weather but the storm is blowing over quickly. They're experts in a few very relevant disciplines from more or less neutral countries. Switzerland, India, New Zealand, Indonesia, Iceland... a few from right here in Japan. We're going to go over that bird with a fine-toothed comb and take lots of photos, videos... the works. Until that's finished, you two and the bird are equally important. Once we have backup evidence, we can concentrate more fully on keeping you in pocket. That's the best we can do."

The reality was Tim did not know whether he could still be 'found' in light of his health upgrade but he wasn't about to tell Pip that. Pip had stuck with him no questions asked. They would livetogether or die together.

"Oh, yes," Salty added, "we may split you two up for insurance. Less likely they'll get you both if you are in different places, yes?"

He left them alone. They were a bit stunned. It never occurred to them that they might be separated no matter how much sense it made now. The only sound was that of the rain still dashing against the sides of the building. Suddenly, what they wanted more than anything was for the storm to move off.

A week later, Christina found herself sequestered in a small room in the main hall of *Shuri* Castle with Huck, Charlie, Isaac, French and some guy she didn't even know called John Clayfell. They were watching the initial proceedings unfold on a fairly large television monitor and, whether anyone else realized it or not, Christina tried to keep herself from jumping on John Clayfell's back and pummeling his head. And then she had to. He was in front of her and just to the left studying the monitor. In truth, the only one in the room who had not thought of doing the same thing was Charlie. Charlie had spent some time reconciling what he knew about Nikolai/John.

Letting go a guttural yell, she landed on his back with her arms around his neck. Although he was surprised, he held onto himself, did not throw her over his shoulder or defend himself in any way except to try to break the hold onto her arms to prevent being choked.

"Get off, Christina!" his voice sounded strangled. "Someone get her off."

"Christina!" Charlie said, grabbing her around the waist.

"Let go, damn it! Let go!" French tried to pry her arms from around Nikolai's throat.

Charlie managed to pull her off but she landed several fist blows into Nikolai's back and kicked him in the leg. He turned to face her and she caught him squarely in the crotch. He dropped.

"You know," she said panting, "it isn't even just that you help the people who are trying to murder my children... it's that I want to know who the hell killed my mother! Who killed her, Nikolai? Who... did... it?"

"Hey, wait! Shut up!" Huck cried. "Look at the TV!"

The scream from Huck was so uncharacteristic they all turned to look.

"That's my boy! That's my boy!" he cried.

The large screen showed a very weary, saddened Tim Verzet. He was sipping water and waiting. Someone unseen on his end must have indicated it was time to speak. He set the water down and cleared his throat.

"Madame Soderholm, greetings to you and to the members of your panel. My name is Timothy Andrew Verzet and I hail from California in the United States. I and my comrade, Philip Yarmouth...", he wiped his hand across his eyes, voice breaking. Then he cleared his throat and went on, "Pip Yarmouth and I flew an aircraft to Okinawa about a week ago to present to your panel and to the Japanese government, too, as evidence of global chemical warfare and a planned universal genocide. I believe there is a team of experts finishing their inspection of the aircraft and preparing a written report for you and, again, for the Japanese government. The aircraft is an atmospheric dispersal method for toxic chemical agents. As far as I know, that is its sole purpose for existing. Pip and I were two of many pilots who flew these terrible missions. In light of the chances we took, the danger we are in and the great sacrifices... we made, I beg the panel to hear our story. Thank you."

Tears streamed down Huck's face as he watched. French put his hand on Huck's shoulder.

"That's my son," he whispered.

The image on the television monitor changed to Choshin Soderholm, visibly moved by Tim's distress.

"I understand, Mr. Verzet. I am thankful that I've have had some information from both the government of Japan and the police here in Naha. We look forward to accepting what you have brought at such a terrible cost to yourself and to Mr. Yarmouth. Thank you."

Christina's small band in the side room was still.

"Huck," Charlie said finally, "do you have any idea what that's about?"

Huck was wiping his eyes with an over-sized blue handkerchief.

"Yes, I know what that is," Huck said, looking pointedly at Nikolai and smiling, "He's brought one of the aircraft here. What do you think of that, you bastard?"

Pip and Tim sat for long minutes, stunned, that they'd be separated in this final leg of the race with the finish line so close they could almost reach out and break the tape. Salty was right, though. Tim knew that more than Pip did. One of them had to get to the panel and start talking.

"I didn't give much thought to what would happen once we got here, Pip," Tim said, "because I didn't expect us to make it."

"I didn't either," Pip said.

Pip sighed. It was so easy for him to process a situation and move on. Tim would be eaten up by the things he couldn't control. Pip reached for a sandwich, picked up the plate and offered it to Tim. Tim reached out then changed his mind, shook his head.

"Come on, pilot," Pip chided him gently, "you're basically a P.O.W. now. Eat when there's food."

Tim laughed half-heartedly. Good old Pip. He reached for his sandwich… tuna salad. The coffee was good, too, generously doctored with cream and sugar. These men were soldiers and warriors. They knew what was needed.

"I'm going to take a chance on getting some sleep." Tim lay on one bottom bunk. Pip finished his coffee then curled up on the other. As always they both stuck out over the ends because of their height if they straightened their legs out. They got a good four hours' sleep before there was a knock on the door. The door opened immediately thereafter letting a wide band of fluorescent light stream into the darkened room.

"Sorry, men," it was Salty, "we're moving. We're going separate directions, as well."

Pip and Tim sat up, ready to move. They had not so much as untied their shoes.

"Let's go," Salty leaned in and gestured toward them to follow.

Another detail joined them, waiting at the end of the long hall they had come in through earlier. Apparently they would each travel with half a dozen men. Some of the Marines were staying behind. There was no sound of rain or wind against the windows and roof. It was dark... but was it still dark or dark again? They had no idea. They stopped at the door waiting for instructions from Salty.

"Okay," he said, "Verzet, we're going first. There are two identical sedans outside. Obviously you're not being told where you are going. Once in the sedan, you'll be under a blanket again in the back. Go!"

Tim was hustled outside into the night. The door to the black sedan was already open, a plainclothes officer standing by the back seat door, another in the back seat. He recognized one of the Marines as the driver although he was dressed in street clothes. Salty slid quickly into the passenger seat. Tim was shoved into the back and down onto the floor. He crouched on the floor and they covered him with an army blanket. Because of his height, he was extremely uncomfortable. His ankles and knees were bent at ridiculously unnatural angles. He had no idea how long the trip was but he hoped it would be quick. Drive fast. The same thing would be happening to Pip behind them. God speed, pilot.

He sensed a right turn onto the road in front of the airbase. The driver sped up immediately. It might have been thirty seconds later – he would never remember the sequence of events very clearly – when he heard the faint sounds of an explosion, followed by people screaming. Then what could only have been a vehicle exploded, shaking the car he was in. The driver of his car hit the accelerator. The tires squealed briefly and they were gone, traveling as fast as they could away from whatever was burning.

"What the hell was that?" Tim said from under the blanket.

"My guess is that was your buddy," Salty replied. "I'm sorry."

"What the hell?" Tim said again.

"Unknown. The car was one hundred percent clean. If it was a missile, we saw no signature of any kind. I can't use the radio or a cell phone right now but I'll find out what happened."

On the floor where he still crouched, Tim wept silently. Forty minutes later, he was hustled into a house or an apartment. He was still under the blanket so he did not see anything that would identify his surroundings. Once inside he threw the blanket off his head. He followed Salty into a western-style kitchen. He sat at a simple metal kitchen table while Salty pushed buttons on his cell phone. Four additional guards were there to meet them and allowed them inside but never left their stations by doors or windows. Tim's eyes were red and burning from forty minutes of weeping, his cheeks red and flushed from a quietly raging anger. He pushed the glass of water away that someone set in front of him, never taking his eyes off Salty, who murmured monosyllables into his phone. Eventually Salty signed off and snapped his phone shut. He looked at Tim squarely.

"No device under the car, nothing airborne hit the car. No one in the car was wired with anything. All equipment vetted and re-vetted. The men standing in the doorway when the first explosion occurred..." Salty trailed off, seemingly not wanting to finish the sentence.

"Well?" Tim spat the word out.

Salty remained silent, looking at Tim.

"Damn it!" Tim barked. "What did they see?"

"Yarmouth," Salty sighed, shook his head in disbelief, "it was Yarmouth who exploded... sort of."

"Start over." Tim felt his entire body flush. He knew the truth of these statements even if he didn't quite know or understand the mechanism.

"One of the Marines is en route right now. You can ask him yourself. I'm sorry. I really am. If I had to guess based on what you've already told us about bioaccumulation I'd say tracking elements aren't the only thing in there. This is right in the category of stuff we 'know' but 'don't know.' Case in point: remember all the birds that fell out of the sky back in January and all the animals that have turned up by the hundreds and thousands dead... autopsies revealed massive internal injuries almost like they'd had an enormous blow with something blunt. Could be something like that. Could be that once they find you they can use a long-range tool or technique of some sort, electromagnetics likely, to kill you. Probably via satellite. Now, that begs the immediate question… what are we going to do about you and how come you haven't gone up yet?"

Tim felt like a deep cavern had opened up under him and he was falling. It would have been better to crash into the bottom of the Grand Canyon.

Shut up. We got the plane here. That's all that mattered. Pip knew that.

"I had a much higher ranking than Yarmouth," Tim confessed. "My body had been cleaned out of a lot of stuff. What's left in there, I couldn't tell you. That is something we apparently did not need to know."

"Okay," Salty said, "let's just hang tight until my man gets here."

Tim sat at the table. They left the room, left him alone with his thoughts. He was surprised they'd wanted to get this close to him after what happened to Pip. Part of the gig, he supposed. Dying as part of protecting a whistle blower is mentioned in the job description.

Half an hour later a pair of soldiers arrived, covered with dirt and grime from black smoke mixed with sweat. They had been standing by the car when Pip started to get in. They described a scene in which blood started to flow heavily from Pip's ears, nose, mouth and tear ducts at about the same moment. His eyes had gone quite wide, the only sound that escaped his mouth a strangled sort of gurgle, his lungs almost surely filling with blood. These were all classic signs of profound internal injury. Assuming a medical emergency was on their hands, they had all but thrown him into the car as it started to speed away then run back inside to radio the local military hospital. Moments later the car exploded with Pip and three policemen inside it. The guards just inside the building reported no incoming device of any kind. No missile, no rocket, nothing. Tim now knew as much as anyone did about the incident in which one of his dearest friends had perished horrifically but, in his estimation, most honorably.

Christina lay on her back on a meager sofa, some sort of bench with a plastic cushion running the length of it. It was out of place, an alien, here in this stone monument to the Ryukyu Dynasty.

"Why does it all look so Chinese?" she asked no one in particular.

"Okinawa is far more Chinese than Japanese," Nikolai replied. "Have you noted the dragons everywhere? And the red tiles on the roofs?"

Christina did not move, she remained staring at the ornate ceiling. She had seen the dragons. They were everywhere.

"Why did you do it, Nikolai?" she asked, finally.

"It's a job, Christina. In fact, it's a very old profession. One man's espionage is another man's patriotism. It's been a century or two since we've lived in a plain and simple world and, you know what? I don't think we've ever lived in a world where people just minded their own business."

"I thought you were sick."

"I am. I can smell and taste all of it. They tell me if I do a good job, they'll give me the chelating materials. At least I'll be able to get the metals out that way. I will probably just give them to my son."

Christina let that hang in the air for a bit.

"Biological warfare...human resources, experiments. This is what we've come to as human beings. We can even sit there, apparently, working for those who are using these biologics on us, conducting medical experiments on people as a species while our children die...".

"Do you think this is a new phenomenon?" Nikolai asked.

"It's a twentieth century aberration, some disease of intelligence and intent. Maybe some suicidal tendency."

"No. Christina. How do you think the black plague made its way through Europe like a brush fire in the fourteenth century? Any guesses?" Nikolai asked.

No one spoke.

"It was a military ploy, an attack. An army of Tartars in what is now the Ukraine... they had an epidemic of plague within the fortified walls of their city. The Tartars hurled dead, infected cadavers at the opposing army. What followed was the pandemic we call the Black Death. No one knows what the origin of the actual pathogen was but that's how it got out. We're talking about a life form that can and has hurled plague-ridden corpses at enemies. Come on, Christina. Wake up. Twenty five million Europeans died of the plague eventually. They had catapults; we have aircraft that are nearly spacecraft. The only difference is technology."

"No. The difference," Charlie interjected, "is that we are not at war.

There is no war declared on the human race as a whole; just a handful of psychopaths with some followers exterminating us."

"They're going to kill you now," Christina said.

"Yes, very likely they will."

"We'll be killed, as well."

"Not necessarily. My death can be explained. I am a spy, after all. Spies deserve to die horrible deaths; that's been the party line for fifty years. They will kill me out of anger, to make an example of me. If they kill all of us they automatically lend credence to what we are saying... that it's really happening. There would have been a time when that would not have bothered them, their arrogance was so complete. They are in a panic now. Things have got away from them altogether. You should warn your family, though, supposing it isn't too late already."

"I can't," she said. "I don't know where they are."

"What do you mean?" Charlie asked.

Christina sat up.

"They're here somewhere. Otto and I thought the worst thing to do was leave the rest of them to wait at home like sitting ducks. So they flew out the same day we did. They are here somewhere... I don't know where... on purpose. Otto will find me when it seems safe."

There was a knock on the door; five loud raps.

"Yes!" Charlie called.

The heavy, ornately carved door swung slowly on its bronze hinges. A serious young Okinawan man stood in the doorway. His trim figure bowed slightly. Behind him, Choshin Soderholm and Philip Ford appeared.

"Good afternoon, everyone," Choshin was the first to speak. "It must have been a long, anxious day. How are we all faring?"

"It was a long day," Christina replied.

"May I introduce you to someone who will be very important to you over the next few days?"

Choshin gestured toward the Okinawan man. "This is Captain Miyahiro. He is charged with your safety and all the security, in fact, here at *Shuri* over the next two weeks."

"Welcome," he said. "If you would all be so kind as to follow me, we have identified what we believe will be the safest place for you."

They looked to Choshin for reassurance.

"Yes," she said, "this is the case. You can trust Miyahiro completely."

"Please," he stopped and turned to them, "I prefer to be called 'Salty.'"

"That's a nice, solid American accent, Salty," Charlie noted.

"Yes."

This time Salty didn't stop, turn around or make any effort to engage in small talk. He led them down a hallway running the long end of the south hall. At the end, he opened a door. They expected to be going outside but the door led immediately to a staircase down to a lower level. They were being taken under the courtyard to one of the other buildings. Choshin and Ford brought up the rear. Eventually they ended up in what looked like a command center, still under ground, within a setting of about 300 yards altogether of tunnels. Off a main command office, complete with electricity and telephone capability, there were berths much like one would find on an old warship.

"The underground headquarters!" Huck said.

"Just so," Salty replied. "The Japanese Imperial Army headquartered themselves here just before the Battle of Okinawa and stayed here for the duration. Some of it has been restored."

He led them to the berths where their luggage had miraculously been transported. The 'beds' were ship's berths, little more than tough canvas stretched over a frame and held to the metal sides with springs.

"While it will be obvious to those watching you that you are no longer staying at the Arikaki residence we hope that we managed to get your things in here surreptitiously. Obviously we can't start bringing mattresses and things in. This will have to do. There are plenty of pillows and blankets, and the galley is stocked. There is electricity down here so you can watch the proceedings, as well as air conditioning. Believe me, you will need it. Do not connect to any of your personal computer accounts or use your cell phones. Don't even turn them on. Alright?"

"Okay," they agreed.

"Good," Salty said. "I'll be back this evening with one more delivery."

He withdrew leaving only Choshin and Ford with them.

"I just want to tell you here, before your actual testimony which should be tomorrow given the circumstances, that after the Reconciliation is drawn up I intend to hear more about the criminal aspects of this situation and prepare to bring suit to the International Criminal Court in the Hague. My telling you allows you to prepare for that and decide how far you can go individually with this," Ford said. "Some of you won't have a choice."

"Can you be ready for first thing in the morning?" Choshin asked. "I think we'll put you on video down here, as well. We'll keep you... what's the saying... on 'ice'... after that."

Sure," Charlie replied. "We'll be ready to go."

Choshin and Ford left the same way Salty had. There remained a detail of half a dozen men, three at each end of the tunnel. They assumed the men were Okinawan police.

"Oh," Choshin stuck her head back through the door, "don't go anywhere unless Salty is with you and please forgive the supply situation. We just can't be seen bringing things in."

Behind them, French was in the small galley. He began to chuckle. "M.R.E.'s," he laughed. "Now this is what I call a vacation!"

The men started to laugh, as well. "What's an M.R.E?" Christina asked.

"Military issue dried food," Charlie answered. "We are definitely in the trenches now. This is confirmation."

"Here," French said, "come have a look."

He handed Christina a vacuum-sealed plastic package. "Field rations."

"Are they still World War II issue?" Huck laughed. "No," French replied, "they're new, thank God."

"Wait, what is all this? You guys seem to get it," Christina asked.

"Yes, sorry," said Charlie. "This is where the Japanese command hid and directed the Battle of Okinawa during World War II. It's the primary reason it was such a long, bloody battle... this was pure genius. Anyway, I read it was huge. This must be a small restored part."

"I'll bet they had to clear away the bones of Japanese officers who had committed suicide at the end," Isaac added.

"God," Christina said, "that's pretty terrible. What's here then? How do we make 'food' out of these?"

"Well, let's see." Isaac, Huck and French dug around in the cupboard, throwing packs to Charlie who set them on the table and read the labels of some as they flew past.

"Chili with Beans, Beef Ravioli, Chicken with Noodles, Beef Brisket, Beef Stew, Vegetable Lasagna, Lemon Pepper Tuna, Buffalo Chicken," he read then, "hey, wait a second!"

Charlie ripped a package open and held up what looked like a candy bar.

"Hooah!" the men yelled.

"What?" The entire exercise was making Christina cross.

"It's an energy bar," Charlie laughed. "We used to call these Meals Requiring Enemas."

Christina looked alarmed and cross now.

"I'm sure they've improved a lot," Charlie looked at his shoes, then back at Christina. "We can heat these on the stove here at least. I am pretty hungry."

"Yeah, chuck me that bag of meat loaf," French said, laughing.

At eleven p.m., there was noise in the tunnel, talking and movement. They all sat up and listened, afraid that someone had got past security and would be taking them away, maybe back to the United States or just putting a gun to their heads right then and there. It was very difficult not to panic before the unknown and since this was an entirely new experience, every noise, every rattle, every mouse cleaning its whiskers in the passageway, was an unknown.

Salty appeared at the doorway. The guards let him through. With him, he had a single man; Tim Verzet. Huck saw him, left his bunk, and pushed his way through his fellows to get to his son.

"Hi, Dad," Tim said, tears welling in his eyes. He was unshaven, grief-stricken, and had not really slept in days.

"Hi, son," Huck replied softly. "You're right on time. Good job, boy."

They embraced for a full minute, not having seen or spoken to each other since the long night in the snow on the hill in January. Obviously

Huck had not known what Tim was planning because Tim had not planned it until just before it happened. He just knew that Tim was looking for a hook, some way to break everything wide open. Christina felt tears in her eyes, as well.

"This is the safest place on the island right now," Salty said finally. "Right under everyone's nose in a way. There was a rumor this might be a father and son event. Glad it turned out to be true."

"Good God, Tim," Charlie asked, "how in the hell did you get one of those planes out of the country?"

"Oh, Tim," Huck said shakily, "this is Charlie Shepard."

"Shepard," Tim stuck out his hand. "They stood down. That was the main thing. The military stood down across the western U.S. and allowed us safe passage. It was the damnedest thing I've ever seen."

"Jesus, I wish I could have seen that," Charlie whispered.

"Wish we had something to offer you here," said Christina. "Coffee maybe you don't need. Maybe you just need some sleep. Maybe you just need some time with your father."

Nikolai sat in the corner watching Huck and Tim. Tim noticed him eventually.

"Who's this?" Tim stuck out his hand.

"Don't shake his hand, son, he's a damnable traitor," Huck said. Tim knit his brows.

"What are you talking about?"

"Oh, they mean that I have been revealed as an asset. I have been working for the U.S. Secretary of Agriculture these many years and they have managed to corner me here, forcing me to out myself," Nikolai said wryly. "How do you do?"

He stuck out his hand. Tim took it and the two stared at each other.

"I have no idea what I'm supposed to say to that," he said.

"Why are you even shaking his hand?" Christina asked.

"I believe they are waiting for you to tear me apart... since you are so obviously the good guy and I, the bad," Nikolai ventured. "I don't see that happening, do you?"

Tim sat down. He stared at Nikolai for a moment.

"No," he said.

"You see, what he knows that you haven't allowed yourselves to acknowledge is that while I stood on the side, collecting and cataloging… making note of the mood of the people, really… he was flying death planes. It isn't a bigger crime to gain the trust of the people and then betray it. Right, my friend?"

"No, it is not a bigger crime," Tim said. "Believe me, I know what I've done. It's the only way to have solved this, from the inside. We will both be judged. The pilots were the only people who could have done something about this."

"I'll put us in here," Salty spoke up to break the tension. He stood at the doorway to one of the berth rooms.

"Well, there is a difference," Nikolai said, "you get a bodyguard."

"Can I have my Dad in here with us?" Tim asked.

"Yes, I think that'll be fine," Salty answered.

"Okay, Huck?" Tim asked.

"Okay." Huck hadn't stopped smiling since Tim appeared.

They were being filmed in the underground headquarters. The panel was visible on a monitor, reacting to their testimony and asking questions in real time. They heard murmurings and movement as if from a large crowd. However, the camera angle did not waver.

"I must admit," Mai Arikaki said," the burning question for me is who is doing all of this?"

"Yes, I agree," Arturo Maldonado chimed in. "Who is driving this program?"

"Who, we don't know. We see aircraft mostly of the DC-10 and 747 size with no livery at all. Sometimes there are blue and white aircraft, sometimes red and gold, sometimes all white. They never have any windows. We, personally, have brought with us soil, air and water samples gathered over the course of the last ten years. The same areas were sampled over the decades prior to our survey. We can say with complete surety, for example, that the aluminum oxide levels in the water are sixty thousand times more than the government says are acceptable. We have many other samplings over time. The list of toxic chemicals found that could only have come from the atmosphere is long and it is included," Isaac was speaking for the California contingent.

"We can tell you that top scientists are out there all the time constantly talking to the public – trying to convince us that this is a legitimate program. Actually, to be more specific, they say it will be a legitimate program. They don't acknowledge its existence yet. They do seem to have a leader, though."

"Who would that be?" Philip Ford asked.

"His name is Dr. Daniel Bleeth," French said.

The members of the panel seemed stunned. Choshin leaned over and whispered in Ford's ear. They murmured, heads together for a bit, then she nodded to him.

"Mr. Baum and company," Choshin pushed her reading glasses up on her nose. "I have documents before me that indicate we have already had some interaction with one Dr. Daniel Bleeth."

"What?" French exclaimed. "I don't understand."

"Bleeth approached the Japanese government with a petition for sanctuary two weeks ago. He is currently in custody. We have no more information than that."

It was their turn to be stunned.

"However," Ford added, "I certainly would view this as some sort of confirmation that he has something to do with current events."

"One of the seemingly related phenomena that is of great concern to us is the rise in aggressive behavior among humans, particularly young males, in areas which are proved to be saturated with airborne chemicals," Huck put forth. "I particularly have been keeping track of this since the area in which I live appears to be one of those areas. I have collected statistics which track the chemicals in the water and soil over time and compare them to the rise in levels of aggression, at least in reported cases. I'd like permission to submit those to the panel or at least bring them to you attention since they are within the body of information we've brought to you."

"Certainly," Choshin said.

"We would also submit that chemical affecting levels of aggression ipso facto remove a certain amount of intelligent free will. One has to suspect then that learning capabilities are under siege as much as decision-making capabilities."

"Yes, that would be a logical avenue of investigation," Maldonado replied. "I'd like to see those specifically. I, myself, have data from South America as an educator that has thus far been unexplained. I'd like to think this might be a road to understanding that data."

"Finally, in the United States, as you know, we are one of the very few countries that did not stop adding chemicals to drinking water some twenty years ago. Some of those chemicals combined especially with the aluminum oxide falling from the sky simply adds up to a super-toxin in the human body, a super poison that compromises bone structure. Certainly, the toxins and their combinations are deeply suspect in the area of skyrocketing auto-immune disorders." Isaac closed his folder.

"Yes," Dr. Arikaki spoke, "the medical profession has suspected all along the underlying causes of so many twentieth century ailments were environmental. I'd like to see that data myself."

"As would I," Dr. Matambo leaned forward and spoke into his microphone. He did not often interject.

"I'd like to say a few things," Shepard raised his hand.

"Proceed, please," Choshin said.

"I'd like to specifically bring up the topic of water, Madame Chairman. Fundamentally, these airborne toxins are ruining the water supply as it relates to health; not just human health either. Toxic water kills animal life and plant life. So what we are faced with is the poisoning of all life, in a very real way, through the water cycle. I believe that alone violates in the most extreme sense the Geneva Accord and the UN Human Rights Treaties generated just after World War II. If I may, the United Nations revisited this subject as recently as the summer of 2010.

The U.N., Recognizes the right to safe and clean drinking water and sanitation as a human right that is essential for the full enjoyment of life and all human rights; Calls upon States and international organizations to provide financial resources, capacity-building and technology transfer, through international assistance and cooperation, in particular to developing countries, in order to scale up efforts to provide safe, clean, accessible and affordable drinking water and sanitation for all; Welcomes the decision by the Human Rights Council to request that the independent expert on human rights obligations related to access to safe drinking water and sanitation submit an annual report to the General Assembly, and encourages her to continue working on all aspects of her mandate and in consultation with all relevant United Nations agencies, funds and programmes, to include in her report to the Assembly, at its sixty-sixth session, the principal challenges related to the realization of the human right to safe and clean drinking water and sanitation and their impact on the achievement of the Millennium.

These are Developmental Goals read straight from the record at the 108th Plenary Meeting at the United Nations," Charlie said. "It doesn't say anywhere in any UN document merely access to water, it says access to safe water is the basic human right... although I might supersede that with air. The right to breathe safe air is probably the most fundamental human right."

"Yes, Mr. Shepard," Ford said, "these phenomena break both the letter and the spirit of countless treaties. There is no question of that."

"Mr. Ford, I'd like also to remind the world that this program constitutes medical experimentation on unknowing and unwilling individuals. Again, this breaks every international human rights treaty going back to the Nuremberg Code and the Geneva Convention. Again, with the indulgence of the panel, this is a short but direct quote from that document, the Nuremberg Code,

The voluntary consent of the human subject is absolutely essential. That means that the person involved should have legal capacity to give consent; should be situated as to be able to exercise free power of choice, without intervention of any element of force, fraud, deceit, duress, over-reaching, or other form of constraint or coercion; and should have sufficient knowledge and comprehension of the elements of the subject matter involved as to enable him to make an understanding and enlightened decision. This latter element requires that before the acceptance of an affirmative decision by the experimental subject there should be made known to him the nature, duration, and purpose of the experiment; the methods and means by which it is to be conducted; all inconveniences and hazards reasonable to be expected; and the effects upon his health or person which may possibly come from his participation in the experiment.

"I honestly wonder what else is needed having said that?" Charlie concluded. "I suppose an argument could be made that these toxic dumps are not, in fact, experimental but that the end result is well known and anticipated. There is also documentation for that in the stack of data we provided. That would simply be a different legal charge."

"Yes, Mr. Shepard," van Hal said, "I have some deep interest in this component of your case. I am Dutch myself. My parents and I lived in Amsterdam during the Second World War and I have some feelings based on experience with regard to unbridled medical experimentation. It was because of those experiences that the Nuremberg document was created. I would venture that the majority of the world populace is not in favor of a repeat of those events."

"No, sir," Charlie answered. "Additionally, in terms of health, we see a provable reduction of sunshine hitting the surface of the planet, which affects us simply in terms of Vitamin D absorption. Bad things happen to people who can't get Vitamin D, as you know. That deficiency can be traced back with some surety to the blanket of chemicals constantly hanging in the sky over us blocking the sun."

"Yes, now that you bring that up," Father Sullivan interjected, "let's have a word about the sky in general. Let me just say for the record that I am an astronomer as well as a priest. This has been a lifelong avocation and I think a religious one. There was a time when we learned sixty percent of what we know about the scientific universe via radio astronomy... in other words what we could not see. Then that was taken from us when the sky was filled with satellites and their noise. However, we always comforted ourselves with the idea that we still had the basic visual astronomy with which to work provided we could eliminate enough artificial light."

He tapped a pile of papers before him on the table.

"Here I am reading," he continued, "that some twenty percent of my visibility is obstructed by this layer of chemical plasma. I am going to look into that."

"Yes, sir," Charlie replied again.

"This is a tremendous amount of evidence," Choshin offered, "Good, solid evidence. What I would suggest after having given the matter some thought is this: why don't we hear from Ms. Galbraithe and consider the four of you as a unit? Then we can hear from Msr. Louis as his case is infinitely more complex. Will that suffice?"

As one, they looked at Christina, who nodded. She cleared her throat and straightened her papers.

This is it, Mom. Whatever you want to say now is your chance.

"I think when enough pressure is brought to bear on the sovereign human being, certain effects are seen. They are predictable effects even if the stressors cannot always be predicted. They take many guises; they always seem to wear a mask. What always astonishes me is the relentless nature of the attacks on the sovereign human. There is never a surrender from the other side given an avalanche of data or evidence over millennia. They never seem to be able to find something else with which to occupy themselves. There is never a plan that might end in a conclusion of some sort...something like the sovereignty of the human being is the one sacrosanct attribute to our lives on this planet. That is why we can produce so much evidence of previous grievances and bring to the table all of the agreements fashioned among civilized humans to stop. So I can't help but conclude that we enter the black and white arena, the nature of good and evil, that single burning human question. Often it has to do with making others submit so that one human can make it to the top of the dog pile. This must have to do with instinct alone because it can't have anything to do with thought or reason. After all, it's like the idea of achieving riches or fame...particularly fame. Then what? I can't think of a more boring goal. So it must be some animal part of our nature that leads us to this kind of thing.

I am here simply because my mother was killed and my children are dying. I think those are profound reasons. Reasons enough. I am every mother, they are every child. Apparently we will never learn the lessons of totalitarianism. We are not, therefore, a bright lot, are we? We continue to craft treaties because we must and should define ourselves, remind ourselves. We do this despite the idea that every human's free will allows him or her to accept or reject.

However, in my mind, those who repeat this evil scenario over and over and over are like old men who can't prevent themselves from hiding in the disgusting dark corners of pornographic movie houses doing terrible things to themselves in public. They are slaves, surely, incapable of exercising free will. My own mother believed in the virtue and rightness of might alone. Then because she was weak the mighty ran her down in the road. I am just a mother. These are just my children. This is why I am here."

Choshin removed her reading glasses and sat for a bit.

"Young lady," Father Francis said, "I think you've got it in one."

"Let's have a brief break, shall we?" Choshin stood, followed by her fellows, and left the hall. Christina felt strangely calm, like she had managed to climb to a new footing somehow on a higher plateau; something more sure, more secure, somewhere she was less likely to topple over in the wind of emotion. The poison, the infection almost, of her mother's death had to be taken somewhere for healing. Was she the healed, in this case, or the healer? The insane part of it had slipped off her shoulders.

Nikolai was up next. Christina doubted the poison, the insanity, of his situation had budged much. She did not pity him. He could redeem himself here even though he had not sought it or worked for it, he had been dragged to it. When she watched him, though, he did seem resigned. Was resignation the same thing as redeeming oneself? Did it count if it was against your will? These were interesting questions. Soon enough, the panel was seated again.

"Msr. Louis," Ford led this part of the hearing, "how do you prefer to be called? Clayfell or Louis?"

"For these purposes, please continue to call me Nikolai. I'm quite accustomed to it and I think trying to keep all that straight could add confusion to a situation we are actually trying to untangle," Nikolai replied.

"Very well," Ford replied. "I also want to add for the official record that I, Philip Ford, am not asking for nor am I interested in delving into particular legalities having to do with your activities over the last two decades, Msr. Louis. I will be very interested in that at a later time. For now, we are solely concerned with gathering information regarding a quantifiable and apparently provable breech of several international human rights treaties with, it seems, verifiable deaths and illnesses as a result."

"Yes," Nikolai agreed.

"Our burning question remains unanswered, sir. Who, in your actual experience, do you know or work for who has some sort of authority over or responsibility for these events? By events, I mean specifically the chemical saturation of the atmosphere in an international scope."

"I currently work for the United States Secretary of Agriculture, Robert Custer."

"I see. And what is it you do for Secretary Custer?"

"I operate several social media sites, for one thing, presenting myself as an activist campaigning against geo-engineering and collecting people. I collect people as part of these groups, people who are against geo-engineering and we learn things about them so that we might manage them. Where they are located, what sorts of communications they enter into together, what exactly do they know or think they know? And I can collect medical information. The medical information is slightly paramount to my boss. Lab results across the population indicate levels of chemicals and toxins entering the bloodstream and staying there. People talk about their symptomology quite a bit. They can refer back to what's been applied to that area of the country and deduce whether or not goals are being met."

"What sorts of goals does your boss have, Msr. Louis?" Matambo asked.

"He has sizable investments in two industries: pharmaceutical and agricultural."

"And so…?" Matambo prodded Nikolai.

"He has never said as much to me, you understand, but I am convinced that disease is created for profit. Disease and incapacity."

"These are theories that have been floated elsewhere," Dr. Arikaki said.

"What about the agricultural investments?" Maldonado chimed in. Agricultural protection was one of his primary interests."

"He is the largest shareholder I can name in Sceptre Corporation.

There are a few others, I simply don't know who they are. Sceptre has patented seeds, any kind you can think of, which are resistant to the chemicals being sprayed. My assumption is that the idea is to kill off healthy, normal seeds and then have the market cornered by having the only seed that can grow in a bastardized environment."

"So, if your assumptions are correct, Secretary Custer is using this and the Sceptre Corporation to create a market... a captive, unwilling market, for his products and services. And he intends to be the only such offering these products and services," Choshin concluded.

"This is what I think is going on based on my work, what they ask me to track, etc."

"If your job is, in fact, to track the effects of geo-engineering then that gives credence to the notion that first, there is a geo-engineering program associated with the U.S. and a big one and that, at the very least, the Secretary of the Agriculture is very much aware that the citizenry is being negatively affected by it directly," Ford stated.

"Yes, sir, I would think that an apt conclusion."

"Msr. Louis," Ford added, "is your lab result documentation accounted for here in what you've provided to us?"

"Yes, sir, I believe it is all there."

"Is there any other individual you can now name who controls you and your activities with regard to this program?"

"No, not to my knowledge."

"Well, I don't need to hear anymore at this time. Anyone else?"

The other members of the panel indicated they had no questions for Nikolai. He was surprised but as Ford had said, no one was interested in the legalities of his activities at this point. He wondered how long that would be the case. He knew that in less than two weeks, the other members of his group would be free to leave, if they felt it was safe to do so. He would not be. He could only hope to stay on Okinawa in custody. It was known. He felt Salty was an incredibly competent guard. He didn't mind staying in custody; however, he minded getting killed in custody.

"Well, it feels as though we should be stopping for lunch as we have packed a tremendous amount of information into just a few hours this morning. I imagine frequent breaks will be needed as we go through this. I am recommending tea. Let's plan on a tea break every morning at ten a.m.," Choshin announced. "Let's meet back here at eleven and plan on luncheon at one p.m."

"Agreed," Ford replied. "next up is a video statement, as well."

That will be Tim, Christina thought. He was someone who would be driving the poison out with his confession. Tim was still due for his breakdown though. The one that came with the C-clamp that fixes you to some surface so utterly and completely and unforgivingly. Then the clamp is loosened and what was being held in, enough for three or four people, was let loose, flowed into the world, leaving the previously crucified to resurrect themselves...well, resurrect something. So much of what had been in there would have been seared out utterly. It was what Mai had described as the path of the *Uta*. Complete, total disintegration and rebuilding. The seared out parts made spaces for capacities which, when acknowledged, seemed mystical. In actuality, they were more human than the dead matter that had been taking up that space.

Tim waited in his berth. Christina brought him some tea. They did not speak.

Promptly at eleven a.m., the panel reconvened. In the underground headquarters of the Japanese Imperial Army, under *Shuri* Castle, Pilot Tim Verzet sat before a camera, watching a monitor just to his side. The monitor showed him the members of the panel during his interview. Salty sat just to his left. His father was there, as well, calm and confident.

"Go ahead, Mr. Verzet," Ford said.

Tim cleared his throat.

"My name, as I said previously, is Timothy Verzet. I have been a pilot for an organization called Bluesky Airways. This company owns and operates hundreds and hundreds of very large, high capacity aircraft that are used to disperse a variety of toxic chemicals into the atmosphere all over the earth. I willingly joined this group roughly one year ago, maybe a little less, not because I knew what they were doing but because I knew something dastardly was going on. Someone close to my family was killed because of what he discovered about this organization purely by accident. My father was also becoming very ill. I knew once I was inside the organization, I would very likely not be able to get back out. I flew some of these planes and I know the planes were dispersing chemicals while I was the pilot. I freely admit all of this."

"Understood, Mr. Verzet," Ford said. "Before we get too far into this, can you please give us names of those who, in your estimation can verify your account?"

Tim knew Ford was asking for names. He was more than willing to do this.

"Two names I want to give you, Mr. Ford," Tim replied, "Mickey Unger was the boss at the airfield where I was assigned, the primary airfield. That's *Gila* Airfield in far southern New Mexico. He has ties higher up and all the operational information one would need for the mechanism below him. The other name is new to me with regard to this business. However, I spoke to this person myself enroute here and he asked for 'his' plane back. That is Nero Pearle. You may have heard that name. He is also involved deeply in Sceptre and I believe the mega-corporation, Pantheon, is his, as well. The aircraft I flew here was designed and built in their Skunkworks."

"Yes, Mr. Verzet. That name is very familiar to me," Ford responded.

"So, we know some of the 'who,' and the where, what, when and how... we just don't know 'why?'" van Hal said, almost as if he were thinking aloud. "If I may, I'd like to ask you about the fellow who helped you fly that plane here, Philip Yarmouth."

"Yes, of course."

"We have been told an horrific story about this fellow and what happened to him after you and he safely landed on Okinawa. Can you elaborate to the extent that it applies to the chemicals being used?"

"Yes, I can," Tim stopped to sip some water. "A big part of the agenda... the goal... if you will, of applying these chemicals over time is the idea of bioaccumulation. That means the particles are nano-particles and there is very little protection against them even when you find out about them. Most of them settle down on us at night. We spray during the day and take advantage of the inversions at night. That's when most of it comes down. Some of it makes the cell membrane more and more permeable. Your body is a remarkable adaptable machine and it becomes accustomed to these chemicals which 'join' in a way to your own DNA-driven uniqueness. That is called bioaccumulation. The cells are essentially electrical in nature anyway and these chemicals are designed to help each and every one of us give off a special electrical bio-signature. We can be tracked and identified in that way. We can be manipulated through use of more or less electric or electro-magnetic signal and that, I believe, is what lies behind the heightened aggression the fellows were talking about earlier. As I rose in the ranks, I was treated to what they referred to as a 'health upgrade,' meaning they cleaned a lot of that out of me. However, there is another use for this bioaccumulation apparently. My friend, Pip, was located and he was blown up at a cellular level – from the inside out. Aluminum oxide is a severe incendiary all by itself. Although we still haven't figured out what happened exactly to make the vehicle he was in explode, it will be found to have something to do with this kind of bioaccumulation, I guarantee."

"My condolences, Mr. Verzet," Father Francis said, "although condolences probably aren't of much use to you."

"Thank you, Father. It is appreciated, I assure you."

"And you've never seen anything like this happen before?" Maldonado asked.

"Not for sure. However, one of the pilots had taken a chemical mixing plant hostage just as we were leaving New Mexico with the plane. The plant blew sky high. That could have easily been the pilot or the company, either one. I assume I have not disintegrated because of the health upgrade. At this point they can't just start blowing pilots up."

"I hope that's true, son," Father Francis said.

"Mr. Verzet," Choshin interjected, "before you go, I just want you to know that the technical team has gone over your aircraft quite thoroughly. We have thousands of photographs, video and pages and pages of chemical analyses on the contents of those barrels in the belly of the plane. Many copies have been sent to world governments. Either they will be incensed or they will be scared to death that this is out in the open…but out in the open it most definitely is. Thank you. I wish it were in my power to grant you amnesty but it is not. May God protect you, sir."

At that moment, the panel rose and began to applaud Tim. Though the camera did not turn toward the visitors in the hall, had Tim been able to see what he heard, he would have seen hundreds of people on their feet, as well, applauding his audacity, his courage and what would surely be a victory in the end. At that moment, Huck began to cry.

Nikolai and Tim were taken, after their testimony, somewhere even more secret, somewhere only Salty knew. That happened when Salty appeared in the underground command center to ask about Bleeth. Apparently that very morning he'd been found dead in his cell in Tokyo.

"Both of you seem to know a great deal about how things operate within this organization," Salty began. "I heard you, Tim, talking about the death of your friend and what that could mean. Msr. Louis has kept health records concerning victims for years. I hope one of you can shed some light on this particular death."

"What happened?" Tim asked.

"He was found in an isolation cell dead. He was covered with what we thought were bullet holes. An autopsy revealed that he was skin and bones only... and fish. He was filled with a tubular shaped catfish found only in the Amazon."

"Well, that's as creepy as it gets but I've never heard of it. Sorry," Tim said.

"How did anyone get to him?" Nikolai wondered.

"We don't have that answer," Salty said. "We're moving you and Tim to an even more secure location for the time being. Ford wants the both of you at the International Court later."

Crosswalk

After two full weeks underground at *Shuri* Castle, Christina and her colleagues were more than ready to leave and to feel the sun on their faces. Every M.R.E. had been tried by everyone, a game that lost its lustre quickly. Tim and Nikolai had been taken away shortly after their testimony and since then there had been nothing but silence in that regard. Salty brought them newspapers in English from many countries. Due to the sensational nature of the first day's testimony, opened by Christina and company and followed by Tim Verzet, the world media had the story at the very top of the news, where it both belonged and would never have been had it not been for the intense events of July 1.

"Are you worried about Tim, Huck?' Christina asked on their last night underground.

"You'd think I would be but I'm not. Tim fought his own war and there were casualties, for sure, but it was the definitely a just war. He saved millions and millions by doing just what he did. He may have helped save the planet. I believe he will be given amnesty once the International Court of Justice has his testimony," Huck was calmly sure.

"It'll be hard to wait for that to be signed and sealed, though," Isaac said.

"I'm going to The Hague when this is over, to wait it out while he's there," Huck answered.

"Here's the Singapore newspaper," Charlie said, picking up one from a bundle left just inside the door. He opened it on the dining table – a monstrously large set-up that clearly was meant to be a map table for commanders planning strategy.

"Front page again," he said, smiling. "Nice photo of the entire panel. Must be because yesterday was the closing day."

The Shuri Reconciliation is close to being completed as a document unto itself now that the hearings are finished. The panel, an honored group of activists representing the world at large, has heard testimony from groups who wanted their issues to be heard before the final document was crafted. Much of the document was already in place at the beginning of that effort and so the finished product is expected to begin traveling the world shortly. First stop: Japan, where the government has already agreed to ratify and sponsor the Shuri Reconciliation on an international level. The only dissent is coming from the United States and the crumbling EU.

"Nothing ever changes," Christina said.

"Wait, here we go," said Charlie.

Renowned Human Rights Activist and Attorney, Philip Ford, will be opening a case under the Crimes Against Humanity statutes at the International Court of Justice in The Hague within the next week. The ICJ has already agreed to hear the case. At the moment, two men will be charged. The ICJ is a permanent tribunal prosecuting cases of genocide, crimes against humanity and war crimes. Charged and under arrest are, at this time, purported high-level CIA asset, Charlie Unger, and billionaire industrialist Georg Nero Pearle.

The Prosecutor sought charges against United States Secretary of State Robert Custer. However, the United States and Israel recently 'unsigned' the charter and have indicated they have no intention of participating. As a result, Interpol has issued a red warrant for Custer such that he may be legally detained and questioned under their authority. Scheduled to testify at this time is the head of the Joint Chiefs, Hap LeBlanc, as to the potential role of the United States military. Interpol is said to have issued a red warrant for Lord Carroll de Geier, as well, as he is a person of interest in this case. His son, financier Solomon de Geier, is reported to be bringing testimony against his father to the ICJ.

"Yikes," said French. "Maybe I'll go to the Hague with you, Huck. This is going to be one hell of a free-for-all."

"How did they get Nero?" Isaac wondered.

"Oh, I know that," said Charlie. "The Swiss extradited him. He was hiding in Switzerland across the lake from his own estate. That was probably one of the reasons he bought the place, figured he could cross easily enough and be unreachable. The Swiss have proved to be out of patience of late, though. God, I love the Swiss."

"Oh, look, there's a photo of de Geier being handcuffed," Christina pointed to a grainy black-and-white picture.

"Let's see," said Charlie looking around, "is that the only newspaper today? No, wait. *The Times* is wedged under the door, hang on."

"Coffee," said French. "I'm making coffee."

"Okay," Charlie said, Times spread over the Singapore newspaper, "bigger picture here...*Gila* shut down...aerial photos of more airplanes than I've ever seen in one place. Sceptre and Pantheon both under subpoena. Wonder how that will turn out and how long it will take? Lt. General Toby Morrow appointed to look into the role played by the US military. You know what, my friends, as long as those planes are grounded I feel like we can do anything."

"Charlie, what are you going to do once we're free to leave?" Christina asked.

"Get back on the radio. Tell the people what's going on. You can be sure the spin will start somewhere. All of the underground newsfeeds that were established have to be kept healthy, human nature being what it is. You?"

"Otto sent me a note. He contacted the panel day before yesterday. He took the children out to Mai's house on the island at her invitation. I'm going there for a bit. Then we have a life to get back to... I have a bit of unfinished business."

"Your Mom...".

"Yeah."

"Besides, Hugo is still out there. He has to be in a lot of pain right now. If he isn't, he will be."

"Isaac?" Charlie asked.

"There's a ranch or two to run, animals, and all that. If Huck and French are going to Europe, someone has to go back and take care of things. Better do that, I guess," he smiled. He really didn't want to do anything else.

"Says here, the proceedings at the ICJ can be viewed as streaming video with a half hour delay. I'll be watching that," Charlie added.

"Me, too," said Christina.

It was a four hour ferry ride across the Sea of China to Kumejima, where Otto and the children waited for her. Mai's husband took the boys back to Naha to give the family some private time together. He took Hugo, as well, who was traveling to live with a grandmother in Quebec City. There did not seem to be much the panel could do about Hugo. He had family in Canada and they wanted him. Arikaki would put Hugo on an airplane as soon as they reached Naha. Christina had not even seen him to say goodbye. Kumejima was rice fields, sugar cane and beaches. The lagoons were light green and crystal clear. Her own three children were brown from snorkeling and sunburned from biking. That they were, despite the profoundly evil events being met by so many so close to them, was a testament to the abilities of children. It took some doing to create a wound big enough to emotionally hamstring a child who only wanted to play.

"Mama," Anja cried when she spotted Christina getting off the ferry. She and David ran and threw their arms around her. Hank and Otto followed behind. Hank had got so brown in the sun, it was astounding. None of his father's Irish skin for Hank.

"Mom," David shouted, "I've got six stream snakes in a tank!"

"Yes, he does," Hank did not seem pleased, "and they are right in the room where we sleep."

"Do you know what they call Kumejima?" Anja asked.

"What?"

"Firefly Island. Wait until you see. It's magic"

"Hi, honey," Otto laughed and kissed her lightly, "and how was your day?"

The warmth and the sun had worked firefly magic indeed on the spirits and energy of her two youngest children. They seemed to have come some way back to their old selves. That made her want to find a place to cry; cry loud and long for the restoration of their lives. She did not know how the world would heal. That was the next major international project.

Otto drove them to Mai's island house in a little blue Volkswagen with a rusty undercarriage. It was a single-wall beach house with a bit of yard leading to a four foot cliff down to a very narrow beach. Coconut palms just far enough apart for a hammock stood to the left of the yard. Wild lilies grew everywhere on the island. That was it. That was all there was to it because here on Firefly Island not much was needed. The sea reclaimed everything man-made in pretty short order so the inhabitants did not invest themselves or their energy in fancy goods. This was a grand restorative after two weeks under a stone castle and months plinking away at her keyboard in a quiet corner of the big house. She made Otto stop on the way just so she could step out of the car and hold her face to the sun. There remained the white mist; the unnatural veil across the heavens, but there was not an aircraft to be seen. She hoped that would be the first result. It was the one that mattered.

The next day they took her to look for cowrie shells on the ever-windy beaches. It impressed her that life intended never to be denied no matter what happened. It was a thing as strong as the implacable sovereignty of the human being. Life simply will not be denied. The break was almost over when she received a call from Charlie Shepard.

"Hey," he said from very far away, back in Carmel, "the hearings are opening today. Have you got computer access?"

"Yes, I do."

"Choshin told me the first thing they will do is play a videotaped interview with Bleeth. I have got to know what that guy said. He didn't live too much longer after that."

"Yes," Christina agreed, "that is worth shaking the sand out of my bathing suit for."

"Also, Christina…".

"Yes?"

"Now that the Reconciliation is making international rounds through diplomatic channels, Choshin is determined to get an international movement together to restore the environment. There is some talk that it may take a couple of generations. I… I'm going to do that… full time. I'm just telling you in case you want to think about it. I know we've been through a lot," Charlie said.

"We have. I will think about it but I have to finish the book. That's a big contribution, I think."

"Right. Well, let me know. Okay?"

She and Otto made sure the computer was on and connected well in advance of the beginning of the trial. There was a thirty minute delay but since she was on a tiny Okinawan island and the trial was being held in the Hague, the thirty minutes was the least of it. She and Otto finally determined that if the trial started at nine a.m. in the Netherlands, they would need to be watching the same day at three p.m. on Kumejima, then account for the half hour. The streaming worked after a few stalls that made her heart stop. She was somewhat desperate to hear what Bleeth had to say. So many people in the movement had been waiting for the day when this guy finally admitted these things were going on and he was one of the master-minds. This was a very big deal. Dr. Daniel Bleeth was videotaped within an office-like room at an embassy in Tokyo. It was unclear which embassy. Certainly not the U.S. She thought perhaps she saw a Swiss flag in the corner but the view had been too brief.

His rapid-fire staccato voice began with the essentials.

"I am Dr. Daniel Bleeth, currently a United States' citizen and I am in Japan seeking asylum because I believe that if I stay in the U.S., I will be harmed or killed."

"Dr. Bleeth, who do you believe wants to hurt you?" There came a disembodied voice.

"The people I work for, work with…", Bleeth said.

Christina could not believe it was the same Bleeth she had seen a few short months ago. If anything he was much thinner and there were dark circles under his eyes. His lips were red and cracked.

"Who would that be, Dr. Bleeth?"

"Primarily I work for Georg Nero Pearle and Carroll de Geier, both of them are major shareholders in Sceptre Corporation and its technological arm, Pantheon. I also work with the US Secretary of Agriculture, Bob Custer."

"What do you do within this context that imperils your life, Dr. Bleeth?"

"I am the Chief Scientist behind their global geoengineering projects, which serve several purposes, most if not all of them illegal. In every country."

"Elaborate, please…".

Christina listened as Bleeth verified everything she and her friends brought to the panel a month or more ago. He verified everything Tim Verzet and Philip Yarmouth had risked their lives for and for which Yarmouth had lost his life. The tape stopped after two hours of general questioning. Then it began again, time and date stamped in the lower right corner, some two hours later.

The unseen interviewer continued, "Dr. Bleeth what sorts of chemicals are the most predominant in these experiments?"

Bleeth's eyebrows went up.

"Oh, well, we started with aluminum oxide. We started with that because Sceptre had agricultural products it felt it could make resistant to alumina rather quickly. It just made sense. Simultaneously people began to worry over-much about UV rays from the sun and global warming. Aluminum oxide blocks a fair percentage of these. In the end, when we were discovered, as we knew we must be, global warming could be blamed. Solar flares, too."

"What else, please?"

"Barium. Barium was next because the military was using it as an aerosol to enhance battle simulations and high frequency communications, both sending and receiving. The thing is, barium affects the weather, too, very aggressively and decisively. Once you figure out how to manipulate barium you can cause drought, storms, floods. It's weather warfare. Barium is really contraindicated for life. It's a bad thing, trust me. Remember those cathode ray tubes in the old television sets? Barium used to scavenge the oxygen inside those tubes and create the vacuum."

It's bad for human life, would you say?"

"Oh, yes. It stimulates muscles, the nervous system, causes heart problems, tremors, anxiety... even paralysis. The thing to remember though is that some people have a high tolerance to barium in their systems and some people have a low tolerance. That's a really swell thing when you're trying to hide something like this. The argument is, well, if it's falling on everyone, how come not everyone is keeling over?"

"Are there others?"

"Sure. They are just not quite as important. Cadmium, mercury, arsenic, sulfur dioxide... and many combinations of the above."

"Turn it off," Christina said. "I know all this and now I've lived to see him admit it. I'm glad he's dead and I'm glad it's over."

And finally it was time to go home, time to pick up their lives right where they had dropped them. The book needed to be finished and published. The children would have actual lives to look forward to, they would live, and with any luck the poisons would be forced out of their bodies. She would think about joining Choshin later. Maybe she could think about something like that again after she sewed costumes for a child's play or talked Hank through finals week or got the golden retriever to stop digging under the fence. Anja needed support to get into art school. There were vegetables to pick and there would be winter wood to stack. The mittens would not knit themselves and the cold wind would arrive, like it or not. She had buried herself in that little corner now for some time.

Naturally, she knew this world did not quite exist anymore and she would join her friends for the work of a lifetime. Still, if she could just put her feet up by the woodstove one more time and knit, it would sustain her for some time to come.

There was another task, as well, something left unfinished. She suspected it would simply be that way forever. When she arrived back at the big, drafty green and yellow house, she put a call in to the prosecutor.

I need to know where Walters is,' she said. "I need to see him if permission can be obtained for me
to do that. And, yes, I know he's in a coma and completely unresponsive. Please? Is there something we can do? You and I both know he's never going to see the inside of a courtroom."

In the end, Walters' attorney granted her permission if he supervised. She didn't care who was there. He was in a long-term care facility in the next town. She did not tell anyone she was doing this. She didn't even know why she was doing it. So many mysteries had been solved; people had risked their lives and died for the solutions, for the truth, for the tiniest bit of justice. On that summer morning a year ago, she had known none of this. Nothing.

Walters lay in a bed, a hospital bed, head slightly elevated, eyes closed, breathing raspily. He was bald. Completely bald and so his head and his ears, which stuck out a bit, made him look like someone from another world. Six months he had lay here while she wrestled with the dragons she had only been able to see once he slammed into her mother and made Christina stop and look around. Really look. She pulled a chair up to the side of his bed. His attorney sat in the hallway reading a newspaper. His cell phone rang. He answered it, spoke in low tones.

She looked long, then spoke.

"You stupid son-of-a-bitch. Who are you? What happened?" His stillness was less active than death.

This had to be good enough. This was all she was ever going to get. It could be that he was just some poor schmuck who should have stopped driving long ago, who could neither read nor write, a man with no wife, no children to make life worth living. He just ran her mother down, an incredibly difficult, soul-injured woman, who had nearly made it to the other side of the crosswalk. A woman who just wanted to go to church on a Sunday morning in a little seaside town. This event, so seemingly empty of any meaning except to underscore the random meaninglessness of life, had gone a long way toward redeeming the world. She was never going to get any answer other than this and if she had to live with it then the rest of the world by God would have to live with it, too. George Walters. Placeholder for a future understanding. She sat with him until the sun dipped below the horizon, then she picked up her things and left. Forever.

Charlie called the next day. He wanted to fill her in, as she had made him promise to do.

"Hi, friend!" he said. "Tim is finished testifying. He's been cleared of all charges at the ICJ and granted amnesty back in the USA. As you know, the ICJ has no jurisdiction over Americans because we refuse to play by the rules. However, I talked to Huck later and he said all Tim wants to do is fight fires now. Fires are easy, he says."

Christina laughed. "What about Nikolai?"

"Done and gone. Picked up Hugo and disappeared. I hope he can stay alive for the kid's sake but my guess is we'll never know."

It was November again. Soon David would be fifteen. The wood was stacked on the porch and the black iron Vigilant stove burned intensely and steadily. Some years it just seemed to do better than others. Hank was at school in New York; Anja was at school in Canada. The golden had stopped digging under the fence and Fancy radiated her miraculous, winter, under-the-covers warmth. David was the only one home now. He could be convinced at times to wear a coat in the cold air and even to bring in firewood and take out the trash every Thursday.

"Mom," Christina heard him call from the mud room. "It's snowing! I'd better get the trash out before I have to dig it out."

She pulled the drape away from the window. It was indeed snowing heavily. She watched David drag the big green cans to the curb one by one, snow collecting on his wool cap. On his way back the second time he stopped and looked toward the side of the house. He pointed and laughed.

"Mom, come here!" he called.

She wrapped her arms around the big sweater she wore, slipped into her black rubber boots and stepped outside, down the steps and halfway down the driveway to where her son stood, laughing and still pointing. On the side of the house, a branch she had declared dead and gone climbed the house to the second story. On this dead branch stubbornly clinging to the side of the old house bloomed a rose; a single red rose in the snow on a branch that she had declared dead and gone over the summer. It was a perfect rose, a brilliant red against the white snow.

"Hey, Mom," said David, "I think maybe Grammy opened her fortune cookie."

Epilogue

Less than eight hours after Christina wrote the last sentence of the book, the old green and yellow house burned to the ground. Anja and Hank were away. David was asleep on the floor where the blaze was the hottest and most furious but Otto got him out safely. Otto went back in for the dogs and the golden retriever and Fancy also made it out. In fact, the only casualties were one lost cat and the hoop gardens. Christina went back in for the book, which also made it out.

It also happened to be the wee hours of Palm Sunday... they estimated the fire had started about midnight. They said it was electrical. Who could ever be sure given the timing? The book, though, sailed out into the world, for better or for worse and because of it, people started to look up.

Afterword

I first gave an interview for this book in late January, 2012, in London. Shortly thereafter I returned to Maine, to my office which, at that time, was on the third floor of a condo overlooking the shore. For the first time in the eight years I had lived there, a small fixed wing airplane flew past my window close enough to see the pilot. That happened two days running. The third day, while walking on the beach, I was circled by a black helicopter. What could I do? I turned and stared right into the cockpit, refusing to move. It went away. The following day, I was at the market with my daughter. As I climbed back into my car and started the engine, I realized there was a man, a lone man, sitting in a van not quite directly across from me. He glared at me, sort of reminding me of a bird of prey. This wasn't anger, just hunting. I stared back at him as I slowly drove away. It was clear he intended for me to see him.

In March, I signed the contracts to have this book translated and published in German. I then had my passport 'stolen' in Spain. En route to the embassy to get a temporary passport, my bus was stopped, boarded and searched twice. When I returned to the US, I immediately sent for a new passport to the State Department.

A few weeks later, someone approached me on Skype pretending to be an extremely high-ranking military official. I asked him what 'he' could possibly want with me. The response? "Are ya scared?" (his spelling). A few days later, I got a call from the District Attorney's office just to let me know that the attorney for the man who had run my mother down in the street had aggressively argued that the perpetrator was too ill to serve time behind bars and so the case should be dismissed. He had been charged and convicted of manslaughter, had pled guilty. The judge dismissed the case.

The day after the German-language edition of this book was launched into the public, I was notified by amazon.de that someone had hacked my account.

My tech adviser, Mark McCandlish (aka Charlie Shepard) went

through this on the phone with me. He said, "You know, the thing is, you don't have any idea what your mother saw. You don't have any idea if she was actually murdered...and if they had just left you alone, you probably wouldn't have even written the book. So it makes you wonder if something else isn't going on here." True enough.

The fact is, if the man who killed my mother had just been prosecuted in a normal fashion, I probably never would have written the book because that would have validated the incident as an accident. So, to Whomever made sure this guy never saw the inside of a courtroom or a jail? Thank you. I think the world and I owe you a debt of gratitude.

Namaste.

Cara St.Louis
August, 2013

CPSIA information can be obtained at www.ICGtesting.com
Printed in the USA
LVOW10s1932120216

474885LV00029B/949/P